FALL OF THE FAE

BOOK TWO OF THE STOLEN FAE SERIES

MJ LAWRIE

M.J.LAWRIE

For my amazing husband who puts up with plotting madness, writing frenzies, editing insanity and book cover indecisiveness.

You're amazing.

Thank you for everything you do.

ONE

*T*he human's skull slams into the marble floor with a hollow thud. The sound makes me tingle.

It's almost as satisfying as his long, agonised gasp as he chokes on his blood.

The shrill and victorious cry of the half-naked Fae girl who leaps onto his limp and battered body startles him. He looks up at her with wide eyes, full of terror.

Blood decorates her pale skin, dripping between her breasts, past her belly button and soaking into her silk underwear.

The man's dying eyes watch her raise the carving knife in her hands.

He tries to shake his head. The pitiful human starts to beg.

This only makes her laugh harder. The mere idea that *she* would ever show this fucker an ounce of mercy is the funniest thing this girl has probably heard. It's undoubtedly one of mine, considering that when we first got here, she was tied to the bed, face down and legs spread wide, with him about to ram his pathetic excuse of a cock into her.

She buries the knife in his big, round belly, sinking her weapon deep inside, just as many have done to her before.

The girl withdraws the blade and drives it back inside him, splattering herself more and more in bloody war paint as she fucks him with that knife.

Good girl... I think to myself.

The human male's final moments on this earth are full of pain, humiliation and misery. That thought alone tugs at the corners of my mouth, pulling it into a wicked smile.

The Fae girl stands and looks at me, a crazed excitement in her brilliantly blue eyes.

'Go and find Brennan,' I tell her. 'He'll remove your collar.'

She nods and runs off, giggling to herself.

I turn and walk on, stepping over the disembowelled body of another human who is pitifully trying to scoop up his insides and put them back in.

I make sure to stand on his intestines as I pass. The organ, still warm and wet, squelches between my toes.

I don't bother to look back. He'll be dead soon. As will all these disgusting, vile, pitiful humans who paid to degrade and violate the Fae. As well as those who took their wages from Serge in exchange for keeping my kind sealed away inside this hell of a brothel.

My bare feet gently glide from room to room. The sights I see as I enter each one fill me with pride.

So much blood. So much pain. So much death.

An endless amount of retribution.

I fucking love it!

The last time I was here, Serge ruled this place.

His brothel. *His* den of torture and degradation. Behind each door contained a vile horror story. Fae tied up or strapped down. Stripped bare of clothes and freedom. Of dignity and safety. Forced to perform. To use their gifts and beauty for the pleasure of humans. Forced to fuck and be fucked.

How the tables have turned.

Because today... *today*... we have reclaimed every Fae in this place.

I have freed them all, with a little help, of course.

The once-prisoners now wield the whips and canes, striking their former "clients".

Only humans don't heal as we do. Unlike the girls who felt nothing as they were beaten and wanked over, these men feel the pain of each blow. These men aren't getting released. They aren't getting out of here alive.

The girls laugh and mock the men who weep, beg and piss themselves.

Just as the Fae did to them once. They begged for release. For a day of rest. For pity or mercy from these human scum.

Karma, man. It can be a real bitch.

I love it.

The air is filled with music. Heavy beats blast through the speakers above us, and the dim lights cast many shadows. From some rooms, strobe lights seep out, making everyone's movements jumpy and otherworldly. From others, blinding lights expose the grizzly events happening inside.

I walk on, past bodies and blood. Past discarded weapons left wet and warm on the floors of this once pristine establishment. Past a man who has been choked to death on condoms forced down his throat. Past a girl with a long, fluffy tail. She raises her hand. Her nails are long, sharp claws. She brings them down, slashing a man's throat before giggling and skipping off down the hall, hand in hand with another fae girl.

I enter the White Room. No longer is a girl chained to the floor, bent over and shared by men who claimed she stole from them.

I still can't recall that girl's name...

She is now safely away from here, taken to a safe house along with the others we freed, who didn't want to hang about to claim retribution with us.

Today, the fire in the fireplace holds several heated pokers. Another dizzy spell hits me as I step through the threshold. I grab the doorframe to steady myself and shake away the fog that tries to descend. My hand slips and leaves behind a trail of blood. The deep cut on my hand throbs in protest as it continues to weep red. Licking my lips, I feel dehydration on the tip of my tongue.

I don't know how much longer I can stand for.

Long enough to see this through, I tell myself. *I can rest later.*

Three of Serge's bodyguards lie in pieces around me. Literal pieces.

A fourth pulls at the chain around his neck, tethering him to the marble floor.

Lucca now rules over this room. He is the master here today.

His hair, now purple and black, hangs over his eyes and sticks to the deep layer of sweat on his forehead. He stands tall, decorated with weapons and stained with blood. A darkness dances in his eyes as he lingers behind his captive.

He was precise as he hunted through the brothel, seeking out men from his past who took advantage of him in his youth.

He remembers them all. Every man who took turns with the young Fae boy with wings, captured by Serge and locked away in the dark for the twisted pleasure of those with enough cash to play with him.

Many of these men ensured he remained in chains.

Lucca's wings stretch out as he circles his former tormentor. No longer is he a child, helpless, lost, and afraid.

No. Now he is a man. Now he is free.

With my blood in his system, he's free to use his powers without the threat of turning into a Dark Fae.

Free to display his glorious wings.

Free to take revenge.

'Let's see how you like having something forced down your throat,' Lucca says, grabbing the man's hair and yanking back his head.

As the human shouts, Lucca thrusts a red-hot poker into his mouth and down his throat.

I linger in the doorway, watching like a sadistic voyeur as Lucca snarls the words 'Never again' at the man.

Never again...

Never again will we be collared.

Never again will those we have liberated here tonight be forced to obey the rules of humans in exchange for keeping a grip on their souls. Never again will we be forced to submit to them in exchange for Gilt.

All the Fae who have tasted the blood that still seeps through my fingers can proudly say those words.

Never again.

Lucca glances in my direction as he wipes blood and sweat from his brow before he yanks out the poker and drops the dying man at his feet.

'Pup,' he says with a wink. 'Having fun?' His eyes land on my hand. 'You good? You're looking a little pale.'

'I'm perfect.' I nod down the hall. 'Would you start gathering the others and ensure they all have their collars off? I'll make a portal soon to get them back to the cottages.'

He glances back at the men he's left on the floor.

'Thank you,' he says, turning back to face me. 'Thank you for giving me the chance to kill these bastards.'

'My pleasure, Lucca. My absolute pleasure.'

He heads towards me and momentarily stops at the door's threshold.

'Are you sure you don't want me to stay?' he asks, glancing back over his shoulder to the room. 'You don't have to do it alone.'

'I'm positive.'

'Well. Have fun,' Lucca whispers, leaning in to kiss my cheek.

'Oh. We fully intend to.' I look at the gagged man tied to the chair beyond the bodies. 'Don't we, Serge?'

Serge's frame spills over the side of the metal chair he's strapped into. Blood seeps from the gash in his head where Lucca struck him with a bat before manoeuvring him into position. His suit is pressed and expensive. His jewellery is tacky, and the stench of his cologne is gag-worthy.

Despite the death he has witnessed, despite watching his friends, clientele and staff being brutally tortured and murdered before his eyes, he sits still and silent. No struggling. No attempts to speak or bargain.

I walk in a little more, my eyes on his. They have a golden glow.

'Ivan gave you a power.'

Of course, he says nothing. He can't, being gagged and all.

I walk in a little more. He watches my every move.

'But you are still here. Running this shit hole. Ivan can't value you that much if he left you here instead of keeping you by his side.'

I stop before him and pull down the gag, revealing his crooked smile and golden teeth.

'My sweet Raven,' he drawls in his thick Russian accent, looking me up and down with a stomach-turning grin. 'I was so hoping to see you again.'

'What power did he put in you?'

'Let me go, and I will show you.'

'Where is Ivan?'

'I can take you back to your Daddy. He misses you. Or maybe I can be your Daddy. Would you like that?'

I lean down so I'm level with his eyes. He watches my chest as I bend down, and I let him look. I let him leer at my cleavage and wait for him to lift his gaze to meet my own

'I owe you pain, Serge.'

'I owe you a good fuck,' he replies, just as calm as I appear. 'I wonder. Will you scream for me as your mummy screamed for me? No.' He tuts and shakes his head. 'You don't scream, do you, sweetheart? My nephew, Jonah, always said that you took it so well. So quietly and obediently.'

I flinch. Just a little, but he sees it.

'He misses you,' he tells me. 'How about you stop your little temper tantrum, huh? You've proved your point. I'll tell you what. How about you suck my dick, and I'll think about telling you where your Daddy is.'

I keep my smile as I reach down and undo his zipper.

He lets out a gritty and low laugh as I take him in my hand.

'The only one who is going to suck your dick ever again, you filthy, grotesque, repulsive and impotent fuck, is you.'

He's so busy watching my face that he doesn't see me slip out a small knife I had strapped to my thigh.

A small snip. That's all it takes. He twinges, his nasty grin faltering as he tries to understand what has just happened. Then he looks down at his crotch and sees his pathetic pecker in my hand. Blood quickly starts to spread over his lap.

He takes in an enormous breath and lets out a raging scream. One that gets cut short when I shove his cock into his mouth and seal his lips closed.

I return his gag and force it back between his lips.

Now he thrashes and pulls against his restraints. *Now* he screams.

I step back, dodging the puke that spills from his lips and out of his nose. I walk around behind him and press my fingers to his head.

'You don't need to tell me anything, Serge. I can see your truth. Let's take a look, shall we?'

I channel my power, sending it through his body. Sending it to his mind, pulling out the truth of his memories.

Images flash before my eyes. Hideous, disgusting and degrading images.

But he has no idea where Ivan is. Serge has been put in charge of all the brothels now. That's all he's been trusted with. Much to his dismay, as he believes he should be permitted to do more than enslave us for sex and money. I let him go with a shove and step back. The loss of blood and the exertion of power makes me wobble. The room spins, and I must take deep breaths to stop myself from falling over.

'The power to turn minerals into metals. That's your gift? Making gold? How pathetic.'

I look up to see Brennan standing by the door. In one hand, he holds a large duffle bag with all his computer tech to disarm the collars. In the other, he holds a gun.

'Raven,' he says in his usual numb tone, looking at Serge thrashing and bleeding. He slightly raises a brow. 'Need any help?'

'I don't think so, Brennan. But thank you for the offer.'

'Please tell me that you didn't just put that man's severed-'

'I sure did,' I sigh happily, patting Serge on his shoulder and joining Brennan by the door. 'How are we doing?'

'Collars are off. There's a group ready to leave. A few others are with Lucca. Celebrating,' he adds with a tired eye roll. 'You've been asked for. He wants you back in the hall right now.'

'Does he now.' I sigh and turn back to Serge. 'Tell him to wait. I wanna watch Serge die first.'

Brennan points his weapon and fires a bullet through Serge's skull without missing a beat.

Furious that he would dare to end that fucker's suffering early, I stare at Brennan, ready to spit fire.

'As I said. He wants you. Now.' He nods down the hall expectantly. 'He's impatient.'

'Is he ever anything else?' I groan. 'I'm going.'

I leave the room and return to the halls, feeling Brennan's disapproving stare on the back of my head.

Only Lucca was as keen as I was to return here. To finally step out from the shadows we had shrouded ourselves in since escaping the facility two weeks ago and fleeing from the man I once called "Dad".

Brennan came because he was told to. Tessa outright refused. Rhea has no idea I'm here, and El is keeping her safe whilst we're away.

And Reid and Cyrus fought me on every front, refusing to let me come. Refusing to expose us before we were ready. Before I had recovered.

But finally, they agreed. Finally, they bent to my will. With conditions. Obviously.

They're desperate to get back into my good graces. And my bed, seeing as they are now bonded to me and I to them.

Freeing those trapped here was one reason I was so adamant about returning to this place.

The other was Serge.

The man who raped, tortured, carved up and killed my mother.

Finding and killing him, along with Ivan Walker and that piece of shit Jonah, has become somewhat of an obsession.

One that, in part, ended today.

A few steps is as far as I get before I have to stop and take the help of the wall.

My head falls forwards, and my eyes close as another wave of weakness ripples through me.

I've given away too much blood. I know it, and so will they. They always do. They feel my fear. They sense my anger and know when my body is at its limit.

I stumble as the world spins.

An arm wraps around my waist and slides smoothly across my belly. Warm breath lands on my skin, creating a trail of goosebumps over my body.

He caught me.

He always does.

'Having fun, Princess?' Cyrus sings softly in my ear.

I peer back at him and see his devious smile.

He takes my still-bleeding hand and brings it to his mouth. As he presses himself closer to my back, his erection pressing into me, he glides his soft tongue over my self-inflicted wound.

'Finished with Serge already?' he asks.

'Brennan ended the party early.' I sway in his arms.

'You've overexerted yourself. I feel your body's weakness. You've given away too much blood. We told you-'

'I'm fine,' I insist, letting out a long exhale, hoping it will stop the room from spinning. 'I had to do this, Cyrus. I need to see this through. To see them all get what they deserve.'

'I know. You and Lucca both. But you're reaching your limit. We should leave before you fall.'

'I won't fall. Not with you keeping me up.'

'I'll always be here to keep you up, Princess.'

His feet move, and his body sways, guiding mine with it. And together, we slowly dance in the doorway, moving gently from foot to foot to the music and the screams.

I lean back into him, relishing his touch and company in this depraved display of vengeance.

Slowly, he turns us, remaining behind me so we can both see down the halls of the bloodbath brothel.

'Look at them all,' he whispers in my ear.

Cyrus moves his lips to my neck, kissing and nipping at my skin. My head spins as the blood I've sacrificed tonight takes more of a toll, making me feel giddy and drunk. He grips me tighter, keeping me on my feet. Keeping me in the moment.

In the flashes of light, we watch a few half-naked Fae dart from room to room, laughing and celebrating their newfound freedom. It's hypnotic, seeing our kind so free and powerful. So happy.

'Is it everything you hoped it would be?' Cyrus asks, still slowly swaying from side to side and rhythmically rubbing himself against me, making his cock harder and his heart race faster.

'Yes,' I whisper.

'My girl is happy?'

'Ecstatic.'

Cyrus lifts the hem of my dress, bunching it up around my waist as he nudges my feet apart.

'What are you doing?'

Still trailing firm and hungry kisses on my neck, he pulls aside my underwear and eases his fingers inside me.

'You're so wet,' he whispers, clamping his teeth down on my earlobe, making me moan. A long and lust-filled exhale escapes him, travelling down my chest.

Gripping the door frame, my eyes never leaving the scene before me, whilst relishing his touch.

'Undo my zipper, Princess,' he says, adding a third finger and pressing his cock further into my arse. 'I need to fuck you.'

My breath comes out jagged and sharp as his fingers work me. My body reacts to him perfectly, brimming with need, passion, and pleasure.

'Zip!' he repeats. 'I did as you wanted. I got you here. I helped you set them free. I gave you Serge to do with as you wanted. Now it's my turn to get what I want. Just as you promised.'

I remain where I am, soaking up his skill and feeling my sweet release ebbing closer and closer.

'I won't let you come until I'm buried deep inside you, Princess. I know how you like it. I'll have you seeing the Goddess in a matter of seconds if you say yes.'

I laugh and make no move to satisfy him at all.

He does it himself, freeing his straining length from his trousers. His breaths are frustrated as he rests himself at my entrance.

'You can't keep this up forever,' he warns. 'Denying me is also denying yourself. Say yes.' He growls, resuming his wanton lips to my neck and tormenting my clit with his thumb. 'Or I swear-'

'What?' I mock. 'What will you do, huh? Force me? Go fuck someone else? What will you do, Cyrus?'

I look at him. He lifts his face and meets my gaze. I see the anger at my refusal flicker behind his eyes. I see it twitch on his lips, just as I have seen it every day since we sealed the Bond in the woods. I haven't let them touch me. And the Bond means they can't find satisfaction with anyone else.

'You're right there, Cyrus. You could just stick it in. It's. Right...' I shift, resting his tip at my entrance. 'There.'

His words come out in a menace. His eyes never look away. 'Not until you say yes. That exact word. Yes!'

A high-pitched giggle draws my focus back to the *"party"*.

I watch two girls embrace before rushing off to seek more retribution.

That seems to be all my mind is filled with these days.

Revenge. Payback.

Cyrus and Reid are no exception.

They need to pay for what they have done to me. Their marks still cover my skin, trailing up my arms and resting over my heart. Their deception and manipulation live there, too. Buried deep in my heart. My soul. My mind.

I gasp as Cyrus wraps his fingers in my hair and yanks my head back.

He snarls his words in my ear as he looks down at me.

'Damn you, woman. What else must I do to earn your forgiveness? I have done everything you asked.'

'My dear Mate. It will take more than this to erase the shit you and Reid have done to me. All you care about is your own pleasure and getting yourself back between my legs -'

He pulls his cock away and sinks his fingers back inside me once more, sneering as he watches me gasp and grab his wrist in response to his forceful and sudden entry.

'You can't keep playing this game,' he warns. 'Soon, you'll be begging us to claim you again. This is what I can do with my fingers, and baby, you know what my cock is capable of. It will be a matter of days until you beg me for it.'

I grip the doorway for support. My other hand entangles in his long, dark hair.

He fucks me hard and steady with his fingers, taking my weight and whispering the most delicious words into my ear.

We don't care that others watch us as they pass.

The markings on my arm start to heat up. Reid's Markings. His tether Bond put on me back when I thought he was a human Authority Agent. The Bond he can pull on whenever he likes, like a leash on my soul. That both of them can use to summon me from hell itself, and I would have no choice but to go to them.

Reid is calling gently, something we have been practising together. A signal we can share, just us. A gentle nudge to ask for a portal. To show that the other is safe. To get their attention.

Reid calls now. He's ready to return from bringing the Fae we liberated to safety. That, and I know he can sense my body's reaction to Cyrus. He won't want to miss out.

I reach out my hand and watch a portal swirl into life, using Reid as my anchoring thought. His face. His scent. His body.

My eyes are glued to it as Cyrus continues to work me from behind. I watch the golden specks of light swirl and kick up a gale.

The portal forms and Reid strides through. Our eyes meet as soon as he emerges. His white shirt is undone at the top, and his sleeves are rolled up to his elbows. Blood splatters his skin and marks his clothing. He stops, seeing Cyrus's fingers buried between my legs, and his lip hitches into a half smile.

He continues towards us, each step purposeful and steady.

'Why, Little Bird, you look like you're having fun.' His hand glides across my cheek, neck, across my chest and past my stomach.

And then settles between my legs. His fingers entwined with Cyrus's inside me.

I lean back, resting it on Cyrus's chest, and let out a shameless moan.

Brennan and Lucca start funnelling the Fae towards the portal. I see Brennan briefly glance at the three of us before stepping through, followed by some anxious-looking Fae who stare at the portal with wonder.But I'm more interested in what's happening to me right now.

'Is she still being difficult?' Reid asks Cyrus as he looks down at me between them.

'Is she ever anything else?' Cyrus replies.

'Shame. She's so close to coming too.' Reid smirks. 'But if we can't have ours...'

They both pull away, leaving me empty and cold. Leaving me unsatisfied.

And worse, leaving me unsupported.

The blood loss steals away the last of my strength, and my legs give way. Cyrus catches me from behind and scoops me up in his arms.

The two watch as I struggle to keep my eyes open.

'You're spent. Too spent,' Reid scorns, sweeping the hair from my face and shaking his head angrily. Then, sirens start in the distance. Authority sirens. 'It's time to go.' Reid nods towards the portal. 'Get her through before she passes out and we get stuck here.'

With purpose, they both stride towards the portal.

Reid strikes a match and tosses it at the cans of petrol left in the corner, ready for this moment.

We leave, the heat of the flames licking our backs, and just as we step through the other side, my eyes close, and the darkness claims me.

We've won this battle. But the war... that's barely begun.

TWO

I awake in my bed. Alone. A small plate of food is laid out for me, and what I guess counts as clean clothes. The shirt is torn and so stained I don't think it could ever truly be clean, and the leggings are just as bad. Yawning, I roll out of bed and make my way down the landing to the bathroom. I turn on the shower, strip off and sit, letting the water wash away the smell of fire and death from my hair. I hold no energy in my body. Everything aches and I long for more sleep.

The darkened and distorted shape of another appears from the other side of the glass shower door. It slides open. I'm looking at a mirror image of myself. Well, except for the scar, of course. On my face are three deep lines, still pink from healing. They go clear across my eye and have turned the iris a pale blue.

She has no such marks.

'I could kill those idiots,' Rhea scorns, her focus dancing over my pale and tired form. 'You're not an all-you-can-eat buffet. What were they thinking, taking you to that awful place and serving your blood to all those people?' A deep growl emanates from her chest as her anger spikes and a dark shadow forms under her eyes. The ever-present threat of her darkness whispers through her skin, threatening to explode and wreak its vengeance.

'Temper, Rhea. If you go Dark on us and wreck the cottage, the guys will be pissed.'

'No, they won't,' she grumbles. 'Because I would have already torn their arms off and beaten them to death with them.'

She can't hold back her smile as she reaches out and rests her hand on my cheek. To say that her relationship with my two Bonded Mates is tricky would be an understatement.

'I can be annoyed with them, Raven. And I can be annoyed with you, too.'

I sink into her touch, still desperate to soak up every ounce of her I can. She's a miracle. My miracle. She lets out a heavy sigh as my weight falls into her palm.

'I can't lose you again,' she says. 'You shouldn't be taking stupid risks like this. What will I do without you, huh?!'

Of course, she's angry. I don't blame her. After so long under the control of Ivan, the threat of being retaken by him must be all-consuming. But her words still sting. They're the same ones said by Ahri, who used me as a shield and a diversion for the cruelty that could potentially come for her.

'If anything happens to me, I don't want you to think you'll be in danger.' I sit back, pulling away from her hand. 'The others will look after you. They'll protect you from Ivan.'

'I didn't mean that!' she tuts with a scowl. 'I can't lose *you*. *I* have nothing to do with it.'

I lift my gaze and meet hers, frowning in confusion as I sense no hint of a lie.

Rhea shrugs and deepens her scowl. 'Besides. From now on, if anything happens to you, it will also happen to me. We stick together. No more sneaking off to kill pimps without telling me, you hear? I can't believe you went along with their insane plan.'

'I made them take me. It was my plan-'

'And if they weren't so desperate to get back in your good books, they would have said no to *your* insane plan. What if Ivan was there? He could have grabbed you. He could have killed you!'

With a heavy sigh, I slump back and close my eyes.

'He wasn't there, Rhea.' I debated whether I should tell her. But I think she would want to know. 'Serge was, though.'

Her head shoots up, and the dark shadows return in her eyes.

'He was?'

'He was.'

'Is he...'

'Yes. Very dead.'

'Did he suffer?'

'Not as much as I would have liked, but he didn't enjoy his last moments in this life.'

'One down,' she says, gripping my hand in hers.

'Two to go.'

She joins me in the shower, even though she is still fully clothed.

'I should have come with you. I should have helped.'

'You help in other ways, Rhea.'

'I cook and I clean.' She rolls her eyes until they land on me. 'Making a sandwich isn't the same level of helping our cause as breaking into a brothel and freeing all those poor Fae.'

'They have to eat,' I reply with a smile.

'And boy, do they eat. I don't think they have had a decent meal in weeks.'

'Ever, more like. The first real meal I had was with Reid when he took me to that disgusting Authority pub.' My stomach growls at the memory of the sausages and bacon. 'Otherwise, it was bin diving.'

'They fed me dog food,' she says. 'Talk about disgusting.'

Her eyes glaze over as she recalls her time as Ivan's pet beastie. A harrowed expression steals my sister's features.

'They'll pay, Rhea. For all of it.' I grip her hand and bring her back to me. 'Now tell me. How are the Fae we brought back getting on?'

'Other than eating everything in sight, they're not doing too bad. I mean, most of them have stayed huddled together in one room. A couple are too scared to leave the house. Some have sat on the grass and watched the sky this entire time, just enjoying seeing it for once. And others have just slept. There's been a lot of crying and hugging and joy too. It's a little overwhelming for everyone!

'It's only been a couple of days. They'll adjust. Freedom is scary at first. If you can call hiding in an old farmhouse and a crappy cottage in the middle of the woods freedom.'

'Considering the alternative, we can definitely call it an improvement.'

Our eyes fall on each other as we sit in the shower, water soaking us and the sound of rushing water filling the void between us.

The alternative. I'd rather be dead than return to the alternative.

'Your clothes are getting wet.'

'Well, it's just water. I'll dry.'

Her eyes linger on the three long lines of scars that cover my left eye and trail down my cheek.

'Has your vision returned any more today?' she asks.

'It gets better every day.'

'I'm so sorry-'

'Nope. You promised you would stop that. Apologising for things beyond our control is banned. We agreed.'

'We also agreed to stick together. But you still ran off yesterday without telling me.'

'Well, from now on, we stick together. You and me. No matter what.'

'You. Me.' She rolls her eyes and nods to the door. 'And the two lunatics who tethered you to them with their magic tattoos.'

We both laugh softly before she reaches over and grabs the shampoo.

'Let's get you cleaned up. You smell like fire and petrol.'

She shampoos my hair, rubbing it clean and combing it through with conditioner. With gentle hands, she scrubs my hands and feet, ensuring no remnants of the trip to the brothel are left on my skin. It still feels strange to have her here. To have her look after me. I keep waiting for the snide comments. For the *"This never would have happened if you had just blah, blah, blah..."*. Or for her to shrug her shoulders and tell me that I deserved this, so I should deal with it alone. But she never does.

'Where are they?' I ask, glancing at the bathroom door.

'Who?' she replies.

'The two lunatics.'

'Sat at the top of the stairs down the landing,' she says. 'They haven't moved since you came in here, and I doubt they'll leave before you come out.'

'They're just sitting there?'

'Yep.'

'They saying anything?'

'Not for me to hear. They shut up when I walked past, but they looked annoyed. I don't think it helped that whilst you slept, every time they tried to come in, you kept making a portal under their feet and dropping them back into the lounge.' She giggles. 'Over and over again, they landed on their asses in front of everyone. It was so funny.'

'I didn't, did I?'

She nods and keeps grinning like a cheeky schoolgirl.

'I bet that pissed them off.'

'Just a tad.'

The water starts to get cold, so she shuts it off, drapes a towel over me and waits.

'What?' I ask.

'Tessa really doesn't like you, does she?'

'No. No, she doesn't. Why? What did she do now?'

'I kinda snapped at her because she was bad-mouthing you to the new arrivals last night. They were all saying how great you were. How brave. And then some of them started talking about a little moment you and the guys had in the hallway. Something a little... steamy?' She looks at me uneasily. 'She didn't like that. So she started calling you unstable. A man-eater. Husband stealer. A loose cannon who can't control her powers or...'

'Or?'

'Or her vagina. Then she called you a whore and I kinda lost it.'

'Lost it how?' I ask, finding it all a little too funny.

'I slammed my hand on a table, which broke in two.'

'Couldn't you have slammed your hand on Tessa and broken her in two?'

'And when I shouted for her to shut up, I sounded like a demon. I scared some of the others. Made a little girl cry.'

'That's unfortunate. But I wouldn't worry. They see everything you do for them. How kind you are. And they see Tessa being petty. It will be okay.'

She stands and starts to haul me up.

'I would watch out for her. She's not trustworthy. And she wants Reid for herself.'

'Well, thanks to the Bond, infidelity is one thing I don't have to worry about with those two.'

'Yeah. But I think you should worry about them being insanely overprotective, possessive and super horny. That, and a crazed ex-wife is living under our roof.'

'We killed Serge yesterday. We freed every Fae he had held in that brothel. Our army is growing, Rhea. I'll take the wins where I can get them.'

'Our army?' she says, cocking her head to the side. 'I wouldn't call us an army. A few fighters, yeah, sure. But mainly, it's traumatised ex-sex workers and a few kids.'

'It's more than we've ever had before,' I remind her. 'And we've only just started.'

My feet barely leave the shower when the bathroom door hurtles open.

Cyrus and Reid look at me. Rhea plants herself between us and their steely gaze.

'Can we help you?' she snaps, exuding a severe amount of courage as she is overshadowed by these two overbearing and solid men looking right through her.

Cyrus's eyes follow the length of my towel, that darkness I saw in the brothel returning.

I wonder, does it ever actually go?

Reid blinks and adjusts his gaze to my twin.

'She needs to sleep,' he barks as if he's furious that she's the one keeping me awake. 'Take her to her room.'

'Okay. Calm down.'

'Now.' Reid blocks the hallway to the stairs and gestures to the bedroom at the end of the landing. 'Stay with her, Rhea.'

I sense it. Not a lie. My powers have nothing to do with it. This is just me and their evident desire to keep me away from whatever has the veins bulging in their necks.

As if she could hear my thoughts, Rhea turns to face me, mirroring my own expression of suspicion.

There's a clatter downstairs and the sound of panicked voices.

'What's going on?' I ask, staring Reid straight in the face.

He replies with a warning glare. One I'm in no mood for.

I step forwards as the voices below become more rushed and the gasps become louder, but both boys step forwards, stopping me entirely.

'One day, you'll figure this shit out. You don't call the shots. Not where I'm concerned.' I feel the power inside me spike, and the gold in my eyes burn to life just as Reid goes to grab me.

'Don't you fucking dare!' His eyes flash wide with rage. 'Raven, I swear to the Goddess, if you portal out of this room-'

I open a portal below my feet and simply fall through, my feet landing at the base of the stairs. It seals before anyone can follow me down, and I walk quickly towards the lounge, ignoring the thunderous footsteps of Reid and Cyrus up above.

The doorway to the old sitting room is crowded with others, all gathering into the cramped space with the only television this abandoned farmhouse has. We have all taken refuge in this lost and forgotten house nestled in this deep woodland with a sister cottage next door. The newly freed Fae from the brothel, all dressed in baggy clothes that cover their bodies in a way they haven't been permitted to do for years, step aside and let me pass through. They glance at me nervously, ensuring that when our eyes meet, they look away out of some form of misplaced respect or fear.

The kids we saved from that nightmare orphanage or took from the brothel, still hold that harrowed stare on their faces. They're held by those we saved yesterday.

The path forwards clears a little more as I head deeper into the lounge, where I find them all staring with wide eyes at the old television in the corner of the room. Some sit on the floor. Others perch on the mismatched sofas. Most stand, their backs pressed against the wall. And when my eyes meet the screen, I see why they are all so horrified.

Ivan Walker is on television. His sly, well-rehearsed smile. His cold eyes that betray it. He stands tall, dressed in his designer suit and decorated with his gold watch and diamond cuff links.

Listening to him speak is nauseating.

I see what he is trying to do. He's the world's new hope. Its guiding light in the war against darkness.

The darkness being us.

Fae are turning Dark all over. First, it was dozens a week. Then a day. Now it's an epidemic, and we cannot be sure how many have been lost. Ivan has told the world that it is a natural devolvement of our kind. That we are lost, and there is nothing to be done. Soon, we shall all be monsters with a thirst for humankind.

However, he has made it so this loss can become a great advantage for this great nation.

The mad scientist has gone public with the theft of our powers. But he claims it is salvaging a resource from a dying creature. The truth that he is stealing us and tearing our powers from our bodies in his torture room has failed to come to light. The fact that we are turning Dark due to his thievery has not come up once and never will if he has anything to do with it.

Besides, even if humanity did know, they wouldn't care. They hate us.

Praise to Ivan, who has taken it upon himself to capture the monsters with grey skin and twisted bodies and rescue the gifts that lie dying within them.

And praise Ivan for developing a way to control the creatures, too.

Yes. He has turned us Dark. And he has turned us into his slaves, controlling the will of the Dark Fae and compelling them to do his bidding.

He has an army of monsters.

He has many powers.

He has humanity under his control because everyone knows nothing gets the masses in line, like shovelling fear down their throats.

And now, as I watch this monster in human form, I witness him make public that the powers are now up for sale.

He's started a fucking business.

Never mind that the rest of the world is currently cowering in the shadow of England's sudden acquisition of power. This small island was once shunned by others after the appearance of Fae. It was a cursed and diseased island. Now, those burdensome creatures hidden behind brick and iron have made England the most powerful and feared nation in the world.

Oh, wait.

'Who the fuck is that?' I ask no one in particular as I kneel before the television, staring at the grey-haired man standing beside Ivan on a silver stage with an enormous English flag hanging behind him. There's a commotion behind me as the two boys and Rhea finally catch up. They barge their way through and stop on either side of me. I feel their angry eyes on me, but I couldn't give a shit. I reach out and tap the screen.

'Who is that man?' I repeat.

'The American President,' Reid replies, reaching down and hauling me to my feet. He snatches a blanket left on one of the makeshift beds by his feet and thrusts it into my arms. 'You're in nothing but a towel. Cover yourself up!'

'Why is the American president with Ivan?' I ask, still glued to the television.

Ivan answers my question. As Reid tries to cover me with the blanket, I listen to Ivan declare a partnership with America, who have agreed to unite with England against any who would dare threaten this great nation and attempt to steal their newfound resource of power, wealth and profit.

They are talking about us as if we are some oil reserve that they have declared theirs, no matter how much the other countries want a piece.

England will not share.

Well, except with America, apparently.

With a shit-eating grin, Ivan clarifies that any attempts to interfere will be met with sheer force.

He cuts to a shot of his immense Dark Army, standing in perfect lines, all stock still and facing forwards. Their bodies all twisted and elongated from their transformation. They are pure killing machines.

The promotional video announcement ends with a message.

Their power is our gift to you. Their burden has become our strength.

Followed by a telephone number to call if you want to discuss the powers available for purchase.

I just blink, looking at the screen as the ridiculous segments continue. More and more old men with ridiculously expensive suits stand there, condoning all this. Cheesy emotive music plays in the background as Authority superiors discuss how their new gift will be used to serve their people.

Politicians. Business people. Philanthropists.

Pimps and murderers.

Reid is still fumbling about, trying to get the blanket around my shoulders.

'He's joined with America?' I murmur. 'Why?'

'Power. Will you cover up?!' Reid snaps as he grabs the blanket I let slip down.

'We don't all have powers. Not everyone he turns Dark has a gift to steal. Surely the President knows that. It's not like he has millions of us to-'

'Just get yourself covered!'

'And he only has a small amount of my blood. He needs it charged with that chair thing so the powers can be transferred. It doesn't make sense.' I look at him, still getting frustrated at the blanket. 'Will you stop! Forget the blanket.'

'You are the Queen, and you're basically naked. Everyone will see-'

'Oh, for fuck sake!' I snap, snatching the blanket and tossing it to the floor. 'We have bigger things to worry about.'

'I don't. Not right now!'

'You saw how many Dark Fae he has now. That army was massive. We need to get into the cities. We need to get more of our kind out before he turns every single one of them Dark and steals their power to sell on.'

'We can talk about it in private.'

He looks at my barely concealed body, his lip twitching, and then at the many sets of eyes on me.

I turn to Cyrus, who is still watching the screen behind me. With a blink, he turns his attention to me.

'We need to go to the remaining Fae cities,' I try. 'We need to bring more here-'

'Yeah. I'm with Reid. Get your arse upstairs and quit embarrassing us all.'

I growl. I actually growl in anger as he hitches his brow at me in amusement.

I rip off my towel and throw it on the floor. Before they can go to grab me, they're both thrown across the room. My eyes glow as my power surges and the other Fae in the room scurry backwards.

Many of them have gifts. But the gifts they have were deemed fit only for the brothel. So seeing effective powers still frightens them, I guess.

'This house is filled with tortured and traumatised Fae. Most have been stripped down and forced to do things they didn't want to do. Do you think they, or I, care that I'm not wearing any fucking clothes? This fight has no room for meaningless jealousy and idiotic feelings of ownership. I have already made it perfectly clear you do not own me or my body.'

Lucca chuckles from the sidelines, looking between us with glee and excitement. El takes hold of Rhea's hand as she attempts to get involved.

'Brennan,' Reid starts. 'Will you-'

'Brennan. If you so much as twitch, I will throw your arse through a portal.'

His eyes go rapidly from left to right. He stays put.

And so do I. Stark naked and raging, as I struggle to keep hold of the power I have no idea how to control.

'You tried to keep me upstairs and hide this from me? What gives you the right-'

'Because you will want to do something stupid,' Cyrus retorts. 'And get yourself caught or killed.'

'You think it stupid to try and save innocent lives?'

'By leading *these* innocents into death? Yes, I do. Even if we reached a Fae city without being seen or caught, suppose we managed to get anyone out. What do you plan to do with them, Raven?!' Cyrus bites back and gestures to the others. 'Look at us. We're forty-five already, sharing a two-bedroomed shit-hole farmhouse and a three-bedroom cottage in the middle of nowhere. No money. Scavenging for food and fresh water. Brennan is constantly growing crops so we can eat, and we're patrolling twenty-four-seven. And what? You want to lead this lot into a fight we can't win with powers they can't control? Powers that are useful for nothing more than satisfying perverts?'

'We can't just abandon them!'

'Shall we perhaps free a few more and bring them here to live in filth, hunger, and fear?' Cyrus snaps. 'Shall we give them all your blood? Do precisely what your father wants to do and bleed you dry until there's nothing of you left?'

'We have to kill Ivan.' Reid's words carry loud and clear through the room. 'He's the head of this snake. We kill him and destroy his machines. That's the priority. Then we can work on saving the rest.'

Reid walks towards me, grabbing the blanket by my feet and thrusting it into my hands.

'We already have too many souls to look after. Trying to save more right now will only put everyone at risk.'

'Coming from the man who would Trigger people to add to his collection.'

'That was when I had a position of power and the means to protect those I turned.'

'Yeah. Protect. Or sell to pimps. Or blackmail.' I press the blanket back into his chest and stand toe to toe with him. He looks down at me as I peer up. 'You protected me, didn't you? When you Triggered me. Blackmailed me. Exposed my existence to Serge and led my father straight to me. You protected me when I was in chains and Jonah-'

'You need to shut your mouth before I shut it for you,' he snarls.

'I'd like to see you try and lay a finger on my sister,' Rhea warns, letting go of El's hand and stepping forwards. Her skin darkens in a warning.

Reid falls silent as he looks in her direction.

He knows that Rhea can turn into her Dark-self at a whim. Her body triples in size. Her entire being becomes a weapon.

Her ability to control her transformation is improving with each day. But the risk that Ivan becomes aware of her turning is too great. She hears him sometimes, trying to summon her back. His weapon. We can't risk him retaking her will. But she can still become one hell of a monster if she chooses.

And it seems this threat may just be enough to encourage Reid to shut his mouth. His attention returns to me.

'Get upstairs. Get some fucking clothes on and get some sleep. We'll talk about this later.'

'Fuck you.'

He leans in close. 'Don't tempt me, Little Bird. Because you owe me big time for getting you to that whore house and believe me when I tell you I fully intend on collecting what you promised me. So perhaps choose your words with more care because I will fuck you. Right here. Right now. And you will love every fucking second of it. As will I.'

His words make my heart double in speed and my mouth dry.

I hate how easily my body betrays me. Yes. I promised that if they helped me free those Fae, I would return the favour. I never said when, and they said they would remain patient if that's what you can call this. Patience doesn't seem to be their strong suit.

Good job my stubbornness has always been mine. As Reid reaches out his hand and rests it on my hip, I slam my hand into his chest and shove him away. He staggers back, helped along by my newfound strength, acquired when I inherited my mother's wings.

He gives a dark laugh and shakes his head.

'That's your last warning, Little Bird. Get upstairs.'

'We can't just sit here and hide,' I insist. I face the others, pleading for support.

I get nothing except averted gazes and a few feet that shuffle back.

'Rhea. You agree with me, right?'

'Well...' she begins. 'I- I don't... actually.'

'I don't believe this. *You* of all people?'

'I'm sorry!' she says desperately. 'I just don't think tossing you at a bunch of Dark Fae that get ravenous when they smell your blood is a good idea. Especially when Ivan still holds the ability to control them all. And, like the guys said, where the hell would we put them all once we freed them? Where would we go?'

'We would fight!'

'Fight who?' Cyrus interrupts with a condescending scoff. 'The entirety of humanity?'

I'm getting no support from my Mates. And none from their friends, nor my own sister! So I turn to those who have first-hand experience of humanity's cruelty. Of the sheer misery we are forced to endure.

'And you?' I snap, pointing at one of the girls we freed from the brothel, the bruises on her face from her last night within those hellish walls still puffy and prominent. 'Do you think we should abandon them too? You're safe, right? Fuck everyone else?!'

Her lips part as if to speak. All that comes out is a faint squeak before she flushes crimson, spins on her heel and scurries away.

Everywhere I look, all I see are averted gazes.

Or the intense and smug stares of Reid and Cyrus, who have seemingly proven their point.

I'm outvoted.

And what's worse, the harder my heart races, the worse I feel. The blood loss is easing as I heal, but I'm still down enough to make me feel dizzy. As I go to argue, opening my mouth and getting ready to release my venom and scorning, the room spins, and I stumble.

Annoyingly, Reid catches me.

The heat of his rage penetrates my very core, and his hot, angry breath ruffles my hair. Despite his obvious annoyance, his hands are gentle, and he easily takes my weight.

'I will force you back upstairs if you carry on,' he threatens in my ear, a low rumble shuddering from his chest as he almost growls his words. 'You're as pale as death and scaring the others.'

I shrug him off me and step back.

'They should be scared,' I remind him. 'They should be terrified. They should be angry!'

I look up at him, throwing back ten times more wrath than he's shooting me. His brow hitches, and as his feet step back, taking him closer to the stairs, I feel the burnings of our bonded markings stir as he takes hold of his leash on me. He takes another step, and I stumble forwards, unwillingly following his lead.

'Don't you dare use that leash on me, Reid.'

'Upstairs,' he repeats in a low warning, that light tug still firmly between us.

With a grunt, I reach out, grabbing at the invisible tie that links us together. I tug as hard as I can. Reid stumbles forwards abruptly, hauled towards me by that same leash he just had on me. I pull him so hard he lunges too far and lands on his hands and knees at my feet.

Slowly, he lifts his head and bores his fierce eyes into mine. The entire room shares a stunned gasp, followed by a painful, icy silence.

I should be running. I've seen that look before. And I have seen what follows shortly after.

But my anger burns too hot for me to care. I think it's the only thing keeping me on my feet at this stage.

A stream of black smoke wraps around my wrist. I follow its trail, seeing it emanate from Cyrus's outstretched hand. It seeps from his entire body, shrouding him in an otherworldy fog. Of course, the smoke belongs to him. No other Fae has that gift, as far as we know. It's a deeper black than it was before. Stronger. More solid. All of their powers are. Since consuming my blood and removing the need for Gilt, they can build up their stamina without worry. And release as much power as they can muster.

Powerful or not, the same tether that they have on me, I have on them.

Fuckers.

With a grunt, I pull on Cyrus's bonds too, and he joins Reid on the floor, landing on his side with a thud.

'Fucking... hell,' Lucca mutters, his eyes wider than I have ever seen them.

The blood has even drained from his usually self-assured and unbothered face, leaving him ashen and mortified at what he sees. When he rests his eyes on me, a look of concern replaces his mortification. Like he's watching a deer about to be mauled by two lions.

And yet, my anger refuses to abate. I look down at the two men at my feet.

'Don't you dare forget that I can pull you just as hard as you can pull me,' I spit at the pair, who both look ready to kill me on the spot. 'Nor that I am the sole reason you can use those powers without the threat of turning into a monster. If I choose, I can go after Ivan Walker whenever I please and drag you *both* along, kicking and screaming!' My entire body shakes as I speak, and the edges of my vision blur when I blink.

I have no choice but to release the hold I have on them. My strength is all but gone. I have to choose where I place what remains of it, and keeping on my feet, holding my ground, seems, first and foremost, my priority.

As they shift, pushing themselves up and back to their feet, neither looks away from me. Neither of them blinks. I'm not even sure they're breathing.

'Fellas,' Lucca tries, slowly edging towards us. 'Let's keep our tempers, shall we? It's been a hard couple of-'

'Shut up, Lucca,' bites Cyrus. 'You stay out of this.'

Lucca's anxious stare flits between the two as he slowly edges closer. I know I'm in the shit. Lucca's obviously hearing their thoughts and not liking what he's hearing.

Their fists are clenched and the muscles in their arms are solid.

'Raven,' Reid says through gritted teeth. 'Go upstairs. Now.'

'Reid,' I snarl back. 'Go fuck yourself. Now.'

His foot barely has time to move before I've created a portal and disappeared through it, sealing it shut before anyone can follow me through.

That steals away all my remaining energy completely. I land back upstairs, alone in my room, glad I could keep my composure for as long as I did.

'Oh... fuck...' I grumble, feeling my eyes roll into the back of my head and my body give way.

As if I'm made of lead, I fall forwards and slam into the floor, my cheek colliding with the wood and scrambling my brain.

Unable to move, I just lie there. Naked. Seeing stars and with a loud ringing in my ears.

It's a matter of seconds before the door opens, and two sets of feet thunder on the wood as they get closer.

I can't defend myself. I can't fight back.

And when their hands slide under my arms and lift me to my feet, all I can manage is a half-angry, half-terrified whimper.

I'm fucked.

My eyes land on them both as they fail to get me to hold my weight under my sagging legs. I hang from their grip like a ragdoll, utterly at their mercy.

Mercy I'm sure they severely lack.

Reid scoops me up in his arms and holds me between them both, trapping me between their anger and wrath.

'If you hurt me,' I warn as harshly as I can manage. 'I swear... I'll-'

'Obviously, we're here to hurt you, Raven,' Cyrus snaps back with a harsh scoff. 'After fighting with you because we don't want you to get hurt, we, of course, rushed after you to beat on you.

Fucking idiot. What a stupid thing to think. You'll catch on soon, won't you? The last thing we want is to see you get fucking hurt!'

'You're angry.'

'Furious,' Cyrus corrects. 'Doesn't mean we would ever lay a hand on you. What kind of men do you think we are?'

'The same as every other man I've ever met,' I mutter, my eyelids getting heavier and heavier. 'The type of men that would mark me without my permission and Trigger me to own me.'

'Oh, for Goddess's sake. You're our Mate, Raven. In this entire world, you're the one we care about most.' Cyrus grabs my chin and forces me to stare deep into his eyes. 'Sense a lie in my words, do you? Hmm?!' He waits. 'Well?!'

I shake my head.

'Happy now?' Reid tuts. 'You've added a black eye to the never-ending list of your injuries. Do you enjoy putting yourself in harm's way? Or are you just trying suicide by sheer idiocy?'

'Stop yelling at me.' My words come out in a whisper, one choked by sobs caught in my throat. 'I hate it when you both yell at me.'

This is too much for one person to feel. So much anger and rage. So much guilt. So much fear and dread. I loathe how my lip trembles under the weight of it all. And how hot tears sting in my eyes.

'I hate feeling this way,' I admit in a whisper. 'I just want to be free. To be happy.' I barely manage the last word as it gets mercilessly strangled in my throat. 'To be safe...'

Their hard stares melt away. Their tensed muscles ease, and sadness swims in their eyes.

'When will it sink into that thick skull of yours, Little Bird?' Reid sighs, looking down at me in his arms. 'Of everyone in this world, the two you can trust never to hurt you are us.'

'Trust you?' I scoff at the words. 'After all you've done?'

They both groan in exasperation and turn to walk towards the bed. Cyrus pulls back the covers, and Reid gently places me on the mattress.

They both look down at me. My bare skin utterly exposed. Every bruise. Every scratch. Their gaze lingers on them all.

'Whatever we have done, we've done for you,' Reid states.

'Now that's a lie,' I scoff, feeling the effect of the words tingle on my skin. 'You didn't Trigger me for my sake. You didn't tether me to you for my sake.'

'Not solely for your sake, no. For ours too. But we've done other things for you. Do you forget our little day trip to Serge's brothel? That was one of the last places you should have been. But you insisted, and we obliged. We got them all out and killed the humans who held them. We let you kill Serge. Because we knew it was important to you.'

'No. You did it because of what I promised to give you in return.'

'Perhaps. Yes. Partly because you promised to give us a night back in your bed if we helped you,' Reid replies, unashamed and unapologetic about his motives. 'But also to prove to you that we work better as a team. We don't want to fight you. We want to fight *with* you. But if your demands mean losing you? Well, you won't enjoy our steps in ensuring you do as you are told.'

I have nothing to say to that. No strength for the words that I would need to do any of my retorts and threats justice.

Silence surrounds us all. A painful void of distrust, anger and hurt.

'Well. We won't be collecting payment for our brothel excursion tonight,' Cyrus shrugs, looking straight at Reid on the other side of the bed.

'Doesn't look like it,' Reid replies.

They both take a corner of the duvet and pull it over me, covering my naked form.

'You're not going to kill yourself in this fight.' Reid's entire body tenses as he speaks his promise. 'You need to calm down and start thinking clearly.'

'You promised me revenge.'

'And you'll have it. But your obsession with vengeance will end you if you don't fight smart. The odds are stacked against us. Just slow down. We'll get the blood we're due.'

A creaking floorboard has them both looking at the door.

'Is... is she okay?' Rhea asks anxiously from the doorway.

'I'm fine,' I mutter, painfully rolling onto my side and burying my head into the pillow.

'I'll stay with you,' she offers.

'No.'

'Raven, I'm sorry I disagreed with you, but-'

'I just want to sleep. Can you all go?'

'C'mon. She's pissed off and exhausted.' As Cyrus leaves, he takes Rhea's elbow and starts guiding her out of the room. 'Let her get some rest. She's a bitch when she's tired.'

'I'm a bitch when you're all being cowards,' I mumble tiredly into my pillow.

Cyrus and Rhea disappear down the hall, and I'm left with Reid's slow and steady breaths still lingering at my bedside.

He leans down and whispers into my ear, 'You need to start behaving. Or I'll be forced to bring you to heel.'

'You said you would never hurt me.' I remind him with a sneer.

He kisses my cheek. 'That won't stop me putting you over my knee, Little Bird. Nor tying you to this bed and never letting you out. We will never let you go. Sorry. But you knew what you were doing when you made the Bond. Now you deal with the consequences.'

'I'm not your prisoner.'

'No. You're our heart, body and soul. And if you think for a second we will risk you for anything or anyone, then you are sorely mistaken.'.

'Even if it means our race-'

'Even if it means the world burns, Little Bird. We'll ravage you in the ashes.'

Another soft kiss and he heads to the door.

'And if you could stop creating portals in your sleep, that would be great. I'm sick of falling on my arse.'

'Then stop sneaking into my room.'

He closes the door behind him, plunging me into darkness.

How can I just lie here in this bed as others are suffering and dying? How can they all just be okay with that?

How can we win this fight when there is no way to win....

THREE

*M*y sleep is restless and miserable. I can hardly call it sleep at all. Every time I close my eyes, I suffer through vivid, horrific nightmares. The following days and nights all bleed together as I recover, lick my wounds and drown in guilt and anger.

Each morning, I'm presented with food by one of my two pain-in-the-arse Mates. And stared at until it's all consumed. Not that I don't want the food. I know what a hungry belly feels like, and I have no inclination to endure it if I don't need to. Food is limited with so many Fae to feed, and with it being so risky going out in the world to get it, we have to be careful how much we consume.

It's been three days since my outburst. I haven't left this bedroom since. I don't have the strength for the others at the moment. Or the patience. But seeing as we're seriously crammed in, I've hardly been alone.

Rhea sleeps beside me at night and spends most of the day sitting in the corner, huddled in a chair, staring at the same page of a book. Her eyes glaze over as she sinks into herself on and off for hours, lost in thought or perhaps memories, as she often goes pale and starts to shake. I'm pretty sure she can't read, as the books are sometimes upside down, and her eyes never follow the lines.

Every bump or loud noise has her gasping and glaring at the bedroom door. Every attempt I make to ask her if she's okay is met with a forced smile, an over-enthusiastic nod and a choked attempt at an easy laugh before she returns to her book.

Reid and Cyrus waltz in and out as they please, sleeping beside me if there's room or in the chair if there's not. They stomp about, glaring at me sideways and slamming drawers as they pull out fresh clothes, enraged by my refusal to respond to any of their attempts at a conversation.

I hear them heading up the stairs. I often pretend to be asleep when they come in, so I keep my eyes closed and my breathing slow and steady as they come in. They each take turns kissing the top of my head before they leave the room. Sitting up, I see a bowl of dry cereal and a glass of water left for me. As Rhea sleeps beside me, I eat silently and dwell on my thoughts.

The bed jars as Rhea violently twitches in her sleep. Peering over my shoulder, I see her hair plastered to her face in a thick layer of sweat. Her lips are parted and dry as she whimpers and gasps.

'Rhea,' I say softly, turning to face her.

She continues to judder and moan.

'Rhea?' I reach over and rest my hand on her arm, giving her the softest of shakes. 'Wake up. You're having a-'

Her scream cuts off my words. Well, it starts as a scream. High pitched and full of fear. But in the blink of an eye, it becomes dark and demonic. It turns monstrous.

And so does she. Her skin drains of any colour, leaving her grey with sunken eyes full of deep shadows. She screeches so loud it hurts my ears. I throw my hands over them to try and protect them. She's quick. Quicker than me, and before I can get to my feet and get away from her, she's lashed out, swiping me away as though I'm something there to hurt her. Something she needs to be rid of. Something to kill. Her strength is fierce as her darkness takes hold. Her blow sends me clear across the room, slamming me into the wall by the bedroom door.

The whack leaves me dizzy, with a vicious ringing in my ears.

And as quick as it came, the darkness leaves her. Her black eyes return to normal, and her skin pinkens. The rage is gone, replaced instead with horror.

'I'm... I'm so sorry-'

That's as far as she gets before the bedroom door explodes into splinters and a storm of black smoke hurtles through, crashing into her and throwing her clear across the room, as far from me as possible.

The smoke swirls into a solid mass and Cyrus stands between us, his wings wide and every part of his body looking ready for a fight.

Rhea is on the floor, cowering with her hands up.

'It was an accident!' she pleads, pushing herself as close to the wall as she can. 'I swear to you... I didn't mean-'

He takes a step towards her.

'Cyrus!' I say sternly, despite my words slurring and my head still spinning. 'She didn't mean it.'

Reid rushes in next, followed by El, Lucca and Brennan, all falling through what remains of the door and all looking ready to fight. Except for Tessa, who lingers in the doorway, watching with a cruel smirk.

My attempts to try and stand are worthless. I hit my head really hard. Reid kneels at my side and steadies me as I try to get up.

'Maybe you should stay down,' he says through a heavy breath. His words drip with anger as he looks at Rhea. 'What the fuck did you do?'

'I... I was having a nightmare and... I don't know! I Just...' Her desperately regretful eyes land on me. 'I'm so sorry, Raven. I swear... I didn't mean to.'

Reid takes my arm in his hand.

'You cut her.'

Blood seeps from my forearm and trails between his fingers.

'Did you do this with a Dark Fae hand?' he asks, his voice deep and terrifying.

'I... I don't know...' Rhea whimpers, still crouching on the floor.

'I warned you!' Cyrus snarls, throwing a pissed-off look at Reid. 'I said it wasn't safe for her to be alone with Raven.'

This situation is pretty damn shit, and I think it's about to get worse unless I step in.

'She didn't mean it,' I tell them. But they're not listening.

Shocker...

'If you've added another scar to her body,' Cyrus warns, spinning back to Rhea. 'I swear to the Goddess-'

'I said she didn't mean it!' As I throw my words at him, the contents of the room tremble and I feel my eyes burn gold. 'You don't threaten her,' I add, as the room reacts to my anger.

The fucker rolls his eyes at me and lowers his wings.

'I didn't mean it,' Rhea says again, her voice trembling and choked with sobs. 'I didn't. I'm sorry.'

'I'm fine,' I insist, still trying to get the room to stop spinning. 'I've had worse.'

I swear, the room chills at those words. I'm not up for this right now. Not the anger of the boys nor the fear of my twin. And the relentless staring of the others is enough to make me scream. Never mind Tessa's smug smirk as she stands in the hallway.

'Can you all go?' I ask with a sigh.

'We're not leaving you alone with her.' Reid shakes his head.

'El, take Rhea downstairs, would you?' I ask, peering up at El. 'Take her for a walk or something?'

'Erm...' Lucca butts in with a scowl. 'I don't think so. She's bloody dangerous.'

'Of course,' El replies, walking across the room and barging into Lucca's shoulder as she passes. 'Come on, Rhea. Let's get some air in the garden.' She reaches out and helps Rhea to her feet before cautiously guiding her past the others, who all watch with steely gazes. Even Lucca, who I would expect to enjoy the drama.

El and Rhea are gone. The four boys are still standing there, however.

'I said I'm fine,' I repeat. But no one moves. 'I just want some privacy.'

Lucca and Brennan both fold their arms and look at Reid. My words are pretty meaningless to them. There's only one person's orders they'll follow.

'We're fine,' Reid tells Lucca and Brennan. 'We've got her. Go make sure Rhea's stable.'

They both nod and leave through the hole left in the door-frame.

'Let's get you on your feet,' Reid says gently, easing me up.

'I said I'm fi-' As soon as I'm on my feet, my stomach turns and with an almighty heave, I throw up. Puke covers his shirt and trousers and splatters on his shoes. It covers my legs and lands on the ends of my hair. 'Oh shit,' I groan, utterly humiliated. 'I'm sorry.' I sway a little, and he tightens his hold on me.

'Don't worry about it,' he says, guiding me into Cyrus's arms before he quickly starts stripping off. 'I wish puke was the worst thing I've ever been covered in. Help me get her out of those clothes,' he adds with a nod to Cyrus. 'Let's clean her up.'

I stand there as they strip me, and I let them guide me into the shower. Reid joins me and washes off the mess as Cyrus washes my hair. Reid's naked body is close to mine. I watch him wash as Cyrus keeps on task, washing me with gentle, soapy hands.

'If you keep staring at me like that, I might think you're up for some play time.' Reid tucks my freshly washed hair behind my ear. 'Which is a shame because you're not strong enough for us at the moment.'

I blink the world back into focus, realising that I was just staring at him. At his perfect form and delicious skin. His hand settles on my cheek as he shows me a comforting smile.

'You okay, Little Bird?'

'I don't know,' I reply. 'I don't think I am.'

From behind, Cyrus takes my arm and lifts it a little. Blood seeps from the wound and lands on the shower floor, mixing with the water and creating a trail of pale red towards the plug hole.

'That might leave a scar if she was Dark when she scratched you,' Cyrus says, softly placing his palm over the wound.

'I'm more scar than girl at this point,' I add in a sad whisper, lowering my head and loathing the scars on my face. 'What's one more?'

Cyrus leans over. His lips land on the deep scars over my cheek.

Reid follows, and his lips land beside Cyrus's. Their soft, warm and tender kisses send heat through my entire body. But that's all they do. Just a long and gentle kiss.

'I'll grab some towels,' Cyrus says. 'You got her?'

'Always,' Reid replies, resting his hands on my hips.

Cyrus leaves. The water continues to fall over Reid and me. My eyes linger on the tattoos marking so much of his toned body. I stare at the Mate marks that go from his heart to the back of his neck. And then I look at my matching ones, which spread from my stomach to my heart.

The tips of my fingers dance over his tattoos. There are so many more than the ones that belong to me.

Promises, he told me once. Each tattoo is a promise made. His tether is a promise never to let me go. Our bonding marks are a promise to remain faithful to each other.

'Do you still hate them?' he asks, mimicking my actions and trailing his fingers over the marks on my skin.

'Only the ones you put there without my permission.'

He opens his mouth, ready with some smooth or smart comeback.

'What else have you been covered in?' I ask, keen not to engage in an argument.

'Erm... what?'

'You said you wished puke was the worst thing you have been covered in.' I look at him, the water falling like warm rain over us. 'I'm curious as to what exactly could be worse than puke.'

'Your blood,' he replies as if that's obvious. 'I'd take all the piss, shit and puke in the world if it meant never being covered in your blood again.'

'So romantic.'

He gives me a wink and when the corner of his mouth hitches into a smile, I can't help but let out a soft laugh.

'And how the hell did you get her to do that?' Cyrus asks as he appears armed with a couple of towels. 'Thought I'd never hear her laugh again.' He opens up a towel for me as Reid shuts off the shower.

I step into it, and he wraps me up.

'Think you're gonna be sick again?' Cyrus asks, staring intently into my eyes. 'You have a headache? Seeing double? Are your eyes sensitive to the light or anything?'

'I'm not concussed. I'm just exhausted.' I wrap the towel tighter around me. 'I can't seem to get much sleep. My brain won't shut off, and when I do go to sleep, I have nightmares.'

Reid is roughly drying his hair with a towel.

'You sleep well with us,' he says, lowering the towel and running his hands through his mess of damp hair. 'So sleep with us.'

'I'm not fucking you.'

'Did I say fuck? Or did I say sleep?' He raises his brow. 'Just us. No Rhea. No El in the chair. No Lucca curled up like a damned dog at the foot of the bed. Just. Us.'

Before I know it, I've been led to the bed and tucked under the duvet. Someone has put an old curtain over the broken door and cleaned up the vomit as we washed. The window is open a little, letting in a cool breeze. The morning sun seeps in from under the curtains, and I hear the hustle and bustle of the house waking up for the day.

Despite that, they both slide into bed with me. One on each side.

And no more words are said. They fall still and silent, burying their faces in the pillows as they face me. Their eyes close, and that's it.

They stay that way until I close my eyes and fall into a much-needed, restful, peaceful sleep.

My dreams are absent as I sleep. Nothing but silence and still-ness touches my slumbering mind as my body finally relaxes into some much-needed rest. I occasionally open my eyes when something in the real world dares disturb me. When one of the boys moves, or their voices make their way into my ear as they talk.

I open my eyes. It's evening, and they're sitting at my bedside, eating and talking in hushed whispers. When they see my eyes flicker, they rest their hands on my head and usher me back to sleep.

I'm so exhausted, I obey.

I open my eyes again and it's night. El is in the room, talking to Reid in a low tone. He nods at her words as he deepens his frown. From behind, Cyrus wraps his arm around my middle and pulls me closer.

'Go back to sleep,' he whispers. 'There's nothing for you to worry about.'

I roll over and bury my face in his warm chest, gladly obliging. The reason I sleep so peacefully with them both is a mystery to me. But if this is what I need to get enough rest to recover finally, so be it. My need to sleep even overrides my curiosity about what Reid and El are talking about.

The next time I open my eyes, a beam of sunlight streams through the slight gap in the curtains and falls on my eyes.

As I blink the tiredness clear, I swallow and feel something firm around my throat.

'I like that,' Cyrus murmurs sleepily from behind me. 'Do it again.'

His other arm is under my pillow, and he's spooning me, keeping me pressed against him with the arm he has draped over my naked chest and his hand, which encircles my throat.

'Again...' he encourages, flexing his fingers a little.

I swallow and he feels it in his palm.

'Hmmm. Yep. I definitely like that.' He squeezes a little more, moaning softly in my ear as he shuffles closer to me, even though he's already as close as possible. He's topless and in nothing but boxers. His skin meets mine, and we both break out in goosebumps.

'You slept well,' he says, bending his knees to curve with mine. 'But you always do with me. And I sleep like a baby with you in my arms.' He lets out a long exhale. 'It's perfection.'

'Only you would fall asleep with your hand around my throat, sleep like a baby, and call it perfection.'

'It's how I show love, Princess.'

'Is that right?'

'I don't choke just anyone, you know. Only those I really care about.'

Squeeze. Squeeze.

I can't help but let out a little laugh which he shares. The deep chuckles land on my neck and warms me from head to toe because only I would feel safe and sound with him there gripping my throat as I sleep.

'How long have I been asleep?' I ask.

'A day and a night. Feel better?'

'Much.'

We lie there for a while as the sun goes about its business, rising in the sky. We doze in peace, enjoying an easy silence and a simple embrace.

Beyond the bedroom, the house stirs. It's rarely silent with all these people crammed in such a small space, but it's unbearable when the scramble for breakfast begins.

Reid especially hates it.

So when the curtain covering the bedroom door is thrown open and he comes striding in, it's no surprise. He leans over and looks down at me in Cyrus's arms.

'Did you get some decent sleep?' he asks.

'Yeah.' I look down at his feet. His shoes are caked in mud, and the morning's chill lingers on his clothing. 'Where have you been?'

'Getting ready for training. We've assessed the Fae we rescued from the brothel; some of their gifts could come in handy. We thought we'd do training with you too. Do you feel up to it? You certainly slept enough so-'

'Really?' I'm so excited at the prospect my words come out as a high-pitched squeal. I go to sit, but the hand around my throat has other ideas and I'm kept on the bed. 'Let me up,' I scorn, throwing a warning glare at Cyrus, whose face is still half buried in my pillow. That and his lazy smile.

'In a minute,' he says. 'After a kiss.'

'Don't be a dick.'

'If I were a dick, I'd be pushing for reimbursement on our deal. Remember? We take you to the brothel and we get you for a night.'

'You had me for a night and a day, remember?' I jeer, knowing damn well that's not what he means.

'You know perfectly well that last night doesn't count,' he smirks, pushing himself up on his elbow and looking down at me.

'We have work to do. Training! I'm not wasting a whole day satisfying your urges.'

'I'm asking for a simple kiss.' He gives a slight shrug. 'That's all.' He leans in and runs the tip of his nose along mine. 'It's just a kiss, Raven.'

Before I know it, I've given a slight nod.

It's just a kiss. It's not giving in completely.

'Good girl,' he whispers. But instead of leaning in to claim his kiss, he turns my head away from him and towards Reid instead. 'Him first.'

Reid sits beside me, the mattress dipping beneath his weight. Reid looks down at me, his eyes drifting to my mouth, and he leans in.

His eyes remain open as his lips rest on mine. A million emotions scream at me through his dark gaze. He's angry. Frustrated. Hurt. And extremely fucking horny.

He moves, his lips parting mine as he sinks into my kiss. His tongue teases, and his warm breath mixes with mine. His kiss goes deeper and gets hungrier. His fingers knot in my hair as he tugs at the strands, guiding my face towards him as he claims his kiss. My heart races in my chest, and the urge to throw my arms around his neck and pull him on top of me is too much. I ball up the sheets in my fists, hoping to fight the urge to give in, pull him down, and let him ravage me. Reid throws off the duvet, exposing my naked form. Cyrus sits, his full attention on my body. On how my stomach has clenched. How my thighs press together. How my toes curl and flex as Reid devours my mouth with his.

Cyrus reaches over with his free hand, refusing to release his hold on my throat, and takes my knee. He pins it down into the mattress, spreading my legs wide. I pull up my other leg, closing my intimate parts from view. Despite the fact I'm aching with need.

I have to keep my head. I can't let them win!

Reid catches me before my thighs can meet and forces my leg back down, clamping his palm on my thigh and refusing to let go.

I'm now spread wide.

His eyes are still open and flash with warning.

'You said a kiss,' I gasp breathlessly.

'It is a kiss. You keep your sweet legs open for us, hear me?'

His lips crash back into mine, and his desperate kiss resumes. I meet his desperation with my own, relishing every tongue stroke and nip from his teeth.

'Stubborn bitch is soaking fucking wet,' Cyrus tuts, looking at my exposed pussy. 'Such a waste.'

He blows on me, sending a ripple of pleasure through my core. Reid catches my pathetic whimper. The bed dips as Cyrus leans over. Reid's lips have barely left mine when they're replaced by Cyrus's, my face guided toward him by Reid's fingers still entangled in my hair.

My fingernails dig into my palms as I sink into our kiss, my legs still spread wide and everything inside me screaming for more contact to allow a release I've denied us all for weeks.

Cyrus claims my mouth with roughness and possessiveness, uncaring that another was just there. His eyes are open, too, and he watches me beneath him, flushing red with heat and squirming so shamelessly. His teeth clamp down hard on my lip and I yelp, the taste of blood seeping into our mouths. He smirks and slowly drags his fingertips up my inner thigh.

'We've said we're sorry,' he whispers between kisses. 'We've done everything you have asked.' The tips of his fingers dance ever upwards.

Reid's lips are on mine again.

Then Cyrus's.

Then Reid's.

Soon, I can't tell whose tongue is whose. Both their hands are at the top of my thigh, and their fingers are millimetres from my entrance.

'Say yes,' Reid pants with a low growl in his chest. 'We feel your want. We know your body is as desperate as ours.'

Their fingertips are as close as possible.

The bedroom curtain opens.

'Hey, guys. We're ready for-WHOAH! Hello, vagina. Shit. Sorry folks!' Lucca bellows with laughter as he throws his hand over his eyes. 'That's a treat for the eyes first thing in the morning.'

The guys each take one of my legs and slam them shut before throwing the duvet over my body.

I stay in bed, mortified and so fucking turned on I don't think I could move even if I wanted to.

'Never heard of knocking, Lucca?!' Reid grunts, slowly blinking as he glares at his best friend.

'Nah. I always find I miss the good stuff when I do stupid shit like knocking.' He peers through a small gap between his fingers and, seeing I'm decent, lowers them completely. 'Besides. No door.' He points to the curtain. 'Remember?'

'What do you want?' Reid groans.

'We're all set up in the woods, so when you're ready, let's get cracking. Unless you need a few minutes to finish up here?' Lucca looks at me and, no doubt, hears my mind both cursing and thanking him for his interruption. He flashes me a wink. 'Angry and horny,' he smirks. 'That's the best kind of fuck. Sorry I interrupted, Pup.'

'Fuck off,' Cyrus replies, sitting with a grunt.

'Sure thing.' Lucca turns to leave. But not before turning back with one final comment. 'Real nice pussy, Pup. It's a thing of beauty. I can see why the guys are wild for it.'

He explodes with excited laughter as he legs it, followed closely by Cyrus, who looks ready to tear his head off.

I sit, pulling the duvet up to my chest and look at Reid.

'Why do you keep pushing this?' I ask quietly. 'Is that all I am to you? Something to fuck?'

'You're our Bonded Mate, Raven. When you sealed our Bond for good in the woods, you made sure of that fact. We were ready to leave. To spare you this mess, but you kept us here. You refused to let us go. "You're not leaving me". Those were your words.'

'Can't you just masturbate?'

'It's not about that. An orgasm isn't what we're craving.' He leans in and kisses me again. Taking my hand, he puts it on his chest. 'You feel that? That's you.' His heart races beneath my palm and hammers wildly beneath his shirt. 'It's about that.' He rests his hand over my heart too. My heart races almost in time with his. 'We're built to be together. And we're not. We're broken men without you. We need you back so we can be whole again.'

'I... I can't...' I look away, unable to hold his intense gaze for another second. 'Not yet.'

'You can't hate us forever, Little Bird. We won't let you.'

'You don't get to decide that.'

'Well. You're ours. And you made us yours.' He lifts my arm and plants a lingering kiss on the tattoos marking my skin. The ones that match his. The ones he put there without my consent, tethering me to him for the rest of time. A leash. A fucking leash on which he can pull and choke me if he wants.

'We're not going anywhere. Just as you wanted, we're here for good. We want to be here for good. You're our girl. No one else compares. Not at all. Never.'

His words make me smile. I sense no lies at all.

'But we won't be your ghosts for much longer. This is cruel, so you need to think about how you want this to go and make a choice soon.'

'Choice?'

'Forgive us and move forwards with us. Or...'

'Or?'

'Or we're going to have a pretty serious fucking problem. And the last thing Cyrus and I want is for you to get hurt.'

He leans in and kisses my lips. It's a kiss I don't return.

'Are you threatening me? You gonna force yourself on me if I don't-'

'We will never rape or assault you, Raven Rivers. So get that shit out of your head this minute. Consent, my girl, is fucking key. Everything we long to do to you, you'll thoroughly enjoy. But if you refuse to submit to our Bond, it will end bloody and brutally. We told you. Men spurned after the Bond is made don't tend to keep their sanity for long. Why do you think we tried to leave?' He taps the end of my nose. 'You're the one that made us stay. You knew the risks when you accepted us. It sucks, baby. I know. Actions. Consequences. We all have to deal with them. Cyrus and I are tethered to you. We're fucking addicted. We want to worship you in every way. Make all your dreams come true. Protect you. Liberate you. See you smile and make you come. The Fates sewed us together, and I'm afraid nothing short of violent, bloodthirsty and terrifying events will ever separate us.'

'I can't tell if that's the nicest thing or the most terrifying thing anyone has ever said to me.'

'I don't think it's an either-or. Sometimes, being scared is exciting when you know that the one scaring you will never hurt you. Not in a million years. Now. Get dressed.' He stands and heads to the door. 'We have work to do. Let's show these baby Fae what their queen is capable of.'

FOUR

I descend the stairs and join the house of chaos. People go about their business, living what is probably the first normal kind of life they've ever had. Half a dozen Fae are making food in the kitchen, baking bread and prepping the meat from whatever has been killed in the woods that morning. Brennan's ability to manipulate vegetation and plant life has made living off the grid much more manageable. He can grow wheat, vegetables and fruit every day.

Overexerting gives you one hell of a migraine and leaves you so tired you want to do nothing but sleep for a week, so Brennan's been super grumpy and snappy, but needs must.

In the dining room, a group are being taught to read. Not just the children, but a few of the older Fae who Triggered and were sold off to the whore house before they ever got the chance to learn. In the lounge, the television is playing the news, retelling the new developments in the human world. I don't stay to watch. Humans relish in this new resource they have been given. And just like they have done with every other thing that has benefited their lazy, destructive and disgusting lives, they will use it up till its destruction.

All mined and hunted to the end, spilling out pollution and poison instead.

Fucking humans.

They're extra sensitive now that my home city has been destroyed. Their factories are dead and there have been supply issues for specific products. Rumour has it that the air has started to clear, and the smog clouds are dissipating for the first time in decades.

Shame everyone who lived within its walls are dead, Dark or missing.

I nod briefly to those who see me and offer a smile. They all smile back.

In the lounge, Brennan is sliding on his jacket, covering the various guns and knives decorating his torso. On the table behind him are several computers, dozens of cables, tools and several collars previously worn by the Fae from Serge's brothel. He's been experimenting with them and developing a tool to disarm and remove a collar quickly and easily. Something portable without the need for a computer or extra tools.

He yawns and pinches the bridge of his nose.

'Migraine?' I ask, recognising that look. He's overexerted.

'It's nothing.'

'How's the tinkering going?'

'Almost there.'

He throws open the door, and as I pass, he hands me a black leather jacket of my own to put on.

Stepping outside, I'm glad to see familiar faces.

Rhea is standing with El, talking away in deep and meaningful words by the looks of it. My sister wears the same frown I wear when I'm uneasy and anxious. Her eyes dance around at the others, watching them closely for any signs of danger as she tries to pay attention to El's words.

El wraps a black scarf around my sister's neck, ensuring she's warm in this chill. Rhea's eyes fall away from the others and as she watches El, her unease fades in that second.

'Ready?' Brennan asks, stopping by my side with his eyes glued to a phone screen, his fingers typing at speed.

'Yep. Where are we going?'

He points into the woodland towards a clearing in the distance.

'Same place as before.' He lifts his gaze and scans the gathering crowd. 'Don't want any of the baby Fae wrecking any more of the house than they already have. The place is barely standing as it is.'

Rhea spots me by the door, and again that unease returns to her face.

'Is Rhea training today?' I ask quietly.

Brennan scoffs, shaking his head. 'No. Rhea is not training today. And if she were, it would be a million miles away from you. God forbid the golden girl gets put in harm's way.' I feel the eye roll as he carries on watching his screen. 'I'm amazed she's not muzzled in the basement after the other morning.'

'What happened was an accident,' I groan. 'And I would love to see anyone try and put my sister in a muzzle.' I zip up my jacket. 'It's been a while since I slit a man's throat.'

Brennan side glances me, his head still unmoving. 'You slit a man's throat a couple of days ago.'

'That long ago, huh? Must be a slow week.'

I walk past the little cottage set off to the left of the farmhouse and head towards El and Rhea.

After I got her back from the Darkness, after she took my blood and returned to her true form, Rhea's been off, to say the least. Nightmares. Screaming. Anger. Paranoia. That I can understand. I can expect. It makes her unpredictable and a little scary, but I can cope with it. It's the silence I can't take. The endless staring as she gets lost in the past. She stares at the door for hours, waiting for Ivan to return and lock her back inside her monstrous Dark Fae form.

I'm trying to be there for her. But I'm barely able to be there for myself at the moment.

This only increases my gratitude to El, who has taken Rhea under her wing.

In El, Rhea finds great comfort and a true friend, just as I did when I first met her.

'Morning,' El beams as I approach.

Her massively oversized hoody hangs past her knees, and her heavy black boots end at her thighs. Only she would wear an old jumper as a dress and pull it off.

Her hair has been braided, separating the two colours of pink and blue on each side of her head, and her makeup is as perfect as ever. The deep blue lipstick. The intricate eyeliner that disappears in her hairline and the eyeshadow of black and purple.

'You ready for some fun?' she asks, smiling from ear to ear. 'Hopefully, you'll be keeping your clothes on today? Not that I mind, of course. But if I have to hear Reid threaten another person every time he hears them comment on your incredible rack and arse, I may have to become a professional bodyguard for all the Fae we saved.' Her mischievous laugh is contagious. 'I can't wait to see you in action again.' She looks over her shoulder at the other Fae, all gathered around, looking uneasy about using their powers. 'Some of this lot have got some skills. It's exciting.' She lets out a happy exhale and takes another glance around her. 'It's been so long since I've seen our kind so free to use their powers, I'm still half expecting them to go all... erm...' She catches her words and looks at Rhea. 'Well... you know... grrr.' She finishes with a shrug.

'I'm ready, is my answer to your original question,' I reply, smirking at her sudden awkwardness. 'And thank you for your compliment on my arse and tits. I hope you don't repeat them in front of Reid and suffer his wrath.'

She snorts and gives my arm a playful whack. 'I can take him. Don't you worry. I'll never stop sharing my appreciation for such a work of art.'

There's a deep cough as Brennan clears his throat from behind me. My permanent shadow whenever Reid and Cyrus aren't taking up that role. He nods towards the direction of the clearing, impatience and annoyance dripping from every pore.

'If you're in a rush, Brennan, go,' I sigh.

'Not without you, *Your Highness*,' he replies, lowering his head in a sarcastic bow.

Fuck me. Brennan has never been overly warm and friendly, but something has seriously crawled up his arse these past few weeks. His indifference towards me seems to have become disdainful, and I'm not entirely sure why. Of course, I know that since Ivan returned, everyone's lives have been turned upside down. Many have ended. But some have been saved. Some have been freed.

In a way.

Rhea is still shuffling her feet and looking at the ground.

El looks between my sister and me and gives Brennan a whack on his arm.

'Give them some room. Raven's not going anywhere.'

His eye twitches, but he steps away.

I take my sister's hand.

'Raven,' Rhea starts. 'About yesterday morning. I'm so sorry-'

'It's fine. Don't worry about it.'

'I will worry about it.' Again, her eyes fixate on my face and fill with tears as she examines the scars. 'The cut on your arm... is it-'

'It's fine.'

'Will it scar?' she pushes.

The truth is I'm not sure. I haven't looked at it since Reid bandaged it as I slept. It aches, but then again, so does most of me these days.

'You had a bad dream, Rhea. You woke up in a start and lashed out. I've done the same.'

Her lip trembles. 'What if I killed you? What if next time-'

'You already planning on tossing me across the room again, are you?'

'No!' She looks terrified. 'No, I didn't mean-'

'Rhea. Stop!' I take her face in my hands and offer her my warmest smile. 'I'm joking. Please, stop this. What happened was an accident, and I'm not angry at you. I'm not scared of you.'

'Your erm... erm... your... Mates? Is that what I should call them?'

'I can think of a few words you can call them by,' I add.

'They're angry with me.' Her words are low. 'They're scared.'

'They're not scared of anything, Rhea.'

'No. They're not scared of me.' She lets out a laugh at the mere idea before it turns sad. 'They're scared of having to kill me to protect you.' She blinks, her eyes glistening with tears. 'And they *will* kill me if they see me as a threat to you. And it scares them because they know you would never forgive them if they did. And yet, they still would.' She rests her hand over mine as it lies flat on her cheek. 'To keep you safe, they will destroy anything threatening to hurt you even if their actions drive you away from them. I've only been around them for a few weeks, and I already know this as fact.'

'Well,' I tell her, stepping closer. 'I can swear to you that they would never dare lay a finger on you. And there will be no need to because you're not a threat. Not to me. Not to any of us. The ones who should be scared are the ones we're coming for. They better be fucking terrified.' I lean in and kiss her cheek, pulling her in close for a hug as I do. Brennan overtly clears his throat. 'Let's go.' I say. 'Before Brennan has an embolism or throws me over his shoulder.'

FIVE

We head into the woods and make our way to the clearing. I'm not surprised to find a few others already there. Not every Fae we have here has power. Some just Triggered and had their beauty, so they'll watch from the sidelines, but Brennan tells me they will practice a few fighting moves or how to shoot a gun.

After all, they need to defend themselves. Powers or not.

As we emerge into the clearing, many eyes land on me. Leaves fall from the branches above, yellow and dry as they succumb to the autumn. They flutter down, one after the other, gliding gracefully to the woodland floor to be crunched underfoot.

'Excuse me,' Brennan grunts as he brushes past me.

He slides his phone back into his pocket and heads towards Reid, who is still finishing his morning coffee as he watches me from across the clearing. His eyes narrow as he listens to whatever Brennan is reporting, and he nods.

Reid gestures for me to come too, so I head over. He hands me his coffee and pulls my hair free from beneath my jacket.

'Is Lucca still alive?' I ask, sipping his drink and enjoying it immensely. 'Or did Cyrus catch him?'

'Still alive,' he says, still fiddling with my hair, plaiting it so it falls neatly down my back and clear of my face. 'You ready?'

'Born ready.'

'Good girl.' He takes my face in his hands. 'Don't hold back. Mean every move you make. And focus.'

The idle chatter of the few spectators disappears, and I swear, the air gets even colder. Reid looks past me, and a flicker of annoyance sweeps across his face.

I turn.

Tessa has stepped through the brush and stopped dead ahead of us. Her eyes are so full of hatred every time she sees me. And even more so when she sees me with Reid.

Their marriage is over. It was long before I was in the picture, but she's not ready to walk away yet. Not without burning a hole in my head with the hateful stares she continues to throw my way.

Reid and I watch her as she stands there, back as straight as an arrow. Hair perfect. Skin flawless. She suits a royal life. Everything about her is poise, elegance and etiquette, except right now as she tries to blow up my brain with the intensity of her gaze.

With a groan, Reid returns his attention to me.

'Ignore her.'

'Easy for you to say. It's not you she's fantasising about boiling alive.'

'Actually,' Lucca says, 'It's strapping you to two horses and watching you get pulled apart that she fantasizes about.' He shrugs.

'I'm sorry. What?'

'Her father used to do that to unfortunates he would catch stealing. Until we made that specific practice illegal,' Reid adds.

'Suddenly, I'm glad I live in the human world.' I swallow and step closer to Reid, making him let out a low chuckle.

'No one gets to tie you up and stretch you out except Cyrus and me, so don't worry about that,' he says, enjoying the blush of my cheeks immensely. 'Now. Drink up and get ready. Time to practice.'

I down the coffee, and he takes the mug. Everyone gathers, excited to watch.

'Aren't they practising too?' I ask him as I suddenly become surrounded by a distant crowd.

'They will. But they're excited to see you,' Reid says. 'It will do them good to see your powers. Let's start easy.'

'She shouldn't find that hard,' Tessa scoffs. 'Easy is her middle name.'

I take off my coat, revealing my markings that tie Reid and me together, and watch smugly as the jealousy creeps into her perfectly refined little face. And with a whoosh, I reveal my wings.

A wave of admiring gasps ripples through those gathered as they fan out. Goosebumps cover every inch of my body as I feel them, so strong. So powerful. So free.

Pride is all I see on Reid's face. And I relish in it.

'A portal within sight, if you please.' He reaches out his arm, inviting me to respond.

I do. I reach out my hand, summon my powers and channel it into the world. The portals form swiftly now. Much quicker and more refined than they used to be. When made with skill instead of fear, they're much calmer. No howling winds. No inanimate objects flying around. Just a swirl of gold and black. A portal is on my left. Another on my right.

'Anyone want to go through?' Reid asks, looking at the children huddled together.

He's been trying hard to get them to speak. To get them to react and smile. But they're so traumatised, it's hard going. But a little hand goes up. A young girl, maybe five or six. She gets to her feet and stumbles through. When she emerges, her blank face suddenly breaks into a beautiful smile. And with a giggle, she returns to her seat, accompanied by applause.

'Now, to the anchor,' Reid says. 'Cyrus. He's out there somewhere, waiting.'

Easy. I think of his face. His smell. His voice. How I feel when I'm with him. How his name feels in my mouth. How his tongue feels on my tongue.

The second portal fades from sight, and we all watch the one which remains. A few seconds pass, and Cyrus walks through.

A small ripple of applause travels around me.

'Second anchor, please, Princess,' Cyrus says, joining Reid and facing me. 'Lucca's out in the woods.'

I focus hard. I think of Lucca. His cheeky grin. His bellowing laugh. His love-sick puppy dog eyes every time he looks at his Mate El.

Sure enough, he strides through, showing that I managed to move the portal from Cyrus's location to his.

'Great job, Pup,' he says as he heads towards El. 'I still love going through those portals.' He leans in and seals his lips around hers, claiming an almost indecent kiss.

Reid and Cyrus stand before me, their faces serious.

'You good?' Cyrus asks.

I nod.

'You see that large oak tree over there in the distance?' Reid asks, turning and gesturing to the horizon. 'It's the tallest tree in the canopy.'

'The one with the left side that looks bare?' I ask, straining my eyes to the far-off tree and focusing on keeping both portals alive.

This is about endurance as well as precision.

'That's the one,' he says. 'There is someone at the base of that tree waiting for a portal.'

'Who?'

'Point is not to know.' He gives a slight shake of his head. 'No faces. No names. They are at the base of the tree. Give them a portal.'

I dig in deep. I haven't been to the base of that tree. I have no person to use as an anchor. No previous knowledge of the location.

I stare at that tree. My eyes would bleed if they could.

'You can do this,' Reid encourages. 'C'mon.'

I hear Tessa scoffing behind me and muttering insults to me under her breath.

Bitch.

The pressure in my head builds until I feel that hateful trickle of blood slide down my nose.

'It's not happening today. Shut it off,' Cyrus says, waving his hand through the air dismissively.

But I'm not done trying yet.

I stride towards the portal and let my fingers skim the swirling surface.

Base of that tree. Base of that tree. Go to the base of that fucking tree!

More blood spills down my face.

'Raven. Stop.'

I ignore Cyrus and keep pushing. I feel the resistance of the portal. It's unwillingness and reluctance to shift to locations unknown.

The harder I try, the wilder the portal becomes, speeding up and becoming unstable. The air around us whips at our bodies, throwing the debris of the woodland floor about.

It feels ready to budge. Ready to yield.

'I said that's enough!' Cyrus barks, slapping my hand and forcing it down.

The portal fades, and the power and pressure ease. An enormous breath leaves my body in both frustration and relief.

I take the towel he hands me and press it to my nose, stemming the flow.

'I almost had it.'

'Had what? An aneurysm? Yeah. I saw.'

'Drama queen.'

'Pain in the arse.'

'Is she okay?' Rhea asks as she rushes over, taking the towel and taking over the very simple task of cleaning me up.

'I'm fine. I need a minute, and then we'll try again.'

The boys nod and take a step back, giving me some space.

Rhea... not so much. Not that I mind.

El joins us and helps with the cleaning.

'Maybe you should stop,' Rhea starts.

'It's a nosebleed. I'll be fine.'

After a few minutes of tutting, the girls leave, and I resume. Trying... and failing... to make a portal appear in a location I cannot see or have ever visited.

It's infuriating.

Others get bored of watching me fail and begin practising their own shit. In small groups, they test their limited powers. From the girl who grows fur to the one who can turn you on. That makes for interesting watching. It infuriates her that she can't get her powers to work on Cyrus. Our Bond makes it impossible for him to get hard for anyone but me.

Both a blessing and a curse, I think.

Most have no gifts beyond their Fae beauty, so they practice fighting.

Some go for hand to hand with Lucca and El.

Others go to Brennan for shooting or playing with knives.

I sit on the sidelines, a towel pressed to my nose, trying to ignore the nausea I feel in my belly.

Rhea sits with me, enjoying the show. The guys start to demonstrate and get a little competitive. Soon, the clearing is a full-blown arena of battling winged warriors all showing off. When the shirts come off and the fists come out, El sits with Rhea and me, and the crowd gathers again.

The aim, I think, is to pin down their opponent for ten seconds. El tries to tell me the rules, but all I see are muscles, strength, skill and sweat.

Ain't no one caring about rules with that kind of view.

Lucca and Brennan put on one hell of a show.

El is nothing but squeals and applause, watching the youngest of the four guys kick some serious arse. Lucca has the speed. He moves like lightning, dodging every blow and kick delivered by an increasingly frustrated Brennan. That, and he can read thoughts. He knows what's coming and can react with ease.

'My man has moves,' El admirers as her Mate laughs loudly at Brennan missing his attempt to get him in a chokehold.

But things really heat up when Reid lands before Cyrus, his wings wide, his shirt off and the ground trembling from the impact of his landing.

Hot. Fucking. Damn.

The audience is silent as we all watch.

Reid takes a powerful strike at Cyrus, throwing a right hook at his face. I gasp as it seems ready to find its target. But Cyrus lunges back, his left hand landing on the ground before he pushes himself back up and returning the blow, landing it in Reid's side. The victorious and cocky laugh Cyrus produces has me smiling.

I do love that laugh.

The air hisses past their bodies as they battle with immense speed and skill. Blood splatters knuckles, and sweat beads down their bodies.

Panting, Lucca slumps beside El, wrapping his arm over her shoulders and planting a bloody kiss on her cheek.

'Grim, Lucca,' she complains, wiping it away.

'My lip wouldn't be split if it weren't for Pup over there,' he chuckles.

'Why? What did I do?'

'It's hard to concentrate when all I can hear are your dirty thoughts.'

He looks at the two still going at it, thoroughly enjoying trying to beat the shit out of each other.

Reid comes out on top after a brutal kick to Cyrus's chest. He lands in the dirt and skids a few metres before stopping close to where I am.

'You okay?' I ask him as he groans.

'Been better,' he wheezes, holding his side.

'I win,' Reid declares.

Cyrus rolls over and continues to groan.

'Up you get, Little Bird,' Reid calls as I help Cyrus to sit.

Reid spits a mouthful of blood on the ground before facing me, his entire body tensed and broad, like a fucking God looking down on his worshipers. He gestures to the arena.

'My turn?' I repeat.

'Let's see what you got.'

'Yeah. That's not gonna happen.' Rhea stands and brushes off the dirt from her clothes before standing between us.

'He's joking,' I tell her.

'No, I'm not,' Reid replies, gesturing towards the clearing. 'Practice time. Come and kick my arse.'

'You're not gonna fight my sister.' Rhea's words of warning are absolute. 'You'll break her into pieces.'

'Only if she's lucky,' Lucca adds with a wink.

'Not fight,' Reid corrects her. 'Train. Raven, up you come.' He spits again, clearing the last of the blood from his mouth and turns away, rolling his shoulders and loosening up his neck muscles.

Cyrus walks towards Reid and faces me, looking ready and excited for this.

'Okay.' I step forwards, and Rhea blocks my path. 'They won't hurt me,' I tell her.

'I don't want to risk it. Just watch a little more.'

Her efforts are sweet but unnecessary.

Besides, I need to train.

El's hand reaches up and takes hers. 'She'll be fine. The guys wouldn't hurt a hair on her head. Trust me.'

With encouragement from El, Rhea steps aside and begrudgingly sits back down.

I step into the arena.

The two men circle me like hunters encircling their prey, and again, the crowd falls deathly quiet.

'So, what are the rules?'

'Don't land in the dirt. Ten seconds down, and you're out,' Reid replies with a shrug. 'Same as everyone else. You win if you last longer than three minutes. You ready?'

'Win what, exactly?'

'Oh. You want to make this interesting?' Reid asks, his brow lifting.

'Maybe.'

'Okay. What do you want if you win?'

'I want to visit one of the remaining Fae cities and see if we can get more out. Give them my blood and bring them back with us.'

They knew that was coming. They share a look, but their cockiness fails to falter.

'Okay. Deal,' Reid says simply. They both step towards me and stop close. 'But if we win...'

'Let me guess. Sex.' I roll my eyes. 'You're extremely layered men, aren't you.'

'If we win, we want you to forgive us.'

'Forgive you?' I scoff.

'Yes. If you win, we will go to one of the remaining cities as you wish. If we win, then we start with a fresh slate. No more snide comments. No more throwing our mistakes in our faces. We move on and you give us a real chance. And yes.' Reid leans in and lowers his voice. 'You let us back into your bed. Trust me. You won't regret it.'

Cyrus steps closer. 'You win. We do what you want. But if we win, we will fix this. Us. Properly.'

'It's two against one.'

'Then you can use your powers. We won't use ours. No smoke and no light.'

I hesitate, but the chance of getting what I want is too tempting to pass up.

'Okay.'

They both blink in surprise.

'Okay?' They both repeat.

'You're on.'

I reach out and shake both of their hands.

They step back so we're a few metres apart. They plant their feet in the ground, ready to charge.

'We won't go easy on you.'

'You never do,' I retort, digging in my own feet. 'Start the timer.'

'GO!' they bellow at the same time.

Their feet dig in as they charge. My wings emerge, and I soar upwards. They're quick and react the same, leaping upwards into the air to give chase.

They're skilled fliers. More so than me. They're close on my heels, so I create a portal below and dive into it. I come out by the arena, swooping over the heads of those below who gasp and yelp, ducking for cover. The boys are through before I can get a chance to seal it closed, determination and focus on their faces. I turn and create another portal. They can't stop themselves in time and soar through, coming out back at the cottage. As I seal it closed, I hear their distant yells of anger.

I turn, my wings lifting me upwards.

They're soaring towards the clearing.

'TWO MINUTES LEFT!' Lucca yells as they pass.

I duck and dive, throwing portals in their path and also in mine. But they're quick learners and dodge most of them. Each one I pass through, they emerge right behind me.

Bastards.

I glance back and see only Reid.

Where the fuck has Cyrus gone?

I continue dodging Reid's outstretched hands and slip through his grip every time.

'ONE MINUTE LEFT!'

Thanks, Lucca.

I bank a hard right, past a large Oak tree, and hear a sharp whistle above. I look and scream as Cyrus's feet head straight for me.

They collide with my belly and push me to the ground. I land in the dirt, my back colliding with the hard earth, and cough from the winding he's given me.

His feet plant either side of me before he presses his boot on my chest and he peers down, his head tilted to one side and a half smile on those beautiful lips.

He starts to count. I lift my foot and slam it between his legs as hard as I can. His eyes widen as he grabs his dick and falls on his side.

'Not... cool...' he whines.

I'm up again and running. I lift myself with a beat of my wings but feel something grab my ankle.

Looking down, I see Reid keeping me grounded as I try to fly to freedom.

'No, you don't.' He strains, yanking me down hard.

Thud.

He slams me into the ground, my wings fading from sight.

Reid grabs my wrists and pins them down. Cyrus grabs my ankles.

The bastards start to count.

My powers link with the panic.

Suddenly this isn't a game and graphic, violent images start to bombard my mind of me in the woods, held down by Jonah and his friends. All laughing as they tore at my clothes. All boasting about what horrific acts they were going to do to me. They held my wrists. They held my ankles. They kept me in the dirt.

'STOP!' I scream. 'LET GO! PLEASE!'

'LET HER UP!' Lucca yells. 'PTSD FLASHBACK! LET HER GO!'

Too late.

Cyrus and Reid yell as a surge of power erupt from my body, hurtling them backwards.

My mind is filled with one thing. And one thing only.

Him.

The terror he sparks has my powers exploding again. I open a portal beneath me, but this time, it's unintentional.

I scream and reach out for something to grab, terrified that I've no idea where the hell this gateway leads.

I land with a crippling thud on my back.

Groaning, I look up at the swirling portal high above my head. A clear sky looms even higher. The smell of the woodlands is gone. Instead, a stench of rot and filth has replaced it.

That, and an eerie, constant, low growling that is almost deafening.

I turn my head, blinking away the spots marking my vision.

My entire body runs cold. An icy chill engulfs me from the top of my head down to my toes.

Everything slows. The whole fucking world.

I'm looking at hundreds of Dark Fae. All stood in a large pen but in perfect lines. Their snarling is impossible to control, unlike their behaviour, which is under the control of a madman. I'm on a stage or podium, elevated above them all.

And to the right are three men. I think they're men. But they don't look entirely human. All their eyes glow gold, but they have no pointed ears or any hint of Fae beauty. One has pale, sickly green skin. And as I look harder, I see vines growing under his skin. They slither and move inside him, and thorns protrude from his neck and cheeks. The second looks like he's been burned. His flesh is charred and black. Smoke seeps from his pores and he glows red and orange, like burning coal in the heart of a fire.

The third looks as though some of his body has become metal. Not sleek, but rusted and degraded. Not all of it, just some. His left arm is mostly covered. Some of his face and neck.

They all look as if they're in pain but trying not to show it, grimacing stoically and swaying as they try to remain on their feet.

They face a long line of men who survey the army of stolen Fae and admire the three mutated humans. They lord over them, puffing smoke into the air from their thick cigars, laughing and boasting about their victory over us all.

One of the men turns and sees me. Still in slow motion and suddenly drowning me in silence. Like I'm back in that portal without air or life. The man turns, and he smiles.

Jonah.

Dressed in his Authority uniform, decorated in medals celebrating his atrocities. Our eyes become glued to one another.

He turns and faces me fully, his eyes shining as he utters my name with longing. The other men all turn to look too.

Most are unknown to me, but all are wealthy, wearing suits and silk ties. Or they're Authority and decorated in uniform.

Except for the man in the very middle.

My father.

Surprise smacks him hard and leaves him speechless at the sudden arrival of the daughter he's been hunting for being dropped into his lap without any effort on his part at all.

Jonah takes a step towards me. His fingers flex in excitement at the prospect of finally getting them back on me. But he stops. They all do. Their eyes drift upwards.

The floor trembles and I'm cast in shadow. Rage now engulfs Jonah's face as he sees Reid standing over me, his face rigid with twice as much rage as Jonah's could ever hold.

And suddenly, time speeds up. I'm back in the world, hearing the snarling and smelling the stench.

'GET THEM!' Ivan roars, his eyes going gold as he wields the power he stole from Rhea.

The Dark Fae all screech and start to charge towards us as the men in suits and Authority uniforms leap aside to get the hell out of their way.

Reid sends a ball of his blinding white light at Ivan and Jonah. He's paying no attention to the creatures charging towards us. None whatsoever. Reid goes to charge, ready to attack, consumed with hatred and vengeance. Ivan has a gold flame on his hand, the same flame he stole from me when he had me in that chair.

The Authority pull out guns and the three humans to the right, the one still burning, the one covered in vines, and the one of metal, all face us too.

Cyrus's arms slide under me, and he lingers for the slightest breath, staring at those bastards. Those devils.

'What the...' he breathes, staring at them. 'What are they?'

Reid is going mad with his light, desperate to kill anyone and everyone, whereas Cyrus and I watch as the three mutants come running. One is now covered in fire. He starts to scream in agony but keeps coming for us. The one covered in vines reaches out his hand. But a vine explodes from his chest, killing him instantly. And the one of metal charges forwards, his feet slamming hard into the stage. I sense that the metal is iron. He opens his mouth and roars. Shards of iron come flying from his mouth, all splattered with blood, tearing his insides as they leave his body.

'What the fuck are they?' Cyrus hisses as he steps back, holding me tight.

They're sick and twisted. But they're also fucking dead.

The Dark Fae, however, are not.

'Go!' I tell him, seeing them charge closer. 'We have to go! REID!'

Cyrus soars upwards towards the portal, leaving behind the podium full of our enemies and the incoming army of lost souls. Reid is still trying to fight everyone.

So I pull on our tether marks. I use the very Bond that I loathe and watch as Reid is yanked away from them all with a shout.

We all hurtle through the portal and land in the woodland clearing, where everyone lingers.

'Where did she land this time?' Tessa says with a jeer, clearly mocking my inability to control my powers fully.

'Shut the portal down, Raven!' Cyrus says, lowering me to my feet and backing away from it.

Reid is back on his feet and actually goes to go back through, overcome with utter rage and wrath. I pull him back with the tether and drag him across the dirt to keep him here. To keep him safe.

'SHUT IT DOWN!' Cyrus yells, pointing at the portal.

His tone alerts the others that the shit's about to hit the fan big time, and they all leap to their feet, grabbing a weapon and facing the portal.

But the image of Jonah seems imprinted on my brain. I don't understand how he's suddenly in my head and I can't get him out!

'RAVEN!' Cyrus shouts. 'FIX YOUR FUCKING MESS AND SHUT IT DOWN!'

'I CAN'T!' I yell back, trying with all my might to get it to stop. 'I DON'T UNDERSTAND-'

Two Dark Fae explode through, all snarling teeth, twisted limbs and sharp talons.

Everyone screams and starts to run

Everyone except Lucca, El, Brennan, Reid and Cyrus. They all run towards the fight.

The fog clears in an instant. And whatever was keeping my thoughts on nothing but Jonah ends in the blink of an eye. As the others take on the two Fae that have already broken through, I turn to the portal, take back control and cast its form to the wind just as three others are halfway through.

The wind dies down, and I'm left looking at three writhing forms. Their bodies are lost from their chests down, yet they still stare at me, clawing their way across the ground in desperation to get to me.

Their master ordered them to. They won't stop until they die, and now, because of me, they will very soon.

There's a chorus of gunfire, and I spin just in time to see Brennan send several bullets through the skull of one of the Dark Fae.

'No!' I yell, rushing towards them all. Towards the last Dark Fae left alive. It's got a hold of El.

Lucca has a gun trained on it. His finger rests on the trigger, and before I can think, I throw myself between them.

I can save it! I can bring back another Fae from the Darkness!

Lucca fires and I catch the bullet in my shoulder.

The Dark Fae screeches as I fall to the ground, clutching the wound. My blood is in the air. The scent of life. The sweet promise of light. It tosses El aside and leaps high, pouncing on me instead.

Teeth as sharp as knives dig into my arm, and I cry a blood-curdling, agonized cry, struggling to get the damned thing off me.

BANG!

The Dark Fae jolts and slumps on top of me. The back of its head is clean gone. Its brains exposed and chunks of skull splatter my cheek.

The echo of that fatal gunshot continues, swirling around the clearing like a siren of death.

Everything else is silent.

The weight of the dead Fae is crushing as it remains slumped over me. I peer down. Its face is so close to mine I can feel its final breath still leaving its body.

My blood drips from its teeth and lands on my skin. It was so close... so close to coming back.

Reid stands over me, the gun still in his hand from the fatal shot.

'Why...' I whisper. 'Why would you shoot them?'

His eye twitches as he stares down at me.

I try to shift, but the creature's weight is too much, as is the pain from the gunshot and the bite.

'Raven!' Rhea calls, running towards me.

Reid raises his gun and points it at my sister. She skids to a stop.

'She got herself in this mess. She can get herself out,' he says to her.

'She's hurt. She needs help!' Rhea's words are met by the cocking of his gun.

'I won't shoot to kill, but I promise you it will fucking hurt, Rhea.' Reid's words are utter truth. I sense no hint of a lie.

'Stay where you are, Rhea,' I say, staring at Reid and his gun.

'But-'

'I'm fine. Just stay there.'

I summon all my strength and painfully slide myself from beneath the creature. Stumbling, I reach my feet and look down, my hand pressing into my arm as blood seeps through my fingers.

Brennan is frantically checking the monster's necks. He lifts his gaze to Reid.

'There are no collars on them. They're not being tracked.'

'Well, that's something,' Lucca tries with a smile. 'How about we all go inside and have a nice cold beer or-'

Hatefully, I lift my gaze to Reid.

'Murderer.'

'Is that supposed to come as a shock to you or something?' he says coldly. 'Or have we not met?'

'It had my blood. It was minutes away from-'

'We agreed to terms. Blood is given in controlled circumstances. Not you throwing yourself in front of a bullet and letting one almost tear your arm off.'

'You could have just pulled it off me. You could have just-'

'No.' He shakes his head with his brow raised. 'You could have just lost the match. You could have played by the rules instead of throwing yourself through that portal. You could have not thrown yourself in the path of a bullet. What if one had pulled you back through the portal you, for some reason, refused to close? Ivan would have you already. What if one of them escaped and told him our location? All the Fae you begged me to help you save would be slaughtered or recaptured.'

'I could have saved them.'

He lowers his gun and points it at the five dead Fae surrounding us. 'This is you. This is your fault.'

Those words are a punch to the gut.

'This is not my fault.'

'No?'

'You shot them.'

'And you cut three in half.' He looks at the still-writhing creatures who remain compelled to get me, just as Ivan ordered. 'I already made it clear that I will set the world on fire before I see you taken from me. Before I see you butchered and killed. Before I see you back in the hands of...' He seals his lips together and violently shakes his head, refusing to say the name I know he was about to say. 'How could you use that bastard as an anchor?'

'Who was it?' asks El. 'Who was the anchor?'

'Jonah,' Reid says plainly, looking at me with accusatory eyes.

'I didn't mean to,' I reply through gritted teeth. 'I don't know how it happened, but he just-'

'Anchors are only made with a deep connection. Emotional and physical. There has to be a longing there, and you feel that for him?! What the hell is wrong with you-'

Before Reid can finish, I step closer and slam my fist into the side of his face. He stumbles, not as much as I wish he had, but I manage to draw blood thanks to my newfound strength, courtesy of my new wings.

'If you think for one second that I have any longing for that man, then you can go to hell and stay there. You were the one trying to kill them all on your own when we should have been getting the hell out of there.' I turn to Cyrus standing behind me, watching with an unreadable expression. 'And you both held me down, even when it was obvious that I was freaking out. Lucca even told you to let me go, but you didn't. All because you wanted to win.'

Reid rests the tips of his fingers over his lips and feels blood. His eyes flick to me and are so full of wrath it should have me cowering.

But I'm done cowering.

'I get that you're frustrated with me. I get that I'm annoying. That I don't do as you want. That I follow my own conscience instead of your orders. And I get that my refusal to let you stick your dick inside me is pissing you off.'

A low growl emanates from his chest.

'But I want you to think hard about what you just said to me. To your Mate, who you claim to care for above all others. Do you think I have a strong emotional attachment to that man? A longing? Really?'

'No,' he replies through clenched teeth. 'Of course not. I just don't understand how you managed to use him as an anchor-'

'You're jealous of him or something? Has he been allowed to do something to me that you wish you could?'

'No. Don't be-'

I slam my hands into his chest and he staggers back, still looking at me with silent anger.

'You got something to add, Cyrus?' I snap, looking in his direction as he takes a step forwards. 'Because now's the time.'

Silence engulfs the two men as they watch me.

'He appeared in my head like a bomb going off,' I tell them. 'You had me pinned down. I couldn't move. I couldn't fight you off and I panicked. It's never happened like that before. I have to try hard to create the link I need to make an anchor. I have to want it. He just forced his way in like a fucking crowbar prising apart my brain. He felt pushed in. Not called. I couldn't stop it. I had no control. Okay? And damn you for ever suggesting that I would want to see him unless it was with his intestines around his neck as he dangled from a tree.'

'She's telling the truth,' Lucca says. 'She's too scared of him ever to be able to form a link strong enough to-'

'Shut the fuck up, Lucca!' I shout. 'No one fucking asked for your input, alright?!' I groan and roll my shoulder, the pain starting to override the adrenaline. 'You fucking shot me. You don't get an opinion, and you don't get to listen in on my thoughts.'

Reid steps forwards, his hand reaching out to help with the wound. I slap it away.

You bet I fucking slap it away.

'You know what?' I say, tears threatening to claw their way up my throat as I get ready to say the words my anger is pushing me to say. 'The match is over. Neither of us won. Neither of us will ever win. This is a sick joke of a relationship. I wish I never sealed our Bond.'

His eyes flick to my arms, and he sees the hairs on my skin stand on end as my lie is exposed. Reid looks visibly relieved at that fact.

'You are lucky that Cyrus and I were there to get you out of that situation-'

'Lucky?' I scoff, wiping away the tears before they fall. 'Reid. Nothing about my life is lucky. Where I've been. Where I am. Where I will end up.'

'You're the luckiest fucking girl in this whole shit hole of a world.'

'Really!' I bellow with laughter.

'Really,' he spits back. 'You're *lucky* that you escaped Ivan when you were a child. I doubt anyone else would have gotten away with their lives as you did. You're *lucky* you survived Rhea's attack on you all those years ago and that all you have to show for facing a giant Dark Fae as a child are your scars. You're lucky we're the ones, Cyrus and I, who found you in that cesspit city and Triggered you so you could be strong. You're lucky you have us here to protect you!'

'To own me, more like!' I yell back. 'I'm not lucky, Reid. I'm a fucking disaster. A magnet for death and pain. And I'm nothing to you except a weapon and a fuck toy. Quit pretending otherwise!'

'YOU'RE EVERYTHING TO ME! TO US BOTH!' he roars. His words bounce around us as spit flies from his lips and he puts his red face in mine. 'You should be thanking the fates and the Goddess that you have us as your Bonded Mates.'

'Oh yes. Thank you.' I turn to the sky. 'Thank you, Goddess. Thank you, Fates.' I throw up my arms as if to offer my soul to them. I roar at the endless sky. 'I thank you for my endless blessings. For all the people in my life who have treated me like shit. For Ahri and her dad. For the degenerate fucker that made my life hell at school. For Jonah, Ivan and Serge. Thank you for making me fall in love with two deranged, psychotic, overbearing arse holes who want to control every aspect of my fucking life!!'

My words echo again and again in an endless loop, returning to us over and over. My words. My stupid fucking words.

Reid blinks, looking at me without anger. But with shock.

He looks at my arms and sees no sign of a lie. His mouth opens. 'You're falling in lo-'

'Don't.' I step back as he goes to reach out for me. 'I didn't... I didn't mean that.'

'What are you talking about?' Rhea asks, breaking the tension-filled vacuum. 'W-what... what do you mean... who is Jonah?'

My eyes close, and I regret my haste to spit my venom in a second.

Rhea has no idea about Jonah. No idea about my past. No idea about my life really at all.

I grew up on the city streets, bunkering down with a man who pretended to be my father. That's all she knows. That's all I want her to know.

Ahriella. The Old Man. The deals they would strike with Jonah. Even school and the hell Darius would put me through. It's all a secret the others agreed to keep for me.

Rhea's only just started to sleep through the night. She's only stopped crying when she sees the scars on my face.

The poor girl is haunted by flashes of her life as a Dark Fae and riddled with guilt about everything else too.

I have no intention of her discovering anything about my life before we found each other again.

'It's nothing, Rhea,' Cyrus says, still watching me almost unblinking, the same look of surprise on his face as still remains on Reid's. 'Raven and Reid are upset and angry with each other. It's nothing to worry about.'

'Raven?' she urges.

I turn and put on the best smile I can.

'It's nothing. Don't worry.'

I can tell she doesn't buy it. Why would she? I'm offering her bullshit. No one enjoys receiving a steaming pile of lies.

'I'm gonna go fix myself up.' I turn and start towards the house.

'I'll help,' she offers.

'I'm fine on my own. Stay with El.' I walk quickly, almost running away from them all.

'Raven. RAVEN, WAIT!' Reid calls after me.

'Midnight!' I call back.

'You can't safe word a fucking conversation!' Cyrus argues as I keep walking.

'Watch me.'

The heat of their stares burns my back, and once I reach the woods, I run. When I reach the farmhouse and spot all the others lingering about, cautiously watching the surrounding area for any straggler Dark Fae that may have escaped, I divert and run deeper into the woods.

Soon, the tears break through. They spill down my cheeks, and the sobs aren't far behind. When I'm surrounded in solitude, I fall to my knees and just howl.

I'm stuck. Trapped in this fucking nightmare with no way out. Facing an impossible fight against those that utterly terrify me and, yes, falling in love with the two men I should hate.

My hand seals around my mouth as I let out a scream. Tears blur my vision and I struggle to hold it all in.

I am so fucking scared.

So lost.

So broken.

I have no idea what to do.

SIX

'Are you dead?' Lucca asks as he steps through the brush and looks at me lying on the floor, looking up at the sky. 'Because if you're dead, I'm not gonna be far behind you.'

'Not dead,' I reply, watching the clouds slowly drift overhead. 'Just hiding.'

'Can I join you?'

'If you want.'

Lucca makes his way to me and falls heavily onto his back so we're side by side, watching the clouds.

'They're looking for you.'

'I know. They've been tugging at the Bond.' I lift my arms, showing him the intricate black tattoos that they put there. 'Just light enough to know they want me back, not so hard as to actually move me.'

'I thought you all promised you wouldn't use those unless it was an emergency.'

'They're not really using them. Just reminding me that they're there and that they could. It kind of feels like a cramp. It's more annoying than painful.' I drop my arms back into the debris of the woodland floor and let out a long breath. 'How did you find me?'

'I could hear your thoughts.'

'You're getting stronger then?'

'We all are, thanks to you. Our powers are like muscles. Now we're allowed to exercise them again properly, they're getting stronger every day.'

I look over. His eye is a mess of bruising and swelling.

'Lucca... what happened?'

'You should see the other guy,' he smiles. 'I really fucked his knuckles up with my face.'

'Who did that?'

Like I need to ask.

'Not important. It was nothing less than what I deserved. If someone had shot my Mate in the shoulder, I'd do much worse than give them a black eye.'

He turns his head to face me and tries to seem okay. His Lucca charm isn't as strong as it usually is.

'I'm really sorry I shot you, Pup. I swear to the Goddess it was an accident.'

'I know that. Of course, I know that. And so should the idiot that hit you. I was the one that jumped in the way. It had nothing to do with you.'

'You should go back to the house. Everyone is freaking out, and that wound needs dressing.'

'I'm fine. It was just a graze.' With a heavy sigh, I look back up at the sky. 'It's all my fault, really. How stupid could I be? Making a portal that led straight to the very people we're hiding from.' I swallow dryly. 'Straight to *him*.'

'Not as stupid as you may think,' he says quietly. His tone carries with it a slight chill. 'Your trip today was no accident. Your thoughts being consumed by Jonah was less instinct and more.... Payback.'

I sit. So does he.

'Explain.'

'As I said, our powers are growing.'

'Yeah. I got that.'

'Well, just before you went bye-bye through the portal, I heard someone thinking.'

'Uh-huh.'

'It was Tessa.'

My teeth grind. '*Uh-huh.*'

'She's an extreme empath. She can take emotions and feelings from one, keep them for herself or pass them to another. But now she's been flexing her muscles, and it would seem that she is getting rather good at finding certain emotions and firing them up. When the boys had you pinned, I heard your thoughts. I knew you were having flashbacks to the day in the woods with those scum bags. I heard you, but I also heard Tessa. She had sensed your fear of Jonah, that how the guys held you down made you panic. And she turned your fear voltage up to full power. That's why you went to him.'

'Tessa did that to me?'

'She really hates you, Pup.' He rolls his eyes and looks at the trees. 'She passed out soon after you fell. Her power exhausted her. If you're interested, she's still out cold in the bush she was hiding in when she fainted.'

He lies back down on the ground, his arms folded across his chest.

'You left her there? Why not tell Reid or Cyrus?'

'Honestly?'

'Do you have any other choice since I'll know if you're lying?'

He gives a soft laugh. No. Of course not. No one does with me.

'Because Tessa's family. I love the idiot like a sister. But one of those really annoying, ungrateful, bratty sisters that think she's better than everyone else, you know? And if they found out that her jealousy almost hurt their Mate, I'm not entirely sure that it would end too good for her.'

'You're protecting her?'

'Someone has to. Idiot sure as shit isn't going to do it herself. But you're the one that got thrown to the monsters of your nightmares, so I figured you get to tell. If that's what you wanna do.'

'Tell?'

'Overbearing arse number one and overbearing arse number two probably would like to know that the ex-wife is trying to fuck over the new girlfriend. But Tessa, you see, she's on real thin ice as it is. After the incident with the food poisoning-'

'I didn't stop throwing up for three days. It was disgusting.'

'And then there were the fleas she put in your bed.'

'Itchy. Really annoyed Cyrus.'

'They were fond of his arse.'

'Maybe he should have kept it out of my bed. Then they wouldn't have kept biting it,' I grin.

'She's circling the drain and is not their priority.' Our eyes meet. 'You will always be their priority, Pup. You, above all others. Until you, or they, take their last breath.'

I know what he's asking, but I also know that he would never ask it with anything less than the words he has already chosen.

He loves Tessa. She's family. She's in trouble. Angry. Looking for payback.

The guys will not take her actions lightly.

'Ughhh,' I groan. 'Fine.' He holds out his arm, and I fall into his chest, looking up at the sky with him. 'You talk to Tessa and tell her she needs to back off. I'll keep it to myself if she leaves me alone.'

'Thanks, Pup,' he says, wrapping his arm around me and kissing the top of my head. 'I owe you one.'

'Lucca, you fucking shot me. You owe me more than one.'

'True...' he laughs. 'I'll pay up. Just tell me when.'

'Oh, I will. Don't you worry.' My body relaxes as I lie with him. 'Did you hear about what we saw?'

'Which part?' he asks. 'The army of monsters. Daddy dearest and he who must not be mentioned. Or the three freaky stooges who died when they tried to attack you with wonky powers?'

'The stooges,' I answer. 'One looked like he was burning from the inside. The other was like he was rusted metal. And the third guy looked like he had plants growing inside him. They all looked like they were in agony, but they didn't make a sound.'

'Yeah. That was mentioned. They're looking into it. Cyrus said they were human.'

'I don't know what they were.'

'Ivan does like to mess with shit he shouldn't,' he sighs.

'Science meets magic,' I sigh back.

'So...' he starts. 'Did I hear you say the "L" word to Reid and-'

'Not talking about that.'

'I've never seen them stunned into silence like that before.'

'Where's Rhea?'

'A seamless change of subject. She's with El, who's making sure she's okay.'

'*Is* she okay?'

'Rhea is demanding to know what you were on about whilst you were dancing the foreplay-hate-dance with lover boys. Maybe you should tell her about what happened with-'

'I'm glad Rhea and El are getting on so well.'

'Another successful change of subject.'

'You know, I still can't get used to looking up and seeing a clear sky. I don't think I'll ever get tired of it. Nor the air. I keep going to put on a mask when I get dressed in the morning. But I swear, even now, I can smell the city. That stench is embedded in my senses.'

'I wish you could experience home. Now that was fresh air.'

'I wish I could, too.' I close my eyes and feel so at ease I think I could sleep. 'Can I ask you something?'

'Always.'

'Did it make you feel any better?'

'What?'

'Killing those men at the brothel,' I say sleepily. 'The men who hurt you.'

'A little, yeah. But they weren't sorry for what they did. They were just sorry their actions caught up with them. So it's a hollow victory really.' He shifts a little. 'Did it make you feel better killing Serge?'

'I didn't kill him. Brennan did.'

'Well... did it make you feel better torturing Serge?'

'A little. Not as much as I hoped it would. But I'm glad he's dead. Lucca?'

'Yeah.'

'Does it ever get any better?' I take a shallow breath and feel the pull of sleep seriously tugging me. 'When do the nightmares stop? When will I be okay?'

'I don't think people who have been through the shit we have will ever be okay.'

'Great...' I whisper. 'Comforting.'

'I can't lie to you, remember?'

'But you and El work. You guys are great together.'

'Yeah. We are. In our own twisted fucked up kinda way.'

'Why can't I be like you guys? Why can't I... Reid and Cyrus... I wish we could just be...'

'Pup? You okay there?'

'Tired...'

He shifts and gives me a shake.

'Ahh shit. Pup. Your thoughts are getting real quiet.'

He sits.

'Tired...' I whisper again, my body heavy with the need to sleep.

'Nope. Unconscious. Man,' he groans, getting to his feet and cradling me in his arms. 'I'm gonna get another black eye for bringing you back unconscious.' He starts to walk. 'And for the record. You do have what El and I have. Love. Passion. Friendship, fire and then some. You guys just need to realise that you can trust each other and quit trying to best each other. You're on the same side.'

'Doesn't feel... Like it...'

'They're on your side. To them, *your* side is the only side. I know because I feel that way for my Mate. They will follow you anywhere. I just wish one of you would ease up on the self-righteous obsession to be right all the time.'

'Shut up.'

'That's never gonna happen.'

'Don't I know it.'

Sleep claims me.

And so, again, do the nightmares.

SEVEN

*T*alk about crowded. The bedroom is full of people when I wake up. The guys are asleep on the floor, their backs against the wall and their legs stretched out. On the bed, El and Rhea are fast asleep. Lucca sits on a chair, but his head is on El's pillow.

Sitting, I feel the pinch of the bandages on my shoulder. The blood-soaked cloths are still on the bedside table from where I'm guessing they cleaned me up. Hunger stabs at my insides, and thirst has dried my mouth. I leave the room and head downstairs. Space is so lacking, and people sleep wherever they can find space. Each room is rammed with Fae. I pass them all as they sleep through the early morning hours and head towards the kitchen. Brennan is awake. I swear he's always awake. Always on watch. He walks through the hall to the front door to do yet another sweep, guns at the ready.

'I'm going to make some coffee and toast. You want some for when you get back?' I ask him.

He gives a nod and leaves.

Always a man of many words.

In the kitchen, sitting at the old dining table with several mismatched and wonky stools, an unwelcome face greets me. I say greet. Scowl would be more like it.

'Tessa,' I grumble.

'Whore,' she greets back.

'How's the head?' I ask, seeing her bloody handkerchief pressed to her nose.

'None of your business.'

'Wow. Someone woke up on the wrong side of the bed. Or should I say bush?'

As I pass, I pick out a twig from her hair and place it on the table beside her. I busy myself with making coffee, knowing she's watching my every move.

'I heard you had some trouble earlier.' I hear her smug grin through her words.

'Yeah. Five Fae were killed, and Ivan Walker almost found our location. Good job he didn't, or everyone here would be dead.' I turn, stirring my coffee as I stare at her. My words knock her smile clean off her face. 'Was it worth it?'

'I don't know what you're-'

'I'm a walking lie detector, Tessa. Besides. I know it was you. I know what you did, same as I know that you woke up alone, in a bush, blood smearing your pretty little chin and your head pounding. You want to watch how far you push your powers so soon. I would hate for your head to explode.'

'It's not my fault you can't control your powers and opened a portal-'

'It won't be my fault if the boys find out what you did. It won't be my fault what they choose to do with you.'

'I am family. I have been with them for decades. You're nothing compared to that.'

'This is the last time I cover for you.'

She scoffs at my words.

'I'm serious, Tessa. Fuck with me all you want. Piss about with your childish little pranks. I've seen it all. I've been at the end of every form of torture you could devise. Every cruelty.' I lower my mug and walk over to her, leaning over her as she sits and tries to hold her composure. 'But if you dare put the other's lives at risk again. If you even think about it. I'll-'

'You'll what? Tell on me?' Her lip curls in cruelty. 'They will never get rid of me, whore. No way. There's nothing you can do about it.'

I grab her hair and slam her pretty little face into the table. I hold her easily, even as she thrashes and claws at me.

'You're under the impression I need anyone to look after me. I've survived monsters you could barely conceive in your dreams. I am not scared of you. But I promise that you should be fucking terrified of me. My sister was in the crowd when those Dark Fae followed me through that portal you manipulated me into. My friends. My lovers.' I shove her harder into the tabletop. 'If your pathetic little attempts to get back at me over Reid and Cyrus being my Mates ever endanger anyone I love ever again, I will cut you down without hesitation.' I lean down close to her ear. 'You use your powers on us, you spread your venom or stir your shit, you so much as look at my guys or me in a way I don't like, I will open a portal into a Fae city sewer and drop you right in it and watch you drown in excrement. And you know what?' I look down at her as she struggles beneath my grip. 'No one will ever know where you went. And I highly doubt anyone would care.' I hold my arm out for her to see no trace of a lie. 'I'm not your enemy. Not yet. I suggest you focus on those who want to kill and enslave us all instead of lashing out because of your jealousy. Got it?'

I give her head a little thud into the wood when she refuses to answer.

'Yes,' she snarls. 'I've got it.'

I let her go with a shove and straighten myself up.

'Good.' I take my coffee and leave, letting the kitchen door shut behind me so she can lick her wounds in private.

'That was hot.'

I stop and turn to see Cyrus lingering by the door.

'Has anyone ever told you that you should wear a bell?' I sneer. 'You're a sneaky little fucker.'

He pushes himself from the wall and strides over, stopping close and looking down at me. I have to tilt my head up to keep him in my sight. Him and his cocky half-smile.

'What did you hear?'

'Just you threatening Tessa like a possessive little lunatic. Just the way I like you. What did she do this time? Not fleas again, I hope.'

'Not fleas. Forget it. It was nothing.' I swivel on my heel and start towards the front door, but he takes my elbow and guides me back.

'Are you okay?' he asks in all seriousness. 'Seeing who you saw today, it must have been hard.'

'It was harder to be accused of having feelings for him, if I'm honest.'

'That was fear talking. Nothing else. It's amazing how quickly fear turns to anger, and it's nearly always misdirected.'

'Is that so?'

'Like when I was a kid, my mother always told me not to run so fast. But of course, I ran as fast as possible and fell flat on my face. She would rush over. All worried that I was hurt. When she saw I wasn't, she was furious that I had disobeyed her. Only because she couldn't bear the idea of me getting hurt.'

'I wouldn't know what that was like. My mother was raped and butchered, and my father locked me up and experimented on me.' I yank back my elbow. 'Excuse me.'

'Well, you know what it's like now because if you took a second to pay attention, you are surrounded by people who care about you.'

My feet slow as he follows me. Again, we're face-to-face.

'Your sister. El. Lucca. Brennan. They all love you. And you have Reid and me. Trust me when I tell you that you are fucking cared about in this house. For Goddess's sake, we all fell asleep in that room because we were all so worried about you and didn't want you to wake up alone.'

'I know that,' I admit. 'Of course I do.'

'Then why are you so fucking angry all the time? So combative?'

'I... I can't...'

'You're in fresh, clean air. No collar. No need for Gilt. Your gifts have saved all the lives that are under this roof. Your days of starving are gone. You have powers beyond your wildest dreams. You're stronger than you have ever been. You're stronger than the best of us and a queen!'

'I know that.'

'Then why are you so fucking angry at us all the time?!'

'You know why! Everything that happened. Every lie. Every-'

'Are you still genuinely pissed that Reid Triggered you?' He snatches my arm with rough hands and clamps down hard on my skin. 'Because of him, you have power. Strength. A way to protect others and fight your enemies? To protect yourself and those you love? Are you seriously angry about that?'

'Get off me.' The more I struggle, the tighter he grabs. 'You're going to leave bruises.'

'Good. I like leaving a mark.'

'Pig.'

'Answer the question.'

My mouth seals shut.

'Are you still angry with us for our tether on your arms? Even though you know full well that you can drag us about just as much as we can drag you? You will never be taken from us and will always be found if you are. Why is that something to be mad about?'

Lips. Shut.

'Are you still angry that Reid was married even though you know it was an arrangement he had no interest in taking part in?'

'Get off me.'

'Maybe it's that-'

'Maybe it's the fact I can't trust a single one of you as far as I could throw you.'

'You could throw us very far, given your wings and strength.' He steps closer. 'Pretend you didn't say what you said earlier if you want. But we heard you loud and clear. You're falling in love with us. Or you already have. Maybe if you looked a little harder, you would see that we're not all that different and that we too are-'

'The last person I loved hated me, Cyrus. She hated me and went out of her way to make me suffer whilst I went out of my way to try and protect her!'

'Fuck Ahriella. That bitch is either dead or Dark, and if she ever does come back, I'll personally repay her for what she put you through.'

'I don't want her dead or Dark. I just wanted her to love me, and she didn't. No matter what I did, she hated me.'

'That's her deal. Not yours and not ours.'

'You know. I preferred you when you were abrasive, mysterious and sultry.'

He walks up to me quickly and pins me to the wall. His hands wrap around my wrists as he holds me in place.

'And I prefer you just like this.'

'Fuck you.'

'Oh, baby. I wish you would.'

'That's the bottom line, isn't it? The only reason you care? You want to get laid. Being bonded to a girl who keeps saying no must be annoying.'

'Unbelievably so.'

'And being bonded to someone willing to stand up to you must drive you mad.'

He leans in, his front pressing against mine.

'Not in a million years. I love arguing with you. Nothing turns me off quicker than a meek little shadow who shies away and refuses to stand her ground. The damsel in distress isn't my type at all. A blood-soaked warrior woman with a bad temper and a filthy mouth is right up my street. When you stand up to me, toe to toe, and spit your venom with as much fire as you can muster, it doesn't just turn me the fuck on. It makes me fucking proud to call you mine.'

His hand rests on my hip and he comes close, his warm lips an inch from mine.

'You are perfect.'

'I'm not.'

'Yes.' He makes me look dead in his eyes. 'You are absolutely perfect. My kind of perfect.'

Our eyes look deep into each other, and neither of us moves.

The faint whirring of helicopters sounds in the distance. We both look up. The closer they get, the louder the sound becomes until the glass starts to shake in the old window frames.

'They've found us.' Cyrus snatches my hand in his. 'MOVE!'

EIGHT

*W*e run upstairs, yelling for everyone to wake up. To grab their shit. To run.

We reach the landing, where Reid emerges from the bedroom.

'They're here,' I pant, terrified breaths choking my lungs. 'Ivan's found us.'

'CODE RED!' Reid yells.

Everybody is on the landing within seconds, running around and yelling for everyone to move.

We're ready for this. Bags are always packed. Emergency supplies are ready and raring to go, piled up by the stairs. The safe place is chosen. I've been there before. I know it well.

I'm frozen in fear. Ivan. Jonah. The chair. Death and pain.

Reid's hands take hold of my face.

'I will not let them touch you. I swear it. I will die first.' He waits, watching me as I blink up at him. 'Do you hear me, Raven?'

'If they get me, kill me.' I whisper the words, but he hears them loud and clear. And I mean them. 'I can't, Reid. I can't go back.' I grip his wrists so tight I see him flinch. But he doesn't let go. 'Don't let Jonah or Ivan get me.'

'They won't get you.'

'Swear it. Swear it, Reid! Don't let them get me again.'

'I swear it. On my life, I will not let you go. Never.'

He leans down and kisses me. And I kiss him back.

'Let's get out of here. Ready?' he asks me, his thumb trailing back and forth over my skin.

I manage a nod and he steps back.

All eyes are on me as I reach out and create a portal.

'GO!' I order.

No one hesitates. They all start charging through carrying bags, boxes or kids. Cyrus runs around the ground floor, grabbing anyone he can and sending them my way. Reid is doing the same upstairs.

I reach out my other hand and create a portal to the cottage so the others can get to safety. The strain of making two separate portals causes the familiar pounding in my skull.

The entire house trembles as something explodes outside. Cyrus plants himself at my side.

'Only a couple have gone through the portal from the cottage,' I tell him. 'What are they doing over there?'

Cyrus hesitates, watching me uneasily. 'Make a portal. I'll go.'

'Sure?'

'Do it.'

I do. He runs through, and within seconds, the Fae from the cottage start pilling through and leaping into the second portal to the next safe house.

At the back of the crowds still scrambling about here are El, Lucca and Rhea, urging everyone to move as quickly as possible.

More and more funnel through. Rhea and the others reach me.

'Get to safety,' I tell them, nodding at the first portal.

Rhea looks at me. 'Not without you,' she insists.

'I'll be there soon. Please, go.' I nod to the portal, but she shakes her head.

'Not without you.'

Another explosion, and we all stumble as the entire house shakes, showering us in plaster and ceiling dust.

'HURRY UP!' I scream at the stragglers. I could almost cry with the strain.

Gunfire echoes outside, followed by yet more explosions. Brennan suddenly leaps through the portal from the cottage. His face is bleeding and he's clasping his side, struggling for breath.

'Close down the portal,' he orders, pointing a gun at it.

'Cyrus is still over there-'

El and Rhea scream as a Dark Fae lands before us, its arm ablaze.

'The house is overrun!' Brennan barks, shooting the monster before it gets too close. 'And on fire. Shut it down, Raven!'

'Cyrus is still-'

With a yell, Cyrus falls through with a child in his arms and a Dark Fae on his back. El pulls the vicious creature off and starts dragging it clear of them both as Brennan takes skilful shots to kill it.

'Shut it down!' Cyrus orders. He grabs my arm and yanks it, annoyed at my hesitation. The portal to the cottage flutters out of existence. 'Everyone else is dead. There's no one else left over there to save.'

Windows shatter downstairs, and snarling and screeching get louder. We hear a few screams from those still down there, followed by their pain-filled cries as they are slaughtered.

'We have to go. Right now!' Reid looks at El and Rhea. 'Girls-'

'There are still some down there!' I argue, watching a few stragglers scramble up the stairs. At the rear, Tessa is urging them on, dragging those who have been injured. Her wings are a barrier of protection between those she's helping and the monsters and bullets giving chase. Brennan is pulling all of them towards the portal, shoving them through without a care.

'Is that everyone?' I shout to Tessa. Blood starts to trickle down my nose.

'All that I could save,' she calls back as she gets to the landing. 'They're killing everyone.'

Cyrus throws his black smoke at the stairs, smothering three Dark Fae scrabbling towards us.

'All of you. Get your arses through the fucking portal!' he orders

His attempts to grab Rhea make her latch onto my waist.

'I go with her. Not before her.'

There's another explosion and the foundations violently shake.

Perhaps if the house were not as old, it would have withstood it. But this place is old as shit, and everything comes down. The roaring of the roof as it caves in above us, as the wood bows and breaks, is deafening. I look up and see it coming.

I pull at the portal, tugging it closer to us all.

Brennan and Lucca get swallowed to safety first. Then Cyrus and Reid, who reach out to me.

The floor below gives way before Tessa, El, Rhea and myself manage to get through the portal, and we all fall through the floor. The portal abandons me, and we all plummet down with the bricks and mortar.

We hit the lounge floor and look up to see imminent death coming for us all. We'll be crushed. The entire house is coming down. My eyes scrunch shut. I barely get to twitch my fingers, and I know without a doubt we'll be crushed before I can create a portal.

There's a loud crash. But nothing lands on me. No heavy chunks of brick or plaster.

Instead, a shrill and malevolent screech echoes all around me. One that almost drowns out the crumbling building.

I open my eyes and come face to face with the Dark version of my sister. The great beast. The deadliest of all Dark Fae. She towers over El, Tessa and me, catching the falling house on her back.

'PORTAL!' her demonic voice demands, straining under the weight. 'HURRY!'

I slam my hand down on the floor and a portal opens below us. We fall through and land outside.

I close it down before too much debris can follow us through.

We all lie on the ground, coughing and wheezing from the dust we've inhaled, our bodies littered with debris. I roll over and gasp in the air as I sit.

My head. Goddess, help me. My head is burning.

'Is everyone okay?' I ask, swallowing the blood as it trickles down from my nose.

We're in the clearing out in the woods. The sound of destruction and chaos echoes all around us as the Dark Fae tear through what remains of the two houses only a small distance away.

My arms start to tingle as the boys threaten to use their Bond marks on me.

'Yeah, yeah. I hear you,' I moan, sending back a light tug myself so at least they know I'm alive. 'Everyone okay?'

'Ow,' groans El. 'Very ow.'

'Tessa, you good?' I ask, seeing her doubled over and clutching her side.

'I'm fine,' she snaps back. 'Why are we here? Why didn't you make a portal to the safe house?'

'I don't know. I just made a portal,' I grumble back, not appreciating her tone one bit. 'Maybe you put the image of the clearing in my head. I don't know.'

'I most certainly did not.'

'I got us out, didn't I? Rhea, are you-'

In the distance, the farmhouse explodes in a full blaze, illuminating us as the orange light seeps in through the trees.

But that's not what has my body running ice cold.

A low snarling starts close by. So close I feel it on my neck. I turn and see Rhea, still in her Dark form, glaring at me.

'Turn back, Rhea,' I try to say as calmly as possible.

She just keeps snarling. Her enormous hand digs into the ground as she crawls like a demon dog.

'Rhea... please.'

She keeps growling at me, with no sign of her soul behind those eyes. She leans in close and stops, her heavy breath landing on my face.

'Fight it, Rhea. I need you.'

El and Tess stagger to their feet.

'Raven... should we-'

I hold up my hand, stopping El's attempts to interfere. Rhea could kill them both without breaking a sweat.

'Sister...' I plead, looking desperately into her eyes and praying that I see her looking back at me. 'Together. Or not at all.' I rest my hand on her leather-like cheek. She blinks a few times and sniffs.

The screams and howls of the other Dark Fae are getting louder as they turn their focus from the house to us. The girls look anxiously in the direction of the incoming horde.

Rhea's talons wrap around my arm. She pulls me to my feet.

'Run,' she growls. 'Go!'

'Not without you. Never without you.' I wrap my fingers around her wrist. 'Turn back, and we'll go.' I wait, the fire of the farmhouse illuminating her features. 'Now, Rhea!'

Her immense form shakes and shudders, and slowly, her skin returns to normal. Her body twists and snaps back into its normal form. Finally, she sheds herself of the darkness.

Her clothes are gone. Naked and filthy, she staggers before I catch her. El throws her jacket around her shoulders. Together, we face the trembling treeline.

'They're coming,' Rhea whispers.

I reach out my hand and create a portal.

I scream in effort as I pull the portal towards us all.

Tessa goes. El and Rhea next. Before it reaches me, a chain is thrown around my neck from behind.

An iron chain.

The portal fades instantly, my powers suppressed by the poisonous metal. My skin burns as it's wrapped around and around, stealing not only my power but my voice. My air.

I grab it desperately, my fingers burning and my nails clawing at my throat.

And I look up to see Jonah standing over me with an evil grin. 'Gotcha.'

NINE

*J*onah.

Blood smears his face and sweat clings to his clothes. His wide eyes look down at me as I lie at his feet, clawing at the chain locked around my neck.

Jonah's gaze bores into mine, full of adrenaline from the attack and exploding with excitement at his victory.

'I told him,' Jonah says with a maniacal laugh. 'I told your father I was the one for the job. That I could find you when everyone else had failed.' He looms over me, saliva thick on his lips and heavy pants smacking me in the face. 'Miss me?'

I let out a furious scream and slap him hard across the face, being sure to drag my fingernails deep across his cheek. He yells and steps back. After a brief inspection of the scratches I've left and when he sees the blood on his fingertips, I expect him to strike back. He just laughs as I struggle to my feet and try to run.

I get yanked back and land in the dirt, struggling for breath as I try with all my might to free myself.

'C'mon, my sweet Raven,' he sighs happily, taking a firm hold of the chain before pulling me behind him. 'Let's get you home.'

I manage to get on my hands and knees as he keeps pulling me behind him like a dog on a choke leash. He starts to whistle as he leads me through the sea of monsters he brought with him.

They all snarl and swipe at me. Jonah's entire body holds a hateful swagger, and I am further from safety with each step he takes. From Rhea. From Reid and Cyrus.

The iron stops me from calling them. It stops me from being able to do anything except stumble and trip, gasping for air and screaming in agony. It doesn't affect Jonah at all, even with his stolen power.

Ahead, I see a large convoy of Authority vans surrounded by agents dressed head to toe in black uniforms and holding guns loaded with iron bullets. They have them aimed at me, the woods, and the sky, ready to shoot at anyone who dares intervene.

But I know there's no one. I sent them all miles from here. Even if they flew at their top speed, it would take at least three hours to get here.

The location had to be safe. It had to be clear of this mess we knew would find us one day.

Two humans open the doors at the back of a van. They step aside and allow Jonah and me to pass. I feel the iron in the van before I get close, and when he drags me in behind him, I scream a throat-tearing scream as I fall onto its dirty floor. The whole inside of it is lined with iron.

My ears ring from its effect. My skin chars and hisses on contact.

If I thought Jonah's smile couldn't become more twisted, I was wrong because when the van doors shut, sealing us inside together, his smile becomes demonic.

'Let's play,' he says, his eyes flickering faintly with the gold of his stolen power. 'I can't wait to show you what I can do.'

We speed off.

The van tosses us about as it takes hard corners and brakes sharply. It feels like a getaway, but Jonah couldn't be calmer.

'Let's see now,' he says, digging around in a satchel he has thrown over his shoulder. One by one, he pulls out clear little bags filled with different kinds of herbs, leaves or flowers. 'Don't suppose you recall the gift your father gave to me? A strange power, but I have had so much fun with it these past few weeks. I can take the medicinal qualities of plant life and enhance them through touch. Do I want you sleepy?' he muses, looking at one holding dark brown leaves. 'Nah. Not sleepy.' He puts it away. 'Do I want you numb?' he asks, admiring another pouch filled with red petals. He looks at me and scoffs. 'Where's the fun in that? Nope. Not that one.' He returns it and continues looking. 'Ahhh...' He pulls out another bag. 'This one. Let's make you submissive and compliant. I've always been curious what it would be like for you to fuck *me* instead of me fucking *you*.'

My attempts to threaten him with a violent and agonising death if he dares use his stolen gifts on me in this way come out mangled and incoherent. The chain is still around my throat. Tight, but not tight enough to stop me from breathing. Laughing, he steps over me and places a boot on either side of my hips. His nasty little eyes look over my body with devious intent until he sees my tattoos. Then jealousy and anger sweep over his face.

'It's not fair that they get to leave their marks on you, and I don't. You were mine first, after all.'

'Fuck you,' I manage.

'Poor choice of words, considering your situation.' He falls to his knees and looks down, his eyes violating me with his unwanted gaze. 'You should be nicer to me. Your father has great plans for us all. If you want your part in them to be bearable, perhaps you should rethink how you treat me.'

I would rather fuck an iron dildo than willingly fuck you.

That's what I want to say, but all I can do is growl like a feral beast. I've never been sealed up in so much iron. It's as if my entire body is destroying itself atom by atom, cell by cell, organ by organ.

He grabs my top and tears it to pieces, leaving me in only my bra. My skin is even more exposed to the iron. I sob, my hands and feet curling in pain.

'You see this?' he says through heavy breaths, holding up the clear little bag. 'If I consume this, I take in its properties and can wield them on whomever I please. I've used it a few times on some of your kind. But I bet it will be even better with you.'

Panic would take hold if not for the pain and agony.

He opens the bag, reaches in and takes hold of the contents before bringing it to his lips.

He chews it. The gold in his eyes glimmers brighter, and he looks down at me with a deep breath and a shudder.

He places his hands on my cheek. As soon as he touches me, my body reacts. A calm washes over me. An absolute stillness. My brain empties of all thought. I look up and see only Jonah. He looks down at me with a soft and wondering smile.

'There you go,' he whispers, his words an echo in my ears. He leans down. 'Kiss me. Kiss me how you kiss them.'

I reach up and wrap my fingers in his hair, just as I do with the boys. I press my lips to his and sink into his hungry kiss. His tongue glides over mine. His teeth bite my lips hard and he pins me to his mouth painfully tight. His disgusting moans as I kiss him fill me with repulsion. And yet I still kiss him, just as instructed. My body is not my own. My will is gone.

'Use your hand. Get me hard,' he pants, refusing to part from my kiss.

I sob as I reach into his trousers. My hand feels his already hard and ready weapon.

'Stroke me. Now!' he growls.

I want to scream. I want to cry and shout. But I just lie beneath him and do as he commands, watching him throw back his head and hiss in grotesque pleasure.

His hand goes down the waistband of my trousers, and his fingers find their target. I manage a small whimper, not the death scream I have inside me. He works me. But not roughly. Not with aggression or haste. He's slow. He's steady. He watches closely as I lie beneath him.

'You're going to come for me,' he declares. 'I know you don't want to. I know you'll fight it. But your body is under my control. You will move with me, and I will feel you come around my fingers. I'll be honest,' he says, watching as I obey and feeling my hips move in time with his fingers. 'I have no interest in making a girl climax. None whatsoever. You're for *my* pleasure. That's all. I don't give a flying fuck if you enjoy yourself or not. But your fellas will know that you enjoyed me. Your freaks will know that I made you moan. And then they won't want you. They will hate you. They will see you as you finally are. Mine. And that you want to be mine.'

I keep doing as I'm told. My body isn't mine. But this is worse than all the other times he's had hold of me. So much worse.

Because what he's doing is working. No matter how much I fight it. No matter how much I resist, my body is finding its release. And I have never felt so disgusting and horrified as I do right now. Gritting my teeth, I stare into his eyes. There's no bigger turnoff. No stronger reminder of his filthy soul than his eyes.

But he enjoys that. He relishes in the hatred he sees. Adores the anger and the fear.

I'm about to... I can't...

Tyres screech, and he's thrown forwards as the van swerves left to right, tossing us about in the back until there's an almighty crash. The sound of metal twisting and contorting drowns out our yells. The van flips on its side and skids for a few seconds before coming to a stop.

How I manage to stay conscious, I have no idea. But despite the pain, the iron, and the chain still around my neck, I force myself up on all fours.

I have back my will. His effect on me has faded.

Jonah's still alive. I hear him groaning as he attempts to stand.

The door of the van is ajar, crumpled by the crash. I waste no time and crawl towards it. I throw my whole weight at it, and it opens

I drop onto the cold tarmac of the road. I don't care I'm bleeding. I don't care the iron chain is still around my neck. I don't care about what just caused the crash.

Run. I have to run!

'Get back here...' Jonah groans painfully, stumbling to his feet and grasping his head. 'BITCH!'

Gunfire makes me jump and throw my hands over my head, but as I hear the firefight, I also hear the screams of the human Authority agents.

I look up and can't help but smile.

I don't know how, but they've found me.

In the sky, I see a winged warrior swooping down and launching lethal attacks on the surviving Authority agents shooting their weapons upwards.

I pull and tug at the chain still at my throat, but the damn thing is stuck firm. I open my mouth, ready to scream for help.

'Oh no, you fucking don't.' Jonah's hand slams over my mouth, and he starts dragging me away from the warzone on this dark country road and into the bushes.

He pulls a knife from his pocket and presses it to my throat.

'Don't make a sound.' His hands are back on me. I can't disobey. 'When we're out of here, I'm cutting off your fucking legs. Let's see how far you can run from me then!'

He's not lying. Not even a little bit.

I watch the darkly dressed blur attack the humans, but they don't see me as I'm hauled away from sight.

The trees steal us from view, swallowing us into obscurity.

My feet drag behind me as Jonah hauls my body with him, huffing and puffing with effort.

I dig my fingernails into his arm as hard as possible, drawing blood before I claw down, ripping his flesh. With a livid grunt, he tosses me to the floor.

'BITCH!' His foot collides with my face and I slump, blood exploding over my face. 'You know...' He breathes heavily, wiping blood and sweat from his face. 'While we wait for the Authority to kill whoever was stupid enough to try and save you, I'm gonna do it.'

I weakly try to slap his hands away from me as he pins me down.

'You hear that?' He snorts and spits the blood from his mouth before rummaging in that damned satchel. 'That sound? You hear it?'

I do. It's Dark Fae. Lots of them.

'If that winged prick gets past the Authority, they won't get past the small regiment of fucked up little freaks we had follow-

ing us. I hear your sweet sister Ahriella is among them. She's easy
to spot.' He pulls out something black and mangled from the bag
and thrusts it in my face. I blink through the daze. 'She's the one
missing her left hand.'

I see it in the darkness. Through the blur.

He has a Dark Fae hand.

'Now hold still. I think it's only fair I stake my claim too.'

I scream as I feel the red-hot scratching he inflicts on my
side. Tears spill down my face at the pain as he chuckles like
a deranged lunatic. I can't fight him. I can't kick or thrash. He
told me to lie still.

I watch the sky, relief flooding me as a glorious flying shadow
soars downwards. It lands beside us and grabs Jonah before
tossing him away, far from sight through the many tree trunks.
My will returns. My body becomes my own.

But I don't reach out for the man.

The hooded figure looks down at me. I know without a
doubt... that it's not Cyrus or Reid.

It's none of my people.

'Who... who are...'

He pulls me to my feet before wrapping his arm around my
waist and pressing me close to his body.

'Pleasure to meet you, Your Majesty,' a deep voice sings to me
from beneath the hood. 'Forgive my impertinence. I know it's
wrong to hold a queen so close.'

He lowers his hood, and I blink at the beauty of the Fae man
smiling at me. His eyes are oddly familiar. Their deep colours
dance with gold. His firm jaw holds an air of superiority and
calm. His long, dirty blonde hair is pulled back and tied up, and
a few loose strands follow the curve of his face.

He looks into the distance, towards the sound of the Dark Fae scrambling over each other to get to us.

'And that's our cue.' He pushes off from the ground, the air whooshing as it speeds past my ears.

Below, the Dark Fae pile after us, screaming in fury that we've got ourselves out of reach. And I watch, stunned, as they organise in such a way I know that Ivan is inside their heads.

They all scramble on top of each other, making a mound of bodies to leap off. One of them manages to grab the man holding me. The stranger's wings beat harder as he tries to gain more height, but more Dark Fae hands grip us, and soon, we're being pulled back down.

The stranger changes tack, and instead of going higher, he goes down and forwards, dragging them along after us. Forwards we go, pulling with us the multiple monsters trying desperately to claw us back. We reach a clearing. Ahead, I see an endless sky, a dark ocean and a steep drop.

The winged stranger strains as he surges towards the cliff's edge, where that endless sky meets an endless sea.

Each beat of his mighty wings brings us closer. The Dark Fae may have wings, but they're deformed monstrosities and can't fly. I kick at their bony fingers. I try to help break free of their hold, trusting that whoever has me now must be better than those who had me a moment ago.

We reach the cliff's precipice, and the stranger turns his efforts back to height. We take off, but they still refuse to let go. More climb on. And more. We're hovering over the cliff's edge with the sea below, and we break free of the group with a jolt.

But a few stragglers remain latched to us. They climb up the stranger's legs and wrap themselves around his wings. We make it a few metres before he can't keep us airborne.

'Hold your breath, Your Majesty!'

We fall into the cold ocean below.

The icy water engulfs me, the chain around my neck dragging me down.

I can only see those golden eyes fighting in the murky water. More Dark Fae dive in, swarming towards us like fucking piranha. The stranger grabs hold of me. I point at my neck. I can't do anything with this chain restraining me.

He takes hold and starts to pull as hard as he can. The urge to take in a life-ending gasp is almost too much.

We're both pulling at the chain as more Dark Fae encircle us, grabbing and clawing, trying to return us to the surface.

Finally, the chain gives, snapping in two and falling from my body.

Pain tears through my heart as the iron leaves my body, freeing the power of the Bond-tether. Reid and Cyrus are both calling me with everything they have. Neither are holding back as they summon me to them, uncaring what I could be dragging back with me. I start gliding through the water like a torpedo. The stranger grabs hold and comes along for the ride.

I reach out my hand and pray to the Fates, the Goddess, to anyone who will bloody listen to give me the strength to create a portal.

Nothing happens. I'm gliding ever closer to shore with a swarm of golden eyes giving chase.

Focus!

Create the anchor!

Cyrus's eyes. His smile. Reid's hands in mine. His soft breath as he sleeps by my side.

Their kiss.

Their scent.

Their everything.

The last breath of air leaves my body as three tiny bubbles pass through my lips. I look into the darkening water, my vision blurred and painful. I have to take a breath... I have to! The stranger's strong arm wraps around my waist and pulls me flush against his body. We both sail through the sea, the rushing water pounding in our ears. He has to hold on tight so he doesn't lose me. But he is going to lose me. They all are.

My eyes start to close.

His lips crash onto mine and open my mouth. His fingers seal my nose closed and a blast of air forces its way into my lungs. It keeps going, filling me up with warmth. With life.

The stranger stares back at me as he breathes his final breath into me.

I take hold of him, clamping my fingers into his shoulders as I take his life-giving gift. The pull of the Bond is vicious. I entangle my legs around his waist so I don't lose him. A move he welcomes because he closes his eyes and caresses my tongue with his, turning his mouth to mouth into a kiss.

The golden eyes disappear. The monsters can't keep up with us, and soon we're in utter darkness.

Until it explodes into a blinding golden mass of light as a portal forms at my back, swirling and heaving water in its wake.

The tug from the Bond pulls me straight through. The stranger keeps hold and comes for the ride, his arms now encasing me and his tongue well and truly in my mouth.

The cold, rushing water carries us through the portal's void. It falls deathly quiet and still for a second, as it always does when I pass through. It leaves the stranger and I frozen together, clamped onto the other and lips still pressed together.

Then everything comes crashing back.

The world spins as we're thrown through, crashing into the ground.

Sea water pours endlessly through the portal behind me, washing us away. I try to get him off me, but he refuses to ease up! The ocean continues to pour through the portal, filling up the room. I hear yelling, but the words are muffled by the water still hammering into us all.

'Close the portal!' I hear. 'Before we drown!'

I pull back the power and shut down the portal, and in a second, Cyrus is standing over me as I lie in the water with the man still atop me, lips on mine and arms holding me firm. With a rage unmatched by any other man, Cyrus grabs him by the throat and pulls him off me, freeing me to cough, gasp, and splash about. There's yelling and threats as I try to get myself up and out of the several feet of water.

My arms are weak, and I struggle to hold my weight. I fall and am submerged again.

That's right, I think to myself. You just carry on beating the shit out of the guy who saved me and leave me here to fucking drown!

I'm pulled up and held.

'I've got you,' Rhea says, panting and panicked as she wipes my wet hair from my face. 'Can you breathe? Shit, Raven... you're bleeding! Your side!'

I nod but keep on coughing as I cling to her. When she places her hand on my bleeding side, I hiss a swear word. But she keeps the pressure on.

I look over and see Cyrus throttling the guy who saved me. He's dragging him away, spitting venom in his face as his black smoke seeps from his body and his fingers grip his throat.

'STOP!' I yell. He doesn't. 'CYRUS!' I scream.

My words thunder around the room, and the rage inside me, mixed with the fear, has the room shaking. Cracks explode in the walls, and a threatening rumble deafens us. Rhea holds me tighter and looks at the ceiling above.

But that does nothing to stop Cyrus from repeatedly slamming his fist into the stranger's face. Blood splatters into the water and up the walls. I don't know if it's pain that has the stranger not fighting back or just stupidity! But he takes the blows, one after the other, not even attempting to defend himself.

'Touch her...' Cyrus snarls. *Thump.* 'You die...' *Thump.*

Then I see Reid wading through the water towards them both. He has the same look on his face as Cyrus.

A familiar surge swells in my chest from the powers inside me. Of the ones I don't know, understand, or can control. The same ones that caused the cracks marking the walls and ceiling. I know I want Cyrus to stop and Reid not to start. And I know that my words will not be enough.

I reach out my hand.

Cyrus bellows furiously as he's yanked away from the stranger by an unseen force. He still reaches for the man, despite soaring backwards through the water and coming to an abrupt stop when his back meets the wall. Reid meets much the same fate as he is thrown in the same direction. He side-slams into the wall beside Cyrus and falls to his knees.

I struggle to my feet, impatiently batting Rhea's attempts to keep me out of it and with her instead. I'm up and stumbling towards them, planting myself between my two Mates and the man who saved me.

I stand there, facing Reid and Cyrus as they return to their feet. The room continues to tremble as my emotions seep out through uncontrolled powers. I can't stop it. My body is trembling just as much as the room is! Each stab of pain I feel from Jonah's injuries makes it so much worse.

Cyrus charges forwards, stumbling as the floor beneath his feet jars and shifts from my magic. He doesn't stop. His focus is on nothing but the man who came through the portal with his tongue in my mouth.

I block his path, and he stands over me, his dark hair soaking wet and blood dripping down his face and arms. His chest rises and falls with speed, and a look of anger consumes him.

'You protect him?'

'I need-'

'Where the fuck are your clothes?' Cyrus quickly takes off his jacket and wraps it around my shoulders. 'Did he hurt you? Look at me.' He stares deep into my eyes and then looks past me to the man. 'I swear if you've so much as-'

I throw myself into Cyrus, burying my face in his chest and grabbing his shirt. His scent surrounds me. His hammering heart fills my ears. His solid form is my protection. My safe place.

'Shut up,' I sigh, relieved to be back with him. And surprised at how relieved I am. 'Hold me. Don't let go.'

Cyrus's arms wrap around me. I melt into him and give him my entire weight, which he takes with no problem. And as he does, the swell in my chest, fuelled by panic and rage, eases. The room stops shaking.

As Reid goes to resume the assault, I reach out and grab him, pulling him into us both. I refuse to let go of his shirt as I move between the two, making sure I'm surrounded and safe. Removing any remainder of Jonah. Replacing it with them instead.

No more cracks seep up the walls, and the dread and horror fade.

'He saved me. Stop.'

'Saved you?' On Reid's hand, his light glows bright and deadly. 'He had his tongue down your throat, Raven! You have no clothes and you're bleeding.'

'That wasn't his doing.' I let out another sigh, so fucking glad I'm back where I belong and far from Jonah. 'He got me out.'

Reid looks at the stranger. 'Who the fuck are you?!'

There's a series of guns cocking. Brennan, Lucca and El both point their guns at the man.

'What's the matter?' laughs the stranger as he wipes the blood flowing from his broken nose with his sleeve. 'Don't you recognise me, Elias?'

'Who are you? One of Ivan's?' Reid guides me to Cyrus fully and steps between us.

'He has wings,' I tell him. 'He's one of yours.'

Reid and Cyrus both look at me with a frown.

'Wings?' they repeat together.

'Big wings,' I add.

'I'm glad their size impressed you, My Queen.' The stranger smirks before lowering his head in a slight bow. When he lifts his gaze, he sends it to Reid. 'For the record, she kissed me back.'

'That's impossible,' Cyrus whispers, his arms holding me firmer.

'Long time no see, Cyrus Black.' The stranger still holds a cocky smile as he enjoys a stunned Cyrus. 'You're still chasing Elias around, I see. Stuck firm in his shadow.' He looks at Brennan, El and Lucca. 'And the rest of the gang too. Some things never change. Except this.' He gestures to me. 'Swapped the wife for the queen, huh, Elias? Dreams really do come true. For you.'

'Stick?!' Cyrus says in disbelief. 'How the fuck-'

'Stick?' I repeat. 'You know him?'

'My name is Ezra, Your Majesty.' Again he gives another bow. 'Ezra Reid.'

'Ezra... Reid?' I look at Reid. 'Reid... as in...'

'He's my brother.' Reid's eye twitches, and I see no love in his eyes for the man before us. 'Half-brother. And he shouldn't be here. It's not fucking possible.'

TEN

'So. You and the Princess finally got it together,' Ezra smirks, nodding from Reid's markings to mine. 'She wasn't quite as dead as you thought then, hey brother?' He looks at me. 'I was there the day it was discovered. That the great Elias was fated to a baby. Oh... the disgust he expressed. The utter-'

'Shut the fuck up,' warns Reid, the light on his hand glowing brighter.

I see Ezra eye it nervously, and the smug grin on his face falters ever so slightly. Then he looks at Reid's ears and is repulsed.

'What happened to the points of your ears?' With a scowl, he looks closer at the heavy scars. 'You've been cut?'

'Brother?' I repeat, still stuck on that revelation.

'Half-brother,' Reid replies coldly, his wings emerging. 'You shouldn't be here.'

'It's a good job I was. Or where would your precious Mate be, huh? Careless of you to lose her so easily. Again.'

'It's impossible.' Reid shakes his head. 'You being here is impossible.'

'Improbable. Nothing's ever impossible. For example, you sharing a Mate with Cyrus over there and that Mate being the Queen, making you both Kings, seemed unlikely to me when that first was announced. But here we are-'

'What are you doing here? How?' Cyrus demands.

'I think you're looking for the words, "Thanks for saving my Mate. What could I ever do to pay back that immeasurable debt?" Or something similar.'

'You didn't come over in the event. You were back home with Father in the Thirteenth Kingdom when we were sent here.' Reid steps forwards. 'How did you get into the human realm, Stick?'

Ezra walks to Reid and stops. I see their similarities clearly now and know why he seemed so familiar. There are strong traits they share. Their eyes. Their jaw lines.

'You need to come with me,' Ezra states. 'I'll explain everything.'

'Come with you where?' Reid replies.

'Somewhere safe. Somewhere you and your people will be protected. Fed. Kept warm.'

'I'm going nowhere with you until you tell me what I want to know. And don't think I haven't seen you look at her ten times already in the short time you've been talking to me.' Reid steps into Ezra's eye line, blocking me from it. 'I strongly suggest you keep your focus on me and as far from her as conceivably possible. Hear me, *Stick*?'

Ezra's wings slowly spread, matching Reid's design but not size.

'If you want to stay here, then fine. Stay. And die.' He looks hard to me. 'But I'll be taking the queen and doing what you have failed to do this entire time you've had her.'

'Oh yeah? And what's that?' Cyrus scoffs.

'Save our home realm, our people, and stop the human tyrant king Ivan Walker from destroying everything.'

'He telling the truth, Princess?' Cyrus asks me, never looking away from him.

'Yeah,' I reply. 'There's no lie.' As I stand with his arms around me, the burning in my side becomes more unbearable. I feel the warmth of my blood seeping down my leg. I rest my hand on the wound and swallow the extreme discomfort.

'And where is it exactly you'll be taking us?' Reid asks.

'It's far. We'll need a portal.'

'She needs to know the location to create a portal.'

'Seems we have a problem then. I tell you what. You stay here, and I'll take her off your hands-'

'You so much as twitch in her direction,' Brennan warns from behind us. 'You'll need a bag to carry the many bits I will blow your head into. Raven stays with us. She stays with Reid and Cyrus. End. Of.'

I suddenly swell with affection for the gun-toting man of few words.

'Need I remind you that she is here because of me and despite you?' Ezra argues. 'Goddess only knows where she would be right now if I hadn't saved her from that freak of a human.'

'Which human?' Reid and Cyrus demand together.

'I don't know. They all look the same to me. But he had some twisted powers in him. Powers you let them steal from-'

'Jonah?' Cyrus asks, looking down at me and cutting Ezra off. 'Did Jonah-'

'Nothing happened,' I tell him, looking away as I lie through my teeth. I don't want them to know. I never want them to know.

'Only because of me,' Ezra announces.

'Ezra got me out before anything could go too bad,' I tell Cyrus.

Cyrus looks as I struggle to conceal my wince when he glides his hand down my body to my hips.

'Too bad? You're hurt?' He moves the jacket to see. A deep smear of blood has him cursing. 'Shit. What the-'

'What is it?' Reid says, returning quickly to us and taking a look for himself. 'You're bleeding.'

'I'm ok. It can wait.' I return the jacket and hide the wound with a glance at Ezra. 'We have more important shit to be dealing with. Can we trust this guy?'

'You tell us. You're the lie detector,' Reid replies.

'He's your brother,' I remind him.

'Half-brother,' he corrects, still staring at my side. 'Was he telling the truth? Does he have somewhere safe?'

'I... I don't...' I shake my head, hoping to clear it a little.

Right now, I'm not much use for anything. I'm in pain. I'm exhausted. I'm half-naked and full of adrenaline.

Reid rests his hand on my cheek, appearing to understand. A simple and absolute gesture as he removes any responsibility and expectations from me and takes control of the situation.

'Brennan. Put Stick in the secure unit,' he orders. 'Make sure he's disarmed and made comfortable.'

Brennan doesn't need telling twice. He presses the gun to Ezra's temple as El searches his pockets for any weapons. Knives and daggers are pulled out one after the other. No guns, though.

And Ezra doesn't fight. He simply stands there, watching me with a confident smile.

Once disarmed, Brennan takes him by the elbow and leads him away.

'Let's get you sorted out,' Reid says softly, slowly pulling open the jacket and cringing as he sees the raw flesh and blood. 'This looks like a Dark Fae wound.'

'Yeah.' I see Rhea shuffling uncomfortably in the corner as the guys turn to face her. 'It wasn't Rhea.'

El stands beside her and takes her hand. With a silent gesture, she offers to take her out of the room. I nod in agreement.

'C'mon, Rhea,' El says softly, tugging her towards the door. 'She's in good hands.'

I see the reluctance to leave me, but she goes. And I'm glad that she does.

Everyone leaves. We're alone now.

Still standing in several inches of seawater, the guys take off the jacket and inspect the wound.

'What happened after the portal closed?' Reid asks, focusing hard on my side.

'Jonah,' I tell him, hissing as he starts wiping away the blood. 'It's always fucking Jonah. Prick wrapped me in iron and threw me in the back of a van. Ouch!'

'Sorry,' Reid mumbles.

'He had a severed hand of a Dark Fae and he cut me with it. He said he wanted to add his claim long with yours.' When I look down to see it as they clear the blood, Cyrus quickly takes my chin and lifts my gaze. 'What did he do to me?'

'It's not important,' Cyrus says, failing to hide the anger in his voice.

'Liar,' I retort. 'What did he do?'

'You're safe now. We're all safe. That's what matters.'

'Not all. How many did we lose?' I ask as Reid returns the jacket to my side, hoping to stop the bleeding.

He stands. 'We're not sure. We haven't checked yet.'

'You haven't checked yet?'

'No. Since you went missing, we've been calling you through the bonds non-stop.'

'Well, have you checked everything is safe? That this place is secure? How could you not bother to-'

'Our concern was you.'

'And the others? You don't care if they're-'

'Our concern was... *is* you.'

'And how the fuck is your brother here, huh? Can you explain-'

Reid's lips crash into mine so hard I stumble back. But Cyrus is there to keep me up. To hold me in place for Reid to have. His tongue licks and flicks mine. His teeth nip my lip, and his breath lands heavily on my skin. This kiss stills everything. It soothes more than I thought a kiss ever could. The world falls away and leaves the three of us in solitude.

'Our concern,' Reid says breathlessly, taking my chin in his fingers and looking down at me through his long mess of hair with eyes of fire and hunger. 'Will always be...' Cyrus unhooks my bra from behind and lets it drop to the floor. His warm hands cup my breasts, and he grips them firmly. Reid's eyes land on mine with such intensity I let out a shuddering breath. 'You.'

My lip trembles as guilt overwhelms me.

'I have to tell you something,' I whisper.

'What?' Reid asks, watching me.

'Jonah. He...'

Reid swallows dryly. 'What did he do?'

'He put his hands on me. He... he used his stolen powers. He had control over me and-'

'Did he rape you?'

'His fingers,' I admit. 'I didn't fight him off. His power took my free will.'

'Where did he touch you?' Reid asks.

'Everywhere,' I weep quietly. 'He told me to come. He made me move in ways that-'

'Did you?' he asks.

I watch him nervously. Terrified of what the truth will bring. Jonah said they wouldn't want me. And they got so angry when they thought I used Jonah as an anchor.

'Almost,' I whisper with a shaking breath. 'Ezra crashed the van before I... before...'

Tears spill down my cheeks. No one makes a move. My quiet cries echo off the walls, and the remaining inches of water slosh as Reid shifts his feet.

'I'm sorry,' I offer with a strong tremble in my words. 'Every second I was away from you, all I wanted was to be back in your arms. I tried to fight, and I tried to resist, but his stolen powers were too strong. I was so scared that I would never see you again. I want to burn every inch he touched and-'

'Do you feel better in our arms?' Reid asks.

'When I'm in your arms, I can breathe again. When you hold me, Jonah is a distant memory.' I look back at Cyrus, who watches me with hard focus. 'I swear to you, I didn't enjoy it. My body just-'

'Sense my truth when I say this to you.' Cyrus leans in close. 'We are not angry. This was not your fault,' he says plainly. 'Your reaction had nothing to do with wants or desires. Sometimes, a body just reacts. It means nothing, Raven. Not a damn thing.'

As Cyrus holds my breasts in his palms, Reid lowers and takes my nipple in his mouth. I hiss as he sucks and pinches it between his teeth.

'What... what are you doing?' I whisper.

'What we do when we're relieved to have you back after you scare the shit out of us and disappear.' Cyrus says the words in my ear as he takes the waistband of my trousers and pulls them clear down my legs. Reid takes them off completely, guiding each of my feet clear from them. 'We're going to remind you why you should never want to leave us. And make sure you know that no matter where you go, we will always bring you back. And we will replace all the hurt and misery inflicted on you tonight with our admiration and devotion. His hands will not be the last ones to touch you.'

Reid looks up at me as he kneels in the water. 'If that's what you want? Do you?'

'More than anything in this world.'

Cyrus lifts me by my hips as Reid throws my legs over his shoulders. Reid is on his knees as he pulls me harder onto his face, clamping his fingers into my backside and urging me closer and closer, grinding my hips in time to his glorious tongue.

He moans. The vibrations of his delight ripple through my core, and I find myself gladly working in time to his rhythm, rocking back and forth, back and forth. It replaces the grotesque show I was forced to put on for Jonah.

'That's it, Princess,' Cyrus whispers, a dirty smirk on his beautiful lips as he watches me writhe in pleasure. 'Fuck his mouth. Let me taste those moans he's so kindly giving you.'

Cyrus kisses me, catching my whimpers. His eyes never close. And neither do mine. There's no comfort in the darkness. Only in them. I will happily drown in them both rather than sink into the blackness again.

My fingers knot in Reid's hair, and I pull. He growls. So I pull again. I feel him smile before I wrap my legs around him, keeping him where he belongs.

I've denied myself for so long. Refused to let myself enjoy their touch. I need it now. I need it to replace all that has just happened. All that could have happened.

I cry out as Reid's fingers ease into me. My back arches, but Cyrus tightens his hold and keeps me in place, chuckling as I react.

They both do. Laughing their devious laughs as they work my body.

'Open,' Cyrus whispers, looking at my mouth. I oblige. He puts his fingers in. 'Suck.'

I do. I lick and suck and bite. Cyrus slides them back and forth as if his fingers are a poor replacement for what he wishes his cock could be doing. He bites down on his lips and watches, pushing his fingers further until he feels the back of my throat.

And he holds them there, watching my eyes water as I choke on them.

That half smile of his grows into a full-blown grin.

'You like that, Princess?'

He pulls out his fingers and I take a deep breath.

Before I know it, he's got his fingers, wet and ready, at my arse.

'I bet you'll like this even more.'

'Fuuuuuck!!' I moan as he eases them inside me. 'Ohhhhh fuuuuuck!'

'Oh no, you don't,' he warns as I throw my head back and look up at the ceiling. 'Eyes on me, Princess.'

I feel it coming. That satisfaction. That euphoria. That pressure building in my core.

Cyrus buries his face in my neck and kisses my skin.

'You stay with us,' he says. 'You never leave. You're ours.'

I reach out, placing one of my hands on each of their heads, and grab their hair.

'You're mine...' I whisper.

'Again!' Cyrus orders, speeding up with his fingers, as does Reid. 'Say that again!'

I reach my peak. My body convulses and I cry out.

'MINE!' I call as I climax between them.

When I've ridden out my overpowering orgasm, Reid gets to his feet, tucking my hair behind my ear.

'Damn fucking straight we are.' He slams his lips on mine, sharing my pleasure as it lingers on his tongue. 'And don't you forget it.'

ELEVEN

*R*eid refuses to let me look at my body as Cyrus cleans the
wound on my side. It fills me with dread over what has
been carved into it. Whatever it is, it's there to stay.

They cover it with a bandage. It feels hot, like it's searing.
Every time I go to see, Reid snatches my chin and shakes his
head in warning.

'We have told you not to look. Do as you're told.'

'He said it was Ahri's,' I tell him.

'What?' he asks.

'The Dark Fae hand. He said that he cut it off her himself.'

Cyrus applies the last of the tape and gets to his feet. I rest my
hand on my side, and he takes hold of my wrist with a flash of
panic.

'You're not to look,' he repeats. 'Ever.'

'Is it really that bad?' I ask.

'We'll get rid of it,' he assures me, letting my wrist go when he
feels certain I won't look.

'What did he scratch into me?'

'You need fresh clothes,' Cyrus says, turning away from me.
'There's some out in the recreation room. I'll fetch you-'

'What did he scratch into my skin?' I repeat louder. 'I can't not
look forever, and I want to know.'

His feet slow, and he stops.

'He's carved his name into your side with a Dark Fae fingernail.' Cyrus's words come out through clenched teeth. He doesn't turn to look at me. 'Specifically, *"Jonah's Whore".*'

I feel the blood drain from my face, and disgust fights with anger for dominance in my chest.

'I'll fetch her some clothes,' Cyrus grunts as he leaves the room.

Fucker. I can't believe... what am I thinking. Of course I believe Jonah would do this to me. It's what he's always done.

I swallow the urge to throw up.

'If it was put there with a Dark Fae claw, it's permanent.' I look down to see, but Reid retakes my chin.

'You don't need to see it. We've said what it is.' He turns me to face him.

'It's not going anywhere, Reid. I can't live the rest of my life not looking at it.'

'We're gonna figure out a way to get rid of it, so I don't want you to upset yourself by looking.'

'Sure you don't mean you don't want to upset yourself by seeing his name on me?'

'Why? Did I lie with the words I just chose to say? I don't want you to see it because I don't want *you* upset. Ok? I know who you belong to, Little Bird. His name on you means nothing. And he'll pay for this. And everything else.' He takes a deep breath. 'Can you just promise me that you won't look at it?'

'I'm not allowed to look at my own body now?'

'Why must you make everything an argument? The wound is clean. We've dressed it in a bandage. We will figure out a way to get rid of it, so until we do, I don't want you to remove the bandage. Okay?' He lowers his face and looks harder into my eyes. 'Okay?!'

'Fine.'

'Good.'

Cyrus returns with some clothes. I'm glad to get covered. Some baggy jeans. A tank top and an oversized hoody that smells of him are perfect. It hangs almost down to my knees, and he grins as he surveys his clothes on me.

'You look cute in my stuff.'

'I'm going to ask, but I know your answer,' Reid says with a resigned sigh. 'Will you get some rest?'

'Not until I've checked on the others.' I shake my head and make for the door.

'Thought as much.'

This place is by far the most derelict building we have been forced to stay in, but safe places are beyond limited. Now, I think they are non-existent.

It was once an insane asylum. Humans locked up their kin behind bars or in padded rooms, out of the way and out of sight. Much like they do... did... to us with their walled-in cities. There are hardly any windows in this place. The few there are, are covered in thick metal bars and high up out of reach. The doors are heavy and made with reinforced steel and bulky bolts. We're sealed in pretty tight. Ironic that the place the humans used to torment their own now protects us from them.

Reid walks to my left, and Cyrus is at my right as we travel down the halls and corridors towards the main room where the survivors have gathered. The grime-covered sign on the door calls it the recreation room.

I'm not sure exactly what kind of recreation the patients here got. No games. No television. No radio. No comfort. The floors are made of chipped tiles, and the walls are heavily peeling white paint covered in mould and what looks like old, dried blood. There are mangled wheelchairs in the far corner and piles of moth-eaten straight jackets heaped beside them. Words are carved into the door frames. Words like "help" or "let us out". I pass one that says, "The devil made me do it".

I shudder.

Even the chairs have rust-covered chains attached to them. I can almost see it in my mind. How terrible life in here must have been for the patients, like their ghosts wander around me, staring into nothing. Lost souls without hope.

I blink them away and replace them with the real souls hiding here now.

We have no electricity, so the room is lit by candles and torches which cast dim shadows over the dingy walls.

And the stench of the mould and dust is enough to make you choke.

We won't survive here for long. Even if we're not found by the Authority, the Dark Fae, or my father, this place isn't meant for the living. Insane or not.

We brought first aid supplies, tinned food, clothes and sleeping bags on our last visit here. We knew the day would come when we would have to run from the farmhouse and the cottage. We prepared.

But there's only so much you can prepare for. This isn't a permanent solution. It can't be! I promised to save them. To free them. But we're in a worse position now than maybe we have ever been.

The dull groans of the Fae that made it out of the attack echo off the walls. The pain. The fear. The hopelessness and grief. I hear it in each whimper and sniffle. In every cry of pain and wail of sorrow.

My eyes scan the room as I count.

'Half...' I whisper. I blink my eyes as they start to sting. 'There's less than half left.'

In the far corner, one of the women we pulled from the brothel is cradling a young girl. A child. One we saved from Serge.

As the woman stares into nothing, I see the young one dead. Her skin is ashen and smeared with blood. Her stomach is a chasm of slashes.

Tessa crouches in front of her and rests her palm on her cheek.

After sharing a few words, the traumatised woman nods and a white whisp travels from the woman's head to Tessa's fingertips. I watch closely and see Tessa shudder before she takes the young one from the woman's arms. As Tessa stands, the woman lies down, rolls on her side and closes her eyes.

'What was that?' I ask.

'Tessa took the woman's grief from her,' Reid replies.

So that's what it looks like when she takes away emotions. As Tessa carries away the body, tears stream down her cheeks. Her abilities as an extreme empath allow her to remove or reassign emotions. But any she takes, she has to keep for a short while.

Tessa must have permission to remove emotions. I remember that from when she came and tried to convince me to give up my feelings for Reid after he was hurt saving my life. But other than that, I'm not too sure what she can or cannot manage.

I nudge Reid.

'Go help her,' I suggest.

'I have more important things-'

'And when you go,' I cut in, my suggestion turning into a demand. 'Tell her not to take other's emotions. She has enough misery to be dealing with. It's not fair on her.'

'She only has to have it for a few hours before it goes,' he shrugs. 'What's the problem?'

'The problem is she was once your wife. She still cares about you, and she is in pain. Be decent. Go show her you're not an uncaring arsehole, would you?'

I glare at him, and he rolls his eyes before heading to her.

'Cyrus, stay with her!' he orders back over his shoulder.

I spot Rhea dressing another's wound and El doing the same to the girl opposite. As I head towards them, the survivors give a slight bow.

I hate it.

I scoop up some bandages and get to work.

We work swiftly, making the rounds and patching anyone we can. Anyone who can get up and help does. Wounds are dressed. Soup is heated and handed out. Water. Pain killers. Clean clothes. And rest.

The recreation room falls quieter as more lie down and close their eyes. We all end up sitting together, catching our breath on a couple of the beds in the far corner.

Rhea falls onto the bed opposite me with a groan, exhausted from everything. El sits next to her as I sit with Lucca. When Cyrus joins us, holding multiple mugs of soup, he sits beside me and shares them out.

'I cannot believe Stick is here,' El says with forced calm. 'How, in the name of the fates, did he get to the human world?'

'I'm sure we'll soon find out,' Lucca replies with a tired sigh, leaning in to inhale the soup.

I get one sip in before Tessa's shrill and angry voice travels into the room from somewhere down the corridor.

We all look, but she's out of sight.Shame her words aren't as she bellows at Reid.

'Don't you dare presume to tell me what I may or may not do,' she screeches.

Reid's tired and almost bored voice replies. 'I'm just suggesting that taking on everyone's misery isn't the best idea-'

'Misery?!' she yells, making me twitch as her voice reaches an unbearable pitch. 'What would you know of misery, Elias?'

'Maybe you should lower your voice.'

'Oh, I should, should I?'

'Yes. You should. No one wants to hear your hysteria, Tessa. Me least of all.'

'And no one wants to hear you and that harlot moaning and groaning like beasts whilst we bleed and mourn for those we lost today. But that didn't stop you from revelling in sensual pleasure as soon as she got here, did it?!'

I feel everyone's eyes land on me as Cyrus snorts in amusement beside me, his grin hidden by the soup mug at his lips.

'Tessa, stop,' Reid warns.

'You should roll up your sleeves and help look after the Fae you are responsible for instead of satisfying your urges with *her* and leaving us to do all the work.'

'For fuck sake...' I whisper, my face reddening. I look at El. 'Were we that loud?'

'I personally found it a much more attractive soundtrack than all the crying,' she replies. 'None of the others in here heard you. We closed the doors. Don't worry about it.'

I bury my face in my hand.

'Hey!' El insists, reaching over and lowering it. 'You did your part. You got us out and nearly got caught in the process. You wanna fuck your men? You're well and truly entitled to. Fuck away.' She gestures to Cyrus, who winks at the suggestion.

We look over as Reid strides inside the room, followed by a distraught and furious ex-wife who grabs his arm and pulls him back. Reid does not react well to that at all and spins to face her.

'Touch me again, Tessa, and you'll regret it,' he warns.

'Oh. I regret a lot, husband.'

'Ex-husband.'

'But I will never regret touching you!' She bursts into tears. 'It's her fault we're trapped here, hiding like vermin. This is all her fault!' She points a trembling finger at me. 'We were fine until she got involved!'

'Fine?' Reid scoffs. 'You, perhaps. Not her. She's much better now than she was.'

'And that's worth all this bloodshed, is it? That's worth living on the run in places like this?'

Reid steps forwards and towers over her.

'Absolutely,' he snarls.

I hastily put the soup in El's hands and run over, stepping between the two. I rest my hand on his stomach and urge him back. He obliges, stepping away.

'Enough,' I hiss. 'Stop it.'

'You're the one who sent me over to her in the first place,' he snipes back. 'You think I want to be listening to her whining?'

'I asked you to try and calm her down. This isn't calming her down, is it?'

'Don't you dare presume to tell me what I need to do,' Tessa shrieks at me from behind. 'Especially regarding my husband and me.'

Reid looks past me to her. 'I'm not your fucking husband-'

'And yet you still assume authority over me and my actions? You think you know best? That you can order me not to use my powers? Well, I shall.' She folds her arms across her chest in defiance. 'I will use them and grow them and make them something you will witness with awe!'

'And you can,' I tell her. 'No one is saying that you can't.'

'I wasn't asking your opinion, whore,' she spits back.

Now Cyrus is on his feet and heading over, followed swiftly by El and my sister.

Goddess damn it.

'Tessa,' I try, turning to face her. 'Now is not the time to-'

'Don't you dare speak to me like you have any authority over me.'

'You've taken too much grief and anger from the others. Go and sleep it off before you say or do something you'll regret!' I gesture to the others all lying on the cots. 'They don't want to hear us arguing right now.'

'But they want to hear you moaning my husband's name, huh?'

'Please. Just quieten down.'

I rest my hand on her arm, hoping to encourage her out of the room.

It doesn't.

Her face scrunches up in hatred before she lunges at me, shoving me over. Her wings explode from her back, and her hands slam into my stomach with a powerful blow.

I go down. Hard.

As soon as I hit the ground, I scream in pain, clutching my side.

Rhea's on me in a second, ensuring I'm alright. Behind me, there's one hell of a scuffle as Cyrus and Reid go for Tessa.

'I'm sorry!' she says in a panic. 'I didn't mean to!'

She scrambles back in horror as El stands between them. Her wings are broad as she blocks their path, allowing Tessa to run from the room crying.

'Raven,' Rhea gasps, easing me up. 'Are you okay?'

The pain in my side is unbearable. Blood seeps down my side, and I quickly lift the hoody to see. The large bandage is saturated. The tape holding it in place starts peeling, and I see the first few letters of Jonah's words carved into my side.

I lower the hoody and scramble to my feet, shoving away Rhea's attempts to keep me close.

'We told you not to look,' Reid says, his sympathy evident as he sees my reaction to the marks.

'I didn't.' I back away as Reid takes a step towards me. I hastily wipe my tears before they fall too far down my cheeks. 'It's bleeding again. The bandage is soaked and falling off.'

I head to the medical supplies and grab a handful of bandages. When I turn back around, Reid is there. I can't bring myself to look at him, so I stare at his chest.

'It will upset you if you see it. Please give me the bandages. I'll fix it.' He holds out his hand.

'I don't want you to see it either.'

'It's just a scar, Raven. It's not worthy of your pain. Don't let him win. Don't let him make you feel less than what you are. You're brilliant and beautiful and-'

'He's in my nightmares,' I say in a hushed whisper so only he can hear. 'He's in the shadows. He's in the corner of my eye. His breath is on my skin with every breeze. His laugh is in my ears with every moment of silence, and now, his name is in my body.

He's there, calling me his whore.' I reach out and rest my palm over his heart, where his tattoos lie beneath his shirt. 'Right next to the Bond markings that link my heart and soul to you two. He's tainted it all.' I step back and shake my head, desperate not to break down in tears. 'I'll burn it off. I'll cut it off or-'

'You will not. And he hasn't tainted a thing between us.' He pulls me in for a hug, wrapping his arms around me as I sink into his chest. 'This is your safe place, and it always will be your safe place. No one will ever change that. And most definitely not a damn scar.'

I grip his shirt and inhale him with a deep breath. Everything inside me calms just a little bit more as he holds me. I'm so grateful to be back in his arms after almost being taken away from them both again. The attack seems to have cleared away some of the anger and resentment. Now I'm just thankful I'm able to have him hold me.

'I don't want to see it,' I whisper. 'I don't... I can't...' I peer up at him and hold out the bandages. 'Will you help me?'

'Yes. Always.' He takes the supplies and my hand before leading me to the old shower room down the hall.

As he reapplies the bandage, images of Jonah's cruelty flash in my mind. Not just his but Ahri's too. If he was speaking the truth, her severed hand did this to me. And yet she was the one who handed me over to him time and time again. Who turned the school against me. Sold me to the Authority after I Triggered. Who stole my money and my future.

This isn't just words.

It's a lifetime of pain. Torture. Savagery and betrayal. All summed up in two words.

Reid finishes up and lowers my hoody.

'Now is not the time for falling apart. Now is the time to be strong. To fight. To win. You let me and Cyrus deal with this scar. And know that it doesn't change a single thing about how we feel about you. You're still the most beautiful creature in the world to us both. Got that?'

I nod. It's not enough as he lifts my chin and forces eye contact.

'You got that, Little Bird?'

'Yes,' I reply.

'Yes, what?'

'Yes... Sir.'

'Good girl. Now come on. Let's go and have a talk with Ezra. See what he's got to say.'

'You want me to come with you?'

'We're a team, right? No more fighting. I want to work with you. Not against. Almost losing you has seriously shifted my perspective and reminded me of the real threat.'

'Real threat?' I ask.

'The real threat of losing you. Enough things are trying to take you. I won't drive you away. So... together. Together, or not at all. Right?' He rests his forehead against mine.

'Right,' I agree.

We stand and head to the door.

Together.

TWELVE

*B*rennan leads the way, along the long corridors, down some stairs, past some god-awful-looking theatre filled with what I can only describe as torture devices, and finally, to a heavy metal door with a tiny porthole window. Brennan stops, pulls out a massive key and hands it to Reid.

Reid looks back at me as he slides the key into the lock.

'You give me a minute with him first, okay?'

He poses it as a question. But it's not. Reid steps inside and closes the door, leaving Cyrus, Brennan and me in the hall.

We all wait and hear nothing.

'What's he doing in there?' I ask them both.

They share a look and an eye roll.

'Ezra is Reid's little brother,' Cyrus tells me, throwing his arm over my shoulder and looking smugly to the door. 'He's giving him the talk.'

'The talk?'

'Reid won't want him to say anything embarrassing. Or incriminating.'

'Incriminating? I don't think there's much that he can say-'

'There is. And it's not for you to hear. Ezra won't like Reid being happy. If he can fuck it up, he will.'

'Is he?' I ask Cyrus. 'Is this Reid happy? Is this anyone's idea of happiness?'

'Happier than I've seen him in...' Brennan looks out into the distance. 'Well... ever, actually.'

'And Ezra won't like that. Hence his tongue down your throat,' adds Cyrus.

'But they're brothers.'

'And how would you feel if Ahriella dropped back into your life with a promise to save us all? Would you trust her?'

'No,' I scoff. 'Never.'

'Well, there you are.'

'They weren't good brothers then?'

'No. They weren't,' Cyrus says. 'Reid's mother died when Reid was seven. Three weeks later, his father remarried. Bitch hated Reid. Made sure he knew it too. Soon after their marriage, Stick was born. She spent ten years pitting the two against each other and ensuring Reid knew who the wanted son was. The real son. It didn't do much for encouraging brotherly love.'

'Didn't his dad step in?'

'He didn't give a shit. Making his son miserable made his wife happy and made the boys stronger. More resilient. When wife number two died of a fever, the two boys were left in Daddy's care.'

Even Brennan snorts at that.

'Reid knew his father was an egotistical bastard with a heart of coal,' Cyrus continues. 'Reid gave up trying to earn love or respect from him at a young age. He focused on his work. On the wealth and protection of the Thirteenth Kingdom. The less time he spent at home, the better. He was happier out of court business and even happier out of reach of his father. But Stick...' He tuts and shakes his head. 'That kid was desperate for his father's approval. The shit he would pull to make it look like he was the golden boy.'

'Like what?'

'One night, when Reid was barely a teenager,' Brennan says. 'Stick let out all the horses after Reid had stabled them. His father blamed Reid. He said he hadn't stabled them properly and sent him out alone to retrieve them.'

'Without clothes,' Cyrus adds. 'Naked as the day he was born, without food or water. Without reins or rope. Without shoes.'

'Shit...' I breathe.

'Took him five days to find them all and bring them back, one by one. But he did. He didn't complain. He didn't ask for help.' Cyrus puffs out his chest a little. 'He smiled the entire fucking time. Do you remember how he would relight candles after Reid had left the room?' he asks Brennan. 'Idiot burned down their father's library.'

'And Reid got the blame?'

'Of course. Reid was the next in line to rule the Thirteenth Kingdom after his dad died. Unless he gets disowned or killed, that's the end of it. Stick wanted him fucking gone so he would be heir instead. His father is... was... I have no idea if the shithead is still alive or not. But he was a psycho. Brutal and unforgiving. Stick wanted Reid to run away from home or for his father to go too far and kill him. But Reid's not the running away type, and the bigger he got, the stronger he got. Soon, Reid was even stronger than his dad. His powers came in. His strength. Stick was always a skinny little runt and he has no magic. Just wings.'

He stops then, catching himself. Cyrus glances down at me and sees my reaction to his lie. He glances at Brennan and then back to me with an "I'll tell you later" expression.

'Ezra soon got the point that Reid was never going to let him win,' he carries on. 'Reid spent as much time as he could with us and decided to wait for the fucker to die. Until it was discovered he and I were destined to be the Mates to a pain in the arse, stubborn and indescribably sexy princess. Then we were called back.'

'A bratty, entitled baby with a silver spoon up her backside is what I actually think you and he called her,' Brennan adds.

'Is that so?' I look up at Cyrus, who still has his arm thrown around my shoulders.

'Maybe. Anyway, the idea of Reid being the heir to the Thirteenth Kingdom and the whole realm didn't do much for Ezra's mental state. Their dad was suddenly thrilled with Reid. His son. A future King. He lost all interest in anything Ezra did to put Reid in a bad light. This made Ezra erratic.' He lets out a long exhale. 'But then you died. The Bond faded. And we got sent here. So who the fuck knows what's going on in his head now.'

'Reid can handle him,' Brennan says with certainty. 'I'm more interested in knowing how Stick got here in the first place. It's impossible.'

'There's no way he could have come over in the event with you all and got separated?' I ask.

'I mean... it's possible,' Brennan says, but not wholeheartedly. 'But where has he been all this time if he did come over with us? And I'm certain he was back home with his father that day. The weasel never left that tyrant's side if he could help it. God forbid he would miss a chance to kiss his backside.' His eyes glaze as he looks into the distance. 'And how did he know where you were, too? How did he know you had been caught and were inside that van?'

From inside, the handle lowers, and the door starts to open.

'I guess it's time to find out,' I say as Reid steps aside and invites us inside.

Ezra's not tied up. Nor is he restrained in any way. He has a chair and a table with a bottle of water that's been half drunk. He's in the same clothes as before, and I see them now as looking extremely unusual. I think that what he's wearing is called a tunic. It's a deep silver with intricate markings delicately embroidered all over it. He has empty sheaths where his blades were until the guys took them. And there are golden cuffs that start at his wrist and stop at his elbow. His long, black coat looks like leather. There's no doubt that he is wealthy.

He taps his fingers on the table. His nails are immaculate, and his hands are covered in tattoos, as is his neck. I can't see more of his skin, but I assume he's marked much the same as the others.

'A pleasure to see you again, My Queen. I missed your beauty whilst you were gone.' As I walk towards him, he smiles with what I assume is his attempt at a seductive enticement.

I soon wipe it off as I slap him hard across the cheek, knocking him off his chair and onto the floor.

'What was that for?!' he demands.

'That was for sticking your tongue down my throat,' I state clearly. I reach out my hand as Ezra holds his cheek. He takes it, and I lift him to his feet. 'And that's for saving me.'

'You are... confusing,' he says, sitting himself down and not taking his eyes off me. But that smile is quick to return. 'I like it.'

'They have questions.' I nod towards the three standing behind me.

'I will answer what I can,' he says coolly.

I walk around Ezra and stand behind him, placing my hands on his head.

'What are you doing?' he asks, trying to look back at me.

I keep him facing forwards and nod my readiness to the others.

'How did you get here, Ezra?' asks Reid.

'It's a long story. And it's easier to show you.'

'Show us what?' asks Reid.

'How I got here.'

'We have time for you to tell us.'

'You don't. It's a miracle we haven't been discovered already.'

True. But I keep that to myself.

'You said you have somewhere safe for us to go. Did you mean that?' I ask.

'Yes,' is his simple reply.

The others look at me and I nod.

Truth.

'Where is this safe place?' I ask.

'I can't tell you.'

'Then I'll beat it out of you,' Cyrus laughs. 'It's not a bother to me.'

'He's telling the truth,' I tell them. 'He has somewhere safe but can't say where.' I press my fingers in deeper. 'I don't know why.'

'You can't tell us or won't?' Reid asks.

'Can't.' Ezra slowly crosses his legs. 'The location is incognatia.'

All three furrow their brows and repeat the word together in a low, disbelieving whisper.

Incognatia...

'He telling the truth, Princess?'

'Yes,' I reply to Cyrus. 'What's incognatia?'

'It's an enchantment,' Reid tells me, his brow still in a deep furrow as he looks at his younger brother. 'An old enchantment from home. To have an incognatia is to have a hidden place. A sanctuary. You can talk about it when you're there, within its walls. As soon as you leave, you can't speak of it at all. Not its location. What it looks like. Who is there. Nothing.' Reid glares at Ezra. 'How the hell do you have one here? It's ancient magic. The knowledge to create one was lost centuries ago. It's not possible you made it.'

Ezra sighs. 'I didn't. We found it. I can't tell you more. Have you lost your memories of the old ways, brother? It's impossible.'

'So you want us to follow you to this "safe place" without knowing where it is?' I ask.

'If you want to live. Yes.'

'Are you working with Ivan?' I ask.

'No.' His words are firm, as is his truth.

'Do you mean to cause my friends or me any harm?'

'No.'

Cyrus looks at Reid. 'Raven says he's telling the truth. He has somewhere safe for us to go.'

The way they observe each other, a silent stare holds a thousand words within it. Then they look at me, their thoughts raging.

'Is it walkable?' Reid asks. 'We have Fae without wings.'

'I can't say how far it is. But I can say your friends without wings will not make it on foot without death or capture.'

Reid's eyes land on me. I nod. Truth.

'How did you get here, Ezra? Into the human realm?'

'I can't tell you.'

I grow impatient. His words may be restricted.

Perhaps his head isn't.

He yells as I focus my powers into his mind, forcing myself into his head. Into his memories of truth.

'STOP!' Ezra bellows, grabbing at my hands. 'STOP!'

I don't, and I force my way inside.

'RAVEN!' Reid yells. 'DON'T!'

Ezra's wings explode from his back as he gets to his feet. The room is lost to a blinding white.

There's a scream.

My scream.

I flood with pain through every cell and every atom. The noise of the room and those inside it are lost to the extreme ringing in my ears.

When I finally manage to blink the world into focus, I'm on the floor, my back against the padded wall of the cell and Reid and Cyrus shaking me.

Yes. I have been well and truly knocked on my arse.

'Are you okay? Hey! Can you see me? Hear me?' Cyrus keeps shaking.

'Unless you want to be puked on again, I suggest you stop with the shaking,' I groan.

'I told you not to do that,' scorns Reid. 'I told you to stop!'

'I was just trying to see.'

'I know. But the incognatia enchantment is too powerful. It would never let itself be seen like that.'

'You could have said.' They help me to my feet and hold me as I sway.

Ezra is nursing a heavily bleeding nose and is glaring at me with much the same disapproval as his half-brother beside me.

'I am not here as your enemy, My Queen,' Ezra insists. 'Reid and I have had our differences in the past, but this is bigger than us. It's bigger than all of us. I have somewhere safe for you to go.

Once there, I will tell you all I can. I swear to you. The fate of us all lies in your hands. Come with me. Let me show you.' He looks at the three others in the room. 'All of you. You must come with me now.'

Reid and Cyrus look down at me.

'What do you want to do, Little Bird?' Reid asks.

'We have to save them...'

The room spins. Cyrus wipes at the blood that has started seeping down from my nose.

'Raven?' he asks. 'You okay?'

'Nope.' I shake my head as much as I'm able. 'Need to sit.' My legs buckle, but they have me. They always do. 'We all go. We have to.'

'I can't take you all,' Ezra argues, sniffing at the blood seeping down his face. '*We* can go. Those with wings. We can fly.'

Cyrus scoops me up in his arms, and my head lolls against his chest.

Shit. That backfiring has knocked me hard.

Reid lifts my shirt.

'She's still bleeding on her side. Her magic is weak from the escape, and now this?' Reid looks at Cyrus. 'She needs patching up and rest. She won't be able to fly anywhere like this, and carrying her leaves us one down in a fight if it comes to that. We start travelling with her leaking blood from the sky, she could be smelled by a Dark Fae and we'll be followed.'

'She's not going anywhere for a while,' Cyrus agrees.

They do that damn staring thing again. They look at each other as if having a whole discussion in utter silence.

They nod, and Reid faces Ezra.

'Fine.' Reid nods.

'Fine?' Ezra asks, a little lost.

'You and me, we'll go to this safe haven of yours and I will decide if it is safe.'

Ezra glances at me before meeting his brother's stare once more. 'Just you?'

'Yes. If it's everything you say, then I will send for the others.' He turns to Cyrus. 'You'll keep her safe.'

'That's not even worth asking. You just keep yourself safe.'

Reid nods and looks down at me.

'You stay close to Cyrus while I'm gone, and I'll-'

'No. No, Cyrus goes with you!'

'He stays with you.'

'Then take Brennan or Lucca!' I feel panic building in my heart as the idea of him going and never returning becomes unbearable. 'Ezra can't be trusted!'

His hand rests on my cheek as he looks down at me with calming warmth. It emanates from him. A silent encouragement to trust him. An unspoken promise that everything will be okay.

'Every time we're apart... terrible things happen.' I'm shaking uncontrollably now and I see them share a look of concern. 'We can travel together. Please. Please don't leave me.'

'I'm not leaving you. We'll all be together again real soon. I promise. Okay?'

'I could make you stay.' I give a slight pull on our bonds. 'I will-'

'And part of me would love nothing more. But I have to go. You have to rest. And I need to kiss you.'

He leans down and rests his lips on mine. I kiss him back, hating that he's leaving. Hating that he's right that leaving is the correct thing to do.

'I will pull gently on the bonds to let you know I am okay,' he says. 'You do the same in return. If something goes wrong and you need me, you pull hard. You pull with all your might for as long as possible until I am by your side. And when I know it is safe for you to come and join me, I will pull hard for a few seconds. Then you make me your anchor and make your portal. Okay?'

I nod.

'You'll be a good girl, won't you?' he asks quietly, his lips a hair's breadth from mine. 'No tears. You're stronger than that.'

'Yes,' I reply.

'Yes, what?'

A slight smile pulls at my lips. 'Yes, Sir.'

After a chaste kiss against his grin, he turns to Cyrus.

'You shouldn't go alone,' Cyrus says, side-eyeing Ezra. 'You need someone to watch your back.'

'I'll take Tessa. It will keep her away from Raven, and I can have a chat about her behaviour whilst we're alone. Watch for trouble.'

'You got it.'

Reid leaves, dragging Ezra with him.

My fists clench Cyrus's shirt as I become swamped with dread.

'You need anything?' Cyrus asks.

'To go back in time, stop my mother from sending us all over here, kill Ivan Walker and forget this nightmare ever happened?'

'That might be tricky. Anything else more within my realm of capabilities?'

'You can take me to the toilet,' I tell him. 'I need to pee.'

'I get all the best jobs,' he chuckles, leaving the room with me still in his arms.

THIRTEEN

'Are you certain sending Reid and Tessa with Ezra was the best idea?' asks Lucca as I lie on my side, half asleep on one of the many cots in the recreation room.

Rhea is beside me, gripping my hand as she sleeps.

'Reid can look after himself. And Tessa is better with him than left here with Raven to cause trouble.' Cyrus yawns, and I hear him rub his face in his palms. 'Stick was telling the truth when he said he knew of a safe place, and if it somehow turns out that's a lie, Reid will remain silent and won't call Raven to him.'

'Probably because he'll be dead.'

'Quit worrying, Lucca. Reid's fine. We're fine.'

'You should get some sleep, Cyrus. You look like shit, dude.'

'I will when we're safe. I don't want to take my eyes off Raven. Especially when she's snuggled up to a giant monster-in-waiting.'

'Rhea was pretty fucking scary by all accounts. El said she almost lost herself when she went Dark. Nearly didn't come back. We could have lost her.'

'Rhea transforming into that dark creature saved the girls' lives. If I had to choose between her going dark or Raven getting hurt, it wouldn't even be a choice.'

Fucker.

I turn to face him with a glare.

'That's a really shitty thing to say,' I whisper.

'What is?' he asks, looking baffled at my annoyance.

'That you would rather I lose my sister again than risk me getting hurt. Very heroic.'

'You'll get this eventually, Princess. Me... villain.' He points to himself.

'You can't be a villain if you care about me as much as you say.' I sit, prising my hand from Rhea in an effort not to wake her. I throw my legs over the side and face him. 'Sorry to tell you, Mr villain. But you're not as much of a bad man as you think you are.'

'Villains can care about people, Princess. Caring about someone doesn't make them a good person. And it certainly doesn't make them a hero. People like me will destroy everyone and everything if it saves the people they care about.' He leans forwards, resting his elbows on his knees. 'A hero, on the other hand, would destroy the ones they care about if it saved everyone and everything else. That's why heroes are pussys. And why I would take being a villain any day of the week. Because believe me, if this place exploded into fire right now, and I had to choose between saving you alone or everyone else in this room? You would be in my arms, and I wouldn't even look back as this place burned.'

'Cheers, man,' Lucca says with an eye roll.

'Don't pretend you wouldn't be the same with El,' Cyrus says with a slight shrug.

'True,' Lucca grins, throwing me a wink.

'Well. Now we all know you are both psychopaths-'

'Was that a spoiler?' Lucca yawns. 'Thought you would have nailed that the first time you met us all.' His laugh booms across the quiet room of sleeping Fae, causing a few to shift and stir.

To be fair, he does have a point. The first time I met Reid, he threatened to shoot me and then Triggered me in the middle of a Dark Fae bar fight. And when I first met Cyrus, he had me cornered in an alleyway, threatening to slit my throat if he ever caught me stealing in his patch again.

'Any luck figuring out how they found us?' I ask Lucca as I rub my eyes clear of sleep deprivation and exasperation.

'Brennan is convinced that those Dark Fae were tracked.'

'They didn't have collars.'

'He thinks an implant. Your Dad-'

'Don't call Ivan Walker her dad,' Cyrus tells him. 'She doesn't like it.'

'Apologies. The raving, homicidal, piece of shit, child torturing-'

'I get it,' I sigh.

'He likes to experiment and create new tech. Almost as much as Brennan. The collars were made decades ago. I wouldn't be surprised if Ivan has put much more advanced weapons in place. Better trackers. More advanced experiments.'

Images of the snarling and demonic monsters flash before my eyes, and I feel my heart hammer in my chest as panic forces its way into my core.

As it does, I watch Cyrus shift and rest his hand over his heart as he focuses harder on me.

'You okay?' he asks, his fingers still resting over his chest. 'You're panicked.'

'Can you always feel what I feel?'

'Sometimes,' he admits. 'When we want to. We can sense your emotions when we focus on you and tune ourselves to your body. Your fear. Your pain. Your happiness.'

'Your arousal,' Lucca adds, with that same smirk.

I feel a gentle pull from my band markings. I run my fingers along them.

'That him?' Cyrus asks.

'Yes.'

'He's tuned into you too, then. He felt what I just felt.'

I return the call, a gentle pull to let him know I'm okay.

'What if I don't want you leeching off my emotions and spying on me?' I ask.

His expression tells me I have very little choice in the matter.

'Can you teach me how to feel your emotions?'

'Nope. It's a guy thing, I'm afraid.'

'What was that earlier?' I ask Cyrus.

'More specific, maybe?' he replies. 'What was what thing?'

'About Ezra. That lie I felt as we stood out the door?'

'Oh, that,' Cyrus laughs. 'Yeah. He has a gift. A pretty strong one too. I sensed it the first time I met him when we were young. But he had just gotten Reid into a load of trouble, and I could tell he was a massive dick. So I lied. Said I didn't feel anything and that there was nothing there for Reid to Trigger.'

'Does Reid know that he has a power?'

'Of course.'

'That's pretty shitty.'

'No, it's not. It's smart. Ezra would have been put on our team. And he is beyond untrustworthy. Having him with us would have led to death and dysfunction. Trust me when I say he is not the kind of man you want to protect your back in a fight. My job wasn't just about sensing power. It was determining a loyal and trustworthy character. And his loyalty and trustworthiness are non-existent.'

'He seems to be on side now. An extra power might come in handy.'

'Well, that's up to Reid. But I wouldn't hold my breath on him changing his mind anytime soon. Trust us, would you? At least on this?'

'Fine,' I sigh. They do know him better, I guess. And what I've heard so far, I've not particularly enjoyed hearing. 'I want to talk to the survivors,' I tell Cyrus.

'Like a speech or something? Looking to make a passionate declaration?'

'Not really my strong suit. No.' I stand. So do they. 'I want to see if I can sense any lies from anyone. I want to know if they had a hand in how the Dark Fae found us. We can't risk taking a traitor to perhaps the last safe place for us when Reid calls me.'

'I checked,' Lucca insists.

'Well. I'm checking again.'

An uneasy silence consumes the room as I make my way around it. Some sleep through sheer exhaustion. Others stare blankly at the wall. And Cyrus, Lucca, and I go to each and every one, checking that they aren't the reason we almost got caught and killed.

I sense no lies from them. Except for a few who insist they're okay when they clearly aren't. They're scared, tired, grieving and angry. They should be all those things. I know I am. But no one here had anything to do with what happened. They are all loyal. All grateful for our protection. All depending on us to fix this mess.

Somehow.

The thank you's. Bless you's. The hands that hold mine as they stare into my eyes and swear to me that they would never betray me. That I am the reason they have hope for the first time in their lives. Even through all this, being out of their collars has given them the first night's sleep without waking in terror and a cold sweat. They would rather die for a fighting chance than be slaughtered in cages. Than to be held against their will to be used and abused.

And as a little girl wraps her arms around me and hugs me with all she has, I hug her back and vow to myself that I will do anything I can, all I can. I will give everything to save them. To save us all from Ivan Walker.

Someone here needs to at least try to be a hero.

FOURTEEN

*T*he hours pass. The wounded are slowly healing and the chatter starts to pick up as word of the mysterious stranger who might have a way out of this hell hole begins to spread.

I glimmer of hope does wonders for the body and soul.

Lucca gives me a sharp whistle to get my attention. He sits on a bed with his back against the wall, lounging about with a beer bottle in his hand.

Where the fuck did he even get a beer?

'Pup, would you check on El? She went to grab some oranges a while ago and hasn't returned yet.'

'Your legs broken or something? Why don't you go?'

'I'm watching the baby Fae.' He smirks as he swigs his beer.

Lazy sod.

'Fine...' I groan.

I leave the recreation room to make my way down the long hall to the east side of the asylum. And I head to what's called The Garden Room. A section of the building where the ceiling is made of glass.

We brought several tubs of soil here when we chose the location as a safe place. Soil and seeds. As soon as I enter the room, I see that Brennan has been working hard in here.

So different it is now. The mouldy walls are hidden from view as leaves, vines, and fruit grows as if they have been here for years, not a single day. The smell of earth and fruit is intoxicating as I step inside. Above, the stars twinkle through the glass ceiling, and I wonder at its beauty. Not a flicker of the toxic smog that plagued our city. Not a cloud. To my right, a brilliantly white flower blooms in an instant. I reach up and take a pear from its branches. Perfectly ripe and ready. I sink my teeth into it and grimace. It's unbelievably sour. I spit it out and check the pear. That's very unlike Brennan. His fruit and veg are usually perfect.

Then I hear hushed voices further in the room, somewhere in the foliage blooming in the moonlight.

'I'm sure that if you keep training, you'll get stronger and stronger. That you'll be able to turn and keep yourself... you.' It's El, her voice soft and sweet as she talks.

She only talks to one person so gently.

'I'll keep training if that's what Raven wants me to do. But with guns and knives. I have no intention of transforming ever again,' Rhea says with a sniffle. 'I'm sorry, but my strength and size when I'm like that just aren't worth the risk. I wanted to save you, so I turned, but I was filled with rage and hatred within seconds. I didn't see you any more. Just something that needed to be torn to pieces. And the darker my mind got, the more I could hear him.'

I peer through the leaves and see Rhea standing with El under an orange tree. She's hugging her middle with tears streaming down her face as El looks on with a face full of sympathy.

'I heard Ivan,' Rhea continues. 'It was like he was everywhere. Inside. Outside. In the air. On my skin. He was calling my name, and if I hadn't turned back when I had, I'm sure he would have me again.'

'You can beat him. We all can.' El steps closer to Rhea and rests her hands on her shoulders.

'No. *You* all can. If I had my powers, my ability to control the Dark Fae, then things would be different. But my power is gone, El. Ivan stole it, and now he controls the Dark Fae. He controls me. Without my powers, I'm just another of his creatures. A bigger, more capable and lethal creature. I can fly. I can talk. I'm three times the size of those things, and if he gets me back, you will lose.'

'He's not going to get you back,' El assures her, reaching up and sweeping her hair clear of her tear-soaked face. 'We've got you now. He'll have to go through us first if he wants you back.'

'You, maybe,' Rhea sadly scoffs. 'Reid and Cyrus want me gone. Brennan doesn't like me because Reid doesn't. And Raven...'

'Raven loves you.'

'She's covered in scars because of me. She's trapped with two men because of me.'

'She's not trapped with Reid or Cyrus. She's fated to them.'

'Forced to be with them.'

'No. Fated doesn't mean forced. It means destined. She can be fated to someone, but she can leave. She could love others if she wanted, but she doesn't want to. That's why she's with them. Because she wants to be. But she can love anyone she chooses.'

As I watch them, I see El resting her fingertips on my sister's cheek, catching her tears and wiping them away.

'She can?' Rhea whispers back.

El slowly nods. And steps closer.

'There you are!' Cyrus snaps as he peers around the door, looking seriously agitated. 'What the hell are you doing in here?'

The two girls step away from each other and look in our direction.

'You heard from him yet?' he asks, nodding to my arm.

'Just the odd gentle tug to let me know he's okay,' I reply.

'Why is it taking so long?'

I know the question is rhetorical, but it's one that's been on my mind too. It's been almost twenty-four hours since Reid left.

'Hi guys,' El says, smiling as she walks towards us, her cheeks blushing furiously. 'Whatsup?'

'Lucca asked me to find you.' I nod to the orange tree where Rhea still stands. 'He's asking about fruit.'

'Shit. I forgot.' She chews her lip. 'I better get back to him.'

She hurries out of the room.

'You forgot your oranges!' Cyrus calls after her.

She rushes back in, face getting redder and her eyes firmly on the floor. I see Cyrus's brow furrow as he watches her.

He looks at Rhea with the same expression as she hugs her middle, tucks herself in and leaves the room too.

'What was that about?' he asks.

'No idea.'

He takes my arm, pulls up the sleeve and looks at the markings.

'What are you doing?'

'Making sure they're strong. If he dies, they'll fade. I'm just checking.'

I pull my arm back.

'He's not going to die.'

'I was just checking.' He shrugs and leaves the room.

'No one is going to die,' I mutter, looking once more at the sky.

Two days. Two fucking days we've been hiding in this shit hole. I've continued communicating with Reid throughout, but he has yet to signal safety, and I can't tell if I'm pissed at him or worried about him.

Why hasn't he sent for us yet? Tessa better be behaving herself.

I've rested. I've eaten. I'm feeling strong enough to get the hell out of here, and I know everyone is just as eager. We remain packed, and they all leap to their feet every time they see me, but I'm yet to give them the news they yearn for.

Come on, folks. Let's go! Leave behind the toilets that don't flush. Forget the stench of dampness and mould. Move on from these grimy grey walls that withhold the sunlight and fresh air.

More bars. More walls.

Part of me wonders if Reid's call will ever come. What if he's in trouble and just giving me these gentle tugs to ease my concern? What if they soon stop altogether?

If he dies, my marks will fade. They're still there. The Bond is still in effect.

Patience, I repeat on a loop in my head. *Just a little longer.*

And until it's time, perhaps I'll stay out of sight.

I'm getting sick of the disappointed groans when I shake my head.

I retreat into the padded cell where we talked to Ezra.

I make portals. Small ones, and only from one side of the room to the other. Eventually, Rhea joins me and sits beside me, silently watching me.

'I think we've established you can make a portal,' Brennan says, lingering by the door with an apple in his hand. He throws it at me. 'How about some physical training?'

'You want me to run laps or something?' I ask, waving my hand and brushing away the portal before me.

Brennan steps inside. 'Punch me.'

He slides off his jacket and drops it by the door. He's all in black. He always is, with various guns holstered to his body and his muscles straining through the thin fabric of his black t-shirt. His hand is outstretched, his palm facing me.

'Punch me. As hard as you can.'

Tossing the apple to Rhea, who sits nervously watching, I get to my feet and ready my fist. I pull it back and slam it into him. My added strength from the gifted wings makes him spin, and he nods in approval.

'Yep. You have a mean right hook.' He gives his hand a shake and returns it to position. 'Cyrus did mention that. Hit it again.'

'Okay.' I pull back and strike, but he pulls it out of the way and clips me around the ear with his other hand.

'Missed,' he states.

'Again.' I gesture to his hand.

He holds out his palm and narrows his eyes as I watch him closely.

This time, as I go to punch, I also grab his arm to hold it in place. He tries to move, but I land my blow before he can.

He laughs, the sound echoing all around us.

'Brilliant,' he tells me.

'Why, thank you. Punching men was a skill I needed to learn early on in life.'

His hand is back up. 'Again.'

We spend some time sparring for a while, throwing punches and dodging each other's attacks. It's enjoyable. Playful. And he shares some handy tips, such as protect your head above all else. Defend yourself before attacking. And there are no rules in a real fight. Play dirty. Attack where it hurts most. Scratch and claw and bite. It's all good.

But most of all, never fight with anger as your fuel. That's how you make mistakes and impulsive decisions.

As I pull back my fist to try and hit his cheek, I yell. Because as I let it loose, I get yanked violently to the left.

I yell and grab my heart before being hauled across the tiled floor, the pull of the Bond dragging me straight at a wall.

Brennan lunges for me as I hurtle with speed. He tries to stop me but gets dragged along for the ride. My face scrunches up in preparation for impact, but Reid's call stops when I tug back on him in equal measure. I slide to a halt, a hairsbreadth from the stone.

Brennan is still wrapped around my middle as we both slump in relief.

'CYRUS!' Brennan yells, quickly returning to his senses and releasing me as he gets to his feet. 'IT'S TIME!' His hand reaches out, and he helps me up. 'That was close.'

'I always forget how much that hurts,' I groan, rubbing my chest.

Black smoke seeps into the room and swirls into Cyrus's form.

'It's time?' he asks, looking at me as I rub my chest.

I nod and turn away, hiding the pain of Reid's pull. My heart may have just been torn from my chest and shoved back in after my arm was torn off and stitched back in place by how painful it was.

'It's time,' I confirm.

With my thoughts on nothing but Reid, I link us. He's my anchor. My guide to the unknown. I give him a gentle tug again, just to double-check it's still safe. He returns it.

'You ready?' Cyrus asks, cocking his gun and looking at the empty space ahead.

'Yes. So are you, apparently,' I reply with a gesture to the gun.

'You know me. Shoot first, ask questions later.' He nods to the bare space ahead. 'Show us what you got, Princess. Let's get the hell out of here.'

I exhale and reach out my hand, calling forth the portal. The wind picks up, and the darkness becomes blinding as the gold starts to swirl wildly. My hair whips across my face as everyone gasps and shuffles back.

'You got it?' Cyrus calls at my side, straining to be heard over the howling.

'It's stable!' I call back, keeping my complete focus on the portal.

Cyrus whistles and Brennan starts towards it. He halts for a second and glances back at us.

'It's good,' I assure him. 'Go.'

He's gone. The first one through, acting as our scout to ensure it's safe. We wait, watching for him to return with the all-clear. Cyrus reaches out his arm across my waist, ready to throw me aside if anything other than Brennan returns.

Each second feels like a lifetime.

'Come on,' Cyrus whispers. 'Please...'

His desperation is well felt. If we have nowhere safe to go, we have minimal options left to us. This place can't keep us safe forever. If the Authority doesn't get us, sickness, hunger or dehydration will.

Brennan reemerges, nodding eagerly.

'It's safe. Reid's on the other side waiting.'

'Truth,' I confirm with the most relieved sigh I may have ever expelled. 'Okay, guys. Get going.'

El and Rhea start herding the surviving Fae towards the portal. It's a slow start getting them to go through. It seems that now there's no one trying to blow them up, they're not as eager to rush through the magical portal leading to who-knows-where.

'SHE SAID MOVE!' Cyrus roars, hearing me strain against the effort to keep it open. 'NOW! OR YOU GET LEFT BEHIND!'

Brennan and Lucca start pushing them all through, much to their displeasure.

Finally, they're all through.

Almost everyone.

Lucca's next. I give Brennan the all-clear to take Rhea through.

It's just us now. Cyrus and me.

'Ready?' Cyrus says, his wings emerging at his back.

'Definitely.'

'Get your wings out. Just in case we need to fight or fly.'

I follow his lead and call my wings. My strength doubles in that instant, and the safety of flight gives my courage a boost.

Together, we walk through the portal.

Darkness mixes with flashes of gold, and the silence deafens our ears. We emerge and welcome a breath.

The portal fades and becomes gold dust drifting slowly to the floor. The howling ends. The wind eases.

Ahead, our people are gathered in silence, huddled together and clutching their limited belongings. Wherever we are, it's dark and damp. Dripping water echoes off stone walls, and the only light source is from a few fire-lit torches held in the rock face.

A cave. Are we in a cave?

Ahead is an endless lake that disappears into the furthest recess of tunnels. The water is so black and still, it resembles a black mirror. The reflection of the stalactites on its surface makes it seem like there's a sunken city beneath its surface.

It's beautiful.

The Fae gathered before us are huddled together and staring past my shoulder.

Cyrus and I both turn.

A dozen or so men are stood with faces of pure shock. Their mouths have fallen open in a hollow "O". They're in the strangest clothes I have ever seen. Leather tunics and black robes decorated with a silver tree of gnarly and knotted branches. They have swords on their hips.

Swords!

Each has long hair tied back. Their ears are pointed, and their beauty most certainly indicates their Fae blood.

'Erm... Hi?' I offer, my eyes on their blades and their hands resting on the hilts. I notice then that their eyes are on my wings.

Their hushed voices echo around us, rebounding off the cave's walls.

"It's her."

"She's alive!"

"The royal wings. Do you see?"

"W-what do we do?"

'Glory to the Queen!' calls a voice.

Ezra's voice.

His words cause the men to fall to their knees with their heads bowed and their hands over their hearts.

Ezra's gaze stays firm on me as he, too, lowers himself down to his knee and bows his head.

Beside Ezra stands Reid. He looks clean and healthy, dressed in fresh clothes that seem more reminiscent of these men's strange wardrobe than the usual shirt and black jeans. He heads straight towards me, and I to him. His lips claim mine indecently as everyone around us stands in silence, watching us.

'What took you so long?!' I glance at the men. 'And why are they doing that?'

'Because you are their queen.' He stands straight and looks down at me. 'You okay, Little Bird?'

'Fine. You?' I look down at him. 'What are you wearing?'

'You like it?'

'You look like a prince from a dark fairytale.'

'Sounds like a yes to me.'

'Welcome, all, to my Keep.' Ezra stands tall and looks at those still cowering behind us, holding out his arms as if showing us some exquisite room. 'I assure you that here, with us, you are perfectly safe.'

A smug grin and proud eyes land on Reid, and I feel my Mate's entire body tense. Even his arm firms around my waist to an almost painful effect.

'I hope you are well recovered, My Queen?'

'Please stop calling me that,' I ask.

'Should I call you "Little Bird"?' he asks, side-glancing Reid.

'You call her anything other than her name, and I'll tear your tongue out and make you eat it, *Stick*,' Reid replies calmly.

'Where are we?' I ask, keen to end this tense stand-off. 'This? This is your safe place? A cave?'

I can't hide the disappointment in my voice. There's no light. No electricity. No clean water. Nothing. It's worse than the asylum.

'This is the gateway,' Ezra tells me. 'The entrance to it. No portals can be made within its walls. And the entrance can only be shown by a willing and earnest Fae.' He gestures to himself.

'It's an extra safety precaution,' Reid says. 'So even if someone is brought here against their will, they can't show the entrance unless their intentions are pure.'

I look around the darkness and shudder in the chill. 'Where's the entrance?'

Reid gestures to the water.

'Down there?' I ask. 'I can't swim.'

'You don't need to.' Reid makes for the water, wading into it without a care. He looks back at me. 'Come on.' He carries on until he's in up to his shoulders. Then he sinks below its surface, leaving nothing but a slight ripple on the surface.

And he doesn't come back.

I glance at Cyrus, who looks just as confused.

I scream as Reid pulls on my Bond, and I go hurtling into the water after him.

I'm pulled beneath its glassy surface, dragged deeper and deeper down.

As the surface disappears and the dark depths swallow me, I suddenly emerge, staggering onto dry land and bone dry.

'You okay?' Reid asks, catching me before I fall flat on my face.

I reply with a whack to his arm.

'You didn't need to pull on me like that. It fucking hurts!'

Clasping my heart and gasping from the lingering pain of the Bond, I free myself from his grip and regain my balance.

Lifting my head, I see I'm as far from the dark and dingy caves as I could be. The air is warm. The scent of firewood and smoke drifts through the air, and the hint of freshly baked bread and pie accompany it. Reid stands at my side, looking at me with a warm smile.

'What do you think?' he asks.

'Wow...' I whisper, my voice carrying in a soft echo. 'Where are we?'

'This is called The Vestibule,' he tells me. 'It's a welcoming area. Pretty, huh?'

Pretty? Pretty doesn't come close. The space is immense. The floors are white marble inlaid with gold swirls. A staircase lies dead ahead, wide enough for ten people standing side by side to walk up together. Two prominent stone figures stand century at the base of the staircase. One woman and one man, both with fierce expressions carved into their faces, but also extreme beauty. At their back they have wings and in their hands they hold swords. Their carving detail is so realistic that I hold my breath, half expecting them to move or speak.

To the right of the vestibule, a waterfall tumbles into a small pool that glimmers a brilliant blue. From the roof, flowers and vines grow from seemingly nowhere. All blooming and flourishing, despite the fact the only light I can see comes from an orbed-shaped chandelier made of glass. The closer I look at the chandelier, I realise it's giving off not only light but also heat.

'It's harnessed sunlight,' Reid tells me. 'Pretty spectacular, right?'

He chuckles as I just nod with my mouth agape.

I turn back to see the door I entered through. But there is no door. I'm facing the same water I sunk into back in the caves. The same black and still surface. But it's on the wall, like an enormous mirror showing me my own darkened and slightly rippling reflection. I reach out, the tips of my fingers caressing its surface. Its chill sends goosebumps over my skin. An icy void. Not wet, just empty.

I yelp as Cyrus steps out of it, landing on his feet with a slight stumble before looking at his dry clothes and then back to the mirror.

'That was weird,' he mutters, turning around and seeing the rest of the space. 'Fuck me...'

We step back as, one by one, the others emerge. Rhea, El and Lucca are first. Then the survivors. Some gasping. Some screaming. Some laugh as they experience something so obviously magic in nature.

Our people are through. And then so are Ezra's. Ezra and Brennan are the last to emerge.

'Please. Follow me.' Ezra leads the way up the wide staircase and follows it to the right.

We pass through a few double doors that reach high above us and consist of carved figures and inscriptions of words I can't read. Hushed whispers echo off the walls, and our footsteps sound much louder than they are as we all remain silent. Ezra pushes open another set of immense double doors and ushers us all inside a room.

Not a room. No. A Hall. A majestic, elegant, unbelievably stately-looking hall.

The floors are white marble. The walls, too, with columns placed throughout to support the incredible ceiling. Black and gold decorate the floors and walls in markings similar to my friends' tattoos. Portraits hang on the walls, of noble-looking Fae adorned in silk and jewels. Above us are at least a dozen chandeliers. Unlike the one in the vestibule containing sunlight, these burn with fire. Those and the fires in the ten fireplaces placed around the room illuminate the space. Tapestries hang floor to ceiling, and long tables and benches made of white wood reach from one end to the other, holding silver candlesticks and goblets and plates and-

'Food!' Lucca almost sings, dragging poor El by the hand as he charges towards one of the tables filled with bread, cheese, fruit, vegetables, water and wine. 'Oh, my Goddess. Fucking wine!' He grabs one of the giant jugs and starts downing it. As he does, he moans loudly and lowers it to peer into it, a look of suspicion on his face.

Please don't tell me the idiot has just poisoned himself.

'Lucca?' El asks. 'What-'

'It's from home,' he says, thrusting it into her hands. 'From the Everlong vineyards. I would know this wine anywhere.'

'Impossible.'

He shoves it into her face, almost spilling the lot down her front. One sip and her eyes begin to glisten.

'It is. Wine from our homeland. How-'

Her words are cut off by the scrambling of the others rushing to the table full of fresh food and drink. They sit and tuck right in, like starving wolves finding their first meal in weeks, laughing and overtly moaning as they finally get a chance to fill their bellies with real food. Cooked and fresh, not from a tin or a packet.

'Where are we?' I ask again.

'We are quite safe, I assure you.' Ezra declares. He glances at Reid. 'Ask him. He was most thorough with his inspection.'

'It's safe,' Reid confirms. 'And comfortable.'

'I repeat.' I look at Reid for my answer. 'Where the hell are we?'

'It's complicated.'

'And my little bird brain won't understand?'

'It's not a simple answer, and I don't think now is the time to discuss-'

'Is this *Clairgathin*?' Cyrus asks, looking up at one of the tapestries with his hands shoved in his pockets. He starts reading whatever the hell is written on the thing. I don't understand a word of it, but it sure sounds beautiful coming from his mouth. He nods. 'It is. This is *Clairgathin*.'

'Clairgathin is a legend lost to time,' Brennan scoffs, striding towards him and picking up a loaf of crusty bread from the table before it can be snatched by anyone else. He tears it in half and gives a chunk to me as he joins Cyrus's side. 'Even if it were real, it wouldn't still be here. No way.'

'Well,' Cyrus takes the piece of bread Brennan tears off for him and uses it to point at the scribing on the tapestry. 'This tapestry calls this place exactly that, and its welcome message seems pretty clear. Now. I know my Elderich is rusty-'

'You learnt Elderich?' Lucca asks with amusement, hiccupping as he returns the now empty jug of wine to the table. 'Wasn't that an elective?'

'Some of us wanted to better ourselves when we were young,' Cyrus retorts. 'This tapestry contains the laws for wanderers, and it's written in Elderich and it clearly calls this place "Clairgathin".' He turns on his heel, facing us all and still points accusatorily to the tapestry before biting into the bread.

'I don't understand anything you just said,' I tell him, handing the bread to Rhea. The last thing I'm capable of doing right now is eating. 'So I'll ask again, and I would appreciate an answer in a language I do understand. Where are we? What does any of the things you just said mean?'

'We are safe, and for now, I think all that matters is getting our people fed, cleaned and rested.' Reid turns to me. 'You especially. I have our room ready for you, and I will run you a bath.'

The flames flicker as an impossible wind starts to blow through the hall. I feel the gold in my eyes flicker as my power surges in response to my anger.

'I don't want a bath. I want to know where you have brought us.'

Reid remains irritatingly silent.

Ezra clears his throat.

'Raven. I urge you to calm yourself and your magics. I will gladly tell you anything you wish to know.'

'You'll stay out of this, *Stick*,' Reid spits. 'You don't get to talk to her without my permission. Or have you forgotten your place? She's mine, and you have no right-'

'Your permission?!' I scoff. 'I'm *Yours?*'

'Oh shit...' Cyrus groans, pinching the bridge of his nose. 'Here we go.'

I could rant. I could rave.

But I don't. I smile and turn to Ezra.

'I would be most grateful for your time. Is there somewhere we can talk in private?'

Ezra makes no effort to hide his smugness as he nods and smiles, giving me a low bow as he gestures towards a set of wooden doors that reach floor to ceiling and lead out of this magnificent hall.

I take my sister's hand and follow his lead.

'Raven. Raven!' Reid's tone holds nothing but warning.

'Give it up, mate,' Cyrus offers as he follows us towards the door. 'The old rules will never work with her, so I would quit while you're ahead.'

'I'll stay with this lot!' Lucca calls after us, scooping up another jug of wine and a handful of red grapes. 'Make sure they're okay.'

'And I'll stay with this idiot to make sure he doesn't drown in wine,' El adds. She watches us leave and gives a sweet little wave.

Not to me, though.

Rhea waves back in the same manner.

Brennan walks with Cyrus, and Reid follows on with a look I know would send a shiver up my spine if I were to look back.

FIFTEEN

'This place is indeed called Clairgathin,' Ezra explains as we leave the hall behind and step into a long corridor. Just as in the other room, this one is lit by flames making it bright and warm. 'Clairgathin is a palace of sorts. An ancient palace and place of study and rest.'

We follow him and a handful of his men down this endless corridor, past doors and more passages that veer off in other directions.

'It's Fae built?' I ask.

'Of course. The fires that light the halls are eternal.' Ezra peers back with a grin. 'Unless a powerful Fae kicks up a strong wind with their magic and blows them out, of course.' He turns and carries on, gesturing to the odd portrait hanging on the wall. 'It was built thousands upon thousands of years ago by a controversial queen obsessed with the human world. She wanted to study its people and the essence of the realm, convinced it held magics lost to time. The human world, of course, holds no magic, and the humans are a rather unremarkable lot, so it was abandoned soon after she died and forgotten by all except the history books and those who read them. This is a version of an ancient civilisation.'

'Ancient?' I mutter, looking at the exquisite carvings that decorate the pillars. 'It looks brand new.'

'The Fae make things to last the ages. We take pride in all aspects of our life.' He glances back at Cyrus and can't help but look him up and down with distaste, taking note of his filthy clothes and rugged appearance. 'The way we present ourselves to the world matters.' He turns back and carries on. 'We thought this palace was lost. But thankfully, we were wrong, and it continues to stand.'

He opens a few doors and lets me take a brief look inside.

Studies. Washrooms. Rooms holding statues. Suits of armour. Rooms for weapons training. For meditating. For prayer. Bedrooms upon bedrooms.

We go up and down stairs. Left and right. I'm utterly lost after ten minutes.

He opens up a set of wooden doors painted a dull green.

'Welcome to the royal library.'

We step inside. Rhea and I gasp so loudly it carries on in an endless echo.

It is nothing like the library I knew at the Academy. It's so grand. Each bookcase is made of hand-carved oak. The shelves are lined with leather-bound volumes. Above is a balcony lined with plush armchairs. There are several fireplaces, all with gentle flames dancing in the hearths. The smell is intoxicating. Earthy with a hint of cinnamon.

I never knew books could be so beautiful.

Ezra strides towards a large table and pulls out the heavy chair at the head of the table, offering it to me. Rhea's hand tightens in mine, so I stay at her side.

He gets the point and quietly sits.

'Are you certain we're safe here?' I ask. 'I've seen countless jewels and tons of silver and gold. Humans sniff that shit out.'

'You may have noticed that there are no windows in this structure. That is because we are deep underground, protected by ancient magic and defences placed here by our ancestors. I assure you, there is no way for a human to locate this place. And even if they did, they would need to be invited.' He sits and rests his feet on the table. 'There is fresh water here. Facilities to grow food. To cook. To live.'

'It's essentially an underground palace,' Reid adds.

'It's more than that,' Ezra insists. 'You can live within these walls for the rest of your life in comfort and safety. It's entirely self-sufficient. Our ancestors were remarkable. Unlike humans who thought a stone wheel was the height of sophistication, we have had comfort and taste in our blood for countless centuries.'

'It was rumoured that Fae and humans once lived side by side in peace,' Cyrus says. 'That the two species would travel from one realm to the other. But wars happened. They disagreed with each other. The Fae soon realised humans could not be reasoned with or trusted, so a treaty was established to stop further bloodshed. Only humans invited to the Fae Realm were permitted access. And likewise, only Fae invited were permitted in the human world.' Cyrus takes a seat at the table. 'Humans forgot this through the ages, and we only remember it as stories told at bedtime. Clairgathin is legendary. The home to a queen obsessed with humans, forbidden to enter their land through the rules of the old treaty but determined to live in their world.' He turns his focus to Ezra. 'How long have you been hiding down here then, *Stick?*'

Ezra glances at me with uncertainty. And then to Reid.

Reid nods.

'Five years. Give or take.'

'Five... five years?' I look at them all. His men and him, dressed in their splendour with warmth, comfort and food aplenty. 'You've been hiding down here for five years?'

'It's complicated.'

'Then maybe fetch someone who understands so they can explain it to me if it's too complicated for you to say,' I reply.

It's almost amusing how they all simultaneously roll their eyes and fold their arms across their chests.

'You have powers?' I ask Ezra. I know his situation. But not his highly armed men. 'You and your men?'

'No.'

'Do you need Gilt?'

'Some of us did.' He clears his throat. 'Some of the men Triggered, as I believe you call it. And they had to be put down.' As he recalls it, a dark shadow etches over his features. I can see it, clear as day. The memories of the screeching creatures and slashing hands.

'How did you get here? No. Don't look at him. I'm the one asking the question.'

'I know that, Raven. But you see, your Mate here has threatened to rip my eyes out if I do or say something he disapproves of, so in the interest of keeping my eyes, I think it best to do as he sees fit.'

'How did you get here after the Event that brought everyone over?' I repeat.

'It's com... a long story. One which I will be happy to tell when told I can.'

'What have you been doing for five years whilst the rest of us starved and lived in shit?'

'Working.'

'Working?'

'Elias. I am running out of things to say.'

'There is a room prepared for you,' Reid tells me. 'There is a bath with hot water. Some food. Clean clothes.'

'A large bed, too, huh? Candlelight? A roaring fire, perhaps? Some nice lingerie, maybe?' I shrug. 'Then go and have fun. I'm not moving until I have answers. How did you find me?' I look at him, almost accusatory. 'You got me out of that van. How did you know I was in there?'

'I'm ashamed to admit that I had been spying on the growing situation outside the palace for some time. I sneak into the human towns and learn all I can from their newspapers or drunken conversations between Authority Agents. I overheard an Agent drunkenly discussing your sudden appearance at the demonstration of powers earlier that day and how they had found your location. That they were sending a team. I followed the Agent down an alley as he relieved his bladder and persuaded him to tell me the location. I left immediately to try and help. Saw the van on the road and just went for it.'

'Sounds like a lot of luck,' Cyrus scoffs, meeting my stare. 'Truth?' he asks me.

'Unbelievably, yes. Not a single lie,' I reply.

'Now that's settled,' Ezra smirks. 'This entire floor is free to you and your people,' Ezra declares. 'There are twenty bedrooms, each with its own bathroom. There are clothes in the closets if needed. You have the main apartment, Raven. We have plenty of food. Breakfast, lunch and dinner are served daily. The library is a great place to pass the time, and if you feel the need to get some air, there is a subterranean garden I can take you to. It's still underground, but the rock is infused with old magic to mimic perfect weather to grow crops.'

'I would love to see that,' says Brennan with the most enthusiasm I have seen him show for something that doesn't fire bullets.

Ezra stands. The chairs scrape as they slide across the stone.

'Let me show you to your rooms,' Ezra offers. 'Rhea, you have a lovely room just down the hall and Raven, you are-'

'I can show her to her room.' Reid's chair legs grind as they move. 'Brennan. Please escort Rhea as Ezra shows her the way. Cyrus and I will take Raven to our room.'

There's no chance of arguing. Brennan follows Ezra and his men from the room and leaves us alone.

'I'm not interested in your attempts to bullshit me here, Reid.' I stand tall. 'I thought we agreed to work as a team. If you think for a second-'

'One night of good sleep and two decent meals.' He stops toe to toe with me. 'You give me that, and I will give you a way to win this war against Ivan.'

'You can what?' Cyrus steps forwards and rests his hand on Reid's shoulder, forcing him to meet his stare. 'What the fuck are you talking about?'

'I will explain everything, but not before she eats and rests. She's a bag of fucking bones and swaying from exhaustion, so if she wants to know anything, she does as she's told. I'm not negotiating because what I have to say is huge, and I know that when she finds out, she will want to do nothing but work.' Reid looks at me, brow raised and his face firm. 'Eat. Sleep. And then we'll talk.'

'You can't be serious.' I look at the pair. 'You can't say something like that and then send me to bed!'

'I'm completely serious. I'll show you to our room.'

'I need to check on the others. Make sure they're alright.'

'We can do that,' Reid replies.

'Well, I would like to see more of the palace. It's incredible!'

'In the morning. I promise,' he agrees, holding out his arm and directing me to the door. 'For the first time in your life, you can sleep without worry, with a full belly, clean clothes and a comfortable bed. We will make sure everything else is as it should be. That's our job.'

His strides echo as he goes to the door and waits for me to follow.

A fire burns in the fireplace. Candles flicker in brass sticks on a large table in the centre of the room. And what a room. There's a giant four-poster bed complete with black silk drapes. A brass bathtub sits in the corner of the room. It steams with the promise of hot water, and the scent of lavender wafts towards me. Beside the tub is a table holding a plate of food and a glass of wine. A silk robe is draped over a chair beside a towel. To the right is a set of ornate doors made of white wood and gold leaf. I walk over and open it up, revealing a second room. Smaller than this one but still just as exquisite. The walls on either side are lined with rails of clothing, all hanging neatly. There are cushioned stools and velvet chaise longues, mirrors, and chests of drawers.

'That's your wardrobe,' Reid says. 'There are some clothes in there you might like.'

'I'm sure,' I mutter, closing the door and looking back at the room. My eyes go upward, and I gasp.

The ceiling... my Goddess, the ceiling.

All impatience and frustration abandon me for the briefest moment as I stare up in wonderment.

'It's enchanted to look like a clear night sky back home,' Reid tells me, still standing by the door. 'It helped ease homesickness. So I'm told.'

'It's beautiful,' I whisper, looking at the stars above, twinkling so perfectly. The odd shooting star soars overhead, and I can see a red moon far in the distance.

'It is. Not a patch on the real beauty of home but still very beautiful.'

Cyrus also stares at the ceiling, and both men look up at the heavens they yearn for.

'The bath is ready for you. It's infused with some herbal remedies that will encourage healing and sleep. And there are some lotions for your hair and skin if you choose to use them.' Reid takes hold of the door handle. 'Bathe. Eat. Sleep. We will be back to check on you later.'

'You're leaving?' I ask. 'Both of you?'

'Unless you want us to stay-'

'Yes,' Reid cuts off Cyrus. 'We're leaving. We have business to take care of.'

'Where will you be in case I need-'

'You're perfectly safe. I assure you.'

I look around the vast room. It's been so long since I was left alone with so much space.

'We'll be back to check on you later, and if you do need us for something, pull on the Bond. That's what it's there for.' Reid gives me a reassuring nod. 'Enjoy your bath. Relax. You have earned it.'

The door closes. The thud rebounds off the stone and makes me jump. And then...

Click.

I run towards the door and try the handle.

'REID?!' I slam my fist into the wood. 'Don't you dare lock me in here. REID!'

But only silence replies to my outrage. I try a portal. Nothing happens. They were telling the truth that portals can't be made here.

With another hit and an added kick to the door, I turn and slump against it.

'Fuckers...'

I head to the bath. The scent and warmth are utterly enticing. My muscles ache in response to it, yearning for it. My stomach growls as if yelling at me to hurry the hell up and get to the eating!

I pick up the fresh bread and take a bite as I peel off my disgustingly filthy clothes and drop them to the floor. Glancing down, I see the patch of bandage on my side. The constant throbbing from it continues.

I step into the tub.

Holy sweet mother.

It's perfection in every way. Almost instantly, I feel my body relax, and the aches and pains ease. Reid wasn't lying when he said it held medicinal properties. I collect the food. A large slice of vegetable pie with creamy mashed potato and gravy. I make light work of it and then drink the wine before lying down entirely and taking a moment to enjoy looking up at the stars.

I have limited experience with a clear sky. It's only in the last few weeks I've been given a chance to see anything other than the city's smog, but I can tell straight away that this sky is not a human sky. It's not only the red moon but the thick clusters of stars that swirl and shine in a deep purple that speaks of its Faeness.

If this is a fraction of the beauty the Fae Realm offers, I can't imagine how it would feel to see the real thing.

I stay submerged for so long that my fingers grow wrinkled, and my eyes grow heavy.

Best not to drown in the bath, I think to myself.

With a tired groan, I step out of the water and slide on the robe.

With the jug of wine in hand, I sit cross-legged on the floor by the fire and watch the flames dance.

I listen to the crackling wood and the hissing embers as I drink.

What possible thing could Reid have discovered that would give us a chance at beating Ivan? This place, hidden deep underground and far from human eyes holds secrets. I know secrets. They taste bitter and make my skin tingle. It's all I have felt since landing here. An uneasy truth. Omissions are hiding in the dark. Another swig and I wrap the silk robe tighter around my middle. It's not cold. It's actually perfectly comfortable. Another twinge from beneath the bandage, and I know I can't ignore it a moment longer. I untie the robe and let it fall open, before peeling away the wet covering.

I swallow the urge to vomit as the swollen and red flesh meets the air, and I struggle to hold back the tears as I uncover what he's done to me.

Jonah's whore.

The letters are carved deep and wide, from my hip, halfway up past my ribs.

Jonah's whore.

I run my fingers over the scabs forming and feel the heat of the Dark Fae nails' venom.

I remember it well from my face, which has only recently stopped sporadically bleeding.

Jonah's whore.

My fingers travel across my stomach and follow the Mate Bond markings belonging to Reid and me. The intricate and elegant tattoo curves with my shape. I lay my palm flat on my back where Cyrus's marks reside.

Is my body no longer mine? Covered in the claims of others. I'm their Mate. I'm his whore.

Wiping away the tears, I return the robe and secure it so I no longer have to see any of it. I collect a pillow from the large bed and bring it to the floor. The fire is a comfort to watch as I lie myself down, drink the wine to its end, and fall asleep with the heat of the flames drying up the tears I let fall one after the other, after the other, after the other.

SIXTEEN

*H*angover. From. Hell.

Note to self. Fae wine is evil.

Pure evil.

Through the throbbing head, the dry mouth and the uneasy stomach, I suddenly remember where I am. That there's so much to do. To learn. I need to talk to Ezra. I need to find out what Reid knows.

'Can you at least wait until we've had some coffee before you start?' Cyrus grumbles from behind me. 'It's too early for your stress and anxiety.'

Rolling over, I see him sitting on a chair beside the bed. His feet are on the mattress and his arms are folded across his chest. Slowly he lifts his head and rubs his eyes.

'I swear, this Bond shit is something else. Feeling faint waves of your emotions can be fun when you're happy and horny, but girl, you need to quit with the negativity and worry.' He stretches his limbs and gets to his feet.

'How would you like it if I spied on your emotions?' I ask.

'You can't,' he yawns. 'It's a guy thing.'

'When did you get in here?'

'After you passed out in front of the fire in a silk robe. You looked damn fine sleeping in the firelight.'

'You locked me in here.' I sit. 'I don't like being locked in places.'

'Up you get.' He takes my hand and gets me to my feet.

I sway and swallow the urge to hurl.

'Where did you and Reid go last night? Why did you lock me in here?'

'Always so suspicious.' He smoothes my hair over my shoulders and taps the end of my nose. 'Now, get yourself dressed. Reid's waiting for us.'

'Waiting for us where?'

'You wanted to know what Reid was talking about yesterday in the library, right? Well, you did as he asked. You slept, and you ate. Now you get your answers, and we get to watch you obsess relentlessly for the foreseeable future. There are some clothes at the end of the bed for you. Reid suggested you might want to have a look in the wardrobe. See if there's anything you might like. But I doubted you would want anything in there, so I left those out instead. Chop chop.'

'Why? What's in the wardrobe? Tutus and tunics?'

'Dresses, mainly. Not your thing, I'd bet. Hurry up, would you?'

Side by side, Cyrus and I make our way down numerous halls and passageways. As we walk, we're joined by El and Lucca. They step out of a bedroom, all giggles and kisses. Lucca's hands are all over her, and his lips can't get enough of her skin.

'I see someone enjoyed a night in a real bed,' Cyrus teases as they straighten themselves up.

'A night in a real bed on our *own*,' Lucca corrects him. 'I don't mind who watches to be honest, but my dark little angel can sometimes be quite shy, so it's been a while. We had lost time to make up for.'

'The poor bastards that shared a room with you back at the farmhouse are very grateful for your patience,' Cyrus laughs.

The two guys walk on. El and I drop back a little.

Her smile fades as soon as she's out of Lucca's line of sight.

'You okay?' I ask. She warily watches Lucca's back. 'El, are you-'

'I'm fine,' she says with a painfully forced smile. 'Couldn't be better.'

I feel the hairs on my arms stand on end at her lies.

'You and Lucca okay?'

'We're fine,' she insists. 'Was nice to be alone with him after all this time finally, you know? I'm just... I'm worn out. You know how it is. I mean, you have two Mates to keep satisfied. I bet you're exhausted too. So, you have any idea what this is all about?'

Her swift change of subject follows a pleading look. She knows I can sense her lies. But she's asking me to believe them for now.

I take her hand in mine.

'No idea. I'm keen to find out, though.'

It's at least ten minutes until we reach a set of large doors. El and I stop, our necks craned back as we take in the sight. Enormous white gold doors stand before us, carved with wings identical to mine. The same shape. The same pattern. There is even gold inlay where gold shines through my wings too. They're enormous, towering over us with absolute grandeur.

'Why do those wings look like mine?' I ask as Cyrus rests his hands on the handle.

He looks back at me. 'Because this is your house. This place belongs to the royal family. It was built for the bloodline of the Portal Wielders. This place was built for you, Princess.'

He pushes open the doors. I expect them to groan. To protest against rust, weight or age.

It opens majestically.

Revealing inside...

'What the fuck?' My words come out in barely a whisper but echo around me several times.

It's a cavern so large I can't even see the roof. A fire burns in a perfect circle around the room, illuminating this great space. Ahead is a raised path of black marble a metre wide. There is a pit on either side of the path a few feet below it, and they're packed to the brim with chunks of stone, marble, gold, rock, glass jewels, and who knows what else. It's like a sea of beautiful rubble. An ocean of broken beauty, as still as a pond.

The elevated path leads to a structure in the very centre of the room. An immense Arch of stone stands on a platform of pure gold. But the Arch is broken. The top half is gone. Reid, Brennan and Ezra are standing around it. They're deep in conversation, speaking hurriedly, nodding and listening to each other intently.

Then Reid sees me. He smiles this sweet and boyish smile. I've not seen him smile like that before.It's beautiful. Serene. Hopeful.

Is that was this place means to him? Hope?

He gestures me over.

I walk along the pathway, looking down either side at the pits below. Some of Ezra's men are shoulder-deep in the stones. I watch them wade through, sorting and sifting as they examine the rocks and place them in piles.

As I pass, they stop their work and bow their heads.

'I wish they would stop doing that,' I whisper to El, who still grips my hand and follows closely.

'What would you rather them do?' El replies.

'I'm more used to people sneering or spitting. Not bowing.'

'Well, if anyone sneers or spits at you now, I think it would be the last thing they would ever do.'

I peer back at Cyrus. 'I dunno. I can think of a couple of guys that enjoy throwing me the odd sneer.'

'Disapproving or impatient glances, Princess,' Cyrus corrects. 'Never a sneer.'

We reach the platform and slow to a stop. The Arch, broken or not, is no normal stone archway. I feel it. I sense it somehow, just as I felt my mother's wings when they were locked away in glass and iron. They called to me. This Archway is doing the same. It's not as loud as the wings. The pull is not as strong, and it's not a voice that sings to me as hers did. It's a whisper. I stare at that shattered structure and feel the whispers on my skin. I feel them in my heart. Soft and sweet and gentle. Warm, almost. I don't hear words. Just... whispering.

'You hear that?' I ask, stepping a little closer to the Arch.

'Hear what?' Reid asks, standing by my side. 'You can hear something?'

'Yeah. Like... a whisper. A pull.'

'Like you heard before? With your wings?'

I nod, wriggling my fingers.

'The air feels a little thicker the closer I get to it. What is it?' I ask.

'It's yours,' Reid replies, looking up at the towering structure, which should reach ten times higher than it does.

'Mine?'

Ezra gestures to the broken stone. 'This is the first portal ever made.'

'That old Arch is a portal?' I ask, staring at it.

'This is how portals first came into being.' Ezra steps back and admires it. 'They were powered with ancient magic and archaic equipment. Before we could harness the magic ourselves, structures such as these were made to do it for us. As we evolved, our ability to tap into the powers of our world came forth, and places like these were no longer needed. Thousands of years ago, these stone portals were used to move from place to place. It was technology. Science meets magic.'

I shudder at those words. Words said to me by the man who destroyed my life, along with so many others. I feel the eyes of my Mates on me, knowing that they, too, are hearing my arsehole of a father speak those exact damn words.

Science meets magic...

'I've never heard of portals like that,' El says, taking a closer look. 'Only Portal Wielders can make portals.' She waves a distracted hand in my direction. 'The royal family. And only one in each living generation. AKA that sexy bitch over there.'

'Well,' says Ezra. 'Before that sexy bitch ever had the gift-'

'You watch your tongue, Stick,' warns Cyrus.

'She called her it first.'

'She can,' Cyrus says. 'Cos, she's a sexy bitch too. You? Not so much.'

Ezra clears his throat and carries on. 'Before the royal family had the Portal Wielding gift, this was the only way to travel between the two realms. These devices stopped working when we began to tap into the powers of the Fae Realm. There was no magic to power them because the Fae now powered them. The stone and metals in this Arch would charge the power. The result would be a portal formed in the Archway. Then you could walk straight through.'

'Through to where?' I ask.

'To another portal. Another structure just like this.' Reid nods to this one. 'If the stories are true, there was once a small network of these things.'

'Six,' Ezra adds. 'There were six in total. Three in the human world and three back home. This one here is the only one left standing in this realm. And as luck would have it, it was still connected to its sister back home.'

'Wait. This one connects to your world?' I ask, my heart picking up. 'As in the Fae world?' I look at Reid. 'Your world?'

'Our world,' Reid clarifies. 'And yes. This portal *was* connected to the one back home.'

Ezra continues. 'Eighteen years ago, the First Kingdom went silent. As traders ventured inside the walls, they found nothing. No one. Just half-eaten meals and unfinished wine. A whole city just empty. No sign of struggle. No bodies or blood. It was as if everyone just disappeared.' He looks beyond Reid to me. 'Then we found your father's hidden workspace. His notes. His experiments. The bodies he left in his wake hidden deep underground. His butchery left from grotesque experiments.' A disgusted sneer crumples his face. 'We don't know exactly how he managed it, but from his notes, we knew that a portal was involved. We had to get to the Human world. We had to try and find those we lost. We had to find you,' he says, looking me dead in the eye. 'The kingdoms need their queen back.'

'Why?'

The men share a look. Reid rubs the back of his neck and looks at me.

'Okay. You wanted to know everything, so here you have it. The royal family, your family, hold the power of the Portal. That's the most powerful gift in our realm. Your ancestors have always ruled because of that. Other kingdoms don't like how they set the rules. Now the First Kingdom is empty, so is the throne. Many kingdoms are making their play for it, and others are defending it, waiting for your return. There's a war going on back home.'

'A war?' I repeat.

Ezra nods. 'We came here to try and find the Queen or her children so we can end the war back home.' Ezra looks longingly at the portal. 'It was a miracle we found this old relic's sister and managed to charge it up. It took years to get it going. The portal Archways were destroyed or torn down over the centuries. Or they simply decayed.'

'You came through this thing? Then... we can go back through it, right?' I ask.

'The portal got us here, yes. But it overpowered and exploded after the last man stepped through.'

We all look up at the missing section of the portal.

'Can't you fix it?' I ask.

'We've been trying,' Ezra replies. 'But you see, the entire Arch was destroyed. Hundreds, if not thousands, of shards got sent all over the place. Killed six of us in the process. Tore them up like confetti. And you see this river of stones below?' He points to the mix below. 'They help charge and channel the machine's power. It was the same back home. The Arch. A sea of stones below. When it powered up, the stones glowed gold. We've been piecing the Arch back together, but the rocks blew into the pit with the other stones.' He gestures to the pit below. 'We've been trying to sort through them all. Finding the splinters and shards from the portal is hard enough. But then we have to ensure all the pieces fit together correctly.'

He turns as one of his men places a small shard into a crack on the right side of the portal. As the stone slots in, it shimmers, leaving no trace of the crack behind. It looks as if it were never damaged. The next bit he places in doesn't stick. No shimmer. The man returns it to the pile and carries on.

'It's a giant puzzle,' I whisper.

'Massive...' El almost groans, looking at the stones. 'And if this one exploded, who's to say the one back home didn't?'

Ezra gives a half-hearted shrug.

'Hope,' he says. 'And prayers.'

'We can fix it. We can help you put it back together, and I can power it up.' My face beams with excitement as I look at them all in turn. 'This portal leads to the Fae Realm. We can fix it. We can get our people out of here!' I look up at the Arch and can't help the excited laughter I expel. But then I remember. 'You've been here for five years.' I feel a hole start to build in my gut. 'Have you been trying to fix it the whole time?'

'Yes, ma'am,' Ezra replies. 'But finding the right pieces is like searching for a needle in a haystack. And then trying to put them back together is a mission in itself.'

The weight of that sits heavily on my shoulders. Unbearably so.

Five years. The Arch is barely standing.

The others start to talk. Talk about the Arch. The war back home. But their words all fall away as I look at the pile of stones left by the Arch. I step closer and kneel before taking one in my hand. It hums a little. I pick up another. It doesn't. The third hums. So does the fourth. The next doesn't.

The two that don't sing to me don't belong in the Arch.

And now I can smile again.

I hand them to Cyrus, step into the stone pile, and sink to my neck.

'What are you doing?' Cyrus asks, looking at me like I'm insane. He stands at the edge, side by side with Reid and El.

'I can feel them.'

'Huh?'

'The stones from the Arch.' I slowly start wading through but struggle against their weight pushing against my body. They press against the cuts on my side and make me wince.

They slip and ripple through my fingers. Dozens upon dozens of cold, hard lifeless stones brush against my skin. I try to move my feet but struggle to find the strength.

'Need some help?' Reid asks.

'I'm fine.'

My wings emerge, slowly forming at my back and giving me an added boost of strength. They gently help me wade through, pushing me forward until I finally feel something other than cold stone. The tip of my thumb brushes against something warm that hums.

I take it in hand and lift it. It's small. Barely bigger than my palm.

'This is one,' I tell them, holding it up for them to see. 'And the ones Cyrus is holding.'

Ezra reaches down and takes it, looking at it as if it's the most precious thing he's ever been given.

'You found these in a matter of minutes. It takes us weeks to find one, and even then, we can't be certain until we fit it in in the exact right spot.'

'Good job I'm here then, isn't it?' I pull out my other hand and show him the sliver I hold. 'Because I just found another one.

This is it! This is the answer. I don't need decades to learn how to make a portal to another realm. We just have to fix this, and we can leave this place! We can all go back home!'

The pile slowly grows over the hours I continue to work, but we're still a long way off. The others have joined us. El and Rhea are gently combing through the stones and offering me any they think may be a part of the Arch as Ezra, Reid, Brennan and Lucca try to figure out how they all fit together in the Archway. Cyrus sits on the pit's edge, his legs dangling over the side as he reads one of the books he collected from the library earlier. I reach up for the water and food he hands me regularly, never taking his eyes off the page. He peeks over the heavy leather binding when I wince or groan against the stones pushing against my body. He says nothing. He just looks and lets his gaze linger before he returns his eyes to the page.

Rhea comes over and looks down at me. As I wade through the stones another step, I hiss against the pain of my aching muscles and tender skin.

'Raven,' she says softly. 'You're in pain. Get out of the stone pit.'

'I can find a few more,' I insist.

'You've been in there for hours. You're wincing.' She even looks at Cyrus as if hoping for backup. 'Can you please tell her?'

'Get out of the pit, Raven,' he says half-heartedly.

'I think there's another one nearby.' I reach further forwards.

'I tried,' he sighs, turning the page.

She faces me and folds her arms across her chest. 'Get out,' Rhea says firmly

'Hold on...'

'Get out!' she says, firmer still.

'Just a sec...'

'GET OUT OF THAT PIT!' she roars, her eyes going black and everyone flinching as her voice bellows off the walls. A voice that comes out as two entities. The monster and my sister mirroring each other. Both so angry. Her rage dims the flames in the room. Her shadow, that of her monster self, looms over me, despite her physical body remaining exactly as it should be.

Cyrus looks up at her, waiting to see if he needs to intervene. Every muscle in his body has tensed, and his entire frame is poised for action as is everyone else in the room. All stood still. All waiting. She swallows her rage and shakes her reason back into place.

As the others all step away, scared of the monster that lurks beneath, I see her fear. The threat of what hides just out of sight.

'Please,' she says quietly, looking me dead in the eye. 'I really can't watch you flinch again. I can't see you in pain. It's making me... feel things.' She side-eyes the others. 'So can you please just get out?'

She stretches out her hand. Cyrus's eye twitches, and he watches her hand as if it's some kind of weapon.

I guess it is or holds the potential to be. The deep scars on my face can attest to that.

I'm back on the pathway and feel battered and bruised all over.

'You have found as many stones as we have in the last five years,' Ezra says, admiring the pile before him. 'My Queen, you are... you are...'

'Choose your next words very carefully,' El warns under her breath. 'They look ready for a fight.'

'Amazing,' Ezra chooses. 'Thank you, Raven. Thank you.' His eyes sparkle in the light, shining with such gratitude and admiration. I find it impossible not to smile back.

'You're extremely welcome, Ezra.'

As I step back and go to examine the pile myself, Rhea tightens her grip on my hand and refuses to let me go. With a shuddering breath, she looks me in the eye pleadingly.

'I'm feeling a little hungry. Shall we get something to eat?' I offer her, hoping to ease her discomfort.

She nods.

I turn and come face to face with a wall of black smoke. I wait with a groan as it forms into a solid mass.

'Cyrus,' I sigh as he becomes himself, standing straight ahead with a sultry stare. 'Let us pass.'

He steps forwards, leans in, and kisses my cheek.

'Be safe,' he says before stepping aside. 'El, go with them.'

Hand in hand, we head out of the room. Feeling the eyes of everyone else following us. And sure enough, El comes too.

'What's the matter?' I ask my sister as we leave.

She glances back at the Arch where Brennan slides a stone into place.

'I don't know. I just feel very uneasy in that room.'

'We finally have a chance! A way out! We have some hope!' I insist.

I take El's hand and squeeze it tight as she shares her excitement with me.

'Let's celebrate,' she says. 'Fae style.'

SEVENTEEN

The great hall is alive with chatter and laughter when we step inside. All the surviving Fae are here, sitting at the tables, looking much better than when I last saw them. They're washed, rested and enjoying the food and wine on offer. It's a glimpse at what could be. A future for us all in the Fae Realm.

As Rhea, El and I walk in, we're greeted with smiles and subtle bows. We sit and help ourselves to a jug of wine before filling our faces with food. We take up a table close to the fire. It's warm, and the whole room smells fantastic. The scent of smouldering wood and charcoal. The smell of wine in the air. The scent of food from the tables.

And that laughter. That easy, relaxed and happy laughter.

I could listen to it all day long.

'Cheers!' El says with a mouth full of bread, holding her goblet of wine high.

'Cheers,' my sister and I sing back, meeting her drink with ours.

I don't know how long we sit here, but I do know I break my vow never to drink Fae wine again. And I break it hard.

My hand sways as I hold my cup out for a refill, and El struggles to keep her eyes focused enough to locate it.

'You sure you won't have some?' she slurs at Rhea, who is clinging to her water.

'I'm not really into drinking,' Rhea says. 'I've never had alcohol before, and I don't like the idea of not having all my senses about me.'

'What you talking-*hiccup*-about,' El slurs back. 'I am in complete control of all my facili...faciti... fajuziawatsits.'

'Clearly,' Rhea grins back, watching El snigger uncontrollably.

'You are the cutest,' El sighs, blinking my sister into focus. 'You know that? I just love that heart of yours.' El rests her palm flat on Rhea's chest and slows her words. 'It's the purest heart I have ever seen.'

'You've seen my heart, have you, El?' Rhea giggles.

'Well. Not literally,' she shrugs. 'But I've seen my fair share of hearts. They're bloody, swollen, and full of lies, pride, and agenda.' Her face falls. 'My heart is just like that. It's a bad heart.' Her eyes briefly flick up to mine. 'All our hearts are black.'

'Don't say that,' Rhea insists. 'You're one of the best people I know.'

El looks at her with sparkling eyes. 'I know that if I cut you open... a-and held your heart in my-*hiccup*-hand, it would be warm and soft and honest and... it would be beautiful.'

Time stills as the two girls watch each other. Their eyes are lost in the others. Their breath barely leaves their lips, and even though I am sitting opposite and merely spectating, I see their world slow to almost a complete stop.

'Well, hello there, my lovely ladies,' Lucca booms as he slams his arse on a chair beside El and takes the jug of wine from her hand. 'Save me some?'

And just like that, whatever I just saw disappears. El and Lucca are lost in some unholy snog, and Rhea clears her throat and slides away a little.

Her eyes drift past my shoulder. Seconds later, I have Reid to my left and Cyrus to my right. They each plant a kiss on my cheek and tuck into the various delights on offer. They pour themselves some wine. They eat the food. And they can not stop smiling.

'I thought you said you weren't going to drink Fae wine any more,' Cyrus says with a nod to the goblet at my lips.

'It's good wine,' I reply, sipping it down.

'You're damn right it is. The fucking best.' He tops mine off, as well as his own.

'You trying to get me drunk?'

'If I'm lucky,' he teases. 'It's about time we had something to celebrate instead of commiserate.'

Reid has his hand on my knee. Cyrus has his at the base of my back. Each of them is sat so close they press against me, and I love that everyone around us is happy and content.

Lucca chokes on his drink and can't take his eyes off the door behind us.

'Oh shit,' he coughs and splutters, wiping wine from his chin. 'This should be fun.'

Turning, I see Tessa.

And she is making one hell of an entrance.

Her pale pink gown hugs her figure and trails behind her on the marble floor. It clings to her hips and loops around her neck, trailing a length of silk down her exposed back. Her hair falls in perfect curls, and her wrists are adorned with jewel-encrusted bracelets. She strides in with her head high and an air of grace I haven't seen on a Fae before.

'I wondered where she was,' El groans. 'Got her priorities in order, I see.'

'What in the fuck knuckles is she doing?' Lucca whispers as we all stare at her in silent shock. 'Where does she think she is? Back in court?'

The rest of us are still in the clothes we fled in. True. The cleaner ones, but it's still stitched-up tank tops and holey jumpers. This girl has waltzed in, looking like something from a fairytale.

Her gaze rests on me, and she makes no effort to hide the smug grin.

She's the epitome of what royalty should be. She's beautiful. Graceful. Elegant.

And here I sit with a scarred-up face, bruises over most of my body and rags for clothes.

'She looks beautiful,' I admire.

'She looks delusional,' El snorts. 'She thinks we're back home already? Wearing royal gowns and-'

'She looks like that back home?' I ask, watching her. 'Did you look like her?' I ask El, nodding at Tessa.

'Me? Not so much. Only dresses I wore were for funerals or weddings. But you most certainly would have looked like her.' She waves a drunken finger between my sister and me. 'Both of you two princesses would have. Every damn day it would have been silk gowns, perfect hair, jewels and tiaras.'

I scoff and drink more wine, unable to imagine myself in anything like that. But the others all nod and agree. As I drink, I see Reid watching her. His eyes never leave her, and I loath how he surveys her elegance and beauty.

I bet he would rather have me in something like that. I bet they both would. Maybe all of them. A queen, with her shit together and some fucking class. I bet I would look ridiculous.

'You would look mighty fine in a dress like that, Pup,' Lucca says with a wink.

'Funny. I was just thinking the same about you,' I tease back. 'Perhaps in a nice purple.'

'If you ask nice enough, maybe I will.'

'Now there's something I would pay to see,' I laugh.

I peer back at Tessa again. Her back is arrow straight, and she glides with each step.

How does a person actually glide?

'Where did she even find that dress?' I wonder.

'Your bedroom, I imagine,' El says. 'That wardrobe of yours is crammed with royal gowns.'

'My room?' I look at the guys. 'You let her into my room so she could take my clothes?'

'No,' Reid replies. 'Obviously not.'

I look at Cyrus, remembering what he said to me this morning.

'You don't think I would look nice in one of those dresses?' I ask, a little hurt at his earlier words.

'I never said that. I just said that they wouldn't be your thing. You hate dresses. You once said you would rather wear a sack infested with fleas than walk about in a frilly frock.'

'That's not a frilly frock, Cyrus.' I look back at Tessa. 'That's beautiful.'

'If you say so,' he shrugs. 'Seeing girls dressed up like that makes me think they're nothing but snobby, dim-witted trophies who know nothing of the world but far too much about what shoes match the season.'

Everyone turns and looks at Tessa as she sits at the table ahead, swishing her hair over her shoulder as she lowers herself down.

'I'll have a word,' Reid mutters, placing his wine on the table and going to stand.

'No. Leave her.' I take Reid's arm and keep him at my side. 'I'll tell her to stay out of my room in the morning. Let her have this tonight. Besides.' I peer back at her. 'It's the first time I've seen her smile.'

'My Lady,' Ezra greets as he stands at the head of the table. 'I have a surprise for you.' He glances over his shoulder to where several of his men have started tuning musical instruments. Ones I can't name and have never seen before. 'It's a thank you. A small token of my immense gratitude for your help today with the Archway.'

'Music?' I ask, smiling from ear to ear.

'Music,' he agrees. 'Now, they are a little rusty. Some of them only started playing after we got here, in a bid to stave off the boredom.'

'They should be so lucky that boredom was their greatest problem,' Lucca scoffs far too loudly.

El delivers a swift kick to his shin from beneath the table, and wine comes out of his nose in protest.

The music begins, and the entire hall falls silent.

It's beautiful. Ethereal almost and wonderfully melodic. Even though it's just sounds, it carries such emotion and makes my heart ache for something I didn't know it ached for.

Home. The Fae Realm.

'My Lady,' Ezra says softly as he bends and holds out his hand. 'Would you care to da-'

'Dance with me,' Cyrus grins, taking my hand and leaping up from his seat.

I spin and almost fall he pulls me up so quickly, and my feet struggle to keep up with him as the wine makes everything a little uncoordinated. Once we're in the middle of the room, Cyrus stops and turns. I crash into his waiting arms and peer up at him.

'I don't know how to dance,' I admit.

'Just follow my lead. Don't worry. No one is watching us.'

'Liar.'

He laughs and pulls me in closer.

'I won't let you fall,' he says. 'Never.'

He starts to lead, gliding left to right with graceful steps. I can't help but laugh as I repeatedly step on his toes.

'Look at me. Not your feet,' he chuckles. 'I'd like to be able to walk in the morning.'

Our eyes meet, and suddenly I couldn't give a shit if I know the steps or how foolish I may look.

I get into it, keeping up his pace and speed as he bellows blissful bouts of laughter and guides me all over the hall. Soon, others join us. Reid has Rhea in his arms. Lucca has El. Brennan has offered Tessa a dance but seeing the disorganised chaos of us all drunkenly swaying about, she declines. So he's accepted an offer from another. Fae surround us, all energetically dancing. With a spin, I leave Cyrus's arms and land in the waiting arms of my other Mate.

'There's that smile I adore,' Reid says, pinning me close.

'Right back at ya,' I reply, seeing his wondrous grin.

He takes the lead, stepping to the music and taking me along for the ride. The rhythm picks up. The gliding becomes clapping and bouncing and waltzing. The room is filled with whoops, laughs, and such joy that my heart could burst.

As the time passes, hours I'm sure, I laugh so hard my sides start to ache. I dance so much I sweat like crazy. The kids are even up and running about. We drink more wine, eat more food, and the rest of the world fades into the distance for a little while. All of it. The harshness. The cruelties. The impossible weight of all we have faced and all that is yet to come.

Even when Tessa attempts to wrap herself around Reid, her fingers sliding through his hair as she leans up to his face with expectant lips, it doesn't bother me. He guides her away and returns his attention to me instead.

It's a crowd of revelry. Everyone dances with each other. The best part for me is seeing my sister relax and enjoy herself. To see her dance and laugh. To see how the others enjoy her joy as much as I do.

I love it.

As Cyrus dips me low and Reid leans down to plant a kiss on my forehead, I realise I have never been happier.

Never. At this moment... I'm in heaven.

As I stumble down the hall, hoping to find a toilet, I can still hear the music in the distance. The cheers. The whoops. The giggles.

As I pass a smaller corridor, I stop.

It's a dead end. A water fountain slowly trickles beneath a lit chandelier. A man is talking to one of the girls from the brothel.

Ezra's man. He talks softly and keeps closing in on her. All the time, reaching out to touch her. Her hair. Her skin. Her clothes. She giggles, but it's that kind of giggle we do when scared and uncomfortable. I did it on occasion too, when I knew that telling the arse hole closing in on me to fuck off would make them angry. Make them violent.

'Come on now,' he drawls, slipping down her shoulder strap. 'Haven't we been good to you? The least you could do is-'

'What?' I demand, my voice echoing off the stone walls. They both turn to face me. The girl lets out a sigh of relief and barges past him, and stops just behind me. Her hands take hold of mine as she makes me a barrier between her and him. 'What can she do for you, huh?'

'We were just playing, My Lady.'

'Playing? Playing what?'

'I offered to pay,' he says with a disgustingly wet belch. He sways on the spot and slowly blinks as he pulls out a couple of silver coins. He drops them. Obviously, we're not the only ones who have celebrated too hard with the wine tonight.

'Pay her for what?' I ask.

He gives a drunken drawl of a laugh.

"I mean... it's not like she hasn't satisfied-*belch*-a man before.'

My silence and stare make him still as he realises that perhaps, this is not a good situation for him. He starts shuffling uneasily.

'We have been good to you. To them all. Opened this place and offered protection. Comfort. Food and water.'

'Is that so?' I smile back.

'And it's been so long since we've seen a lady. Years. The least you could do-'

'You're right,' I declare. 'Of course. Because that's what it is to be a man, right? You have needs.'

'Yes, My Lady,' he says happily, glad I understand. 'It's a burden at times. But so many of the girls have been so obliging. So-'

'Other girls?' I ask, careful to keep a smile on my face. 'You've slept with other girls? They agree to it, did they?'

'I mean, once we explained it, they were happy to. And as I've said...' He laughs and gestures to the girl behind me. 'It's not as if they were pure to start with. No virtues were spoilt.'

'Hmmm.' I look back at the girl. She steps a little closer to me. 'Is that so...'

I kick the doors to the hall open, shrouding myself in the warm glow of the festivities, before I shove the worthless man inside. He lands flat on his face in the middle of the dance floor, too drunk to keep his balance. My wings are spread wide and the girl is firm by my side.

The atmosphere changes instantly, and the others are on high alert.

Reid, Cyrus, El, Brennan and Lucca have their weapons drawn and pointed at both him and Ezra's men, who have withdrawn swords and come to his side. They're unsure where to point them, though, especially as Ezra leaps between us all.

'Put down your weapons!' he bellows. 'Everyone, just calm down!'

'What's happening here?' Cyrus asks me, his eyes and gun on the man at my feet. 'You okay, Princess?'

'What's happening here is the same thing that happens everywhere. Men. Fucking entitled men who think they are owed. Who think they have the right to take what isn't theirs.'

'He did something?' Cyrus cocks the gun. 'This piece of shit touch you?'

'Not me. No.' I look at the girl who scurries to her friends. They reach out for her and engulf her in their ranks. 'Good job I passed by the empty corridor when I did, though.'

'My men wouldn't hurt anyone,' Ezra insists. 'They would never hurt a woman or take them by force. Rape?' He shakes his head. 'No.'

'Rape is an ugly word. An ugly word for a disgusting act. It's also a really big word, Ezra. Real fucking big.' I look at the crowd gathered around us. 'I will ask, but know there's no requirement for you to speak out if you don't want to. If you do, no harm or shame will come to you.' The girls share glances and a few nod. 'Have any of you pleasured any of Ezra's men since we got here?'

I wait mere seconds before five of the girls raise their hands.

'Keep your hands raised if it was your choice. If you wanted to. Lower it if a sense of debt was implied. Or something was offered in exchange. Or if you were simply too scared to say no.'

Shocker. All the girls lower their hands.

I turn to face Ezra.

'One day. We've been here one fucking DAY!' The flames in the room burn brighter and all the plates and goblets on the tables shake.

'I...I don't... They wouldn't...'

'Anyone want to say what happened?' I ask the girls.

'He said that if I wanted to stay, I had to earn my keep,' says one of the girls as she points to the man who spoke his bullshit to me in the hall.

'He cornered me in the bathroom,' another of them says. 'Told me how lonely he'd been. How hard it's been for him to go all this time without a woman. He wouldn't let me pass until I... you know.' She shrugs and looks around nervously.

'Is it just him?' I ask. 'Or are there others?'

The girls shake their heads and only look at him.

'Let me make this perfectly clear.' I look at them all. The men. The women. Ezra. 'We are not for sale. Not a single one of us. We are not here for anyone else's satisfaction. Just because you have a cock does not mean you are owed a mouth, a hand or a pussy to satisfy it. We owe you nothing. You owe us nothing. We are not to be bargained for. Bought. Guilt tripped or blackmailed. And if you think for a second that that is the case, then we will-'

'You can't leave,' Ezra says in a panic. 'I swear to you. I had no idea he had pulled this. Don't go. Not now we have a chance of escaping this realm. The Arch. You can't abandon it.'

'Oh. We won't be leaving. You will.' I gesture to the man before me. 'He will. And any of the men who have dared lay their hands on my friends.' I look at Ezra. 'I want him gone.'

'I'm sure it was a misunderstanding,' Ezra attempts. 'I promise you. It will never happen again.' He turns to his man and looks ready to spit fire. He's genuinely disgusted, and I sense the truth of that. 'You. You have disgraced your family name.'

'I never forced anyone. I never made them do anything they didn't-*hiccup*-want to.'

'Is that so?' I sneer, hating every breath I'm wasting on him. 'Tell me. Which would you rather do? Would you like to be thrown out of here to the humans who will turn you Dark or just straight up kill you? Or would you rather bend over and take a red hot poker up the arse?'

My question lingers in the air as he looks at me.

'I'm serious. Pick one. That will be your fate.'

'You can not b-be serious.' He looks at Ezra for help. But he says and does nothing, so he looks at Reid. 'Say something to her-'

'Pick one. Death out there or being violated in here. Degraded. Used for my satisfaction because, believe me, watching a man like you have a poker rammed up his arse will give me immense satisfaction.' I shrug. 'So pick.'

Silence weaves around us all as he looks between Ezra and me.

'Impossible choice, right? One may say it's not a choice at all. That's what we've been living with out there. Impossible, painful, devastating and deadly choices. Whilst you hid away in this palace, safe and fed and looking at a pretty enchanted night sky, we choked on poisonous air. Killed rats so we didn't starve. Watched as humans took our friends and family from us. Beat them. Strung them up in the streets. We watched as they broke their bones and threatened us with worse if we even thought about intervening. They butchered children. They didn't discriminate. They took us. Sold us. Pimped us out. Be a whore or die. When they cornered us in dark alleys, we either took what they forced on us, or they beat us down and took it anyway. We have been at the mercy of humanity our whole lives. We have been raped and trodden on by them, and we will never be raped or trodden on again. And certainly not by our own kind.' I point a furious finger at his disgusting face. 'And not by you.'

'It wasn't like that.'

'How many of the women you touched wanted you to touch them?'

'All of them! They wanted me!'

The hairs stand on my arms, and I can taste his bullshit.

'For Goddess's sake!' he spits, fury and panic fighting for control. 'The girls are professional whores. We fight for a living. They fuck! I never held anyone down. No one screamed. They should be glad to have a real Fae man to enjoy them for a change, rather than a stinking human! They should be thankful! They should be grateful. No one will want them for wives when we return, so they better get used to their place in life!'

Rage overwhelms me. It downright consumes me.

Ezra's man looks at Reid.

'You need to get her to heel. Unless you want a rebellion on your hands upon your return, you must shut her up. We don't want a woman with a big mouth and ideas above her station waltzing about, and if you want to rule-'

There's a flash of white and a fierce scream of pain. The man falls to the floor, his entire chest a chasm of burnt flesh. The crowd all jump back, horrified at the carnage on the dance floor.

Reid lowers his hand, the glow of his light dimming.

'The girls are not for sale,' Reid states. 'If anyone thinks otherwise, I will gladly remind them of that fact.' He looks down at the man at my feet. His flesh, what remains of it, smoulders still. Reid looks at Ezra. 'Do you have a problem with that?' he asks, nodding to the dead man.

'None whatsoever,' Ezra replies. 'I want the names of any other men who took advantage of those we are sworn to protect.' He surveys the crowd. 'You have my word. All of you. You are under no obligation whatsoever to any of us. This is your home, and you are safe here.'

Every word he says is the truth. He's honourable. Honest. His rage is at his man. No one else.

But there was something about what the man said. His words at the end weren't a lie.

We don't want a woman with a big mouth and ideas above her station waltzing about, and if you want to rule...

Odd words from a group who claim to swear loyalty to their queen.

'Raven.' Reid stands before me and tentatively holds my hand. 'Are you alright?'

'I'm fine,' I reply distantly, still looking at the man. 'You didn't need to kill him.'

'A man like that?' he says. 'Yes. I did.'

I step back, wondering what this unease I feel all of a sudden is. A wave of anxiety sweeps over me, drowning me in dread. Like I'm waiting for a bomb to drop, expecting it any second.

'Raven?' Reid tries again, pulling my attention back to the here and now.

'I need a minute,' I tell him, stepping away. 'Too much wine.'

I turn and leave the room. The crowd separates as I go, allowing me to pass with plenty of room. As I pass Tessa, she watches me with a satisfied grin.

As I leave, that dread fades. I take a relieved breath and feel my body relax.

The wine. It must be. Because those emotions... they don't feel like mine.

I look back over my shoulder. Maybe Tessa is messing with me again.

I return to my room, closing the door behind me and resting my back against its surface. My eyes close as I slump, glad to be alone. I wish that the effects of the wine would pass. That unease. That fear. It was so strange.

The ceiling above glistens like a magical night sky. The fire still burns in the fireplace, and the room is warm and welcoming. I sit on the edge of my bed, the wine making me hum, and now that I'm alone, I have neither the inclination or the energy to return to the party.

I look at the bath and remember the blissful effects the lotions and salts had on my body. The aches from the stones that crushed me in that pit and the dirty feeling I have from what just happened in the great hall, demand a bath.

Reid killed that man. I was so angry. Overcome with wrath as I heard the same sentiments from him that I've heard so many times before.

From Darius whenever he caught me at school. From the old man when he would sell me to pay off his debts. From the Authority. And from Jonah, most of all.

You should be grateful. Glad. Thankful.

But to actually kill him, one of our own. Was that right?

I turn on the taps and let the bath fill up. I roll my neck and shoulders, hoping to ease my muscles a little and replace the sounds of screams and sobs with the gushing water instead. I strip off and sink beneath the water, keeping the taps running.

Bliss.

Well and truly clean, relaxed and fresh, I step out and wrap myself in the silk robe. In the corner of the room are the bags we brought with us when we fled. As I get closer, I realise how they stink. The scent of the cottage, the asylum, the sweat and fear... it oozes from the bags. Not something I find myself too enticed towards, now that I smell of vanilla and flowers.

I keep on the robe and walk around the room, looking at the art on the walls and the meticulously carved stonework. It's all so beautiful. So grand.

I know we are safe here. Everyone can sleep easy, knowing that nothing is expected from them other than to protect and look out for each other. Ezra's reaction was a surprise. I half expected him to defend his man. He didn't. He was genuinely disgusted, and so he should have been.

And that Arch. A gateway to the Fae Realm and a one-way ticket out of here.

We finally have a chance. A real chance.

I stop at the wardrobe doors and rest my hand on the handles.

Before I can talk myself out of it, I open them up. Ahead, a fireplace springs to life and a chandelier hangs overhead. The room is cast in a warm orange glow of firelight. I step inside. To my left hang countless gowns. And to my right hang countless tunics. Shirts. Trousers. Exquisite cloaks and majestic jackets. On the lower shelves are shoes and boots of all sorts.

Women to the left, men to the right. Got it.

In between the rails are wooden shelves displaying countless items of jewellery. Several of them are missing. I'm assuming they are on Tessa's wrists and neck.

My fingers glide over them all. This all must have been in here for years. Decades. Perhaps centuries. Yet they could have all been placed here yesterday.

Not a speck of dust. No rot or dampness, rust or moths have tarnished a single thing.

'Well. Look at you,' I whisper, seeing a shimmer of gold glisten at me from the deep blacks of a silk gown. 'Aren't you pretty?'

I pull out the dress and admire it.

'Fuck it. Why not...' I mutter, placing it on a chaise lounge and stripping off my robe.

I put on some thin satin underwear and slip the dress over my head. I shiver as the cool silk slides across my skin. A few adjustments and I seek out one of the many mirrors.

I stand before my reflection, unable to tear my eyes away.

My hair is silky smooth for the first time in my life. The cream I washed my hair with has tamed the mop of split ends and knots. It falls down my back in loose but perfect curls. The dress is stunning. A midnight black with slight gold flecks that catch in the firelight.

It hugs my figure and leaves my back exposed. From my belly button up, there's no fabric either. It covers my breasts and goes around my neck. The sleek silk trails behind me several feet. There's a long, seductive slit on either side of my outer thigh. When I take a step, my entire leg is exposed.

So this is what could have been? This is the woman I should have become? Except for the scar on my face, I'm almost believable as a lady.

I sweep my hair over the scars and cover them from view.

How things have changed in the few months since I met Reid in that pub. An event that should have meant death or eternal servitude has led me to the opposite.

Now, I'm royalty. Dressed in silk. Decorated in jewels. Wine in my belly. No hunger pains. Not hiding in the attic. Not tip-toeing down the hall.

Not hiding from monstrous men who take what they want from me.

No. Now I have men who will die for me. Who saved me. Unlocked my powers and my strength. Took away the shit I thought mattered. Shit that I stayed in the gutter to protect.

The pretend sister and the flimsy promise of survival if I did what I was told and took what I was given.

I hated them for it at the time. Reid and Cyrus both. I blamed them. Blamed them for exposing the truth of my lie of a life. I was an idiot for clinging onto the slightest thread of hope I could scrounge from the dirt. I hated them for stripping me bare of everything. For making me need them. For giving me no other choice but to fight.

But I wouldn't change it for anything now. Reid and Cyrus reunited me with my real sister. They have given me strength and power. And a reason to go on. To fight.

This isn't just surviving.

I'm happy.

I'm living.

I'm safer than I have ever been. I have people who matter to me, and I matter to them too.

I thought for so long that keeping everyone at a distance was right. Everyone would either turn Dark or die anyway. Why bother risking the heartbreak of caring about them? Why bother loving anyone when there is no hope of a future?

No hope. Just pain. That's all I had in my old life. Before the night Ahri left the attic hatch open. Before the old man stole our money and took it into the city to gamble away.

Before I went after him and met Reid. Before he awoke the powers inside me.

But not now.

Perhaps it's the alcohol. Perhaps it's everything.

But I feel ready now.

I feel ready to face the truth. My truth.

The bedroom door opens, and Reid and Cyrus step through with a belly of laughter and happy chatter.

I run to the wardrobe doors and slam them shut before they can get the chance to see me. The heat of embarrassment washes over my skin and I curse my stupid curiosity.

They all laughed at Tessa when she appeared in all her finery. Cyrus made it clear he thought it all so stupid.

'Raven?' Reid calls. 'What are you doing?'

'Nothing,' I call back. 'Erm... just give me a second.'

I hear them stride across the room towards me. One of them tries the handle. It opens a crack before I slam it shut.

'I said give me a second!' I snap.

'I don't like you hiding like that. What's going on?' Cyrus rattles the handle. 'Open up.'

'Nothing's going on. Please, just give me a second.'

The handle falls still, and I hear them step away.

Thank fuck for that.

I turn, my fingers seeking out the clasps at the back of the dress. Rushing, I return to the chaise lounge, where my robe lies in a pile. I glance back at the door, only to see Cyrus's smoke seeping underneath.

He forms quickly and stops dead, looking at me in utter silence.

Without looking away, he reaches back and unlocks the door, allowing Reid inside.

I watch them stop still as stone in the doorway.

'What the...' Reid whispers, looking at me.

'Please don't laugh.'

I knot my fingers in front of me, wringing my hands nervously as they just stand there gawking at me. Their eyes travel from my head to my toes, and I can't read their expressions in the slightest.

'It's silly. I know.' I look down at the gown and offer a little shrug. 'I look ridiculous, but I couldn't help myself. I just thought... I thought it was pretty, and I know you said you don't like girls that dress like this, but I think that these gowns are actually incredible and I don't care what you think, actually. So... yeah. I wanted to try one on because I've never worn anything so nice, and yes, we laughed at Tessa, and I probably look like a street rat in-'

'You're rambling,' Cyrus says.

'Can you just...' I cringe and die of shame a little inside. 'I'll be out in a second. Would you mind?'

'Raven,' Cyrus grins, looking me up and down still. 'You look-'

'Ridiculous. I know.' I wave my hand dismissively. 'And while we're on the subject of being honest with each other-'

'That's your subject?' Reid smirks. 'I thought it was dresses.'

'No more secrets,' I demand. A little too loudly as they both flinch at my booming voice. 'No more hidden agendas and no more trying to best each other. This whole you versus me thing is exhausting, and I want it to stop.'

'Okay...' Cyrus answers slowly, that amused grin still in place.

'We have a shot here. A real shot at getting out of this mess. To save ourselves and others. And I want to do that with you both by my side.' I clear my painfully tight throat and realise I have just very awkwardly and a little aggressively stated my realisations from a few moments ago. 'I want us to be a real team. I want us to be together. When we return to the other realm, I want to do so as a couple.' I gesture between us all. 'Throuple? Is that the right... I dunno.'

'How drunk are you?' Reid asks.

'A little,' I admit with a deep breath. 'But I mean it. I was angry at you and blamed you for many things. Most of them were your fault, to be fair. But... what I'm saying is...'

'You love us?' Cyrus asks.

'Maybe.' I clear my throat. 'Do you love me?'

They both smile. 'Maybe,' they reply together.

They stand there. I stand here.

A series of cheers echo up from the party in the hall, yet we all just stand looking at each other.

'It's the dress, isn't it?' I mutter. 'I look ridiculous.'

Cyrus slowly walks towards me, his face still utterly unreadable. He stops, his feet and mine toe to toe. He takes the hair I carefully placed over my scar and sweeps it over my shoulder before running his finger softly down my cheek.

'How drunk are you, Raven?' Cyrus asks again.

'Why do you keep asking me how drunk I am?'

Reid leaves the walk-in wardrobe. Cyrus turns on his heel and follows.

I linger here alone, utterly embarrassed and a little crushed at their reaction.

From the bedroom, I hear the door close and the lock click.

The bastards have left and locked me in again?!

My heart hammers in my chest. Rage perhaps fuels it. Or maybe disappointment. I finally tell them that I'm in. That I'm done being angry. That I'm ready to be with them, and they just walk away?

I slowly leave the room, ready to curl up in a ball and stay there forever. I emerge from the walk-in wardrobe and stop.

Reid stands at the door, his hand still on the lock. He turns to face me and slowly starts removing his belt. I watch him slowly slide it free, never breaking eye contact with me.

Cyrus stands at the edge of the bed. That dark, delicious smile is in place. His eyes shine with desire as he unbuttons his shirt.

'Last time I'm going to ask. How drunk are you, Princess?' Cyrus asks. 'Because the things we're about to do to you,' he lets out a low chuckle and bites his lower lip. 'Oh, the things we're about to do to you... we need you to be with us. We need you to be sure. Or do we need to wait until the morning?'

I swallow a tight swallow.

'I'm tipsy. Not drunk. I'm right here,' I state.

'Good.' Reid drapes his leather belt over his shoulders and stops beside Cyrus. 'Come here.'

He points in front of him. I do as commanded and stop where he points.

Cyrus leans down and kisses my neck, sinking his lips into my skin so softly that I erupt in goosebumps. His hands slide beneath the slits of my dress and he grabs my arse, pulling my hips into him. His erection digs hard into my stomach.

Cyrus claims my mouth with his. I open wide and caress his tongue with mine. Our desperate breaths fill each other up.

When I go to touch him, Reid takes my hands and pins them behind my back before sliding the belt from his shoulders and securing it around my wrists.

'You don't touch us until we tell you that you can,' Reid orders in a firm and absolute whisper, tugging at the belt and securing it fast. 'Understand?'

'Yes,' I breathe.

'Yes, what?'

'Yes, Sir,' I whisper through Cyrus's kiss.

Reid finishes securing the belt around my wrists, tugging at it to be sure it's nice and tight.

'You look fucking stunning in that dress, Little Bird,' he whispers in my ear from behind.

Cyrus drops to his knees and disappears under my dress. He slides the silk underwear down to my ankles and takes them off so he can nudge my legs apart.

Still looking Reid dead in the eye, I let out a heavy whimper as a skilled tongue glides over my clit.

'Does that feel good, Little Bird?' Reid asks, his hand knotting in my hair as he holds my gaze. 'Does his mouth feel good on you?'

'Yes.'

'Yes, what?' he demands, tugging my hair back.

'Yes, Sir...'

Reid leans in so we're nose to nose. He wears a gloriously dark half-smile.

'Tell me what he's doing to you.'

'His... his hands... *oh Goddess*...'

'Tell me. What is he doing to you?'

'His hands were on my arse. He's moved them to my opening-'

'Your pussy.'

'He's eased in fingers from each hand. He's... stretching and teasing me as he licks and sucks my clit.'

Cyrus is moaning with bliss as he tastes me. My mouth falls open as I release a shudder, feeling the pressure of pleasure building up quickly.

'You're close,' Reid breathes, still watching me intensely.

'Yes.'

His eyes start to glimmer as I moan louder and harder.

In a cruel move, Cyrus pulls away and stands, surveying me with a smug, glistening grin.

'Why did you stop?' I pant furiously. 'Why, when I-'

In a swift move, Cyrus forces my underwear inside my mouth, muffling my words and silencing me. He seals his hand around my lips to stop me from spitting them out.

'You know, sometimes you talk too much.' He gives my head a slight shake and raises his brow. 'You keep those in there whilst we play. You hear me?'

He can't be serious.

Oh, but he is. Deadly. He pulls back his hand, running his fingers over my lips as if daring me to open them up.

'You are going to be good for us,' Cyrus says.

He lets out a low chuckle as I slowly nod.

'Remember your safe words?' Reid asks.

Again, I nod. My heart thundering in my chest, and my body aching for them both.

'Good girl. Now turn around and bend over.'

My feet remain on the floor as Reid spins me and pushes my head onto the mattress. The hem of my dress is lifted, exposing my bare backside to the pair of them.

'I have waited a long time for this,' Cyrus says heavily, running his hands over my skin, digging in his fingertips as he does. 'Do you remember what I said the last time I had your arse in the air?'

I moan around the satin in my mouth.

'You remember when I told you I like it hard?'

I yelp as he delivers a firm smack.

'That I like it rough.'

Smack.

'And I love to leave my mark.'

Smack. Smack. Smack.

I grunt with every strike, revelling in the sharp sting mixed with his heavy pants. He massages me a little before delivering three more blows. Sweat builds on my brow, causing my hair to stick to my face. With my hands still bound behind my back, I can't lift myself from the mattress, and I watch Reid sip from a glass of wine, enjoying the show.

Cyrus's fingers ease in and out of me. Once wet enough, he spreads my cheeks and spits before easing his thumb inside my arse.

I grunt against the invasion as he torturously fucks my arse with his thumb and, with his other hand, spanks me again.

'That's it,' Cyrus says softly. 'Breathe. We're just getting started.'

Smack.

The sound of his zipper echoes around the room before his trousers hit the floor. He steps out of them and drops his shirt beside them.

'We'll start slow, shall we?' With a lust-filled moan, he slides his cock inside my pussy, his thumb still in my backside. Inch by glorious inch buries deeper and deeper until he's all the way inside.

Smack.

He gets going, ploughing himself into me over and over, gripping my hip with one hand as he keeps that thumb easing in and out of me with his other. Each thrust is hard and demanding, hitting me deeper and deeper each and every time.

Reid keeps watching, sipping his wine and admiring my face buried in the bed and my arse in the air as another man fucks me into oblivion.

Reid sweeps the hair from my face and leans in close, smiling. 'Does he feel good inside you?'

I nod and moan in bliss, his dark eyes penetrating me intensely.

His eyes start to glimmer as I begin to reach my peak, and as soon as they do, Cyrus pulls out.

I scream in frustration as the orgasm slowly starts to ebb away. The fuckers laugh. I'm kept in place as they swap. Cyrus stands by my head, and Reid takes his place behind me. I hear his zipper, and then I feel him. Slowly, his cock buries deep and fills me completely. I groan heavily and try to move. He keeps me firmly in place and holds himself there.

'Deep breaths,' Reid says before he withdraws and slams himself into me so hard I scream.

He withdraws. Then hammers into me again, his skin smacking mine with tantalising satisfaction.

Again. And again. And again.

I feel it once more. The promise of release is building in my belly. Their eyes begin to glow in response to it, so Reid pulls out, and they hoist me up. I sway between them, gasping in as much air as possible while still keeping my mouth filled with my underwear as instructed.

Reid sits on the bed, takes my waist and guides me onto him so I'm straddling him.

He lies back and wags his finger, beckoning me forwards.

'Sit on my face,' he says.

'*Sitonyourwhat?*' I ask with my mouth full.

He taps his lips.

'Sit. Right here.'

I shuffle up his body and he lifts the dress as I get closer. I stop with my knees on either side of his neck.

'He doesn't have all day,' Cyrus tells me. 'Sit.'

I lower myself down.

'I said sit.' Reid grips my hips. 'Not hover.' He pulls me down onto him completely.

With my head thrown back and the enchanted sky above me, I shamelessly grind against him. My eyes water at the extreme pleasure that's taken over my body. Every nerve is screaming. That ache deep in my belly has never been this intense. Reid's deep moans vibrate through me as I rock my hips back and forth. Cyrus sweeps my hair from my sweat-soaked face and watches.

I feel it again. That pressure. The delicious promise of release, and I try, my Goddess, do I try to reach it as quickly as possible.

But they know. They feel it too, and I watch as Cyrus's eyes glow in reaction to it.

I shake my head, pleading with him not to let this end and I speed up, desperate for more friction. More tongue.

'Oh no you don't, Princess,' Cyrus teases.

Reid lifts me by my hips and peers up at me with smug satisfaction as I roar furiously at them both, and the bastards just laugh at me.

'One more?' Cyrus asks Reid.

'One more,' he agrees.

I'm stood at the end of the bed. My legs are barely able to keep me up through trembling. Cyrus removes my dress, untying it at the back so it slips effortlessly down my body and lands in a heap at my feet.

Off comes Reid's clothes, too, and we're all naked. All sweating and panting in anticipation.

Reid stands in front of me. Cyrus behind. Reid takes out the underwear from my mouth and steals a kiss. I taste myself on his lips and feel his fingers ease between my legs. Cyrus tugs at my hair and pulls me away from Reid's demanding kiss, and replaces it with his fingers, forcing them down my throat until I gag around them. They swirl in my mouth, all around my tongue and the very back of my throat.

He then lets me go and puts them, soaking wet, back into my arse.

'So fucking tight,' he whispers.

'You and her arse, Cyrus,' Reid laughs darkly.

'Me and her arse,' Cyrus smirks, pushing his fingers in as deep as they can go.

I long to hold them. Touch them. Caress them. Pleasure them. But my hands are still bound, and they seem to have a very clear idea of how they want this to go.

Pinned between them, I'm fingered hard and skillfully, each keeping in perfect time, pace, and rhythm.

I feel it again. The promise of release. Stronger than before. Enough to make my ears ring and my heart pound so hard it hurts. I feel it in my damn throat.

'Please don't... please... please!' I openly beg them to let me have it. 'Please, let me come!'

Their eyes glow, and I grow dizzy with the sheer intensity of what's coming.

But they pull away.

Before I can scream and threaten to kick their arses, Reid has laid on the bed, spun me around and pulled me down on top of him.

'You got her arse last time,' he says to Cyrus. 'It's my turn.'

'Have at it. It's a mighty fine little hole to fuck.' Cyrus beams, looking me in the eye as he speaks to Reid. 'I've got it all ready for you.'

I'm lowered down. Reid's cock finds my arse and impales me slowly. The cry I let out is a mix of pain and pleasure, and when I'm sat completely, he gently guides me down so I'm lying flat on his front.

My back to his chest.

'You good, Little Bird?'

I nod, and he positions my ankles on either side of his hips. Opening my legs as wide as I can, I look up at my other Mate.

'Cyrus...' I whisper. 'I need you.'

He's on me in seconds, thrusting his length into me and gripping my knees for support.

'I have waited far too long for this.' He leans down and kisses my leg. 'Hold on tight. And feel free to scream.'

They both pound into me mercilessly, wonderfully.

Their hands explore every inch. Every curve. They scratch and grab and caress and pinch.

They fucking worship me. Devour me. Take what they want and give me everything I need, and within minutes, my back is arching. My toes are curling, and I can't fucking breathe! My head falls back over Reid's shoulder as they continue claiming me.

The room trembles as I orgasm. And orgasm. And orgasm! My Goddess, I just keep going. Each time I think it's about to end, I feel it swell again. Rolling pleasure rips its way through me, from my very core to every nerve ending I have.

Someone bangs on the door, asking if I'm alright.

'FUCK OFF!' I scream back, still lost in indescribable pleasure.

When I've ridden out this apocalyptic explosion, I'm flung about, barely able to comprehend what the hell is going on until I'm facing down on Cyrus's chest. They're both still inside me. Both are still fucking the living hell out of me. Cyrus grips my arse cheeks and widens them for Reid as he hammers into me harder from behind. And harder. And harder. I realise I'm groaning like some kind of wild beast, unable to do much of anything except lie between them and enjoy every sweet second.

All three of us climax together, roaring and crying out in release.

Fucking perfect...

EIGHTEEN

*T*he hammering of the door makes me groan. All I want to do is carry on sleeping, but whoever is trying to get our attention isn't fucking off. The third bout of banging and I feel the bed beside me dip as Reid gets to his feet and yawns as he heads towards it.

He opens the door.

'Morning, My Lady. Forgive the intrusion but- oh! Whoah... Elias. Clothes!'

'You brought us breakfast. How considerate.' Reid's tone drips with sarcasm and I lift my head to watch him take a tray of food from Ezra. One complete with a white rose. 'And flowers too. How sweet.'

Reid is stood there completely naked. Ezra's gaze goes from him to me as I sit, and then to Cyrus, who steps out from beneath the covers beside me. The two face Ezra, dicks swinging in more ways than one. I pull up the covers, carefully cover myself, and look between them.

'There's only enough food here for two,' Reid says, looking at the tray. 'How strange.'

'I thought you were... I mean...' Ezra stumbles over his words, unsure what to say or do. 'I thought-'

'You thought we were somewhere else?' Reid asks. 'And you thought Raven was alone so you would keep her company over breakfast in bed?'

'I didn't mean that. I meant... I just thought she might be hungry. I wanted to make sure the incident with my man had not upset her, and I wanted-'

'I know what you wanted,' Reid says quietly, his tone low and firm. 'We spoke about this.'

'About what?' I ask. They remain painfully silent. Already? They're already going back to keeping me in the dark and-

'About the fact that you're ours and not his. Stick does have a habit of trying to take what belongs to me.'

'She's a living soul, Elias.' Ezra scowls back. 'She doesn't belong to anyone.'

'What's up, Ezra?' I reach out for that tray of food. The scent of coffee calls me hard, and I want it more than anything.

Reid places it on my lap and plants a kiss on the top of my head before turning back to him. Waiting for an answer.

'I erm... As I said, I wanted to check on you.'

'She's fine,' Cyrus informs him, folding his arms across his chest.

'I can see that. Will you please put some clothes on?'

'You're in our room. If you don't like it, you can go.'

'Cyrus. Reid. Just put some trousers on,' I groan. 'Or you can all leave and measure your dicks out in the hall.'

They get dressed, begrudgingly. And I look at Ezra expectantly.

'I have spoken to the women who accused my man of indecency.'

'Rape,' I correct. 'Carry on.'

'It seems that he was the only one who bothered them.'

'Raped them.'

He clears his throat. 'I had one man come forward and admit receiving attention from one of the women here. He claims they both had a few too many drinks, and one thing led to another. But that it was consensual.'

'He give you the name of the woman?'

'He did.'

'I want it. I'll ask her myself.'

'I have spoken to her already and–'

'Raven said she'll speak to her herself,' Reid interrupts. 'So give her the name and where she can find the girl so Raven can do exactly that.'

Again, Ezra clears his throat before telling me the girl's name and where her room is.

I thank him and tell them I'll be back in the Archway room once I have bathed and dressed. But he still lingers in the doorway, looking between the two of them and me in the middle.

'Is there anything else?' I ask.

It takes a moment for him to shake his head.

'Then I'll see you in a while.'

He gets the hint and finally leaves. The door closes, and both the guys turn to me.

'You two can get that look off your faces. I need a wash, and we need to get back to work.'

'We don't have to do anything except run our tongues over every single curve and–'

'We have to fix the Arch and get it going. We also need to talk to Ezra and sort out the blood.'

'Blood?' Cyrus asks, pulling on a shirt.

'Yes. Blood. So they don't go Dark Fae on us.'

'Yeah... no,' Cyrus scoffs. 'I don't think–'

'I wasn't asking you for permission.' I rise from the bed, the silk bedding sliding from my body as I get to my feet and walk towards the bath, feeling their eyes on my arse as I pass. 'The only time you will hear me ask you for anything is when I need you to keep working your magic between my legs. Now excuse me. The bath is calling me.'

'Room for two more?' Cyrus asks.

'Always,' I reply.

Back in my everyday rags, I head towards the Arch room. The boys are either side of me, wearing the least ornate clothes they could find in the walk-in wardrobe. I admit, they look damn fine in those loose shirts and tight trousers. They heavily suggested I slip into one of those dresses again, but I knew we'd never get out of that room if I did.

And we have work to do.

The halls hold a few wanderers. All of them greet us happily with their familiar bow and smile. Many are nursing a hangover and gripping onto mugs of coffee like their life depends on it.

We stop at a point where the corridor splits.

'You go on,' I tell them. 'I'll be there in a minute. I want to ask the girl about Ezra's man.'

With a chaste kiss on each cheek, they turn and leave, heading towards the Archway.

I head towards the room of the girl named by Ezra and find her with three other girls we all pulled from Serge's place. She confirms what Ezra said and tells me that just because she was forced to fuck at the brothel doesn't mean she never wants to fuck again.

That's something I can understand, so I leave the girls to it and head on towards the Arch room. A little further on, I hear yelling. Two people are fighting, trying to keep their voices down but failing miserably. I slow my pace to listen and know the voices belong to El and Lucca. I've not heard Lucca extremely angry before. He's raging now.

'This is fucked up, and you know it!' Lucca yells.

When I hear a thud and El yell, I throw open the door and charge in, ready to defend... not sure who. Both can pack one hell of a temper.

Lucca's fist is in the wall, and El is stood across the room at the end of the bed.

She's quick to wipe her tears and turn away from me, and he's just as bad, furious tears dampening his cheeks before he looks away to dry them.

'You okay?' I ask the pair.

'Fine,' they reply together.

Of course, I sense their lie.

'Can I help or-'

'With all due respect, Pup,' Lucca says, prising free his fist from the wall and turning away. 'This is private. If you don't mind.'

I peer past his back to El. She nods her agreement and assures me she's okay. That they're just disagreeing and asks me to go.

I leave, unsure if I should. But I know that El can more than handle herself if things get out of hand. Not that Lucca would ever hurt her. He worships the ground she walks on.

I make my way down the stone halls, past the tapestries of great figures adorned with riches and magnificent wings at their back. Past murals of bloody battles and victories. Past painting after painting of the most incredible landscapes. Of beautiful cities of white marble, never-ending forests that bloom under a blanket of snow, and oceans that surround islands of gold and green.

'Would you like to see your kingdom?' Ezra asks.

His sudden appearance makes me jump, and I gasp as I spin on my heel to find him standing right behind me.

'Sorry, My Queen. I didn't mean to-'

'Raven,' I interrupt, catching my breath. 'My name is Raven. Can you give the whole "Your Majesty" and "My Queen" thing a rest?'

'Apologies.' He rests his hand over his heart and gives a sight bow. 'Raven it is.' He stands tall and smiles. 'So. Would you?'

'Would I what?'

'Like to see your kingdom?' He starts to walk down the hall. 'Follow me. I'll show you.'

I hesitate but sense no lies in his words. And curiosity has its hold on me now. How can I see the kingdoms? I follow, keen to find out.

A few moments later, we're in the same library he brought us to when we arrived. He leads me past countless stacks and aisles, all filled with heavy leather-bound books and rolls of parchment. We come to a fire burning in the fireplace, heating the room. In front of it is a large table of shiny red mahogany. Its legs are carved to resemble the roots of a tree growing into the very foundations. He pulls out a chair lined with deep red velvet and gestures for me to sit.

I do, and he walks into the stacks.

'You are welcome to visit this library anytime you like, Your Maje... I mean... Raven,' he says from somewhere. 'There are some interesting accounts of the history of our homelands here. Some are rather dreary; sadly, a lot is in Elderich.'

'Elderich,' I repeat. 'Your ancient language?'

'Indeed. But I am happy to help translate it if you find some-thing you like the look of.' He returns, his arms full of books, and drops them heavily onto the table.

'Thanks. But Cyrus can read Elderich. He can help me.'

'Indeed.'

He puts aside the ones on the top and places the largest of the books in front of me. One of black and gold bindings with the sigil of a great tree etched into the cover. A tree with thirteen branches, each varying in size and grandeur. The greatest is the one that reaches the highest and acts as a canopy to the others below.

'This is the First Kingdom,' he says, tapping the mighty branch. 'These represent the other twelve.' He traces his finger down and across the others, resting it on the lowest of the branches. The thinnest. The barest. 'This is the thirteenth. The smallest of the kingdoms.' He taps it again. 'My home.'

I reach out and run my finger along its dwindling branch.

Ezra opens up the book. Its pages are thick and stiff, but it's not a book of words. It's a picture book. One with the most intricate drawings and paintings I have ever laid eyes on. The first page shows the First Kingdom. My home, where I was to be born to rule.

A marble castle towers over the glistening city below. It shines, even through the paint. I see flourishing green land and an endless sky with streets of gold.

He turns the page, showing another kingdom. The Second. This one is nothing but flowers and life. Like spring eternal, blooming and growing into a world for Fae to thrive. Buildings made of wood and bridges formed from twisted tree trunks. And an endless sky of pale pink.

The next page, the Third.

'It flies?' I ask, seeing the city pictured in the clouds.

'Yes. It was where the winged ones lived many centuries ago. High in the sky, their purpose was to watch over those below. To protect. And to serve the great Goddess above.'

It's as if chunks of the world lost their gravity and took flight before stopping in the clouds. Waterfalls tumble off the edge, as does the trailing green of the land. Incredible structures of cream stone link up the bergs of land, making bridges to join them together.

The next kingdom is dark, painted with black, blues, and purples as if cast in an eternal night. The buildings look harsher. Made of black steel, perhaps.

'Obsidian,' he says. 'An enchanting material. And to see a city made of it is something else.'

He turns the page.

To a kingdom of snow. Of mansions made of ice, where polar bears roam and wild dogs pull sledges of brilliant white.

Another page. Another world. One of water. Of lakes and rivers. Waterfalls and the sea. The city floats on the waves.

Another page. This one is a desert. Castles of sandstone are dug into dunes. The sky is an endless orange and the sun burns hot.

The next is a forest. Ancient trees and thick vines conceal within them great estates and stone castles.

Then a much more humble kingdom of stone cottages and roads. Markets line the streets, and horses pull carts.

The next is an enormous mountain. Ezra pulls away a thin sheet that covers it, revealing a painting of what the mountain holds inside. Miles of tunnels and acres of caverns, holding life. Fae and vegetation both. A whole city, deep in the mountain

He turns the page.

The next kingdom is dark, with an intimidating volcano on the horizon with lava sliding down its side. The sky is grey, and the houses below seem like hollowed-out boulders.

The next kingdom is deep in a forest. The trees are black and brown. The leaves are a deep red and purple. A city weaves through the ancient trees. Buildings of slate and steel.

Then... the final kingdom. The Thirteenth.

'Wow,' I whisper, my fingertips following the edge of the page as I take in the image of their homeland.

Of the enormous sky that towers over the sparse city below. A sky of the deepest blacks and fullest purples. So many stars twinkle in its endless depths. A deep red moon shines in the distance and reflects in the black river that runs through its centre. In the distance are lines of sharp mountains.

'This is the Thirteenth Kingdom?' I ask.

'It is,' he replies, looking at it with longing. 'We call it Midnight's end. I call it home.'

That word hangs heavy in the air as he says it.

'Midnight's End,' I repeat. 'It sounds magical.'

'It is. In its own way. Every kingdom has its own name.'

'What's my home kingdom called?'

'The First? It's known as Eternal Dawn.'

We sit in silence as I continue to flip through the pages, taking in the extra details of each kingdom and wishing, more than anything, I could see it all for myself. Excitement builds in my chest as I begin to acknowledge the fact that if all goes according to plan, I will very soon!

'Why were you so nasty to Reid?' I ask.

He lifts his gaze and blinks.

'What do you mean?'

'The others told me about what you did to Reid growing up. How you got him in trouble with his father. Why? He's your brother.'

'Yeah,' he sighs. 'He's my brother. He's also the legitimate son of the Lord of the Thirteenth Kingdom. The favourite son of my father. The most popular child at school. The strongest Fae in our land. The most gifted. The funniest. The most attractive.'

'So what, jealousy?'

'I was a child, Raven. And I craved what all children crave. Acceptance. Attention. Love. Friendship.' He shakes his head and looks at his home, etched into the old pages. 'Elias had all that, and he did all he could to ensure I would never have it. He gave as good as he got. Believe me.'

'Did he?' I ask. No one mentioned that.

'He slept with my fiancé a week before our wedding,' he tells me. 'He tormented me through our schooling years. Made my life a misery by bullying me relentlessly. He went out of his way to humiliate me and shun me. He reminded me daily that I had none of what he had. Our father had his heir in Elias. A strong, powerful heir. I was his second son from his second wife. I was pretty pointless to him. I had no powers. I wasn't as good a fighter. I wasn't as clever or witty. Everything I did was ignored or belittled. Elias could do no wrong. I was just overlooked. I acted out. I never intended to hurt Elias.'

'I'm sorry he treated you like that. He never said anything. And I'm sorry about the fiancé. That's disgusting.'

'His deeds are not yours to apologise for.'

'Do you mean him to harm now?' I ask.

'No,' he replies. 'Besides. It looks as if he has been harmed already.' He gestures to his ears. 'Who cut the tips of his ears off, may I ask?'

'None of your business.'

'It's an embarrassment for him, I mean-'

'Nothing about Reid, what he has done, does or plans to do, is an embarrassment. Don't talk about things you have no idea about, Ezra. You certainly won't win any points with me by going after my Mate.' I watch him closely, daring him to say another word on the matter.

'I just want to get us all home,' he concedes. 'Before it's too late.'

'Too late?'

'Before there's no one and nothing worth returning home to.'

'What do you mean?' I ask. 'Nothing to return home to?'

'The kingdoms are at war, Raven. It's been centuries since a war has ravaged our land, but it is now. When we left, several kingdoms revolted against the order of things. The lower kingdoms wanted more wealth. The higher kingdoms wanted to have more power. And many of the lords... well. They want it all.'

'Meaning?'

'The real power lies mainly with the women,' he shrugs. 'The way it works with Bonded Mates means women are revered back home. The men who Bond to them adore them. But therein lies a problem. The women can cast their Mates aside and find other partners. This tends to have a detrimental effect on men. Drives them insane.'

'Yeah. I heard about that,' I mutter, recalling the many times I've been warned of this.

'Well, some women back home can abuse their Bonds. Seize entire kingdoms. Manipulate the men into doing their will. So, there have been movements.'

'Like?'

'Well, a Lord in my kingdom fell for a commoner. Fell hard. Bonded to her. She, however, was wed to another and madly in love. She cared deeply for the Lord but wouldn't consummate the Bond because she did not want to tie him to her like that. Despite the Lord being happy to participate in the sharing of the lady with her husband. But the husband wouldn't allow it, so the Lady said no to the Lord.'

'What happened?' I ask, knowing I will not like the answer.

'The Lord went to their home in the dead of night with his men. Murdered the husband. Took the lady by force. The villagers intervened. There was a fight. A battle.' Ezra lets out a sigh. 'A slaughter. The Lord and his men killed the villagers.'

'Fuck...'

'The Lord pled his case to the other Lords in the neighbouring kingdoms. Claimed she was his by right. By Fated Mate rights. New laws were introduced in these lands that a woman can not deny the man his claim.'

'What? Hold on. You said this was in your kingdom? The Thirteenth?'

He keeps his gaze down. 'It was. Yes. The royal family, you and your ancestors, you kept balance and order. When a Bond was made or declared, it was protected by the right of choice. You were Bonded to Elias and Cyrus as soon as you were conceived. Your mother agreed to honour the Bond. But if it came to a point where you refused the match, no one would have forced you to be with a man that you did not love. Or that you feared. Or just didn't find attractive. It's rare, to be honest. For a Bond not to be wanted. The Fates do what they do for a reason, and it's rarely wrong. But the heart, you see, is tricky. And love is cruel. You can be loved and not love in return. Or you can love a monster and choose to give it up rather than let it destroy you.

And sometimes, Raven, you can love more than one person. But one of those may refuse to be willing to share you. And in your mother's case, when she devastated her entire kingdom for a human Mate, she showed other kingdoms that perhaps women shouldn't have the right to choose who they take as their lover. Motions were made that it was too dangerous.'

'What happened?' I urge.

'When fear takes hold, death comes swift. Women started being killed. Arrested. Punished for their Bonds or lack of them. Everything just imploded.' He takes the book and closes it slowly. 'The war has brought poison to the land. It messed with the balance of nature, and everything has started to turn in on itself. It began to rot like a plague. The Fates do what they do for a reason. They entwine souls. They keep them apart or tear them to pieces. Balance must be restored, or our lands will burn to ash and drown in the blood of our people.'

I run my fingers over that tree on the front cover and imagine it dying. Crumbling to ash and being lost to the wind.

'So, in your kingdom. Women aren't allowed to choose their partners? Bond or not?'

'No.'

'Surely, my mother would have done something about it?'

'The three outcast kingdoms, The Eleventh, Twelfth and Thirteenth, are independent of the other kingdoms. Or they were when I left. They had their own rules. Your mother didn't get involved. She didn't want a war. And when your Bond with the Lord's son was announced, it was seen as a blessing. The Fates intervening to reunite all the kingdoms again.'

'Why wouldn't they tell me that?' I ask, lifting my gaze to Ezra. 'None of the others said that your kingdom treated women like that.'

'They didn't?'

'No.'

He avoids my stare, doing his best to look innocent.

'What aren't you telling me?' I ask. 'I've sensed something has been off ever since I got here. Some secret that no one wants to talk about. What is it?'

'Perhaps it is that,' he offers. 'Perhaps they do not want their lover to know that back home, in their kingdom, you would have had no choice in your match. And that my father, Reid's father, was the man who started it all by murdering an entire village to claim Reid's mother.'

'Your father was the one that killed the villagers? The woman he took was Reid's mother?'

'The Thirteenth Kingdom is a harsh place.'

'Harsh or not. Reid and Cyrus would never have forced the Bond on me. And my mother and her kingdom would never have allowed it to be forced either.' I nod, knowing in my heart that it would not have happened like that. No way.

They wouldn't have.

'The land is poisoned?' I repeat. 'Is it safe to return to?'

'If we don't return, it will perish. If we stay here, we will perish.'

'We'll fix it.' I nod again. 'All of us. Every Fae that was taken will be returned, and we will make it right.'

'All the Fae?' he asks. 'How? They're monsters.'

'They're monsters for now.' I reach over and take the dagger he has sheathed at his side. He watches as I slowly and carefully pull it free. 'You are dependent on the Gilt. That needs to stop. Here.' I slide the dagger across the tip of my finger and take his hand in mine as I let it drip into his cupped palm. He watches each drop as it falls.

'My blood stabilises the Fae gene in this realm. It means that no matter what, you won't turn Dark.'

'No more need for Gilt?'

'No. No more need for Gilt. And Ivan Walker can't turn you Dark either.' I release his hand and nod to the small puddle of red. 'I know it's gross, but it's necessary.'

As I pull my hand back, he takes my wrist.

'Nothing about you is gross, Raven. Not a single thing.'

Before I can react, he pulls my finger and takes it into his mouth. His tongue glides over the cut before he sucks.

Mortified, I try to pull my hand away.

There's a series of low thuds. I lift my head, but it's too late to react. Lucca has arrived and grabbed Ezra by his hair. He's hurled away from me and tossed to the floor. I reach out to stop the raging Lucca and get shoved hard, crashing into the table and rolling over its top before landing face-down on the floor.

'YOU DON'T TOUCH HER!' Lucca roars, half sobbing and rabid as he delivers punch after punch to Ezra, who does his best to protect his face from the assault.

Ezra gets a chance and takes his shot, thrusting his fist into Lucca's side, winding him. He falls, groaning loudly. Ezra is back on his feet, panting and shocked. But Lucca isn't done and just attacks. Wings are out, and fists are flying.

'You don't touch their Mate!' Lucca bellows amongst the crashing and thuds of the fight. 'She's theirs. THEIRS!'

'LUCCA!' I yell as Ezra goes down with a bloody face.

Lucca starts kicking him when he's down. Over and over, as hard as he can to his stomach.

'Lucca!' I rush forwards and grab him. 'STOP!'

With a shove, I get him away and plant myself between the two, my arms outstretched. Lucca rushes forwards and grabs my shirt, bunching it in his fist as he pulls me close, thrusting his tear-streaked and angry face in mine.

'If you betray them, I will tear you limb from limb and bury you in the furthest region of this godforsaken shithole. Do you hear me?' he snarls. Each word rolling from his tongue with truth and danger. 'Do you, Pup? You belong to them.'

'We're not in your kingdom now, Lucca. You don't get to order me to be with them. I'm not their possession. Now get the fuck off me.'

'What has he been telling you?' Lucca throws his angry stare at Ezra. 'What did you say, HUH?!'

Lucca lunges, pushing me onto the table as he towers over me. Tears pour down his face as he looks down at me.

He's scared. I see it now. Absolutely terrified as well as insane with anger.

'You made the Bond knowing what it meant,' he spits. 'You turn them away, betray them or break them, I will end you. Understand?'

'Get off me!'

'DO YOU UNDERSTAND?!' he screams in my face.

'YES!' I yell back, nodding furiously. 'YES! I UNDERSTAND!'

The sound of books flying off the shelves and landing on the floor draws his attention away from me. We turn and see a thick fog of black smoke shooting towards us, the force and speed of it causing chaos in its wake.

'Shit.' Lucca lets me go and stands up, backing away from me as he faces it.

Cyrus must be tapped into my emotions. He felt my fear and panic as Lucca grabbed me and came running.

'I'm sorry!' Lucca yells at the incoming hurricane. 'I swear, Cyrus, I-'

I leap between them, reaching out my hand.

'STOP!' I order.

The smoke halts in a second, less than an inch before it could collide with me with whatever force he planned to plough into Lucca. It swirls there and settles, solidifying until standing before me with sharp eyes and a tense jaw is the man himself.

Cyrus's eyes are on Lucca, who is still behind me.

'I'm okay. Calm down,' I try, resting my hand on Cyrus's chest and feeling his heart raging beneath it. 'It was nothing.'

Behind him, Ezra shuffles as he returns to his feet, wiping the smear of blood from his face. Cyrus barely turns to face him. As he looks back over his shoulder, I see Reid appear.

Perfect.

Knowing Ezra is dealt with, Cyrus looks back to Lucca, ignoring me entirely.

Reid wraps his hand around Ezra's throat and pins him against the bookshelves, holding him there.

'Explain,' he says. A single word. An order. One not to be ignored.

'It was a misunderstanding,' I try. 'Ezra was showing me paintings of your world. Of the thirteen kingdoms. Lucca walked in and thought something else was going on. It wasn't!'

'He had her finger in his disgusting little mouth,' Lucca spits, his eyes still wet. 'She's yours. He can't take her from you. I won't allow it!'

'He had your finger in his mouth?' Cyrus says through gritted teeth, finally looking at me before peering down at my hand on his chest. He takes it and lifts it, seeing the small cut there. 'You gave him your blood?'

'I said I was going to. They need it.' I pull my hand away and step back.

'So you let him suck on your finger?'

'I didn't expect him to do that. I put the blood in his palm.' I look at Ezra, who is still pinned to the shelf by his brother. 'What the fuck is wrong with you? Why did you do that?'

Reid raises his brow, fully expecting an answer.

'It...' Ezra grunts back. 'It was a mistake. I'm sorry.'

'We felt fear. We felt terror.' Cyrus takes a step closer and rests his hand on my hip as he faces Lucca. 'And you were the one on her when I got here. Do you think it wise to scare her? Should I return the favour? Shall I find your Mate? Pin her down? Make her scream in fear?'

'Stop,' I try, hating the hatred in Cyrus's eyes.

'You think El knows true fear? I'll show her fear, Lucca. And I will make sure you feel every second of it through your Bond.'

'You won't.' I turn to Lucca. 'He won't touch El.' I give Cyrus a shove. It's like pushing stone. 'Stop. Everyone, fucking hell! Stop!'

After a moment that seems to last an age, Cyrus steps back. I look at Reid, who still holds Ezra. He drops him, leaving him to gasp and hold his throat.

'It was a misunderstanding. That's all,' I tell them. 'Ezra. Nothing will ever happen between us, so stop trying to score points with Reid by using me to annoy him. If you two want to fight and squabble, keep me out of it. And Lucca. I know you are looking out for your friends, but if you ever grab me like that again, I will portal your arse to El and let you explain to her why you're acting like a dick.'

He swallows dryly at the idea.

'And you two,' I look at Reid and Cyrus. 'I want you to stop tapping into my emotions. Right now. I'm in no danger here.

And it's a serious violation of my privacy. I'm entitled to my own feelings.'

Cyrus leans down to me.

'No.'

'No?'

'No. If you're scared, I want to know. If you are stressed, I want to know. If you're angry, I want to know.'

'Why?'

'Because you refuse to tell us when you are those things, and then you end up getting hurt. So no. We won't. Because you matter to us, and we care if you're suffering. Until you learn to communicate your feelings, you don't get to keep them to yourself.' He points to Lucca with a menacing finger. 'You touch her again, I will rip your head off.' He turns to Ezra. 'You look at her again, I'll tear your heart out.' He then turns his finger to Reid. 'Get your little brother and best friend under control. Or I will.'

Cyrus grips my hand tightly before turning away and leading me out of the room.

'We'll be at the Archway. Sort this, Reid.'

'I'll sort it,' Reid replies coldly.

I don't get to say anything before being dragged out of the library and into the hall. Cyrus doesn't let me go until we're back in the Arch room, where he drops my hand.

He leaves me there and goes to the Arch, where he starts helping Brennan fit the pieces back together.

I just watch him, my thoughts raging.

Hours pass until Reid returns. He speaks to Cyrus alone, far from earshot. They both steal a glance at me in the pit before coming over. They reach down and help me out.

'What did you do?' I ask Reid. 'Are Lucca and Ezra okay?'

'Better than they deserve to be,' Reid replies. 'You can't just wander off with strangers, Raven. It's not safe.'

'First of all. What happened in there wasn't my fault, okay? Maybe Ezra should be told not to stick other people's fingers in his mouth, and Lucca should be taught not to get violent when upset.'

'You still wandered off with a man you know can't be trusted.'

'He only showed me a book.'

'He sucked on your finger.'

'And you slept with his fiancé,' I retort.

'He told you about that?'

'He told me a lot.'

'Before or after the finger sucking?'

'Is it super intimate in the Fae Realm to suck the blood out of a girl's finger or something? Besides, I pulled it away and was about to tell him off before Lucca turned up like a lunatic.'

'Lucca's going through some shit,' Cyrus says, almost dismissing the whole thing.

I can't help but scoff. 'I thought you wanted to tear him apart.'

'That was before.'

'Before what?' I ask. The two share a look but say nothing. 'Back to this, huh? Secrets. Lies.'

'No. Not secrets and lies. Just respecting the wishes of a friend who shared his troubles and asked me not to tell anyone.' Reid attempts to sound patient, but he fails.

'You told Cyrus what Lucca told you,' I tell him. 'Or he would still be mad at him.'

'Because Lucca said I could in the hope that Cyrus wouldn't slit his throat.' With an impatient sigh, Reid drags his fingers through his hair. 'Look. It's Lucca's business. Not mine. And it's not yours. He thought he was protecting you. Just do me a favour and-'

The door to the Arch room opens and Ezra enters.

'Stay away from Ezra when you're on your own,' Reid finishes.

'Why? Worried he might tell me something you don't want me to know?' I counter, watching him closely for a reaction.

'He mentioned he told you about my father and the rules he's imposed in the Thirteenth Kingdom,' Reids adds gruffly. 'I didn't tell you because it wasn't important for you to know.'

'Is that right?' I scoff.

'Have Cyrus and I forced you into our situation?' he asks, brow raised expectantly. 'Because if I remember correctly, we were ready to leave you and spare you this Bond. You were the one that ordered us to stay. And I'm thrilled you did because there is nowhere else and no one else for us.'

'You should have told me. We all have the right to know who protects us. Ezra's men are from your kingdom. One of his men already demonstrated his views on women.'

'And I killed him. I think that speaks for itself. Have we stripped any woman here of her right

to her freedom or body autonomy?'

'No,' I admit.

'I think you will find that we have done nothing but help and protect the women here. So, could you not hold my father's rules against me? I didn't want you to know because it's not something I'm proud of.'

'The rules will change when we return,' I state clearly. 'I don't care if they're separate kingdoms. That shit is not going to fly.'

Reid gives a slight nod.

'If you still want to give the men your blood to stop their dependency on Gilt, then we can do that.'

'We can?' I ask, seriously taken aback.

'I will take your blood with a needle and administer it that way. No cutting yourself. And no tongues are ever to touch your body again.'

'Except yours, I hope,' I grin back, loving how they smile at my words.

'Except ours,' Reid replies. 'Lucca is sorry for scaring you. He feels terrible.'

'Is he okay?' I ask.

'I think so,' he says.

'Is it to do with El? It's just I saw them this morning arguing. They looked really upset.'

'Their business,' Reid says firmly, taking my hand in his. 'Not ours. Leave it be, ok?'

I nod, thinking I'll visit El later and find out what the fuck is going on.

'I want the blood taken now. Or as soon as possible, get them stable.'

'Okay,' Reid concedes. 'Ezra went to fetch the necessary equipment to do it.' He nods at him over his shoulder. Ezra holds a large wooden box. 'After you've made a small donation-'

'Enough of a donation,' I correct.

'After. We want to show you something.' Reid takes the stone that's in my hand and holds it out for one of Ezra's men to take.

'Show me what?' I ask. 'We have work to do here.'

Reid looks at the growing pile of stones by the Arch. 'Looks like you've given them plenty to play with for a while. You've been here for hours. You need a break.'

'A break doing what?'

'It's a surprise.'

Judging by his smirk, I think I may enjoy this surprise.

NINETEEN

I admit that using a needle to draw blood is a much more effective method than a knife. No pain. No bandages. No waste. Reid was meticulous as he drew vial after vial of blood and handed it to Cyrus, who ensured it was administered directly to the men. We get through a third of the men before they call it a day, telling me we can do more tomorrow. I feel fine after a slice of apple pie and a juice drink. They then lead me through the halls, down stone steps, and deeper into the structure. The polished marble ends, and the floors and walls become rough rock. Fire torches line the narrowing corridor, and then I hear rushing water.

'Where are we going?' I ask.

'You'll see,' Reid replies, taking my hand in his as he leads me on, with Cyrus right behind.

I expect it to be colder as we're now so much deeper underground, but it's getting warmer. We carry on and pass through a doorway made of pink stone. As I step through, I gasp, my eyes wide and excitement rising quickly in my chest.

'What the...'

'You mentioned you couldn't swim before. Maybe whilst we are here, we could help you learn?' Cyrus says, walking past me.

Ahead is a large pool carved into the floor, with the most exquisite blue water filling it. Steam rises from its surface, and at the far end, a natural waterfall tumbles from high up in the rocks, crashing below. Stone pillars support the curved roof, each covered in vines and the most beautiful flowers blooming. The steam in the air carries their scent and makes my skin tingle. At the very top of the roof, enchantments make a permanent sunset with the most artistic colours.

'It's... I mean...'

'CANNONBALL!' screams El as she runs out from nowhere, dressed in black lacey underwear. She lands with a splash in the pool, exploding from its surface with a joyful laugh. 'Well, what are you waiting for?' she says, looking at me and someone to her left. 'Get your arses in here! Both of you!'

I peer over. Rhea stands at the pool's edge, just beyond one of the pillars. She's in an oversized t-shirt, clutching the hem as she eyes the water anxiously.

'Come on, girls,' El teases with a splash at us both. 'It's heavenly.'

With a squeal, Rhea leaps in, disappearing beneath the water before El pulls her up.

Clearly, Rhea can't swim either as she splashes and squeaks, clinging to El to stay afloat.

'Your turn,' El beams at me.

'I... I don't have any swimming clothes.'

'You wearing underwear?' she asks.

I nod.

'Then strip.'

Reid takes the hem of my jumper, but I stop him from lifting, shaking my head as I look at him, suddenly desperate.

His eyes narrow as he tries to understand. Then his eyes fall to my side.

'The scar?' he asks. 'You know we don't care about that.'

'I care,' I whisper back. 'Rhea will care.'

Cyrus slides off his shirt and hands it to me.

'It's thin. It won't be too heavy in the water.'

'Uh-huh,' I mumble, staring at his godlike chest.

He chuckles. 'If you keep looking at my body like that, I might have to postpone your swim and take you back to our room.'

'I'm good with that,' I reply.

But Cyrus laughs and shakes his head before stripping to his pants and leaping in.

'Come on, Princess. You're with family here.'

I let Reid remove my jumper and replace it with the shirt before I slide off my jeans and face the pool.

I look up at Reid. I can't hold it in any longer. I have to ask.

'Reid?'

'Raven?' he replies.

'Did you sleep with Ezra's fiancé before his wedding?'

Reid finishes putting me in Cyrus's shirt and meets my curious stare.

'Yes.'

'Why?'

'Because I wanted to hurt him. And because I was young and cruel. I'm not the man I was, Raven. I was not a good man in my youth, and I'm ashamed of many things I did to others. But I want to be better.' He sweeps my hair over my shoulder. 'I want to be a better man for you.'

'I think you're doing a good job at being a better man,' I tell him.

'You do?'

'I do.' I turn back to the pool. 'How deep is it?'

'You tell me,' Reid says from behind before the arse throws me in.

I scream as I soar and seal my nose and mouth shut as I land.

Cyrus has me in an instant and pulls me up, just as Reid jumps in too.

They're all laughing as I grip onto Cyrus. No matter how far I reach, the pool floor is too deep to touch.

'Okay,' Cyrus says. 'First lesson. Let's get you treading water. We'll have you swimming in no time.'

Heaven. There's no other word for it. Just... heaven. The warmth. The joy. The fun. I'm not sure how many times in my life I've had fun. This is brilliant fun.

Reid has my waist as he faces me towards Cyrus at the other end of the pool.

'I can't do it!' I insist, refusing to let go of his wrists. 'I'll sink again.'

'You can do it,' he says. 'You can do anything you put your mind to. That has been abundantly clear in the short time I've known you. Now let me go and swim to Cyrus!'

'If I drown, I will kill you!'

'Then don't drown,' he chuckles. 'Off you go.'

The bastard lets me go and swims backwards away from me.

'Go on, Raven!' cheers Rhea as she sits on the edge with her legs dangling in the water.

'Swim! You can do it!' calls El, who sits beside her, clapping wildly.

'Like I have a fucking choice!' I screech, wildly kicking my legs as I try and claw my way through the water towards a waiting Cyrus.

They all cheer and clap as I slowly, embarrassingly slowly, make my way towards him.

'Almost here,' Cyrus encourages. 'Keep going!'

I reach out and grip his arm as he pulls me into him. My legs wrap around his waist, and I cling on tight as he lets out a glorious bout of deep laughter.

'That's my girl. See? There's nothing you can't do.'

His lips seal around mine and he pulls us both under the water, kissing me hard as his hands caress my body.

Yep... heaven...

I'm not sure if they're doing it on purpose, but the guys are giving me no space or time to sneak over to El alone and ask if everything is okay. They refuse to leave my side and are very careful where the conversation goes. So, I float.

Because I can do that now.

I lie on my back and look up at the eternal sunset above.

'So,' I call over as they all sit by the pool's edge, chatting away. They go quiet as I speak. 'Are all the enchanted skies here from the Fae Realm?'

'I suppose so,' replies El. 'The constellations of the stars are from home. And I've never seen a human sunset this beautiful.'

I watch her as she looks up at the sky. Her perfectly toned body, covered in deep black Fae promises.

'I think this may be from the Second Kingdom,' says Reid. 'Or maybe the first. Probably is the first, as this place belongs to the royal family, and they come from the First.'

'What does the sunset look like in your kingdom?' I ask.

'We only get one sunset a year,' Reid replies. 'We're cast in an eternal night except for a single day of a low sun that passes over in early spring.'

'Really?' I ask, still aimlessly floating.

'The sun rarely rises that far south. Annoys the hell out of Brennan. He does love his flowers,' El adds.

'We do get the shadow plants,' Cyrus says. 'The flowers that bloom in darkness.'

'They're all blacks and blues and deep purples. Most of them are poison.' Reid takes one of the pink roses clinging to the pillar in his fingers. 'Brennan adores pastels.'

'Not what I expected from a man so obsessed with guns,' I mutter. As I look up at the sky again, my thoughts drift to what Ezra said in the library. 'I was thinking,' I start. Making the two guys softly groan. 'Ezra told me a little bit about the troubles back in your world-'

'Our world,' they both respond.

'Okay. Our world. Well, Ezra told me that there's trouble back home.'

'It will settle when you are on the throne again,' Reid says simply.

'What? Am I just going to plonk my arse down and be in charge? There's not going to be any resistance?'

'We'll deal with any resistance,' Cyrus states.

I lower my legs and face them as I tread water. They watch me closely.

'I think we need to prepare.'

'Prepare how?' asks El, slowly swishing her feet in the water and giving Reid a quick side-eye.

'We do what the guys did.' I look at Cyrus and Reid. 'Back home, you said that your job was to find the Fae with worthy gifts and bring them out of them. To Trigger them, right? Cyrus can sense power, and Reid Triggers them. We have the Fae stolen from the First Kingdom here in the human world with us.'

Reid rolls his eyes. 'Raven,' he starts.

'And you all said that the First Kingdom Fae were super powerful.'

'That's not-'

'We could go out there! Cyrus can sense the powerful ones. Reid can Trigger them. And I can give them my blood to stabilise them! Then, they can come back here where it's safe. Where they can eat and sleep and be-'

'Raven, please stop and listen-'

'We have no idea what we'll be walking into back in *your* world,' I remind them.

'*Our* world,' they both repeat, a little sharper than before.

'Our world,' I groan. 'Ezra said that unrest and sickness are sweeping the kingdoms because of the fighting. If we arrive with powerful Fae, who belong to the First Kingdom, whose memories might even return when they go back and are allied to us, it's a no-brainer! Besides, we can't just abandon them here.'

I'm still treading water and starting to get tired. Arguing and keeping my head up at the same time is difficult.

'Is that what you really want? To go back out there?' Cyrus asks. 'We're not exactly unknown. The Fae that pretended to be Authority. The ex-leader of the Fae Undercity street gang. And the daughter of Ivan Walker.'

I open my mouth to argue, but it fills with water. They make no move to come and get me, and I'm in no mood to ask for help.

I release my wings and soar from the water. I hold myself there, flying in the air, dripping water with my hands on my hips. They all look up at me, waiting.

'You said, you all say, that the Fates work the way they do for a reason. That Bonded Mates are tied together for a greater purpose. If this isn't ours, then what is? We have the entire First Kingdom held captive. Being turned into monsters. Being stolen. Turned dark. Their powers were given to humanity, turning them into... whatever those things we saw. And here we are. You two and me. Bonded. One who can sense power.' I point to Cyrus. 'One to bring it forth.' I point to Reid. 'And one to stabilise it. Make it strong and eternal. If the Fates and the Goddess are as all-knowing and preordained as you say they are, then they knew Ivan would tear our home world apart. And they knew they would need someone to stitch it back together. You're right. We are fated for a reason. This. This is the reason. Please.' I beat my wings, placing myself before them both. My feet rest on the water. 'Reid. Cyrus. I'm asking you as your lover, Mate, and Queen. Please, help me bring some of our people to safety. I'll do anything.'

Cyrus lifts a brow.

'Anything?' he asks.

'Anything,' I agree.

Silence falls over the room. Except for the gushing waterfall, that is. El and Rhea look between the three of us, stuck in suspense.

The boys stand.

'Okay.' Reid says, Cyrus nodding in agreement.

'W-what?' I stammer.

'We'll go. But we go where we decide to go. And we make the call about who we Trigger. You do everything we say when we say it, and you don't leave our side at any point.'

'Has there ever been any other option than that?' El says with a grin, nudging an unsure Rhea.

They hold out their hands.

'What's the catch?' I ask.

'No catch. Just a vow to us that you keep your word and that you will do *anything* we ask once it is done.'

'Hang on. When you say *anything-*'

'Don't worry. It won't be anything... unpleasant,' Cyrus grins.

El gives a dark giggle as she looks between us. Rhea continues looking uncomfortable.

I take their hands, and I shake.

'Then it's agreed,' Reid says. 'We'll leave tomorrow evening.'

'That soon?' I ask, stunned at the ease of their agreement.

'Well. We had already spoken about going to recruit others,' Cyrus says, that sly smile on his lips appearing. 'As you said, who knows what we'll be walking back into. And we can't just abandon the powerful lot that got swept over here in the event. It makes sense to go back with at least some First Kingdom citizens. To return with an army. Your army.'

I fold my arms across my chest and show them one hell of a glare.

'You had already decided to go out there, hadn't you?'

'Yep,' they reply together, laughing. 'Just undecided if we would take you, but if you're willing to do *anything-*'

'Bastards...' I smile.

TWENTY

I awake in the morning with a new and refreshing sense of purpose.

We're actually doing something. Not just reacting to what the world throws at us, but seeking out a way to fight back and win our freedom.

Nothing is worse than no hope. No end in sight to just surviving.

I lie on this soft bed with a full belly and a feeling of safety, I know that today we take our first step from surviving to living.

And I'm realising this alone, as the guys are nowhere to be seen. After we left the pool, we ate in the main hall and went to bed. I fell onto the mattress, beyond content and with plenty of wine inside me. I must have just passed out. The sheets smell of them, so I know they slept here with me for a little while. The wardrobe doors are open, their clothes from yesterday are piled on the floor, and their boots are gone.

I sit and go to grab my clothes from the old bag we fled with. But the bag isn't there. I check all over, hoping it got kicked under the bed or something.

Nothing.

Then I check in the wardrobe.

'Fuckers,' I whisper, seeing a dress hanging very deliberately on the rail, a note pinned to it with a smiley face and the word *Anything* sprawled in perfect script.

Anything.

I groan and slide the dress off the hanger.

A few moments later, I'm standing in front of a full-length mirror, my eyes glued once again to my reflection.

The bodice is jet black silk, covered in delicate chiffon of midnight blue when it catches the light. The skirt reaches the floor, and the sleeves are made of lace that wraps between my fingers. The front is cut low in a deep v that shows the Mate Bond markings that travel from my heart to my abdomen. And the same at the back, where the markings follow the length of my spine. They only just show enough skin to boast their place on my flesh. And it more than covers the hideous mark on my side.

I look like something from a gothic fairytale. And I admit... I love it.

They have good taste, and if this is their "anything", I'm happy to oblige.

I turn and go to find them.

As I make my way down the hall, I give a light pull on the tether Bond. I get a slight pull back, guiding me to their location in the main hall.

When I enter, the room falls so silent you could hear a pin drop. Sadly, there are no pins. But plenty of cups, knives, and forks slip through a few fingers and clatter to the tables.

'Yeah, yeah,' I grumble. 'I'm in a dress. Fascinating stuff.'

I head straight to the table where they sit, smirking like schoolboys and smug enough to earn a slap. Ezra's men bow as I walk, and the rescued Fae stare.

I sit rather heavily and stare at the pair.

'Happy?' I ask, reaching over and taking Reid's coffee and Cyrus's toast.

'Thrilled,' Reid replies, eyeing me up.

'Ecstatic,' agrees Cyrus, biting on his lower lip. 'And to what do we owe this pleasure?'

'I hope this is worth your *"anything"*. Of all the things you could have had, me in a dress-'

'Hold on. No, no, no.' Cyrus gestures to my dress. 'This isn't our "anything". Not by a long shot.'

'It is. And you only get one.'

'We know. And we're not about to use it to get you *into* clothing.'

'Looking good, sexy lady!' El says as she joins us at the table. 'Damn. I might have to come and check out your wardrobe. That dress is on fire!'

'Feel free. This is the last time you'll see me in a dress like this. Especially since they used up their "anything" on getting me to wear it.'

'I just told you,' states Cyrus. 'We didn't.'

'Then who did?'

'Me,' grunts Brennan as he sits heavily beside Reid. 'You think you'll be living in jeans and t-shirts back home? You'll know nothing but the finest dresses and jewels, so you better get used to it.'

'You took my clothes and left me that note?' I ask him.

'Yes. I did. You're the Fae Queen. Not some street rat that lifts pockets and sleeps in a gutter. Not any more. Do you think anyone back home will follow your lead if you don't look the part? You think they will?' He gestures to the others in the hall and snorts heavily. 'If we turn up with you looking like an urchin, no one will want anything to do with you. Fae have class. Standards. Expectations.'

'I *am* a street rat, Brennan. And I *have* spent my whole life stealing so I can eat. That's not going to change because I'm in a dress.' I look to the others for some backup. They all avoid my gaze. 'You all agree with him, then? That I'm not good enough unless I'm in a dress?'

'We're not saying that-'

'I guess my scar's going to be a problem too? Can't have a damaged queen as well as an unkempt one?'

'No. They'll like the scar,' Brennan says, picking at a piece of bread and pulling out his guns. 'The scar means you're a fighter. And better yet, a survivor. Which, of course, you are. More so than any queen I have ever seen. Or lady. Or any man, come to think of it.' He starts dismantling his weapons. 'More stubborn and hot-headed too. More loyal and passionate. You are exactly what we need. Not some meek little puppet that will let the wrong people take charge. Again.'

'Brennan...' Reid says quietly. But Brennan utterly ignores him.

'The scar is good. We can work with that. But your presentation has to improve. You must show the kingdoms you care about yourself and your well-being as much as the rest of us do. That you know you belong in our world. That you have grace and class and the lust for everything Fae. You look stunning, powerful and inspiring this morning. You look like you. As you are and as you deserve. Not what this shit hole of a world has done to you. They can't see that, Raven. None of it. A slight weakness, a crack, and they will use it to make you crumble.'

'Who?'

Brennan looks at Reid. 'We all know who.'

'Reid's dad?' I ask.

'Brennan, I don't think-'

But Brennan isn't done and cuts Reid off. 'Things will be different when we return, Reid. Your father's way is not right, and you know it.'

The vein in Reid's neck bulges as Brennan speaks.

'She needs to prepare, and it is your job... all of our job... to prepare her. When we return, the First Kingdom will return with her just as you wish. But things won't be as easy as simply telling the others the Queen is back, so fall in line. And you know that, Reid.' Brennan looks at me with a steely glare. 'Being here hasn't beaten you. Because you, the Queen, are unbeatable. Unstoppable. Unyielding. A force to be reckoned with. A woman to tremble before. Not pity.' He looks again at Reid. 'Don't you agree?' He then looks at Cyrus. 'Both of you. You stand by her, right?'

I feel it again. That pit in my stomach. That sense of dread opening like a black hole over my heart.

'We stand by her,' Cyrus says firmly. 'Both of us, Brennan. You know that.'

'Good,' he replies. 'Then we fetch her people and return together. As one. And we put the past behind us.'

'What past?' I ask.

'It doesn't matter,' Brennan replies. 'As I said. It's in the past. And that's where it will stay.'

The table goes silent, and everyone watches him clean his guns.

I lean over the table and plant a kiss on his cheek. My affection for the stone-faced and complicated man swelling tenfold.

'W-what was that for?' he asks, nervously glancing at Reid and Cyrus.

'Thank you,' I tell him. 'What you said... that was so... I mean-'

'She's very flattered, Brennan,' Reid translates for me.

'It's not flattery,' he says, blushing a little. 'Just truth.'

'Oh, Brennan,' sighs El, looking at him wistfully. 'Such a charmer.'

He clears his throat and looks harder at his guns.

'I know you can't very well go about recruiting Fae in a gown. You'll stick out like a ruby in the rubble. So I will return your rags when we leave tonight. After they have been washed and deloused. But I would like to alter some dresses into suitable attire for you to wear daily here. Something that tells Ezra's men that they are, in fact, *your* men. And that this underground palace belongs to you. The Queen. Not to them.'

'Fine by me. But not this dress. Nor the one hanging on the back of the chair.'

'Ohhh. Why not?' El asks.

'Never you mind.'

Reid takes back his coffee from my hands and gestures to the fruit and bread.

'The others are waiting for us in the library to discuss tonight's plan. We join them once you have eaten. And then I'll take some more of your blood if that's okay. Seeing as we are going to be needing it for those who return with us.'

I nod in agreement and get to eating.

Hours of discussion leave me with a headache and anxiety. The drawing of several vials of my blood probably isn't helping, either. Everyone has an opinion on where to go to find some Fae. Everyone has reservations. And everyone is nervous. We're safe for the first time in as long as I can remember. Yes, we could just stay underground, sealed up in this magical palace, fix the Archway and leave.

But that's not me. It's not us.

So, I let them decide. I let them make the plan. Just as I swore I would.

And when the time comes, the plan is set.

We gather at the Black Mirror, dressed in our rags, with hammering hearts and concealed weapons.

I have on an old black jumper with a large hood. It has more holes than material. I also wear a pair of black leggings and black boots. The guys are much the same. Their oversized coats hang off them. They pull up their collars and sweep their hair over their faces. Lucca is here too. He's managed to pull himself together enough to come but has kept his head down, which is very unlike him. Brennan is checking on the multitude of knives and guns he has hidden. I lose count and wonder how he remembers where they all are and how he hasn't accidentally shot or stabbed himself yet.

Even Ezra is here. Ready and raring, dressed, to his horror, in old jeans and a jacket. He seems more concerned with that than anything else. I'm assuming he has worn nothing but the finery of the Fae clothes all his life. It probably doesn't help that the clothes haven't been cleaned, and we stink.

'Did I always smell this bad?' I ask Lucca as I lean in and whiff my collar. I hold out my arm, offering my armpit for him to try, hoping to fix this unease between us. 'How could you stand to be around me smelling like the arse end of a sewer rat?'

He gives me a playful nudge and laughs.

'We all stank, to be fair,' he smiles. Then his smile falters. He steps closer and lowers his voice. 'Pup. I am so fucking sorry I grabbed you like that yesterday morning. I'm a dick. I hate that I scared you. And not only because I've been threatened with a foot up my arse if I ever pull a stunt like that again. I hated seeing you look at me like that.' He rests his hand on my shoulder. 'Sorry, Pup. Forgive me?'

'Of course,' I insist, placing my hand on his. 'And I'm here if you want to talk about anything.'

'I appreciate that.' He nods. His eyes drift over my shoulder, and he lets me go and steps back.

I turn and see the shadow form of El standing behind me. She gives me a little wave. One I return.

'You all set?' Reid asks her.

Shadow-El nods.

It was decided El and Rhea should stay back. El's currently sealed up in her bedroom with Rhea watching over her as she projects her shadow self. And Rhea's staying well out of the way. Her Dark self is far from stable. The last thing we want is for her to be caught and rejoin Ivan's ranks.

Or to go Dark and kill us all.

Reid starts fiddling with my collar.

'You stay close,' he says.

'Yes, Sir.'

He tries not to smirk. But he fails.

'You do as I say.'

'Yes, Sir.' Now I grin.

'You-'

'I'm yours to command. I gave you my word.'

'If I say portal, you make a portal. You don't argue. If I tell you to run and leave me behind, any of us, you go.' He waits. I nod reluctantly.

He holds out a gun.

'Take this. Keep it ready, just in case.' He tucks it inside my jacket.

'And this,' Cyrus adds, sliding a pocket knife into my trouser pocket. 'Just in case.'

'Just in case...' I repeat with a nervous exhale.

We all leave through the Black Mirror, step out of the Black Lake, and into the cold, damp, dark caves. El stands beside me.

'Will you tell Rhea I love her?' I ask, knowing that her physical body is back with my sister. She is still for a moment, then rests her hand on her heart and points to me. 'She says that she loves me too?'

She nods.

Reid looks at me expectantly. 'Ready when you are.'

I call my power and create a portal. As soon as it's formed, El is through. And we all remain, waiting for her to return. Moments pass in utter silence as we all stare at the swirling mass of black and gold. Dread and nerves gnaw away at me from the inside, hollowing me out and making me feel sick. Lucca grabs my hand and shows me a comforting smile. We all visibly slump in relief when she reemerges with a thumbs-up.

Brennan doesn't hesitate and strides through. Lucca and Ezra next. Then Reid, Cyrus and I.

We all emerge back at the asylum in the recreation room, where the beds still lie bloody and unmade. Empty food cans swarm with flies and maggots. We all gag as the stench left from the toilets hits the backs of our throats.

'I can't believe you were living in this,' Ezra says through a violent wretch.

'Not as nice as your palace, is it?' I snap a little too harshly. I face Cyrus and Lucca. 'Ready?'

'Born ready.' Cyrus pulls out a gun. 'Lucca?'

'With ya,' he replies, gun in hand.

I reach out my hand and create another portal. They waste no time and dart through. As instructed earlier, I shut it down as soon as they disappear.

A moment passes until I get the tug on the Bond from Cyrus, telling me it is safe.

I create the portal once more, and we all step through, except Ezra, who stays behind, ready to receive the survivors.

We step into the room where I stayed with Reid after we visited Serge's brothel. The room where I slept in his arms for the first time. Where he pinned me to the sink, plunged his fingers deep inside me and made me explode in pleasure for the first time in my life.

Lucca clears his throat.

'I'm all for a trip down memory lane, Pup. But can you try a little harder to focus?'

'Maybe stop reading my thoughts,' I hiss back.

'Maybe stop thinking so loud,' he teases.

I step forwards, my eyes on the door to the bathroom. But bump into something solid on the floor.

A man. A human.

'Authority,' I gasp, looking at Cyrus, who is wiping blood from the blade of a knife. 'Was he alone?'

'See any more bodies on the ground?' he asks.

There's a low thud from the old wardrobe in the corner. We all face it.

'You didn't think to look in the wardrobe?' Reid accuses, barely moving his lips as he stalks towards it with his gun drawn. He throws open the door.

'Oh, my Goddess.' I barge through them all and run to the Fae girl hanging by her wrists from the rail inside. She can't be any older than eighteen. She's naked. Her head lolls, and her skin is covered in burns, cuts and bruises. I grab the sheet left crumpled on the floor and wrap it around her, taking her weight as Reid cuts through the rope keeping her strung up.

Lucca rests his hand on her forehead.

'She's out cold. Drugged. That's why I couldn't hear her.' His fingers rest on her neck. 'Pulse is weak.'

'She's half fucking dead,' I hiss, looking at them all. 'I told you we needed to come here sooner.' I reach out my hand, ready to make a portal. But Reid slaps it down.

'Is she powerful?' he asks Cyrus. 'Can you sense anything worthwhile?'

Cyrus's eyes glow gold as he looks at her.

'She has no powers. You Trigger her, and she'll be just another mouth to feed.'

'Good job we have plenty of food then,' I snarl back, taking her hand back and looking at Reid. 'We're taking her.'

'We made a deal. Powerful Fae to help fight.'

'And if this girl were me? And I was just left here instead of saved?'

Reid snatches her hand away and leans into my face. 'Fine. She can come. That's the last one you get to choose.'

I carefully cover the girl up and smooth her hair free of her face as the others check the rest of the room.

'There you go,' Cyrus says to Reid, nodding to the Authority coat draped over the back of a chair. 'Just like old times.'

'I know that's a dig,' Reid says, striding over to grab the jacket. 'But this might come in handy.'

He puts it on. He's right. Of all of us, he's the one that passed as human. The scars on his ears are on view now that he has lost his powers. But they're not pointy like ours. And in the dark, at a push, he could pass.

Brennan throws his duffle bag over his shoulder and stands ready. Lucca presses his ear to the door and listens

Below, the music of the pub blares and a series of loud cheers sound out.

Something about it makes me run cold because this is an Authority pub in the heart of one of the last remaining Fae cities. Anything that makes the Authority cheer can't be good for my kind.

Cyrus takes my hand in his.

'You'll be fine,' he promises. 'Try to calm yourself.'

'Maybe you shouldn't be tapping into my emotions right now. You need to focus.'

'I am focused.' He keeps my hand in his and faces El. 'Ready?' She gives a brief nod.

'We know the plan,' Reid tells us all. 'El and Cyrus head out. See what you can see. Don't be seen. Don't get caught.'

I reach up and caress Cyrus's check. He leans into my touch and closes his eyes. I step close, rise on my tip toes to reach his lips, and kiss him. A slow, soft, and loving kiss. His forehead rests on mine with a sigh.

'You call me if you need a quick getaway. Do you hear me? You use the Bond-tether if you need it. I'll get a portal to you.'

'You worried about me, Princess? I like that.' He grabs my face and steals a second kiss. This one demanding.

He fades into black smoke. I look up at the towering form and swallow a shaky breath.

'Good luck,' I manage.

He wraps around me before disappearing out of the window Lucca has opened.

I face El, hating the risk she is taking.

'Any sign of trouble,' Reid tells her as she takes my hand. 'You go back to your body.'

El nods and walks toward Lucca, who stands at the open window. She rests her hand on his cheek and leans in to kiss him.

'I love you,' he says in a whisper. 'Come back to us safely.'

Her other hand rests over his heart before she leaps out the window and disappears into the night.

Reid pulls up my hood and ensures my hair covers my scars. They're too recognisable. Best they're not seen.

'El and Cyrus will search for any Fae worth Triggering, and he will call you when he has found a safe place for you to portal to. We will go to them, and Brennan will remove the collars so they can't be killed or tracked back to the caves.'

I nod, knowing the plan. But glad to have it repeated.

'Are you certain the device you have made will remove the collars as quickly and safely as you say?' I ask Brennan.

'Yes. I perfected it this morning. It will work. I assure you.'

The Fae cities have all been closed down since we escaped Ivan. My home city was outright destroyed. That's what the news said. Consumed in a fire. But other cities are still alive. Their factories still run, billowing out thick smog. After all, humans aren't about to lock up the workforce entirely. Who else will work in their factories if not the Fae?

Brennan is removing the Fae girl's collar.

I make a portal back to Ezra, who steps through.

'We need you to take this girl through,' Brennan tells him. 'Keep her safe.'

'What happened to her?' he asks. 'What is that device?'

'It tracks us,' I tell him, resting my fingers over my neck. I still find it odd not to be wearing a collar. 'It's fitted with an explosive that can be detonated if we get too close to the wall or gates. Or if we do something the Authority doesn't like.'

Ezra takes another look at the young girl still out cold.

'They're treated like animals.'

'No. Animals aren't treated this badly,' I correct.

Brennan has removed the collar and now takes another device and scans her body.

'What's that?' Ezra asks.

'It will tell me if she has any foreign devices implanted. Trackers under her skin. That kind of thing. I made it after we left the farmhouse. Those Dark Fae must have had trackers in them somewhere. We can't risk Ivan finding the palace and the portal.'

He runs it over her entire limp body. When it does nothing, he shrugs and declares that she's clean.

Her eyes attempt to open.

There's a shrill scream from below and another eruption of applause and cheers. I look at the floor, imagining the horrors that are happening below. I feel Reid's stare burning on me. He knows what I want to do. Go down there and stop whatever the hell is happening.

'You okay?' I ask the girl, gently tapping her cheek as she tries to wake up from her drug-induced sleep.

'Roll her over,' Reid suggests. 'She might puke.'

We try to get her to wake up. We try to get her to speak. But there's no use.

Again, below, a girl screams. And the Authority cheer.

I shudder from head to toe.

'What are they doing down there?' I ask her.

'You know we can't help anyone down in that bar,' Reid reminds me. Unnecessarily. Of course, I know that. I hate that I know that. But I can still know what they are doing.

She tries to talk. It's no use.

So, I rest my hand on her temple and ask again.

'What are they doing down there?'

My power shows me her truth. Well, a glimpse of it. I let go and stand up.

'No!' Reid says, keeping the girl on her side. 'Whatever truth you saw in her head, I don't care. We are not going down there.'

The truth I saw was much of what I expected. Authority, taking pleasure from misery.

'We can't, Raven!' he repeats, staring up at me. 'It's not a case of me not wanting to. If we go down there, we will be discovered and have to leave the city. We might not get to come back! We have a mission, and you gave us your word you would obey us. No matter what.' He waits for my response. For my agreement.

I cringe as they all cheer below once more and loathe that he's right.

Ezra takes the girl back to the asylum, and we wait.

We sit here for at least an hour.

Then I feel the pull. The gentle tug on the Bond from Cyrus.

'He's ready,' I tell them. 'Finally.'

I make a portal. We grab our stuff and go.

We emerge in a dead-end alley piled high with rubbish bags filled with scrabbling rats. I had almost forgotten the way the air choked you in the city. Especially so deep in, where the factories are clustered together. It's late, but they're still running. Spewing out their poison relentlessly.

Lost, again, is the night sky.

Cyrus and shadow-El lead us beyond some bins, glancing to the end of the alley to check it's still clear.

'The houses have all been abandoned,' Cyrus tells us. 'The schools have been destroyed. The markets, shops and bars have been trashed.'

'So where is everyone?' I ask.

'They're keeping the Fae in three locations.' Cyrus points to the east. 'There is a workhouse down there where they are holding the male labourers. Down there are where the women are.' He points south. 'And a little way up there is where they are storing the kids.' He points west. 'The factories don't stop; they change the workers every twelve hours.'

'Have you been able to sense any powerful Fae?' Reid asks.

'A few that would be worth taking with us.' He points to the nearest factory. 'In there is where we should go.'

'We can't go inside the factory. It's too heavily guarded,' Reid replies, shaking his head.

'It's all heavily guarded, Reid. The least guarded place is the factory. Two guards on the door and a few inside with guns.'

'We knew it wouldn't be easy,' I remind them. 'We have to find some Fae and bring them home. We haven't come this far to hide behind a bin and argue.'

'What about the place where they are keeping the men?' Reid asks. 'We should go there.'

'Because they're men?' I almost sneer.

'Yes,' he snaps back. 'The kids aren't going to be much good in a fight. But the men-'

'The factory,' Lucca says, looking at the one Cyrus pointed out. 'There will be men, women and children in there. We can choose some of each.'

He looks at us all, each in turn. He seems confident it's the right call. And when the others concede, he gives a slight sigh of relief.

'The factory,' Reid agrees. 'Let's go.'

'*T*rust me?' Reid asks. He takes hold of my shirt and grips it with both hands.

'I trust you,' I tell him, wincing as he tears it down the middle.

'I'm sorry in advance for this.'

'Do what you have to do, Reid. Make it look real.'

He delivers a vicious backhand to my face. I fall into Cyrus's arms, who keeps me on my feet.

'Did you have to strike her so hard?' Cyrus winces, looking at my lip.

'Is she bleeding?' Reid asks.

'You split her lip.'

'Then I hit her hard enough. Tie up her wrists.' Reid grabs the back of my neck as Cyrus secures my hands behind my back and places my hair over my scars. 'Again. I'm really sorry, Little Bird.'

I take a courage-inducing breath. 'You can make it up to me later.'

He leads me through the streets, shoving and shaking me, doing his impressive Authority arsehole impression.

The harder he shoves me and the more disgustingly he speaks to me, the less conspicuous we are.

'Where's she off to?' calls an Agent standing outside an old pub, smoking a cigar. He watches, with five other agents, as three Fae men bring out box after box of liquor and place them in the van parked outside.

'Keeping me company on shift,' Reid calls back. 'Me and the other guys. Perks of the job, am I right?'

They all laugh and salute him as if he's some legend. Some great virile master. He tugs and shoves, making me trip and stumble. He has a tight hold on me, so I know I won't fall. But it still hurts.

We make our way to the factory. The smoke billowing from the stacks gets thicker the closer we get. When we reach the doors, we see two Authority men standing guard by the doors made of iron. New doors, by the look of it. Back in my old city, the doors were wood. I bet that up until a few weeks ago, these factories had the same wooden doors. I bet those iron bars on the window are new additions too. Reid stops at the entrance, jarring me to a rough halt.

'Evening, Sir,' one of them says, eyeing up Reid's stolen coat and seeing the emblem on his lapel. He's not a big cog. But a slightly larger one than they are. 'Wasn't expecting you.'

'I was sent over to cover for some prick who drank too much and isn't fit enough to work. They told me this was his posting.' Reid looks up at the numbers carved into the stone above the doorway. 'I think this is the one he's supposed to be at. The prick is lucky I owe him. He covered for me a few nights back when I got too pissed on the cheap shit this lot calls whiskey.' He gives me another rough shove, his hand gripping the base of my neck as he laughs a cruel laugh.

'Sounds about right,' one of the men chuckles, eyeing me up. 'What's this one doing here?'

'I was playing with her down at the bar.' Reid sniffs and leers down at me. 'Thought I would bring her along to keep me company. You can have her in a bit if you like. Bet her mouth could keep your cocks warm whilst you're on duty out here.'

'Sounds good to me,' the fucker laughs, his eyes making me feel sick to my stomach.

'She shouldn't be here,' pipes up the other one. 'I think you should take her back to the bar with the other whores.'

Oh shit...

'What's the matter?' Reid says, his tone low. 'You don't like her?'

'I'm just trying to do my job, Sir.'

'This is the job, kid,' Reid replies, moving me to stand before him. 'No one applies to work for the Authority for the pay and the hours. We do it for the perks.' He pulls me to his body, pinning my back to his chest. His hand slides across my belly and then sinks into my trousers. He rests his fingers over my underwear, not touching my skin, but making them believe he is. 'She's a dirty one, this one.' He presses against me and squeezes my throat as if to say, *"play along, will you?!"*.

I gasp as I pretend to feel his fingers inside me. I even let out a little moan, making their eyes sparkle in response.

Pathetic creeps.

'Yeah. Good with her mouth, this one.' Reid's hand comes out of my trousers, and he slides his fingers into my mouth, careful not to move my strategically placed hair.

I lick and suck and moan around them, meeting the lust-filled gazes of the men watching.

Of course it works. The guard unlocks the door and steps aside.

'We'll see you soon, sweetheart,' he drawls.

The door closes behind us, leaving us in a cold, dirty corridor lined with endless pipes.

'You good?' Reid asks, untying my hands.

'Fine.' I rub my wrists. 'I'm used to creeps.'

'Myself excluded, I hope?'

'Maybe.' I walk deeper inside.

It's painfully noisy and cramped. The heat from the steam spewing from the overworked piping smells like sulphur, gas and burnt rubber. We find an old maintenance room and seal ourselves inside.

He gives me the go-ahead, so I pull on Cyrus's Bond. He returns it, so I know it's safe. I make the portal and they step through. Cyrus first, Lucca and Brennan next.

Brennan pulls out his computers and starts tapping away.

'You good, Brennan?' Reid asks.

'Hmmmph,' he replies, pulling out a small silver box with an antenna before he continues furiously typing. With a final slam down on a key, he looks at Reid.

'Twenty minutes. Thirty max, until someone notices I've put a one-kilometre blanket scramble on the building's communication systems and blocked the connection to the collars. No one can call out or in. The bombs can't be detonated. We saw three doors. The front you came in. A loading dock at the back. And a sealed-up fire exit that no one is getting through.'

'Okay. We're going to head to the main operation floor. We kill any Agent we see and get to the Fae as quickly as possible. Ready?' Reid looks at each of us. We all nod in reply. 'Let's go.'

We leave the maintenance room. Cyrus goes ahead as smoke, and El follows behind him as he slams into the soot-covered light bulbs, smashing them one by one and concealing us in darkness.

As I watch them move as one seamless unit, I remember these guys have been together for decades, working as an elite fighting team. Warriors. Skilled killers for the Thirteenth Kingdom.

They know what they're doing.

I stay behind Reid, who keeps hold of my hand, pulling me along and ensuring I'm in the right place. He keeps me safely hidden behind him, just in case. And the others all move in sync with each other, swiftly, gracefully, and lethally. The Authority agents we come across in the halls or who are blocking doors don't even get a chance to react. Not to pull out their guns. Not to go for the radios that won't even work. Not to even try and save their lives. Each one falls, one after the other, landing in a bloody heap with wide and lifeless eyes. They step over the bodies, not hesitating. Not showing an ounce of regret.

Killers.

Beautiful killers.

I'm glad they never came for me like this. I'd be dead before I knew they were even there.

We're getting closer to the main workroom. That's where most of the agents will be. Stood around, ensuring that the workers, *slaves*, are doing all they are physically capable of doing and then some. They'll be there, inflicting pain. Shame. Suffering.

Not for much longer, I think to myself.

The group halt at the double doors made of iron. Reid goes to touch it but can't. Besides, it will be locked. Cyrus manifests into his solid form and takes my waist, lifting me high so I can see through the crack at the very top of the door where a small stream of light is seeping through.

'See anything?' he asks.

'Enough,' I tell him.

'Space enough to portal us past the iron?'

'Yeah. There are at least five Authority Agents on the platform ahead, though. The platform overlooks the work floor below. The agents are holding rifles and pointing them down. Fingers on triggers.' I reach out my hand, feeling my eyes turn golden. 'Ready?'

'Do it, Princess.'

I make the portal. It comes to life beyond the door. The agents all turn, utterly stunned at its sudden appearance. But before they can turn their weapons on it. Reid leaps through. His hand glows with his deadly light, and he doesn't waste a second. Three men are dead by the time Lucca and Brennan are through. And by the time Cyrus and I are through, the platform is filled with corpses, and blood drips through the metal grating to those standing below.

Cyrus points a finger in my face.

'Stay!'

He turns to smoke. The others spread their wings, and they descend on the Agents below.

Gunshots. Screams. Yells. It's all barely audible over the grinding metal of the machines' gears and the steam chuffing.

I run to the railing and look down, seeing something so wonderful.

Something I have longed to see my entire life.

Seeing the Fae fight back!

With the guys appearing with their wings at their backs, fighting the Agents, they waste no time. Not a second. The prisoners have grabbed anything they can as a weapon and have just started attacking. Agents are going down one after the other. Sadly, a few of the Fae workers get hit with a bullet. Iron, by the looks of it, as they fall and scream in agony. But the determination on their faces is something to behold.

The building shakes, and the Fae start to yell, their words lost in the din of the factory machines. But they wave at the guys, desperately gesturing to the ceiling. The dark ceiling above us is concealed in shadow.

I look up and see strange white string or material covering the walls. It stretches from one side of the room to the other.

Then their yells become more clear.

Warden, they yell, pointing upwards. *The warden!*

A skin-tingling chittering reaches my ears. Every one of my hairs stands on end. As I look up, a golden glow emanates from the darkness above. Not just one set of golden eyes. No. Eight.

Eight!

I watch as they move as one. Then I see the first of many legs emerge.

It's a web. A spider's web!

'What the fuck...' I whisper, staring as this monstrous creature emerges.

Massive, with eight spindly legs that crawl forwards. It has a twisted female torso attached to the bulbous body of an enormous spider. Her head is contorted and stretched to make room for the pincers protruding from her mouth. Pincers that drip thick white foam into her long blonde hair.

The Fae below all scream and back up, looking up at the creature put there to watch over them. It screeches and spits something from its mouth.

I react and create a portal, catching the venom before it reaches them, sending it through a second portal I've created at its back. It screams again, the sheer pitch making me and everyone else cover our ears. It comes for me, its many legs carrying it closer. My wings lift me high, and I get the hell out of the way.

'GET THEIR COLLARS OFF!' I yell at the others who make to come and help. 'WE'RE RUNNING OUT OF TIME! I'VE GOT THIS!'

If they're still collared by the time the humans realise what's going on and the systems Brennan blocked come back online, their heads will be pulp.

And this would have been for nothing.

Reid goes to fly at me.

'I said I have this! Get their collars off, Reid. NOW!'

I face the spider monster as it spits more venom at me. I create another portal and catch it. With a grunt, I push the portal towards the creature, but the damn thing is way too fast and scurries across the wall, landing heavily on the platform. Below, the others are hastily removing collars. As soon as the metal is off, they pass around the machines Brennan has been making.

One after the other, collars fall. And our people are freed.

The monster slams one of its legs to the ground and lets out another squeal.

More scuttering sounds and clicking. I look up and shiver with revulsion as dozens of spiders rush out from the darkness, going for those below. Her babies, but still half the size of any man. And like mum, they're half human. Half fucking child! Their wails sound like demonic babies. And they're going for the Fae below.

'LOOK OUT!' I scream to them as I pull out the gun Reid tucked into my jacket.

But looking at them means I'm not looking at my beastie. It spits, hitting my hand with a web made of acid. I drop the fucking gun!

Idiot!

I reach down to grab the gun, but the web burns my hand, making it impossible to keep a hold of it.

The spider creature runs at me. I make a portal, but it scuttles around it with ease, those golden and beady eyes on me completely.

It's too quick to be caught by a portal and hurled into the sea. So I pull out the pocket knife and hold it tight, ready.

The creature lunges, and I swipe my blade, cutting it across its underbelly. It screeches and winces away, its black blood seeping to the floor.

Not enough.

I tighten my hold on the handle and beat my wings hard.

Its twisted human arms lash out to claw at me. My wings send me clear of their reach, and I dive again, sinking the blade in her back, dragging it up with all my might before flying above them all. Below, I see a group of three nightmare spiders surrounding two girls who wave metal bars at them. The others are too busy removing the collars and fighting the baby monsters to help. The girls squeal as I send the spiders to the ocean through a portal I open up beneath them. Lucca kicks one hard, sending it through. He points at me.

'FOCUS ON THAT!' he warns, pointing at the mumma.

I turn back to my own battle, seeing its underbelly as it leaps at me. It collides hard, knocking the wind from my lungs. Its vile legs wrap around my body. We both land on the steel platform with such force that it jolts and starts coming away from the wall. The half-human, half-spider, opens its mouth, those pincers spread, and her venomous web gathers at the back of her throat.

I scream. My powers explode in unpredictable ways. Pipes burst and send boiling hot steam into the air. The platform trembles and my eyes glow as I expel a wave of force from my body, sending the spider backwards.

I'm up on my feet, blade in hand and determination running through my veins. I run and leap, my wings helping me soar. Wrapping my legs around her waist, where humanity meets monster, I plunge my knife into one of her many eyes. She screams as I pull it out and stab her again and again and again before pulling her hair and exposing her throat. And I stab her. The blade disappears up to the hilt. And with another scream, I drag it out sideways. When I let her hair go, her head lolls to the side as if on a fleshy hinge. Her black blood spurts high above my head and lands all over me. My face. My chest. My arms.

Her legs wobble under her weight before falling to the grate, jolting the already precarious structure as it clings to the wall by rusty hinges. Her barely human arm dangles over the edge. Beneath a layer of fine hair covering her skin, I see something on her hand. Something metal wrapped around her fingers like a knuckle duster. I lean down and turn her hand so I can see her palm. At the base of it are two small canisters. When I try to remove it, I grimace. A long spike emerges from inside her hand, covered in the thick black oozing of her mutated blood. It must be three inches long and as sharp as a needle when it's out.

Two vials.

Why I do what I do next, I have no idea. But I've put it in my hand, slid my fingers through the knuckle duster and pierced the needle into my palm.

My head is thrown back as I feel power surge through me. Such twisted and tainted power.

My head fills with voices. I can't understand them, but they're so loud I scream at them to quiet!

They fall silent.

Everything does.

When I look down at the factory floor, the remaining spider mutants have stopped still. Their eyes, each of them with eight, all look at me.

I feel it. The connection to these things. The same link connected them to the mummy monster who lies dead at my feet.

She ordered them to fight. To disarm and to maim.

'Go,' I tell them. My hand out and I create a portal in the floor. 'Now.'

They go. They all slowly walk to the portal, their eyes on me. The blood of whatever Fae they managed to harm smeared on their skin and their many legs. Everyone steps back, giving them plenty of room to calmly and obediently march to their death.

They go. One by one. Scuttering through the portal and falling into the deep ocean below it. And then I seal it closed. The connection I felt with them slowly dies as they sink and drown. I hear their screams in my head. I hear their despair as they slowly die.

A high-pitched wail rings in my ears a dozen times over.

Mother....

Then silence.

I look again at my hand. Blood beads down my palm from where the spike has impaled me, and I know that's the cause. This strange device connecting me to them.

My hair sweeps across my face as Cyrus's wings land him at my side. He grabs my hand, then takes my chin in his fingers, forcing me to look into his eyes. His brow furrows as he rests his palm over my heart, his eyes glowing.

'What are you doing?' I whisper, feeling a little dizzy. Drunk even.

'Sensing your power. You have something else inside you. Something different. Fuck... your eyes!'

'What?'

'They're dividing or something. Your iris' are splitting into two.' He looks again at the thing in my hand. 'What is that?'

'We have to deal with that,' I tell him, looking up at the ceiling with curiosity. 'There's a huge web up there. And eggs. She's had more babies.'

He looks up.

'It's pitch black up there, Raven. How can you see that?'

'I can hear them too.' I look at him, my eyes narrowing. 'Cyrus. I can hear everything. I can even hear your heartbeat.'

'Yeah. I don't think so.' He pulls the device off, making me groan as the needle slides from under my skin. 'I'm not having you turn into whatever the fuck that thing is. No way.'

He kicks the creature and stores the device in his pocket. The effects of it linger for a moment before ebbing away. He takes my face roughly in his hands and stares hard into each of my eyes.

'It's leaving you, whatever it is.'

'My eyes?'

'Going back to normal. You feel okay?'

I nod and let out a long breath.

Below, someone starts to clap. Then more and more join in until I see all the Fae looking up at me, wildly applauding.

'Are their collars off?' I ask. When I sway a little, Cyrus steadies me.

'Most of them. Yes. Do you need to sit down?'

I shake my head and look down, watching them all return to the task of freeing any who still have a collar around their neck.

'Sense some good powers?' I ask.

'A couple. Yes. But-'

'Good.' I face them all, keen to get this moving on. 'You will soon all have been freed of your collars,' I tell them all. 'Now, you have a choice for the first time in your life. And I'm sorry, but you have to make it right now. We have somewhere safe for our kind. And we need Fae that are willing to fight. To risk everything to save others and win our freedom. If you want to stand with us, say now. If not, then step aside.'

Hand after hand raises.

Every hand.

'Do you vow to stand with us?' I ask. 'Will you swear never to betray your people to the humans? To protect each other?'

They nod.

'Say it!' I yell.

They all roar back an unhesitant yes, with fire in their eyes and battle-ready hands.

I sense no lie. Not from any of them.

So I reach out my hand and make a portal.

'If your collar has been removed, go through. You will be safe. I promise. If you still have a collar on, find someone with wings. They will help you.'

They hesitate, looking at the magical swirling mass of black and gold before them.

'Or you can stay here. And be slaughtered like animals. Turned into monsters and used as killing machines.'

They all look at each other. And when one man walks through, the others follow. One by one or hand in hand, they travel through to their new life.

To freedom.

To war.

'You're taking them all?' Cyrus asks me.

'Yep. Go,' I tell Cyrus, pulling my hand away. 'Get more collars off.'

'What's that on your arm?' he asks, reaching out to the sticky web still attached.

'Nothing. Go. Hurry.'

He returns to the others below.

I press my palm into my thigh to try and stop the blood flow, hoping he doesn't see me sway on my feet as I grab the balcony's handrail.

Shadow-El rests her hand on my arm.

'El,' I swallow dryly and gesture to the roof. 'There are eggs up there. Can you destroy them?'

She nods, her arm still resting on mine.

'I'm okay. Please... just get rid of them.'

She steps away and sets to work.

I can hear the sound of all the scurrying feet as the Fae below rush towards the portal.

The panting.

The portal itself.

It's deafening.

As I turn, I come face to face with three women. Their skin is filthy. Their bodies are thin and frail. But the terror and desperation in their eyes are what harrows me.

'Please,' the woman front and centre pleads, gripping my arm with her bony fingers. 'Please. I know we have no right to ask for more. We know you have done so much already. But we beg of you...' Her lip trembles. 'Our children.'

'Children?' I repeat.

'We have children. They took them from us. My two daughters and their sons.' She nods to the two women on either side of her. 'The Authority took them. We can't leave without them. The

3O2 MJ LAWRIE

Authority will make them pay for this. I beg you.' Still gripping my arm, she falls to her knees. 'Help them as you've helped us.'

'I...' I look to the boys, who are still utterly focused on getting off the collars and checking for any hidden or implanted trackers. 'I don't think I-'

Lucca, appearing at my side, pulls me away from the three sobbing mothers.

'You know the plan. We can't deviate.' He looks at the woman, and I know he's faltering in his resolve. How can anyone with a heart look at these women and not feel pity for them?

'Lucca. If we leave, they will make their children pay for it. For what we have done.'

'We can't, Pup,' he whispers. 'I know that it's cruel. But we're already running out of time. We'll never make it across town to where they're keeping the sprogs. And even if we did-'

'Lucca. We were once those children. We were locked up. We were hurt. They did terrible things to us. In all good conscience, can you look at me and say that you didn't wish someone came for you? To save you? Because I know I sure as hell did. Every day. Every night. I prayed to the universe to send someone to help me. *Their* children are praying right now, and we are here. The Fates put us all here for a reason.'

His eyes dance back and forth as he searches for an answer. One he can live with.

His grip loosens. His shoulders relax, and he slowly closes his eyes.

'I'm with you, Pup.'

Relieved doesn't come close. I grab his head and kiss his forehead.

'Thank you.'

'Lucca!' Reid snaps from below. 'Raven. The collars are off. We're going.'

'Yeah. About that,' Lucca sighs, turning to face him. 'We're going to get the kids first.' Lucca lightly shrugs. 'Sorry, Boss.'

The blood drains from Reid's face in pure rage, not only at Lucca's refusal to obey him, probably for the first time ever, but also from my smile at winning him over.

'Lucca,' Reid growls, his tone enough to make me shudder. 'Grab her and bring her down here. Before I come up there and fetch you both myself.' He stands tall and snarls his words.

I side-glance Lucca. But he still looks on, his cheeky "*what ya gonna do*" expression in place.

'If we leave without them,' I call down. 'The Authority will punish them. Punish them for our actions.'

'You promised,' he reminds me.

'I know. I'm sorry.' Another hand rests on my shoulder. Peering up, I see Brennan. 'You won't stop me,' I warn.

'I'm not planning on stopping you. You need someone to get the kid's collars off, don't you?'

My mouth is agape with shock.

'Brennan. Don't you-'

'What is the point of us, Reid?' Brennan calls down as the last man disappears through the portal. 'What is the point of all of us if we cannot save the lives of those we all swore to protect? We all bear the marks of a loyal, devoted and unyielding warrior.' Brennan pulls up his sleeve, revealing a glimpse of his many tattoos. 'To defend the innocent. To protect the weak. To serve-'

'We are not in our world any more,' Cyrus reminds them. 'You will not take her on a suicide mission.'

'I think you'll find it's her taking us.' Lucca pats my shoulder a little too hard, and I almost fall flat on my face. 'Pup talks sense. She talks like we used to talk when we had a purpose and a kingdom to protect and serve. She wants to go. So do I. So does Brennan. And I know, deep down, so do you. You're scared of losing her along the way, but I'm telling you, mate. You'll definitely lose her if you keep holding her back from doing what she was born to do. She was born to save her people.' Lucca steps forwards. 'Not just those lost here. But those who lost their way back home too.'

I swell with affection for the scrappy and erratic man standing by my side.

The portal dies, and the room falls into silence.

Shadow-El leaps down from above and stands at Lucca's side. She's with us too.

Cyrus and Reid look at nothing and no one but me, stuck between their own damn stubbornness and the wants of everyone else.

Without a word, they take flight and with a single beat of their wings, they join us on the unsteady platform.

I focus on keeping my feet exactly where they are, fighting the urge to cower. I don't flinch. I don't blink. I stand tall and firm with the others by my side.

'If you can portal us to the children, from here, we go. Because we will never survive flying or running across town.' Reid shares his angry glare with the others. 'That's our terms. If she can't do it, we return to the asylum.'

Reid folds his arm almost smugly as he looks me in the eye.

'Fine,' I reply through a clenched jaw.

An alarm sounds out. One accompanied by flashing red lights on the wall.

'The systems are back online,' Brennan says. 'They know we're here.'

'And they know she's here,' Lucca says, his eyes on the door across the room. His eyes glimmer gold. 'Dark Fae. I hear their thoughts. Ivan's thoughts. They're coming for her.'

'How many?' Cyrus asks.

'Too many.'

Quickly, I turn to the woman still holding me.

'I need you to think of your child. Think of their face. Their voice. Think of a time they were playing. As vividly as you can.' She nods and closes her eyes as I rest my hand on her head.

'Raven,' Cyrus warns.

'I can do this,' I insist.

I call my gifts. I do as I have practised so many times before and seek out her truth. The truth she holds in memories.

The scrabbling sound of the Dark Fae gets closer as they tear through the factory towards us.

'Raven...'

'I can do this, Reid!'

I see her truth. Her daughters. One no older than six. The other, maybe ten. Their dirty blonde hair. Their dolls are made of sticks and sponges as they play by the fireplace in their old home. Their sweet smiles. The sound of their excited giggles.

A hideous screech makes us jump.

'Raven... they're almost-'

'I can do this!' I bark back at Cyrus. 'Shut up!'

The woman grunts as I force my way in deeper and she whimpers as I push harder. Instead of pulling away, she grips my wrists and holds my hands harder against her.

'Please,' she whispers to me. 'Do what you have to. Just save my children.'

A portal opens, bathing us in golden light. It's solid. It's determined. It's successful.

I open my eyes and see it there.

'I did it!' I whisper, utterly shocked. 'I've made a portal to an unknown place.'

We all jump when the first Dark Fae body throws itself against the door.

Another thud. And another and another until the door flies from its hinges.

'GO!' Reid yells, shoving and pushing anyone within reach towards the portal. 'MOVE!'

The Dark Fae charge across the factory floor, limbs and broken wings flailing in desperation.

Cyrus grabs me by the scruff of my neck and tosses me through.

The portal steals all light and sound as it always does, surrounding us in a vacuum of nothingness. We crash through it and land in a heap on a grey stone floor.

I turn and recall the portal.

Not before the head and torso of a Dark Fae manages to slip through. The portal cleaves it clear in two. But that never stops them. It digs its claws into the stone floor, pulling its mangled half-body along the ground. Not once does it look away from me.

Reid's boot slams into its head. One massive blow and its skull shatters to pieces

I peer up at him and see his annoyance. I think he would have struck me by now if I were anyone else. His eyes move down and focus on my nose. I feel the trickle of blood and quickly wipe it away.

'I'm fine,' I insist. 'Did we get to-'

'MUMMY!' cries a little girl.

Reid pulls me to my feet. The little girl I used as my anchor runs out from behind one of the many bunk beds shoved in this cramped and cold room. More and more little heads poke up from behind the beds, peering at us with fear and curiosity.

'Hey, kids!' Lucca says as sweetly and happily as he can manage, trying not to gag on the stench of piss, shit and puke. 'Fancy getting out of here? We have cake and hot showers.'

The woman scoops her daughter up in her arms and rushes to the bunk bed where her other daughter lies. Sick, I think, as she coughs and gasps with each breath.

'We have to be quick,' Brennan says, manically typing away on his computer. He looks up at us. 'I've scrambled their signal so they can't detonate the collars in a one-kilometre radius of us again.' He starts handing out the devices to remove collars. 'But that Dark Fae got through. It's collared. They know where we portaled to.'

'They'll be coming.' Cyrus grabs one of the devices. 'Get to it!' He thrusts one in my hand and charges off to the kids.

I wipe more blood from my nose and swallow it as it seeps down the back of my throat.

One after the other, the collars fall. One of the women we brought wails uncontrollably as she fails to find her son.

'Where is he?' I ask Lucca, who is working on a collar beside me.

'He Triggered,' he says quietly. 'The kids are thinking about it. They took him last week. No one told her.'

I know where they took him. To Ivan. Where they will wait and see if he also manifested a power. If he did, he'd have been strapped to that chair. That pain would have surged through his body, and they would have stolen whatever gift he gained.

And I know that we can't help him. Not now. He's lost in a sea of monsters, all under Ivan's command.

Lucca looks at the door, and his breath catches.

'They're coming?'

'Yep,' he says, returning to the collar and tossing it to the ground before grabbing another kid and setting to work.

It's minutes before the door slams as the Dark Fae hammer against it. Over and over again, despite the iron on their flesh. The bones that break. The claws that tear on brick.

I remove the collar I'm working on and let the child hurry over to the others gathered in the corner.

The door gives way. And in they come. Dozens, all desperate to get to me. To stop me. Catch me and return me to Ivan. And to kill or capture everyone else.

I look back at the others and reach out my hand. The portal manifests, and Brennan and Lucca scream at the children to get through!

'RAVEN!' Reid yells, his hand outstretched and his white light aglow in his hand. His terrified eyes are on the monsters behind me.

I don't dare look.

Keep the portal open, I tell myself.

The terror on the children's faces as they see the monsters coming is enough to make me pass out with dread.

Keep it open...

It's as if it's all slow motion. Reid throwing his light. Cyrus pushing the children through as he tries to get to me. Brennan shooting bullet after bullet.

A gnarled hand clamps down on my shoulder. I turn, seeing the creature inches from my face. It screams its ungodly scream as white light scorches it, tossing it backwards, burning its body down to its rib cage and sending charred guts spilling to the floor.

But it's replaced with more.

Reid jumps between us, his wings out as he wraps himself around me. A Dark hand reaches out. One meant for me, but it strikes Reid's back instead. He screams in agony as his skin is torn.

With my yell, a surge of power explodes from my core. A deep whooshing sound erupts all around us, and the Dark Fae are thrown back.

My yell leaves my lungs empty, and I stand, holding Reid, who staggers on his feet.

He turns.

'W-what the...'

Surrounding us is a shield that shines in the light with a golden glimmer. Stretching around us all. The children. The portal. Us.

We all watch as the Dark Fae hurl themselves against it. I feel them. Each one as they batter their deformed bodies against it. Streams of the same golden glimmer softly flow from my fingertips, making the shield.

'How are you doing that?' Reid whispers.

'I don't know.' I shake my head, lost for words. I look back at the others. 'Go!'

They continue filing through the portal.

Reid starts guiding me towards the portal as I keep my focus on each hand. The last child is through. Lucca and Brennan too. Shadow-El fades from sight, and Cyrus remains by the portal, waiting. He takes Reid's weight as the wound on his back spews blood. I turn to the portal, ready to get out of here.

As I do, I stop.

On the floor is a Dark Fae. It's silent and, unlike the others, not attacking. Not screaming.

No. Because it's too busy lapping up the tiny droplets of blood on the floor. Droplets that lead straight back to me.

'Come on!' Reid snaps, grabbing my arm and pulling me after him.

'Wait.' I stare at the creature. 'Its hand. Look...'

Reid and Cyrus both turn to the pathetic beast.

The beast with one hand.

'No. No way. That's not-' Cyrus doesn't get to finish his words before it starts juddering and convulsing. Its body twists and snaps. Its skin turns pale and pink.

Now Cyrus grabs me, and both start dragging me towards the portal.

The Dark Fae writhes and changes before my very eyes. The wind from the portal howls. The monsters screech beyond the shield.

And when the one in here with us falls limp on the floor, it's as it was.

As *she* was.

Minus, of course, her hand.

'Ahriella...' I whisper.

My pretend sister. Barely skin and bones. More bruises and scratches than skin. Her usual long flowing hair hacked off short. Weakly whimpering, she looks at me and reaches out her stubby arm.

'R-raven?' she cries. 'S-sister?'

Whatever breath I held has gone. Inside I'm a vacuum. No air. No voice. No thoughts as I look down at her.

I wince as the shield weakens and a claw manages to pierce through.

I look to Cyrus.

I don't know what to do!

I can't make the choice myself. To save the girl that betrayed me. Or abandon the sister I once loved more than anything.

'We take her. Then we can decide what to do,' Cyrus tells me, nodding his certainty and taking the choice from me. One that I would regret in either direction I went.

He runs to Ahri and removes her collar before lifting her naked form in his arms and carrying her to the portal.

We step through, looking back just in time to see the shield dissolve and the monsters charge.

The portal claims us, and we leave them behind, clawing and screaming at nothing but air.

TWENTY-TWO

*I*n silence, I watch as the others are guided through the Black Lake and emerge inside the vestibule back at the palace. My ears ring mercilessly. And the word headache doesn't do my skull justice. Cyrus is close behind me, but neither he nor Reid have said a word to me since we left the Fae city with the children. I turn, hating how Reid limps and winces with each step. His back is still bleeding, but he refuses help from anyone who offers. When I reach out, he walks past me, barging into my shoulder as he goes.

The doors to the great hall are opened, and everyone makes their way through. The children stare in awe at the ceiling, watching the never-ending fire that illuminates the room. Those who stayed behind have prepared for their arrival, expecting hungry mouths and traumatised bodies and souls.

The tables are filled with food, ready and delicious. The newly rescued Fae are welcomed by the Fae we brought here, and all are ushered to the tables.

From the crowds, a woman's high wail is met with a young boy's joyous cry. I can't help but smile as I watch one of the Fae from Serge's brothel run to one of the children we just rescued.

'Mamma,' he sobs, leaping into her arms. 'They said you were dead!'

The two fall to the floor, a mess of entangled limbs and tears.

Through the crowd, Rhea rushes towards us. Her wide eyes rest on me. A relieved smile welcomes me home. Standing beside her, El throws me a wink before going to Lucca. And then, a high-pitched gasp carries clear across the room. Tessa barges through, focusing on nothing but Reid, who groans as he sits at a table. She charges into me as she runs to him, almost knocking me down. Reid pulls off his shirt as Brennan starts to tend to the wound, commandeering a bottle of liquor left on the table. He pours it over the gashes on Reid's back, making him slam his fist hard into the table and almost splintering it in two.

Tessa stands behind him and throws her hands over her mouth in sheer horror.

Cold eyes meet mine.

She blames me.

Reid's eyes are just as cold. Just as distant, even though they look right at me, they go straight through me.

'Raven?' asks Ezra, his hand gently resting on my arm. 'Can I do anything for you? You look-'

'They'll need somewhere to sleep,' I tell him, my words low as I try not to aggravate my head. 'And clean clothes. Maybe... maybe some erm...' I press my fingers on the bridge of my nose and close my eyes, trying to help the pain and sort my thoughts.

It does neither.

'They will all be taken care of. I promise, Raven.' Ezra gives my arm a reassuring squeeze. 'But you need care also, My Queen. You look-'

'I'm fine.'

Lucca stands beside me with an unconscious Ahriella in his arms.

'What do you want me to do with this bitch?' he asks.

She looks so weak. So fragile. So-

'She looks like a sleeping bitch, Pup. Don't you dare forget what she did to you. Now. Where do you want her?'

'Do you have a secure room here?' I ask Ezra. 'One with an effective lock?'

'We do.' He nods. 'I'll show you.'

He leads Lucca away.

I turn to Reid, who is still sitting in the chair as he relentlessly swigs from the bottle of liquor.

He peers up at me as I stand before him.

'I'm sorry,' I try.

'Yeah,' he grunts, returning his gaze to the floor. 'So am I. More than you will ever fucking know. Do me a favour and go away for a bit, would you?'

His words stab at my heart, and when I reach for his hand, he avoids it, choosing to lift his drink to his lips instead.

Cyrus is with some of Ezra's men, busy giving instructions on who needs what. He won't look at me either.

'Raven,' Brennan says. 'Get supplies. I need bandages, needle, and thread to get him stitched up.' He nods to a table up ahead. 'There's a load of first aid stuff ready to treat the wounded. Grab what I need, will you?'

'Of course.'

I reach the table and scoop up what's needed. When I turn, I'm face to face with a furious Tessa, who snatches everything from me.

'Are you happy now?' she hisses, tears brimming in her eyes. 'Look what you did.'

'I didn't mean for him to get hurt.'

'Not just this. All of it. Because of you, he had his wings cut off. He had his Fae ears mutilated. He has been torn from his homeland, and now he has to live with those scars on his back for the rest of his life.' She makes a point of looking at the ones on my face with a disgusted sneer. 'He deserves better than you. Than your disobedience and hot-headedness. You completely disregard the chain of command; because of that, his life has been torn into unrecognisable pieces. He has been a leader and commander for decades. He's the most skilled and prolific warrior in all our kingdoms. And you think you know better than he does? A half-human brat whose entire life equates to a fraction of ours.' She laughs but it's filled with hatred. Her eyes narrow on me. 'You will end up killing him. Do you know that? You will end up killing us all because you are so certain that you know what is right. More certain than those who have lived your years three... four times over! He will see, ha, he probably already has, that you are simply not worth it. And when the day comes that he realises your unsuitability. When he sees you as I do, an entitled brat, demanding she gets her way no matter the consequences to others. When you get one of those he loves killed, he will cut you down and sever the Bond he holds with you himself. You die, the Bond dies too. One moment of pain and he will be rid of you for good, and he knows that. When you die...' She leans in close and sneers. 'They will both breathe a sigh of relief and laugh about how pathetic and foolish they were to ever feel anything for you. And they will wish that they had ended your life so much sooner, just as intended.'

'What do you mean by that? Just as intended?'

'You think you're so clever. But you can't see what is right in front of your scarred and disgusting face.'

'Tessa!' Reid calls. He watches us closely before gesturing for her to come back to him. 'The supplies.'

She spins on her heel and strides back to Reid, resting her hand on his shoulder.

When she leans down and kisses the top of his lowered head, he takes her hand and kisses her knuckles. I feel as if a black hole has opened up inside me. Together, Brennan and Tessa work on fixing his back. And Reid sinks deeper into his bottle.

I make for the door.

Reid doesn't want me here. Neither does Cyrus. I broke my promise and what's worse is they know I'm not sorry I did. I also convinced Lucca, Brennan and El to go against them. To defy Reid's orders. Something they have never done until today.

My feet drag as I walk through the crowd. They see me pass and thank me. They rest their hands on me, offering such gratitude.

Rhea calls my name as I leave. As does El.

I pass through the doors, but before I can reach the hall, a wall of black smoke blocks my path. I wait as Cyrus forms his solid body and stands over me.

'Where are you going?' he asks coldly.

'Bed,' I reply.

'We're going to talk about that shield. We're going to talk about what it means to follow orders.'

'Not now,' I tell him, unable to meet his gaze. 'I'm not feeling too good.'

'Why?' he asks, snatching at my chin and tilting up my head. 'What's wrong?'

'I have a headache.' I pull away from him. 'Go back to the others.'

'Fine,' he says dryly, letting me go.

'Fine.'

I walk past him.

'You need to grow the fuck up, Raven. And quit acting through fear and this pathetic need you have to be a goddamn hero!'

I just keep walking.

'Not going to stick around, huh?' he yells, his anger echoing off the stone walls and smothering me. 'Just going to leave everyone else to clean up your shit? To sort out all the Fae you brought back here? To sew Reid back up? To look after Ahriella? The same girl that treated you like garbage and handed you over so freely to be fucked by-'

'RAPED!' I scream back, spinning on my heel and staring at him. Cracks appear in the walls as I yell, my power still raw and exposed and the flames in the torches burning hotter and brighter. 'I wasn't fucked by Jonah. You and Reid fuck me,' I spit, tears stinging in my eyes. 'Jonah raped me. Just like the men at the brothel did to the Fae we saved from Serge. Jonah beat me. Ahri's dad did too. And Ivan. And Darius. Just as the Authority did to the children now sitting in there eating a hot meal for the first time in weeks, if not ever. With bruises and burns on their tiny and innocent little bodies. Jonah chained me up in iron and threatened to hurt those I loved. Just as the Authority did to those we pulled from the factory. So you can scream at me all you fucking want, Cyrus.' My words get stuck in my throat and it takes all my strength to carry on. 'And you can hate me all you want. You can regret whatever you want to fucking regret with me. But I have lived their lives, okay! I have lived their pain and fear and suffering. You haven't! So until you are wrapped in iron, and beaten, and raped, and threatened, and betrayed, and scared beyond measure, you don't get to tell me to say, do, or feel... a goddamn thing!'

The chandelier between us crashes to the floor, shattering into pieces.

He says nothing. Not a word.

'I have enough death on my conscience as it is. I can barely stand or breathe. My soul is so heavy with the lives my family and I have destroyed. Every Fae here. The war back in your world.'

'*Our* world.'

'I have to save as many as I can,' I tell him, shaking my head and stepping back. 'And if you won't help me, I'll do it alone.'

'They're my family, Raven. They're the only real friends I have ever had. And your choices have continuously put them at risk.'

'Tell that to all the Fae we just saved. Tell them you wish we hadn't saved them.'

'The Dark Fae could have killed you. They almost killed Reid!'

'That would be for the best, though, right? For me to be gone. No more blood to transfer powers to humans. No more Bond forcing you to care about such a pain in your arse.'

He just looks at me, his mouth in a tight line.

'No words. Because you know I would sense your lie if you tried to deny it.'

I turn and I leave, so hurt. So angry. So fucking guilty.

'Oh no. No, you don't. You don't get to walk away after saying such stupid shit!'

He grabs my arm and yanks me back.

I scream at him not to touch me.

But what happens is far more violent than mere words. He's hurtled away from me with such force he slams into the wall. The same golden barrier as before ripples outwards straight to him in one concentrated shot. I hear a hideous snap. He grabs his arm and roars in pain.

El runs into the hall and looks between us.

'What the-'

'You crazy bitch! You've dislocated my fucking shoulder!' Cyrus spits.

'I'm... I'm sorry!' I look at my hands. They're still pulsing with light. Beneath my feet, the ground starts to crack.

'Raven?' El tries, attempting to come closer.

I feel the power swell, and the ground shakes. The cracks spread.

'Don't. DON'T!' I tell her. 'I'm not safe. I'm...' It gets more powerful.

I run. I just run as fast and as hard as I can, not stopping until I reach my bedroom. I slam the door closed behind me and lock it.

My chest feels crushed as panic and self-loathing takeover. And what's worse, the power isn't going. My hands continue to emanate this golden glow. Everything in the room shakes. The torches burn bright, and the whistling in my ears grows unbearable.

My wings emerge in response to it. The throbbing in my head becomes a hammer to my skull. I cover my ears, desperate to make the high-pitched wailing end. To make my head stop splitting in two.

The door slams as someone throws their body against it, bellowing my name and trying the handle.

I start to glow. My entire body is shimmering.

'What's happening to me?' I cry. 'What power is this? What-'

I explode.

Everything goes a blinding white.

Everything goes quiet.

TWENTY-THREE

*T*he grass is long. I sit in it with a little girl in my lap. A child no older than maybe three. She plays with the ends of my hair, twirling it with her finger. She looks up at me. I know her.

She's me. A child version of myself.

I wrap my wings around us both. Child me marvels at how they shine and catch the light. How they look so delicate yet feel so firm. I then hold out my hand and create a golden shimmer in my palm

But it's not my hand. It's my mother's hand. And I realise suddenly that I am in a memory.

Her memory being played out through her eyes.

'This is the gift of the portal queens,' my mother says. 'Your destiny is to protect and defend those in your kingdom. And this power is yours to command. Use it to protect yourself and those you love. To shield the innocent from those who would ever seek to harm them.'

Child me reaches out to touch it.

'My kingdom...' Little me whispers. 'Is this my kingdom?'

'No. This is the human world, my love. We had to flee our kingdom to save you and your sister's life. Evil men came, sweetheart. They came to take you. To hurt you before you even had a chance to see the sun. They stole our throne and forced us out of our home.' With a sigh, my mother looks up at the sky.

The scene flickers wildly between the open fields and endless sky, to a dark cell with no light. My mother huddles in the corner, clinging to her small bump as two figures watch her beyond the bars.

Then back to the grass and the warm breeze.

The child version of me reaches out and touches the shimmer in her hands.

'You must be careful, my love. It is not just a shield but also a weapon. Those who run at it will crush their bones against its strength and shatter their bodies as they try to break it down.' The shield flickers out of existence. 'Our powers come from the world around us, my love. You must use it carefully, for everything is connected. The ground. The walls. The elements. It all draws from the world around us. And sometimes, if we allow our emotions to get the better of us, the world around us will get just as angry. And we could hurt those we mean only to protect. We are simply the energy of the world. We live in harmony or destruction.' She looks out into the field. Rhea is in the distance, dancing in the blades of green. 'Your father seeks to harness it. He seeks to control it.'

'We hide from Daddy because Daddy wants to hurt us too.'

'Yes,' she whispers sadly. 'He wants to hurt you too-'

The scene flickers and becomes suddenly dark. My mother is in the chair. Her belly swollen and in the late stages of her pregnancy. She screams and writhes in pain as the chair's power courses through her. She calls Ivan's name as he stands there, watching her. The chair tears a power from my mother's body. But it can't be contained, whatever it is. And everything explodes in a blinding light.

In a second, we're back in the peace and calm of the field many years later.

'Your father is a wicked man, my sweet girl. A liar and a manipulator. You can never trust him. He stole your sister's gifts when she was still inside me. Tore her power of the portal from her body and sent us all over here with it. To this dirty realm with humans who loathe us. Fear us. We hide now, my dear. That's what we must do to survive this. We must hide because we are hunted both here and back home. We hide. Or we-'

In a flash, I am no longer in that beautiful field.

I'm face down on the bed, naked, as several men chain me to it in iron. My screams rip through my throat. My heart is filled with terror. Not for me. But for the two small children hiding in the wardrobe.

I smell stale liquor on the man's breath as he leans into my ear.

'Your husband sends his regards,' Serge drawls.

I scream and scream as he starts to cut and hack at my beautiful wings with an iron blade. Pain tears through me, more than any pain I could have ever dared to imagine possible. The sound of bone cracking as they are sawn and hacked. The squelching as muscle is cleaved from bone.

They all laugh and surround me, blocking my view from the tiny crack in the wardrobe and the terrified eyes I see watching me from within. My sweet children.

And nothing breaks me more than watching my husband, the man I loved once more than anything in this world, take them from the room. To the chairs of eternal torment I discovered him testing on my kin.

A fate worse than death awaits my children.

My fate is here. And it is of blood and butchery and violation.

I remain in my mother's memory and live her pain as if I were her. I feel her pain as if it were my body breaking and bleeding.

I die with her.

TWENTY-FOUR

*M*y mouth is dry. Muffled sounds seep into my ears as I try to organise my thoughts. But there are no thoughts to organise. None. So all I can do is dwell in the darkness, lost.

The muffled voices become clearer. I hear them closer.

I open my eyes. Everything is blurred until I blink a few times and come face-to-face with Reid.

'Hello, Little Bird,' he says, his eyes looking a little red and puffy. He offers a gentle smile. 'You waking up?'

'Reid? W-why are you lying on the floor?' I cough to try and clear my throat but find it far too painful. It feels torn to ribbons.

He's on his belly. Cheek on the floor, and his hand placed between us. Cyrus is perched on his knees, facing me, just behind him. He's looking bloodless and ghostly around the eyes.

'I'm on the floor because that is where you are,' Reid replies.

'Am I?'

'You are. And you have been for at least an hour.'

It takes me a moment to organise myself and realise I'm on my bedroom floor. My hand is stretched out as if reaching for him, but he hasn't taken hold of me. He just lies there.

'My throat... hurts.'

'Because you have been screaming for the entire hour you have been on the floor. Now. How about you lower your shield, and we can get you up? Get you sorted. Get you safe.'

'Safe?' I croak. 'S-shield?'

Cyrus and Reid both reach over. But before they can touch me, the air becomes solid with a golden shimmer. I'm surrounded.

Surrounded...

I was surrounded. By those men. By the iron.

'Raven?' Reid says quickly. 'Raven. Stay with me.'

He sits up as the memories and images of my mother's death return. Of my death, as I lived it. The room starts to tremble. Reid and Cyrus look up at the ceiling as chunks of plaster rain down. I see now that the room is destroyed. The walls are shattered, and the furniture is all in pieces.

'Raven,' Cyrus tries, moving as close to the shield as possible. 'What I said, what you thought I meant, I didn't! I don't want you anywhere but here. You're the only thing that matters, and the mere idea of you being gone is more than I can bear.'

Flashes of those horrific moments slam into me.

'Lower the shield!' Reid demands, pressing his palm against it. 'Lower it, Raven. NOW!'

I reach out for them both as they start hammering their fists against the shield, as if with the hope of smashing their way through it.

'You'll break your hand!' Tessa screams from somewhere behind me. 'You'll never get through that shield. Leave her. She's not worth it.'

'GET THE FUCK OUT OF HERE, TESSA!' Reid roars, throwing a shot of his white light at her feet. She jumps back, bursts into tears and runs away as he returns his attention to me.

'I will not sit here,' Reid grunts, still sending blow after blow to the shield. 'And listen to the most important person in my life scream in absolute terror and convulse in pain for another fucking hour!' He creates his light, pressing it against the shield.

My eyes roll in the back of my head, and I feel it all again. The hacking and cutting. The fear for my children.

But I know it is just a memory. My mother's memory carried over as I sought the truth of these powers in the memories of her wings.

I scream and go rigid as they try to pull me back in again.

'Where is she, Lucca?' Cyrus yells across the room.

I see Lucca standing by the doorframe, keeping El by his side and clear of the falling bits of the ceiling.

'Back where she was before she stopped screaming,' Lucca calls back. 'The day her mother was murdered. Fuck, Reid. She's in so much pain. Her body is feeling exactly what her mother's felt. You have to get her out of there!'

'How is she in her mother's memories in the first place?!'

As the images relentlessly bombard my brain, I try to stay here with every morsel of strength. To stop my powers from slipping from my control. I look at my Mates, who are overcome with desperation to get to me.

'Her wings,' Cyrus says. 'It must be. They're her mother's. It's her memories. Put your wings away!'

I try. But I can't focus. Everything hurts. Everything screams.

I reach out to Reid and Cyrus. My fingers brush inside that damned shield as I long for this to stop.

Their eyes meet mine. Their fingers rest on the other side of the shield.

'You listen to me, Raven Rivers,' Reid says firmly. 'You may think you get to leave. But you don't. You belong to us, and us to you. And we are not done with you yet.'

'Not by a long shot,' Cyrus adds. 'We are telling you right now. We will never forgive you if you force us to watch you writhe and scream for hours on end. You are stronger than that, so you get your powers under control. Take a breath. Lower this shield and you come to us. Where you belong.'

'D-do I belong...?' I ask, my voice cracking.

'Yes.' Cyrus shuffles closer. 'You belong with us. Every day. All the days.'

'In every way,' Reid agrees. 'Now stop trying to bring the palace down, drop the shield, and quit scaring the shit out of us.'

The shield falls, disintegrating into gold dust between us. They waste no time and pull me towards them, dragging my still-limp body across the floor and into their arms.

As soon as I touch them, feel their skin on mine and their breath on my skin, I return home. And with a relieved sob, I cling to them both. Pulling them into me as much as possible and replacing my mother's fate with my own reality.

With them.

'Good girl,' Reid utters in my ear. 'That's a good girl.'

Cyrus grabs a blanket from under the rubble before draping it over me.

'She needs a bath,' he tells Reid.

'Why?' I manage.

'It doesn't matter. It's-'

'Why?' I look down beneath the sheet. 'I've... I've wet myself... Oh, fuck...'

Mortified doesn't come close. As I try to get off Reid, he refuses to let me go and pulls me entirely onto his lap.

'Do you remember when you spat in my face?' Reid asks me as Cyrus starts pulling off my wet trousers. 'And I wiped it off and licked my fingers clean?'

'Freak,' I whisper mid-sob.

'I told you that none of your bodily fluids would ever put me off. You've been sick on me. Pissed on me. Now all that's left is for you to shit on me, and we'll have the trifecta.'

He laughs, as does Cyrus. And they hold me closer still.

'I'll run a bath for her in our room.' Lucca shows me a smile. 'Don't let it get you down, Pup. Every single one of us in this room has pissed, vomited and shat on ourselves.'

'Or each other,' El says with her best attempt at an amused accusation. 'Lucca got so drunk once, he did all three in the bed. With me right beside him.'

'You got your revenge if I remember rightly.'

'And only you would have got turned on at what I did as revenge.'

She grabs his arms and looks at us all on the floor.

'We'll get you a bath going,' she says. 'You're okay, Raven. We'll look after you.'

They leave, and I bury my face in Reid's neck.

'You got hurt,' I whisper. 'I'm sorry.'

'It's fine.'

'I'm sorry I disobeyed you.'

'No, you're not. But I'll let you make it up to me. Come on. Bath. Before the room comes down on our heads and kills us all.'

TWENTY-FIVE

*T*iredly, I let them wash me. They take their time and gently clean every bit of my skin.

'How many times have you two bathed me now?' I ask, taking the hot tea Cyrus offers as he sits at the edge of the bath.

'We like washing you,' he says, sweeping the hair from my face. 'There's something enjoyable about your vulnerability.'

'And compliance,' Reid adds.

'And your nakedness.'

'Is everyone okay?' I ask, sinking into the water, hoping to hide at least some of my shame from them.

'Our bedroom is a hazard zone, but everyone is fine. Everyone has a bed. Food. Some interesting clothes.'

I smile as I imagine the Fae from the city all stomping about in gowns and tunics.

'What the hell was that, Raven?' Cyrus asks. 'Your powers are becoming so unstable. You're a portal wielder. Yet you sense lies. See the truth in memories. You make things move when you're angry, and now this shield? What happened today? You screamed like you were being slaughtered.'

'I don't know,' I admit, hating that I have no real answers to give. 'That shield just happened. And then we were fighting in the hall, and I got upset, and the power reacted. And then I was in my mother's memories.' I look up at them over the bath's edge. 'I saw something.'

They both still and look down at me. That pit of dread returns again, swallowing my insides into blackness.

'What did you see?' Reid asks.

'My mother said we left the Fae Realm because my life and Rhea's was threatened. She said that we were hunted back home and had to come here to hide. To the human realm.' My eyes close as I recall the memory. 'She was in a cage,' I tell them. 'Pregnant and locked away.' I shudder as the next image in my mind is her in the chair. I throw my eyes open. 'Ivan put her in the chair. He stole a power from her. No... wait... from Rhea. Ivan took Rhea's ability to create a portal while she was still in the womb, and I think... I think that caused the Event that brought the First Kingdom over here.'

'You saw all that?' Cyrus asks.

'Yeah... I did. But bits, you know? Flashes. But I know that's the truth. My mother's truth. And Rhea... she was supposed to be like me. A portal wielder. Her power was stolen from her. Is that why she is connected to the Dark ones as she is? She was made Dark in the womb?'

'There's no point in dwelling on the past, Raven.' Reid takes my hand in his. 'What's done is done, and sometimes not knowing the truth is a blessing. Sometimes the truth serves no purpose but to cause pain. Rhea will find no comfort in learning any of this.'

'You don't think I should tell her?'

'No.' He shakes his head. 'I don't. Why give her grief when she doesn't even know what she lost?'

'Maybe,' I whisper, deep in thought. 'Maybe...'

'I don't want you to do this again, Raven,' Reid says sternly. 'Neither does Cyrus. You are not to look into your mother's memories again.'

'But there could be-'

'You almost blew this place to hell. No,' he interrupts. His hand tightens on mine. 'I mean it. You have your own trauma to live with. I refuse to allow you to seek out more pain and suffering that you have no right to claim as your own. Your mother's death was brutal. Reliving it as if it were your own is not healthy. Not constructive. It serves no purpose but to cause you more pain, and you have enough of that already. So I want you to swear to us both that you will never do that again.'

'I didn't intend to do it in the first-'

'I want you to swear it!'

'Your hand is hurting me, Reid.' I pull my arm free of his grip, sloshing water everywhere as I do.

'Swear it,' Reid repeats, looking deep into my eyes. 'It's too dangerous. Too risky. Swear it.'

'Okay,' I reply. 'I swear it.'

'Good.'

They return to silence, looking at the water in the bath with a glazed focus.

'Where is Rhea?' I ask. 'She... she wasn't in the bedroom when I was...'

'She couldn't cope with the screaming. She had to leave the room for a bit and collect herself.' Reid makes a point of not looking at me as his hand slides under the water to wash my stomach. 'Seeing you suffering as you were... she struggled to hold back the darkness. She couldn't control herself and didn't want to add to the problem by turning, so she left.'

'Where is she?' I ask, a knot tightening in my gut as I think of her.

'She's with the rest of the Fae. Making sure the kids are okay and just keeping herself busy.'

I let out a long sigh and look up at the ceiling. The same stars twinkle here that did in my room.

'Is your back okay?' I ask Reid.

'It will heal.'

'Did Tessa bandage it alright?' I ask tightly. 'You looked like you enjoyed Tessa taking care of you.'

'Did I?'

'You kissed her.'

'I kissed her knuckles. As a thank you.'

'As a thank you, hmm? What does she get if she-'

I gasp as Reid rests his hands between my legs and effortlessly eases two of his fingers inside me. My fingers grip the bath's side, and he shows me his steely gaze.

'Jealousy doesn't suit you. So take it off. It's ugly.'

'I don't want you kissing anyone else. Not even their knuckles. Not even as a thank you.'

'Noted.' He leans down and kisses my knuckles as they grip the bath's edge.

He pulls his hand free and gets to his feet. They both do. Taking their hands, I stand. Cyrus puts me in a black silk dressing gown and lifts me out of the bath.

'Tired?' he asks.

'Exhausted.'

'Shame,' he sighs, looking down at my body. 'Better get you to bed then.'

My mother knew so much. She had powers I have no comprehension of. Perhaps I do too? If looking into her memories could show me something valuable. Something to use against Ivan. Shouldn't I try it again when I know what to expect and how to manage it?

TWENTY-SIX

I left the boys still sleeping in a bed in one of the smaller rooms, which was unoccupied.

After I untangled their sleeping limbs from mine, I pulled on Cyrus's shirt and his black jeans, which I have to fold at the waist to stop them from falling, and I made my way here.

I now stand facing the old wooden door, bolted shut from the outside and protected by one of Ezra's men.

I slide over the bolt across and rest my hand on the handle. That's as far as I'm able to get.

To face her is something I never thought I would have to do again. I was sure she was dead. Even if her body was still walking around, Ahriella was dead to me in any way that mattered.

A hand slides into mine. I turn and smile before pulling Rhea into my arms. We embrace tightly.

'I am so sorry I scared you,' I tell her, feeling how firm she grips me.

'I'm sorry I was so useless and had to leave,' she says. 'Seeing you like that was... it was...'

'It won't happen again.'

'I just felt it, you know? The darkness was trying to get out. And I know the last thing you needed was me there making it worse and trying to kill everyone.'

'You did the right thing. It's fine, Rhea.'

She eases up and we both look at the door ahead.

'Who is she?' Rhea asks. 'The naked girl you returned with. The one with no hand.'

'She was like family. Or at least...' I sigh and shake my head. 'I thought she was.'

My hand settles on my side, where the scar still heals from the very hand of the girl on the other side of the door.

'What did she do?'

'Betrayed me. In pretty much every way a person can betray another.' I look at her and try my best to smile. 'It's nothing to concern yourself with, though.'

I don't want my sister to know the truth about my life back in the city. Of my time at school. Nor at home. Nor at the mercy of Jonah.

'I want to know,' she says. 'I want to help.'

'You do help,' I assure her. 'But I can deal with this on my own.'

'But you don't have to is the point. And you are literally the only one here who thinks you should even try.'

'I adore your sentiments, Rhea. I really do. But there are just some things I don't want you to know. Some things that you shouldn't know. You said it yourself that you're struggling with the darkness.' I see her smile fade away and slip into sadness. I rest my hand on the handle once more. 'I'll be out in a moment, okay?'

With a nod, she steps back, giving me the room I've probably just crushed her heart to ask for.

I open the door and step inside. Before I can close it, Rhea has stepped through, taken my hand and placed herself firmly by my side.

'Together,' she says simply. Firmly. 'Or not at all.'

The door closes, and Ahriella slowly gets to her feet ahead of us.

There's a single bed shoved against the wall and a pot to piss in. A plate of crumbs sits on the floor beside an empty cup. And someone has given her some clothes that look like they were found in the bottom of the bin.

'Raven...' she whimpers, looking between my sister and me. 'You... you found your twin? I thought she was dead.'

'I thought you were dead too,' I reply, feeling a little too smug at her fear and dread as she stands in her little cell. 'You Triggered?'

Ahri nods.

'I was put in this chair. Raven... this chair... you have no idea the pain it inflicts.'

I choose to stay silent. I know the pain of the chair well enough, as does Rhea, whose hand twitches at her words.

'They put you in the chair?' I ask. 'They took power from you?'

'Yes.' She shudders as she relives it. 'I saw it leave me through tubes and wires. Then everything is a blur. My head was filled with deafening orders. I couldn't control-'

'What power did they take?' I interrupt.

She shakes her head.

'I'm not sure.' She lifts her gaze and waits. But I don't know what to say next. She speaks. 'Where are we?'

'Why? You want to call the Authority to let them know?' I feel hatred spike in my chest. 'Wanna call Jonah?'

'I am so sorry,' she starts, openly sobbing as she tries to step closer. 'What happened wasn't my fault, and I-'

Rhea steps towards her with a low growl, stopping Ahri dead in her tracks.

'I... I am...' Ahri's words refuse to come out, choosing to stay firm in her throat and safe from the darkening eyes of my sister.

I tighten my hand on Rhea's and encourage her to return to my side.

'I don't care to hear anything you have to say to me, Ahri. I'm not interested in hearing your lies or your pathetic excuses. What you did to me is unforgivable. All of it. And rest assured that any affection I had for you is well and truly gone.'

'Then... then why did you save me?' Her brow furrows as she thinks. 'I was one of them. I was a Dark Fae, and my head was full of a man's voice. He had complete control over me. He... he told me to do terrible things.' Tears flow freely down her dirty cheeks. 'The things I saw him do.' She looks at her stump. 'He gave my power to Jonah and then let Jonah cut my hand off.'

'You let Jonah do far worse to me.'

She blinks and lifts her gaze before lowering her hand.

'Jonah has your gift?' I continue.

'Yes,' she says quietly. 'The man in charge, he gave it to him.'

'So now Jonah has at least two powers.' I could scream in rage at her. But I know that his stealing her power isn't her fault. It feels like it should be. I want to blame her for everything.

'Are we safe here?' she asks.

'*We* are,' Rhea replies. 'But I'm not sure about you. You see, you hurt Raven. And there are a lot of Fae here, some rather unstable ones, who won't take kindly to that. Two, in particular, may want to see your skin peeled from your body whilst you are still alive. And I would happily hand them the dull and rusty knife to do it.'

Ahriella swallows dryly and looks at me for help. That's almost laughable.

I walk towards her and take her remaining hand in mine.

'You said you saw things. What did you see?'

'Huh?'

'When you were Dark. You said you saw Ivan do things. What?' I keep hold of her, determined to sense any bullshit. 'Experiments?'

Slowly, she nods.

'Tell me. Tell me everything.'

When I finally let her go, I'm more aware of what the hell is happening out there. And what the fuck that spider thing was, as well as the three creatures we saw on that stage. The one of fire. The one of vines. And the one of metal.

And it's not good. Not at all.

As I back up to the door, looking at Ahri sitting on the bed, a teary and emotional wreck, I take my sister's hand.

She looks just as shocked as I do after hearing everything Ahriella had to say.

'S-so what now?' Ahri asks me.

'You get one chance. One, Ahriella. If you step out of line or start making trouble, you will not live long enough to make a second mistake.'

'Wait!' she calls as I turn to leave. 'D-do I stay here? What do I do? I don't even know where I am.'

'Do what you want. Just stay away from me and watch your step.'

I leave, pausing at the door as I see Ezra with his back against the wall, waiting for me out in the hall.

'What are you doing lurking out here?' I accuse, eyeing him suspiciously. 'Were you eavesdropping?'

'No. I wasn't listening. I am waiting for you. I wanted to make you aware that one of the men from the factory seems to have gone missing. No one has seen him since he first arrived. I wanted to make sure you knew, was all.'

'How is he missing? Has he left through the Black Mirror?'

'No. He's in the palace, but we do not know where.' He gazes past me to the still-open door. 'What is your decision with the prisoner?'

'She's free to join the others. But can you ensure that whoever is on guard at the Black Mirror is clear that she will never be allowed to pass through? No matter what she says. No matter what anyone says. She's to remain inside the palace at all times.'

Ezra gives a slight bow.

'Would you like my man here to watch her? Make sure she behaves?' he asks, nodding to the guard at the door.

'That might be a good idea.' I look back at Ahri and hear her sniffling. 'I know her. She likes to make trouble for others if it stops trouble finding her.'

'She'll be watched closely,' Ezra assures me. He gives his man a firm pat on his arm.

'Thank you,' I tell the man, who gives a small bow. 'If you could take her to the dorms the girls have made, I'd be very grateful.'

He goes inside and leads her down the hall. She looks back at me with desperation as if being led to some hideous torture chamber.

But my days of protecting her, or giving a shit about her, are far gone. She served her purpose. She's given me the information I wanted. And my conscience is clear with her final chance.

'I need to speak to the boys,' I tell Ezra and Rhea. 'They will want to know about what Ahri told me. This missing man, should we be worried?'

'It's possible he's just wandered off and got lost,' Ezra replies. 'Or he got drunk and has passed out somewhere. He can't leave, so I'm not worried. I just wanted you to know so you don't think we are hiding anything from you.'

'Makes a change,' I mutter.

'Wait. Before you go,' Ezra takes my arm and stops me as I begin to leave. 'I... I wanted to give you something.'

He glances at my sister for a second. But if he thinks she'll be leaving, he's very wrong. She's not going anywhere.

'Here.' He pulls something out from his pocket and hands it to me. 'This is for you.'

'Is that a dagger?' I ask, taking it from him.

It's in a sheath made of black leather.

'It is. I made it.'

'You did?'

I admire the sheer craftsmanship it must have taken to create such a beautiful weapon. Its blade is at least seven inches long. The handle is around five. The steel shines, and the blade threatens to cut deep and clean with its curved edges. On one side, words are engraved in delicate script.

Protect.

On the other side, in matching letters...

Honour.

The handle is a sleek ruby red notched with black steel into a beautiful twisted design, similar to the markings on my arms.

'It's incredible. But I can't take it.'

'You can. I insist.' He refuses to take it back. 'It was the first weapon I successfully forged. The handle and hilt took me almost three years to perfect. It would mean a lot to me if you would accept it and use it to help protect yourself. Every queen should have a fine dagger at her hip.'

'I... I don't know what to say.'

'Your smile is enough. Maybe, one day, it will bring you comfort. You can look at it and think of me. And of the homeland that it was forged in.'

Before I can say anything back, he gives a low bow and strides down the hall.

'The boys will not like that he gave that to you.' Rhea takes it and pulls the blade free from its sheath. 'It sure is pretty, though.'

'Pretty is an understatement.' I take back the dagger and slip it into my pocket. 'Why are you up and wandering about?'

'I wanted to check on you. Make sure you were okay.'

Hand in hand, we head down the hall and back in the direction of the bedrooms.

'I better talk to the guys about what Ahriella said.' We stop at a crossroads. Her room is to the left. Mine is straight on. 'You should really get some sleep whilst you can. You have bags under your eyes.'

'Oh. That's just my darkness lurking under my skin,' she teases. But she follows her words with a huge yawn. 'I guess rest is a good idea. We've got a lot to sort out in the morning.'

'You're not wrong. Go on. You go to bed. I'll come to wake you in a few hours.'

She hesitates, chewing on her lower lip as she watches me.

'What had you screaming?' she asks. 'When you were in that forcefield thing, you were in so much pain. What happened? And please don't fob me off with some flippant response. You can trust me, you know. You won't tell me about your past. You won't talk about Jonah or Ahri. I understand, and I'm not going to push you into saying anything. But I want you to know that you can trust me. I want to be here for you.' She waits, hopeful eyes shining in the light of the torches.

Silence is all I can give her.

She gives me a small kiss on the cheek.

'Whenever you're ready. I'm here.' And she heads down the hall.

And I turn and make my way towards the bedroom where I left the two guys.

As I walk, I hear yelling. And I inwardly groan as I realise it's Reid. I change direction and follow his voice to the main hall.

I peer inside, seeing that it's empty except for Reid, Cyrus and Tessa.

And she is fucking naked!

Cyrus is off to the side, chuckling as he watches Red trying to convince Tessa to take back her long silver dress. He's shouting in her face as she furiously sobs and attempts to shout over him.

I am there in a second, a jealous rage lighting an inferno in my belly. And before anyone has realised I've even arrived, I have dragged Tessa away from him, slammed her onto a table and unsheathed the dagger Ezra just gave me. The blade of which now rests at her pretty little neck.

She screams as she looks at me towering over her. When I nudge the steel closer, she soon shuts up.

'Do you have any fucking self-respect, Tessa? HUH?' My yell makes the flames flicker.

'H-h-h-h-he-'

'He is MINE! MINE!' Spit flies from my mouth as I bellow in her face. 'Keep your clothes on and your hands to your fucking self, or I swear, I will cut them off and shove them up your arse.'

'I-I-I'm within m-m-my right!' she argues.

'He can't even fuck you, Tessa. His cock only works for me and me alone. It's mine. All of him is. He and Cyrus both.'

Cyrus continues to laugh and nudges Reid as he waggles his eyebrows.

'Not funny,' Reid replies, his mouth barely moving.

Cyrus shrugs. 'Is a little.'

Tessa takes a few courage-inducing breaths before managing to find her words.

'I know that he has been forcibly tied to you. But that doesn't make him yours. And he... he has obligations.'

'Is that so?' I snarl, moving the dagger so its tip digs into her neck, close to drawing blood but not. 'And what obligation is that?'

'It's ridiculous-'

'I'm asking Tessa,' I interrupt Reid.

'In the library. I f-found a book. A rule book.'

'An ancient rule book that hasn't been enforced in centuries, you stupid-'

'Reid!' I snap. 'Tell me, Tessa. What book did you find?'

'A m-male is obligated to provide r-release to his former wife if claimed as Mate by another.' She blinks rapidly and looks at Reid. 'I'm entitled to use him as I please.'

'That is an archaic law,' Reid argues. 'And you know it. No one enforces it. It only exists because the mad Queen who created that law was pissed that her lover was claimed as a Mate, and she refused to let him go.'

'Tell me, Tessa. What part of my actions regarding someone forcing others to do sexual favours for them makes you think that I would let you even *try* to pull that shit with my Mate?'

'To be fair, she tried,' Cyrus scoffs. 'Reid's fingers nearly got devoured by her poisonous pussy when she grabbed his hand and tried to shove them up there.'

'You put his hand-' I don't get to finish before Reid shouts over me.

'I didn't touch her!' Reid says without a single flicker of dishonesty. 'Quit trying to make this worse, Cyrus!'

I look down at Tessa, fighting the overwhelming urge to tear at her neck with my teeth. This is a territorial and primal response I didn't even know I was capable of.

'I have forgiven a lot of the shit you have pulled with me these past few weeks,' I remind her. 'How dare you repay my forgiveness by doing something like this.'

'What shit?' Reid demands.

'But I let it go as a favour to Lucca, who asked me to because he loves you. You're his family. The annoying, useless liability of a little sister who everyone wishes would just fuck off and shut up. But family, still.'

'What has she done, Raven?' Reid continues.

Tessa swallows. I feel the lump pass my blade. She shakes her head, pleading with me not to say.

But fuck her.

'She poisoned my food and made me sick. Put fleas in my bed. She repeatedly left her underwear in my room to make me think she had been there with you. And she's also been testing out her empath abilities on me. Dialling up my fear and dread and panic whenever she sensed it. The day I fell through the portal and landed on that stage with Ivan and Jonah? That was her. Lucca heard her do it. Heard her force her way into my head and fuck with my emotions. And now I think of it, I've been feeling this sudden dread and panic for no reason since we got here. It's you, isn't it?! Trying to mess with me.'

'No! No, I haven't! I swear-'

'I am the fucking Queen,' I remind her, unfurling my wings in all their glory. 'He is mine. Cyrus is mine. This palace is mine. And revenge will be mine to every soul that has dared cross me. And any souls that try. So I will repeat it, Tessa. Keep your clothes on. Keep your rancid cunt to yourself. And keep your hands off my Mates.'

'He only wants you because of the Bond.'

'Maybe. But Bond or not, they are mine. And I don't share.'

'You have two. I want one. The one who vowed to be my husband.'

'The Mate Bond trumps any foolish wedding vow. I'm new to this, and I already know that. And my violent, jealous streak trumps everything else. The dead will attest.'

Her lip trembles.

'It kills me to watch him with you. It hurts beyond measure. It breaks my heart how he holds you. Looks at you. I think I die a little more inside every time I see it.'

I let her go with a shove and stand, letting her scramble upright. She scoops up her dress and faces the three of us.

'And I am sorry that it hurts you. I have tried to be considerate of your feelings, but you keep pushing. The next time you push against me, it will be your last time. I have run out of forgiveness.'

'Are you threatening to kill me?' She looks at Reid. 'Surely, you won't stand there and let her-'

'If I had just walked in on her with a naked man,' Reid starts. 'That man would already be pulverised meat and bone. So be grateful she is far more forgiving than I and take her advice.' He storms over to her, takes her elbow and starts dragging her to the door behind me. 'Move on and stay out of our way.'

'You can't abandon me, Elias. I beg of you! I can't return home without a husband. The shame-'

'I don't care,' Reid snarls slowly.

He looks back at Cyrus and briefly nods at me.

Cyrus takes my hand in his and pulls my attention back to him. I listen to the door open and close before Reid returns to me.

'Sorry,' Reid grunts, looking at the door. 'That was-'

'Forget it.'

Agitated, I pull my hand away and take a seat, grabbing at one of the bottles of wine left on the table. I take a long swig.

The chairs scrape on the floor as they sit with me.

'I hear one of the guys from the factory has gone walkabout. Any idea where he might be?' I ask.

'In here somewhere. Probably drunk and passed out somewhere. A lot of wine was consumed last night. Where did you get a dagger?' Reid asks, gesturing to the weapon still in my hand.

Cyrus leans in a little closer and looks at it, his eyes narrowing.

'Is that... No. No fucking way!' Cyrus snatches it and inspects it closely. 'That's impossible. Fucking impossible.' His disbelief is shared with Reid as he shows him the dagger. 'Reid,' he whispers, passing it over the table to him. 'Is that-'

'How did you get this, Raven?' Reid says sharply, reaching for the dagger.

'It's a gift,' I tell him a little sharply, taking it back before it can exchange hands. 'It's beautiful. Not quite a naked woman begging you for sexual favours, but still beautiful-'

'A gift?' Reid repeats, cutting me off. 'A gift from whom?' As he blinks, his eyes sharpen.

'Ezra gave it to me.'

'Did he now...'

'Yep. It is an exquisite dagger. Sexy almost.'

Reid leans forwards.

'Are you trying to make us jealous?' he asks.

He reaches over and gently takes the knife, admiring it for himself.

'It is a stunning weapon,' he says softly in my ear as he leans over to me, rolling the smooth handle in his fingers.

His lips kiss my cheek, and I turn to face him. I gasp when I feel the tip of the blade rest under my chin.

'What are you–'

'I don't like you walking around with a dagger given to you by another man. Especially an Eternity Blade. Stand up,' he orders with that deliciously dark smile playing at the corners of his mouth.

'What's an Eternity Blade?' I ask, defiantly remaining in my seat.

'I don't like asking twice, Little Bird.' He digs it in a little harder. 'Up.'

I stand, the dagger following me. We stand face to face. Cyrus takes the wine from my hand and drinks it down as he watches us.

'*This* is an Eternity Blade,' Reid says. 'Back home, once a boy turns fifteen, it is customary to spend one month seeking out materials from our kingdoms to craft a weapon such as this. It is the first weapon we fully forge. Some make a sword or an axe. Some make a letter opener. It all depends on the man making it and what he can do. And when we meet our soul mate, we offer it to them. Vowing they will have our protection and loyalty as long as they hold the dagger. They will have us for eternity.'

'I didn't know that,' I tell him. 'Ezra didn't say it had significance.'

Reid steps forwards, pushing me back. The blade's tip threatens to tear my flesh, and as I swallow, I feel it scratch and draw the slightest bead of blood.

My legs hit the table, and Reid's fingers slide through my hair, grasping them at the roots. With a tug, he tilts my head back and exposes more of my throat. His eyes dance down to where the blade rests. He trails it down, past my clavicle, then my chest, and finally rests it over my heart.

His smile grows.

'Thump. Thump. Thump. My dear... your heart is pounding.'

'You have a blade at it. And you're pissed off. Of course my heart is pounding.'

'Am I scaring you?' he asks, smiling as he does.

His fingers wrap tighter in my hair and I hiss in pain.

'I'll give it back,' I state firmly. 'I didn't know.'

'But *he* knew,' Cyrus scoffs. 'Or at least he thought he did. Fucking fool.'

'What does that mean?'

'When Reid and I were kids, younger than we were supposed to be, we would sneak into the old forger's mill and practice sharpening our swords and such. Then we decided to try and make a sword. We mined the steel ourselves. Swam to the depths of the Eternal Lake in search of the finest red rubies we could find. We worked together to make the best sword in history. But we were children and struggled to find enough material. So we ended up making a dagger instead.'

'This dagger,' Reid states. 'But it was forbidden to make weapons at our age, so we hid it in an old barn. Years later, Cyrus and I made daggers with everyone else. Each one far superior to anyone else's because we had already made one in secret years ago.' His eyes flick to the one he still has at my neck. 'Ezra struggled to make one worth a damn. He spent months trying. We never saw his finished piece, but he passed the challenge with flying colours. Much to everyone's surprise. He must have found this one hidden in the barn and claimed it as his own.'

'You made this dagger?'

'*We* made it,' Cyrus corrects. 'Together. From scratch. With materials we found in our kingdom. Which makes it our Eternity Blade. And look whose hands it's managed to find. Damn,' he whispers. 'The Fates certainly are determined for us three to be together. The chances of you holding this is-'

'Impossible,' Reid finishes. 'But it was made for you. Your hands are where it was always destined to be.'

In a swift move, Reid pushes me onto the table. By the time I've sat myself up, he's pulled off his belt and grabbed my wrists. His sadistic smile remains as he uses it to bind my wrists and secure me to one of the table legs. I'm left looking up at Cyrus, who smirks as he sips the wine. He keeps it in his mouth and leans over, tapping my lips with his finger. I open and take the wine from him.

The blade is back at my throat, dancing teasingly across my skin.

I'm not scared. I trust them. But the implied danger makes my entire body alive with anticipation and suspense.

I have no idea what they are going to do.

I love it.

Reid takes my shirt and slices it down the middle with the dagger.

'It's still sharp,' he admires, looking at the weapon in the glow of the fire burning above us. He holds the torn shirt material in his hand and drags the cold steel over my exposed breasts, letting the tip circle my nipples. 'It's light. Easy to handle. It's lethal. Much like you, huh?'

All I can do is take short sharp breaths as he trails the blade down my belly, watching its effect on me closely, as I shudder and twitch. His eyes flick up to mine and seeing that I'm not terrified or fighting, he allows that smile to appear.

'Remember your safe word?' he asks.

'What are you going to-'

'If you want to slow down, say amber. You want us to stop...'

'Moonlight,' I whisper.

'Good girl.'

He places the handle of the dagger between his teeth and tears what remains of my shirt in two. Cyrus stands and slides my trousers down, dropping them to the floor. My thighs press together as the heat and ache between them builds.

'Now, now. Let's not get all shy. Show me that sweet pussy of yours, Princess. It's ours, after all.'

'We're in the hall. Anyone could walk in!' I remind them.

'Lucky them,' Cyrus grins. 'Now open.'

Reid takes one of my ankles and ties it to one of the table legs with the ripped shirt. Slowly, Cyrus takes my other ankle and spreads my legs wide. His eyes never stop watching as I'm exposed more and more. When I'm stretched as far as I can go, he secures my other ankle to the table leg. There's no give in any of my extremities. I'm strapped down and wonderfully at their mercy.

They stand between my legs, admiring me. Reid removes the dagger from between his lips.

'Now. About that "anything" you owe us.' Reid bites down on his lower lip and pulls his attention from between my legs to my face. 'We have chosen what we want in exchange for taking you with us to the factory. And it will also help us with this scar issue.' He nods to my side, where Jonah's name still lingers.

'What do you want?' I ask.

'We want to fuck a baby into you, Princess.' Cyrus smirks at his words.

'I'm sorry. What?!' I pull at my restraints. 'You can't be fucking serious! NO!'

'Not right now,' Reid says calmly. 'And stop pulling against your restraints. You'll bruise.'

'I don't understand.'

'A promise,' Reid clarifies, running his fingers over the black markings on my stomach. 'To Cyrus and I, that when you decide to have a child, you will have ours. We want you to swear in ink that any children you bear will be ours.'

'Isn't my word enough?'

'If you make the vow with the markings, your body will be bound to it also. You will not physically be able to carry a child unless conceived by one of us.' He runs his finger between my legs and sucks it clean. 'That's our anything. And you swore to us-'

'What if I decide never to have a child?'

They share a look and then rest their gaze on me.

'You will live a long, long time. And as Queen, it is your duty to produce an heir.' Reid shrugs slightly. 'When you are ready, of course.'

'How does this promise help me with the scar?' I ask.

'We'll put the promise over it. It will cover it. You'll never see that scar beneath it, we assure you.' Reid unbuttons his trousers and drops them to his ankles.

His cock is hard and ready. He takes it in hand and slowly starts working himself, gliding his hand up and down his full length.

Fuck... the throbbing between my legs is unbearable. Watching him as he pleases himself, letting out blissfully deep groans as he surveys me spread before him has me panting.

'You want my cock, Little Bird?' he asks throatily.

I swallow hard and nod.

'Sorry? I missed that.'

'Yes.'

'Yes, what?'

I drop my head back and roll my eyes, knowing what he wants. I don't care. He can have my words all he wants.

'Yes, Sir,' I reply, lifting my head again and watching him.

He stands between my legs and leans over me, resting his hand beside my head. All the while stroking himself slowly, his tip resting at my entrance.

'Beg,' he says.

'Please, Sir.'

'Please what?' he teases.

'Please, Sir. Fuck me.'

'As you asked so nicely,' he smirks, leaning down. 'I'll happily fuck you.'

His lips claim mine, hungry and demanding. His tongue, still with the faint taste of wine, caresses mine with skill.

'Agree to the promise,' he says through our kiss.

'But what if-'

'If you choose never to have a child, then fine. But we want any baby you carry to be ours. It's non-negotiable. That's the "anything" we-'

'If I ever have a child, I would only ever want one of you to be their father. There's no one else for me but you two. Now fuck me!'

'With pleasure.'

He works my neck before nipping, sucking, licking his way past my breasts to my belly and down between my legs.

The wanton moan I let out holds no fucking shame as his mouth seals around my clit and his fingers dig deep into my thighs.

I throw my head back, writhing in pleasure, and watch as Cyrus stands over me.

He doesn't even blink as he watches me beneath him, tied down as Reid's mouth fucks me into oblivion. He swiftly strips off his clothes and takes his length in hand, stroking it hard.

'Don't you look lovely?'

Breathless, all I can do is look up at him.

Reid slaps my exposed pussy, making me scream and recoil. I look at him with fury, but he simply smiles.

'He asked you a question. Answer him.'

Slap!

'FUCK!' I cry out, unsure if it's agony or bliss. 'Yes! Yes. Shit...'

Reid slides his fingers inside me, and my head falls back as I moan.

Cyrus turns away and leaves my side but doesn't join Reid. No. He's walked towards another table. I hear water splashing from one of the jugs left there.

Reid returns his tongue to my clit, his fingers still swirling beautifully inside me.

'Fuck...' I whimper, pulling at my restraints.

Cyrus returns to my side. He's holding the knife and admiring it. The handle is wet.

His eyes flick from the weapon to me, and he grins before joining Reid between my legs.

Straining, I lift my head to see them both.

Reid stands, and they both share a look.

Then Cyrus spits on the handle.

And so does Reid.

'W-what the fuck are you doing?' I stammer.

'She's right,' Cyrus says. 'It is a sexy weapon. Let's make her come on it.'

'Wait. Wait-wait-wait! What?!'

Cyrus slowly eases the handle inside me, guiding it inch by inch with care.

'Good girl,' he chuckles, watching it disappear inside me. 'You are such a good girl. Always taking what we give you.' He holds it there, still and deep and right up to the hilt. 'Isn't she a good girl, Reid?'

'The best. Now fuck her with it.'

He starts to ease it out of me. Then back In. Out. In.

Cyrus fucks me slowly with the dagger, and the pair share dark and depraved laughs as they take turns to play. Slow and steady. Hard and fast. They slide it out and trail it over my clit before easing it back inside me. Tongue and lips devote themselves to every part of my body. I stop watching and just lie back, pulling at the bonds and shamelessly panting and moaning, uncaring if anyone was to walk in. The handle of the dagger is still buried deep inside. It's hard and unyielding, but even as they drive it into me repeatedly, it doesn't hurt.

It's incredible.

I cry out in fucking bliss, pulsing around it. My voice echoes around the vast hall, and as I come, Cyrus is careful to hold me down so I don't twist the dagger and injure myself.

They let me ride out my orgasm before Cyrus pulls it out of me, walks to my head and looks down at me, sweating and gasping beneath him.

'Enjoy that, did you?'

'Yes,' I manage in a faint whisper.

He rests the handle on my lips.

'Open wide, Princess.'

I do, like the puppet I am for only them. I open wide, and he slides the warm handle between my lips.

I work it how I know they love me to work them, lifting my head so I can take it in as deep as I can, all the way to the back of my throat.

He lets out a shallow breath as he watches.

'I have never been so fucking turned on,' he growls.

His eyes shine as I run my tongue up the length of that handle and lick my lips, never looking away from him.

'Are you just gonna stand there? Or are you going to fuck me?' I ask.

He drops the dagger, no longer interested in pleasing me with it. No. Now he has his erection in hand. He gets on the table, throws his leg over my chest and hovers over me. The tip of his cock is an inch from my mouth and his hand continues to stroke his length.

'You want this?' he asks, nodding downwards.

Reid has freed my ankles and rested them on his shoulders. My hands remain bound above my head as I'm manoeuvred into position.

I peer past Cyrus and watch Reid position himself between my legs and rest his cock at my entrance. He stares straight past me and looks towards the door.

I worry someone has walked in, and I go to look. Before I can, Cyrus steals back my gaze.

'I asked you a question. Do you want my cock, Princess?'

'Yes,' I reply in barely a whisper.

He reaches down, places both his hands on the back of my head, and lifts me towards him. 'Open wide then.'

I do. Of course I do. It's all I want to do. To feel him. Taste him. Hear him hiss in pleasure as my lips seal around him.

His fingers twist in my hair as he rests at my lips, and I'm pulled towards him, his hands lifting my head.

Further and further until my stomach clenches as he reaches the back of my throat.

He holds himself there, watching me with a mixture of fascination and deep lust. My back arches as Reid drives into me, kissing my legs as he pins them to his chest.

Cyrus pulls back my head. My tongue glides along the underside of his cock.

'Hold on tight,' he says.

Reid's unforgiving thrusts mix pleasure with pain as Cyrus manipulates my head as he wishes, lifting and lowering it at his chosen pace and depth. He doesn't move a muscle. His hips stay perfectly still as he uses me to fuck his cock with my mouth.

'That's it,' he hisses, slamming me onto him again and again. 'Take it all like the good girl you are. All of it, Princess. Every inch.' With a deep moan, he begins thrusting, rhythmically rocking his hips just as Reid does between my legs. 'You like me fucking your mouth, don't you?'

My eyes are violently watering, and each time he withdraws, I gasp for breath.

He loves it. All of it. The look in his eyes alone is enough to make me come. The sheer lust and depravity. The want and need he has for me to be at his mercy. To have my submission and even my willing discomfort.

'How's her sweet pussy?' he asks, looking back at Reid as he pins my face into his abdomen, his cock so deep down my throat I'm suffocating.

'Wet.' *Thrust.* 'Hungry for me.' *Thrust.* 'The best pussy I've ever had.'

Reid continues slamming into me with one hand across the legs he has pinned to his chest and the other playing with my clit.

I know I'm seconds away from exploding.

My eyes glow. I look up at Cyrus, desperate now for air.

I come, and I come hard, my body convulsing and writhing between them. My ears ring and my vision is just a blur. Cyrus pulls out of my mouth just long enough to allow me a cry of pleasure and get a few breaths, and then he's back inside me, unwilling to let us be apart any longer than necessary.

Reid's groaning the word fuck, over and over, each uttering of the word gets rougher and more primal.

I feel another orgasm coming. It's building and building.

'Another?' Cyrus laughs, watching my eyes glow and feeling his own start to shine. 'Aren't you lucky, huh?' He pulls my head back, and I gasp in as much air as possible as I claim another release. Again, my cry of pleasure echoes all around us, and he watches with deviant pleasure. He places his tip at my lips, firmly stroking himself back and forth. 'Open.'

I obey, parting my lips for him.

His hand rests on my side, covering my scar.

The muscles in his neck bulge as he spills himself into my mouth, swearing in a breathless shout as he reaches his climax. His muscles ripple over his whole body as he comes, aiming it all at my open mouth

He finishes, and I go to close my mouth.

'Don't you fucking dare. Hold it there,' he orders. 'Don't swallow. You hold it there until I tell you you can have it.'

That smile. Fuck... that delicious smile.

He climbs off me and stands, still watching me obey his command. Watching as Reid furiously hammers into me. Watching my tits as they move with each thrust and making sure I look at nothing but him. His eyes land on my side, and a wonderous look covers his face.

The most beautiful intricate markings begin to form on my side, twirling and twisting across my skin, covering the scar left by the biggest monster of them all.

Cyrus tugs at my hair.

'Watch me,' he whispers.

Reid reaches his limit, and with a loud groan, he slams his palm over my side, covering the scar, and pumps himself to completion inside me.

He stops, drops my legs back to the table and pulls out so he can walk to Cyrus's side and look down at me.

'You're a dirty fucker,' Reid chuckles, seeing my open mouth. He looks at my side, and that same look casts over his face. Wonder and affection. 'The promise is made. The promise of our family to come. Our lineage.'

Cyrus closes my mouth with his finger under my jaw. When my lips are closed, he wraps his fingers gently around my throat.

'Swallow, Princess,' he whispers.

He feels me obey beneath his palm.

'You're fucking perfect,' he says. 'Now, lick Reid's cock clean and say thank you for making you come.'

TWENTY-SEVEN

I float peacefully in the pool water, the two guys floating beside me in silence.

'I wish you hadn't gone on your own to talk to that bitch. And letting her join the others was a mistake,' Cyrus huffs for the hundredth time.

'I wasn't alone,' I sigh, also, for the hundredth time. 'My sister was with me. And Ahri's being watched. She knows that if she makes one wrong step, she'll regret it.'

'And what do you mean by regret it, exactly?' Reid asks, floating to my left and watching the enchanted sky.

'I dunno. Leave her in a room with you two, maybe?'

'Leave her in a room with Rhea,' Cyrus scoffs. 'She's the one she should be scared of.'

'Hmmm.'

'You still in a sex coma?' he asks me.

I grin. 'My entire body is humming. If I fall asleep, just fish me out.'

'Can't let the future mother of our children drown, can we?'

'There you are,' Brennan announces in his tired and dry tone. He stops by the pool's edge, looks down at the three of us floating, and groans before turning away. 'Dare I ask why you are all naked?'

'Shall we give you a talk about the birds and the bees, Brennan?' I ask. 'When an egomaniac and a lunatic meet a pocket-picking mess of a girl, they kiss and-'

'Yeah. I know. I know. Listen, I've been playing with the device you found on that spider woman thing.' He holds out his hand and shows the device in his palm. 'It seems that it's a mobile version of the chair.'

I roll over and indelicately start splashing my way to the edge.

'Let me see,' I ask, reaching up for it.

'Can I turn around? I don't want to lose an eye for looking at your Mate whilst she's naked.'

'You can turn,' I tell him.

But he clears his throat.

'Reid?' he urges.

'If she's okay with it, so are we.' Reid swims over and stops at my left. Cyrus to my right.

Brennan turns and kneels at the pool's edge and hands me the device. Now it's freed of the blood and grime, I can see it clearly.

'There are two vials here,' Brennan says. 'One holds a portion of the power taken from whatever Fae it's been stolen from, and the other would hold your blood. Once implanted, the two are slowly administered to the host over time. I spoke to some of the Fae we pulled out of the factory. From what they understand, the effects aren't permanent and need to be managed. The smallest amount can last for a couple of weeks, but if it's not topped up, the host becomes... different.'

'Spider monster. She was running low?'

'That's the thing. No, she wasn't. Look.' Brennan shifts the device. The vials are half full. 'She had enough. I had a look at what was inside. Raven, the blood in this syringe isn't yours. Well, it is. But it's been engineered. It's synthetic. Ivan only got a small amount of your blood. I'm convinced he's been trying to recreate the properties in your blood to be able to assist with the transference of the power. That's why the spider woman was so mutated, and those who took power using your blood haven't mutated.

'Like Jonah and Ivan,' I mutter.

Reid takes the device and inspects it closely.

'So, fake blood and a Fae power are shoved into one of these and inserted into a human. But the fake blood mutates them?'

'That's what I understand, yes. The factory folk said they saw a crew of Authority come in every ten days or so to top up the warden's mix.'

'What happens if they run out of the mix and the vials go empty?' I ask.

Brennan shrugs.

'Your guess?'

'I can't see mutation as we saw on spider lady reversing. So, if I had to guess, it would be death or full mutation. A loss of all cognitive thought, like the Dark Fae perhaps.'

I let out a light laugh.

'And what is funny?' Cyrus scorns.

'It's their Gilt,' I reply. 'They get a power, and unless they get their fix, they turn Dark or die. Talk about karma.'

'You said that they need to be topped up?' asks Reid, still looking at the vial. 'Both in the blood and the power?'

'I think so, yeah. At least if it's been administered with the synthetic blood, then the power vial would need topping up.'

'And what if they took the power with Raven's real blood? Can it run out?'

'I don't know, Reid. It's possible.' Brennan looks at me with unease and says slowly, 'It's probable, Reid. Looking at the science and hearing the testimonies of the factory workers, I would be pretty certain in saying that every stolen power will have a shelf life when in a human.'

'Reid,' I try, watching as he goes distant and cold. 'We don't know for sure-'

'So Ivan has my power to heal, and unless I get it back, he'll use it up, and it will be gone for good?' He looks up at Brennan as if furious at the answer he hasn't yet had.

'It's... likely. Yes.'

I could slap Brennan.

I reach out and rest my hand on Reid's shoulder. He doesn't even look at me as he lifts himself out of the water and strides across the room.

'Reid!' I call after him.

But he's pulled on his clothes and left.

'Way to ruin the mood, Brennan,' Cyrus scorns before falling back into the water.

But Brennan and I continue to share an uneasy look.

'We need to get that portal fixed as soon as possible,' I whisper. 'Before Reid goes after Ivan to get his power back.'

'Agreed.' Brennan stands. 'I'll keep an eye on him and make sure he doesn't do anything stupid.' He rests his hand on mine. 'Your new markings are beautiful, by the way. You've made a good choice in fathers. They might be rash and irritating,' he says the word irritating a little too loud so Cyrus can hear it. 'But if you're looking for men that will die to protect what's theirs, you've got it in droves with those two.'

'Thanks, Brennan,' I say, still swamped with unease and concern about Reid.

He leaves, almost bumping into Ezra as he walks in.

'What the hell happened to you?' I ask, seeing him pinching an extremely bloody nose.

'Reid. Obviously,' he mutters, looking behind him. 'He just punched me in the face. No idea what I've done now but-'

'You gave me their Eternity Blade.'

'I gave you *my* Eternity Blade.'

'That you found in a barn. Not that you made. Psycho number one and psycho number two made it. I've told you, Ezra. Quit involving me in your childish games with your brother.'

'Half-brother,' both Cyrus and Ezra correct.

'I didn't know they made it,' he tries.

'Obviously,' I sigh, exhausted from the drama. 'Can you turn around?' I ask. 'I'm naked in here.'

He slowly turns, still trying to stop the blood spewing from his nose.

'Just to let you know, we have used up the last of your blood stores to stabilise the factory workers. We need a few more vials, if possible, as there wasn't enough for everyone. And when you are ready, we could use you in the Arch room.'

'Is there something wrong?' I ask, feeling Cyrus swim up behind me and wrap his arms around my belly.

'No. The opposite, in fact.'

Cyrus's erection presses into my arse. I turn and try to push him off, but he sees my amused smile as he cheekily tries to get close.

'What's going on?' I ask, turning to Ezra and watching his back.

Cyrus is on me again, giggling like a damned child as he puts his cock between my legs.

'Come and see. As soon as you are able, that is. I think you'll be most pleased.'

'Cyrus!' I snap as he pushes himself inside me. I turn quickly, utterly mortified that he's doing this in front of Ezra.

'You okay?' Ezra asks, about to turn.

'I'm fine!' I insist as Cyrus slowly screws me from behind, both of us unable to contain our laughs. 'I'll be there in a minute.'

'Oh. That's not fair,' Cyrus says, slamming into me and making the water splash and me yell. 'I'll be at least twenty minutes before I'm done with you, Princess.'

Ezra lowers his head and quickly leaves.

Cyrus spins me to face him, a victorious smirk on his face as he presses me against the side of the pool.

'You're so bad,' I smirk.

'You have no idea.'

TWENTY-EIGHT

*C*yrus has my hand in his and he grips it tightly.

As we walk into the Arch room, I stop in the doorway, my mouth open.

It's almost fixed! The room is full of Fae, all working hard to fix the Archway, each trying to fit the stones together and working as a team. A unit. A family.

When they see me, they beam from ear to ear, wave or bow before getting back to work.

Watching the children run around and deliver food and drink to the workers is a joy to witness. Their faces are covered in chocolate and jam, and their eyes are full of wonder as they explore the palace.

Ezra is at the Arch with Brennan. The two are placing in a stone towards the top of the arch, focusing hard as they slot it into place. It shimmers and becomes whole before they select another and go around the back to continue working.

'Raven!' Ezra calls, spotting me by the doors. 'Are you pleased?' he asks, gesturing to the Arch. 'Not long now. We're almost finished, and it's all thanks to you!'

'It's fantastic,' I call back.

'We're missing a few more stones. Could you help us find them?' Brennan asks, walking up to us. 'We are so close. If we find these last few stones, we'll have it done in the next few hours.' Brennan rests his hand on my shoulder. 'We could really do with your help.'

'Sure,' I reply. I turn to Cyrus. 'Would you go and check on Reid? Make sure he's not doing anything stupid. Plus, I would love for us to be together when the Arch is completed.'

'Sure thing.' Cyrus kisses my cheek and whispers for me to be careful before leaving to find Reid.

I sink into the pit and start searching for the remaining stones.

Lucca makes an appearance. He stumbles in, wine in hand, and walks towards the Arch. As he passes, he knocks over a purposeful pile of deep red stones, causing several others to groan loudly.

'Sorry. Sorry!' he slurs before sitting himself unsteadily at the pit's edge. He dangles his legs over the side and looks at me as he swigs. 'Pup,' he greets.

'You okay, Lucca?' I ask.

'Fucking peachy.' He takes several deep gulps and hiccups. Seeing his glassy eyes and that anger swimming beneath them, reminds me so much of Ahri's dad. Usually, just before he lost his temper and started lashing out with his fists.

'Can I do anything to help?' I ask.

'Oh,' he laughs. 'You've done- *hiccup*- more than enough. Look at all you've done.' He sways as he waves his arm across the room. 'Freed the Fae. Making a way to get home. Found your soul mates and... and...' His lip trembles, and tears spill down his cheeks. A look of utter heartbreak consumes him suddenly.

'Lucca? What is it?'

I rush to him, forcing myself through the stones and heaving myself out to comfort him. He cries hard, burying his hands in his face as he sobs.

Lucca slumps forwards, drunkenly mumbling through his sobs.

'What did you say?' I ask

He lifts his tear-streaked face.

'I'm so sorry,' he whispers. 'Will you forgive me?'

'For what?' I ask. 'What have you done?'

'Everything is falling apart. When... when we get back... it's all going to get worse.' His head hangs as he cries more. 'And El... my sweet El...'

Lucca starts retching.

I quickly grab a pail filled with some black stones and tip it out so he can hurl into it.

As he hurls, Brennan joins us.

'What's the matter?' he asks me, looking at Lucca violently vomiting.

'I have no idea. He just said he's sorry and then something about El.'

'Sorry? Sorry for what?'

I shrug, looking at the extremely drunk Lucca clinging to the pail with white knuckles.

Before I can ask Lucca anything, Brennan asks me to fetch El to see if she can calm him down.

I take off, running down the halls and corridors, searching for her. I get to their room and knock. When I get no reply, I open up and peek inside.

It's empty.

I head to Rhea's room. Maybe she'll know where she is. I run down the stone hallway and knock before opening the door.

I stop, stock still, stunned and speechless.

Rhea's on her bed. Naked with her head thrown back as she moans in pleasure.

Pleasure given to her by El, whose face is buried between her thighs!

'WHAT THE FUCK?!' I snap, rage consuming me. 'Get the fuck off my sister, El!'

'Raven... It's not...' Rhea pants her words as she furiously tries to cover herself.

The two scurry away from each other, trying to gain some form of composure.

I slam the door shut behind me and glare at El.

'What the fuck are you doing?'

'It just... It happened and-'

It hits me. In one hideous swoop, I suddenly see it.

'Lucca just burst into tears in the Arch room,' I yell. 'He looked like his heart was just ripped from his chest. Now I know why! He felt your emotions through the Mate Bond and knew you were cheating on him!'

'It's not...' El clears her throat and smoothes down her hair. 'It's not cheating! He knows Rhea and I are... that-'

'What?' I snap, stepping forwards, the flames in the room burning brighter. 'What are you and my sister, huh? You're with Lucca. He loves you to death!'

'And he knew who I was before he sealed the Bond without telling me I was his Mate!' El snaps back, clearly angry at my reaction. 'I never asked to be tied to one man, and he knows that.'

'Tell that to the man inconsolably sobbing in the Arch room!' I look at Rhea, who sits in silence, staring at her hands. 'And my sister isn't just someone you can play with, El! If you want a fuck toy, find one with less emotional trauma.'

'She's not a fuck toy, Raven!' El yells, slamming her hands into the bed. 'She's more than that. More than anything! I fucking love her.'

Rhea's head shoots up, and she looks at El. Her face shock stricken. And what's more, I sense no lie in El's words.

'You love me?' Rhea says quietly.

El meets her gaze, looking stunned at her admission. Her mouth falls open as she and Rhea watch each other.

'Yeah,' she says in a stunned whisper before nodding her head and sitting straighter. 'Yes.' Her words are much firmer now. 'Yes. I do. I've fallen in love with you.'

'I... I love you too,' Rhea smiles, her hand reaching out for El.

They both let out a happy and nervous laugh as they admit their true feelings.

Then the two share a kiss.

'What about Lucca?' I ask, still standing like the world's most enormous third wheel. 'You've left him? He's broken, El. Does he know about this?'

'It's not really any of your business, Raven,' El retorts.

'It is. He's my friend, and she's my sister.' They remain silent and stare uncomfortably at their hands. I throw my hands up and walk towards them. 'I'm just trying to understand. You and Lucca are made for each other.'

Yes, I see Rhea slump as I say those words. But they're true.

'We are, and I love him too.' El lifts her gaze to me, and I see the pain of it all in her eyes. 'But I also love Rhea. I didn't mean it to happen, but we spent so much time together when she joined us, and the more I got to know her, I just started to fall for her. Of all people, you should know what that feels like to love more than one soul.' She drags her fingers through her hair. 'Lucca felt it. He knew before even I did. That's why he's been so... unlike himself lately.'

'Well, you cheating on him is bound to-'

'This is the first time Rhea and I have done anything,' she says. 'That's not why he's upset. Lucca can live with me playing away. He's been used to that over the years. I've never been a one-Fae type of girl. But not love. Loving someone else is what he can't cope with.' She lets out a long exhale and looks at Rhea. 'I love them both.'

'This is a real fucking mess,' I sigh, to which they both nod. 'The guys made it very clear that men who are rejected by their Mates-'

'I am well aware of what happens to men who lose their Mates, Raven. And the last thing I want is to hurt Lucca. But I can't help who I love, and if I can only be with one-'

'Do you, though?' I interrupt. 'Do you have to choose?' I look between them.

She kisses Rhea's knuckles. 'I can't cope with the hurt on Rhea's face when she knows I have been with Lucca. And Lucca can't cope with knowing I love her. I was being pulled apart by hurting them both. I can't have both without them both suffering. If I have to choose who to spare, it's Rhea. If you knew that Reid or Cyrus was sleeping with another woman, how would you feel then?' El asks. 'See it from her point of view. The guys adore you.

And what's more, they thoroughly enjoy sharing you. They have no problems with it. The opposite, in fact. It turns them on watching you with the other. You're not like that, though, are you? If Reid was able to have sex with Tessa still, for example. Would you let him? Could you bear it if he left your bed to share hers?'

'No,' I concede. 'No way.'

'So how could I ever put someone I love through that? Maybe in time, things can change and work themselves out. But now, Rhea is my priority. And she should be yours too. Besides, Lucca lied to me. He consummated the Bond without telling me. I was in the middle of a week-long bender, and I was so drunk I didn't even realise markings had appeared on my back for weeks. I thought I'd just made another stupid promise to the kingdom again.' She looks at her body with an amused shrug. Her skin is smothered in markings. 'I can't tell you what half my markings represent. I spent a lot of my time back home drowning in wine. If anyone understands that kind of betrayal of trust, I'm sure you can. Lucca tied himself to me without telling me. I would never have willingly tied myself to him if I had known.'

El's words hit home harder than I would have liked. I do understand.

I look at my sister. 'You are my priority, Rhea. Always. And if you are happy-'

'I am. With El, I feel in control of myself. She calms me. Grounds me.' Her enthusiastic nods and hopeful smile, melt my heart. 'I love her, Raven. And I am so sorry Lucca is suffering because of it. And I hope that we can figure this out together. That we can make it work so everyone is happy. I'm trying to get to terms with El and Lucca still being together, and I know I can, given the time. I don't want to break them up. I don't want anyone to be miserable.'

'And I don't want you miserable either,' El tells her, kissing her hand and caressing her cheek. 'I'm not going to hurt you.'

I show them a smile. 'I'm happy for you both,' I tell them with nothing but the truth in my heart. 'It's a mess. But messes seem to be what we're good at. Anything you need, I'm here.'

I leave them to it, closing the door behind me.

I come face to face with Cyrus, who stands with his hands in his pockets.

'Did you know? Is this the 'none of our business' business, and why Lucca's been acting weird?'

He gives that annoying nonchalant shrug.

I fall into his chest, grateful that these arms are mine and mine alone. That although we have our ups and downs, we have each other, and we know that will never change. Cyrus's arms wrap around me, and he kisses the top of my head.

'Poor Lucca,' I sigh.

'Yeah. Poor bastard,' Cyrus sighs, clinging to me tightly.

'There's got to be something we can do? He's been through so much already.'

'We can be there for him. And hopefully, they'll figure it out. Things tend to do that. Work themselves out.'

Peering down at me, he offers me his sweet smile. The one that says, "*I'm here. You're okay. Everything is fine*".

I love that smile.

'Brennan put Lucca to bed to sleep it off,' he says, still holding me tight. 'I couldn't imagine you leaving me for someone else. The thought alone...'

'Oh, please. You know exactly what you would do. Tear out his insides and wear them as a scarf, which is why we need to keep an eye on Lucca. His rival is my sister.'

'He would never hurt her.'

I sink deeper into his embrace.

'Did you find Reid?'

'I did.'

'Is he okay?'

'He's trying to think of a way to get his power back. But there's no way he can think of, so he's drinking instead.'

'Sounds constructive.'

'Promise you'll never leave us, Raven,' he whispers, still holding me close. 'Promise that no matter what, you'll stay.'

He pulls me back into his arms and slowly sways, holding me close.

'I promise. As long as you promise not to hurt me.'

He kisses the top of my head.

'I promise.'

'Just think. This time tomorrow, we might very well be in your realm.' I let out a content sigh at the idea. 'Safe. Safe and home. Together.'

'Together,' he repeats quietly.

I'm relieved I love them.

Shit. There's that word again.

Love.

I think I know I love them. It's not some big revelation on my part. I've let it slip a few times. Love is actions, I believe. Not words. Words mean nothing. Words can be a lie. Actions are not lies. They are true in their single most absolute form.

That word is too easy to use and too heavy to misplace.

They care about me. I care about them. We know that, and for now, it works.

Kind of.

It's an odd thing to think. To be relieved that I love them. Because if I didn't, part of me, a big part, dreads to think what would happen if I rejected them now. I know there's no way they would give me up. Or let me leave. They may think they would let me go, but they wouldn't. I'm sure of it, so yeah. I'm relieved that I love them.

TWENTY-NINE

'*A*re you sure?' Rhea asks me as I continue to wade through the pit.

'Positive,' I grunt, wincing as the stones aggravate the bruises they put there. 'There's no more to find. They're all there.' I wave my hand toward the stone piles collected on the platform.

The Arch room is still heaving, everyone not only eager but impatient to help restore the Arch.

And my Goddess, the progress is incredible. There are a few missing chunks to the left, and the top is still unconnected. But the right side is now complete. Its surface is smooth and sleek. Not a single crack. Not a dent.

Rhea helps heave me out and grimaces as I inspect my bruises.

'They'll heal soon enough. Don't worry,' I assure her. 'And I'm pretty certain I won't need to get back in there again.'

Thank fuck!

Rhea looks past my shoulder and scowls.

I turn to see Ahriella standing at the entrance, her arms folded across her belly as she hugs herself. Her lip is raw from where she's been biting it, just as she always did when she was anxious.

I face her, suspicious and every sense on high alert.

She looks behind me and sees the Arch.

'What do you want, Ahriella?' I ask.

She pulls her focus from the structure back to me.

'I was... I wondered if maybe... do you need some help, maybe?'

'Not from you. No.'

She looks at my body.

'You look... nice,' she says. 'Your clothes are-'

'Thanks.'

She looks at her own outfit. Rags, really. Clothes brought from the farmhouse that have been torn and are threadbare. Then she looks at mine. One of the outfits made for me at Brennan's request. The black trousers are made of material that shines and hugs my legs up to my waist. The top is, in my opinion, a little too much. It has long sleeves that wrap around my arms almost like ribbon, but the front is low, all the way to my belly button, just as the gown was. And the back is just the same, fitted to perfection but very purposefully showing the markings on my skin that tie me to my Mates. She looks at them.

'You have tattoos?'

'Yes.'

'They're nice.'

'They're not nice,' Cyrus says as he strides in behind her, making her jump. He glares at her as he passes and makes his way to me. He stops, still giving Ahri the evilest eye possible. 'They're perfection. What the fuck are you doing in here, Stumpy?'

'I-I-I'm j-just-'

'I don't actually give a shit.' He leans down and claims a kiss, pinning me to him with his strong arms.

I nod to the stone piles when he releases me. 'They're all out. I can't find any more in the pit.'

'That's fantastic. Good job, Princess.' He gives me a soft peck on the cheek and heads to the Arch. 'How's it looking, fellas?'

he calls to Ezra and Brennan, who are working on the back of it.

I look at Ahri, whose eyes are on stalks as she looks at him.

'You remember me telling you about Cyrus?' I ask.

'The leader of the Undercity?' she says in a stunned whisper. 'You and he are—'

'There you are!' Reid declares as he walks past her, barging into her shoulder and nearly knocking her down. He throws her a dirty look as he carries on towards me.

He takes me by the back of the neck and pulls me to him, kissing my lips with sweet passion.

Behind him, Ahriella is looking between Cyrus and us, terrified that something is about to happen. That there's about to be a fight.

'How's it going?' he asks me, looking at the pit.

'All stones are out,' I report. 'Just need fitting.'

'You brilliant girl, you.' He kisses my cheek and joins Cyrus to discuss the matter further.

I could laugh at Ahri's shocked look as she sees the two men utterly at ease.

'What... I mean...'

'They are both her men,' Rhea announces, almost smugly. 'Problem with that?'

Ahri hastily shakes her head and then gasps as she staggers back, her eyes on the Arch behind me.

Cyrus and Reid have taken flight with a handful of stones as they help to fix the top of the Arch.

'What the?!'

'What?' Rhea sneers. 'Never seen a Fae with wings before?'

Slowly, Ahri shakes her head, her eyes on them like they're made of gold.

FALL OF THE FAE

'Your help isn't needed, Ahriella. And more importantly, it's not wanted,' I tell her. 'And don't look at them like that.'

'Like what?'

'Like they're your next meal ticket. They know who you are and what you've done. You should be thankful they've allowed me to let you stay instead of just killing you outright.'

'I wasn't looking-'

'You were. Because that's what you do, you pick the ones you think will protect or provide for you. And then you use them up and trample them into the dirt. So don't look at them like that again. As I said, you're not needed here.'

I turn back to the Arch. Ahri grips my arm tight and pulls me back to face her.

'I said I was sorry, Raven. For everything that happened. Please. I'm scared and alone here.'

'So was I,' I shout back, shoving her hard. She falls on her arse and blinks up at me as I tower over her. 'Being scared and alone I would have survived. But you made sure that being scared and alone was the least of my problems.'

My words echo around the room as everyone falls silent and still.

The ground shakes as the boys land beside me, their eyes on us both, all interest in the Arch lost.

'You should go,' Reid tells her, stepping between us. 'Before I lose my patience with you using up Raven's air.'

Ahri peers past him and looks at me. 'What happened,' she tries. 'It was wrong. I know that now, and I'm sorry-'

'Sorry it came back to bite you,' Cyrus scoffs. 'And cut off your hand.'

'I'm so sorry I hurt you, Raven,' she tries again.

'You didn't hurt me, though, did you? You just handed me over to others to be hurt.' I hold up my hand to the others as they step closer to her. The boys stay put. 'Ahriella. I will never forgive you. And you are not worth my time to hate. So if you can't be quiet and keep out of my way, then don't say I didn't warn you. Now go. You're not trustworthy enough to be in here.' I take Rhea's hand tightly. 'Come on. Let's get something to eat.'

'You can't boss me about, you know!' Ahri stamps her little foot down and shakes as she yells. I turn to face her. 'Y-you're not in charge here. I... I demand to speak to whoever is in charge. To the man who makes the rules.'

'Is that so?' I ask dryly, unshocked at her swift return to an entitled pain in the arse.

'Why do you get such nice clothes? Who are you to tell me where I can and can't go? You're just another refugee.' She scoffs, all be it very forcibly as she tries her hardest to cover up her fear, especially as everyone has stopped to watch us. 'I demand to speak to the man in charge.'

I take Rhea's hand and make for the door.

But Ahri takes my arm and pulls me back.

As she does, Ezra's men withdraw their swords and descend, the tips of each weapon aimed at her neck.

She stops as still as a statue as we're surrounded and trembles even more violently, too afraid to even blink as she scours the many blades pointed at her.

'My Queen. Shall I remove her?' asks one of the men.

'Q-queen?' Ahriella repeats in a whisper.

I step towards her, stopping nose to nose, and spread my golden wings.

I thoroughly enjoy the shock on her face as she sees them.

'I'm in charge,' I tell her coldly. 'I'm the Fae Queen. This palace belongs to me. Your life is in my debt, and these men follow my orders. So I suggest you get your one remaining hand off me, Ahriella. Before they cut that one off too.'

'Atta girl,' Reid whispers proudly. 'About time.'

I don't pull away from her grip. Instead, I wait as she lets go. She does and stumbles back.

'I warned you. One wrong step and that would be your last.'

'H-how are you a queen? You're... you're a...'

'What?' I ask. 'What am I? A scared mess? A monster?' I let out a short laugh.

'You'll find that *I'm* the monster,' Rhea says, taking my hand in hers. 'And you better believe I will tear you apart with my teeth if you or anyone comes after my sister or the Fae she has risked everything to save.'

I look at the man who has been escorting Ahriella around.

'Would you take her back down to her room? And lock her inside.'

He nods and takes her arm. Ahri looks back at me with a tear-streaked face and calls out her desperate apologies.

'Raven,' Rhea pulls my focus away from Ahri as she pulls against the guard. 'I know you're not telling me things because you're trying to protect me. That you're worried I might lose it and go Dark on you. But I want to know what happened between you and her. There's such hatred in your eyes when you look at her. The same hatred that I see whenever anyone says Jonah's name. Yeah, that look. Right there. I want to know, Raven. What happened when you lived in the city?'

My sweet sister looks ready to catch the broken pieces of her heart as she waits, dreading to hear what I might say but determined to hear it anyway.

But she will never know because I would never want to burden her with it. I know that if I discovered anyone had ever mistreated her that way, the way Jonah and Ahri did, I would burn down every human town in the slightest hope I got the ones responsible. In her case, that's a huge possibility.

'I'll tell you everything one day soon,' I promise. 'But until then, please just trust me and don't worry.'

Her sigh is filled with exasperation, but she concedes and steps away.

'I'll get on with the Arch, I guess,' she grumbles.

She walks away, scooping up a barrel of stones. Before I get a second to catch my breath, Cyrus is there, smirking like a kid who just found all the damned chocolate.

'What's got you grinning? Enjoy me arguing with Ahri, did you?'

'I am so fucking proud of you,' he says, clamping his hands down on my hips. 'You're truly coming into yourself. Believing in yourself. We're almost free, the Arch is almost finished, and we have each other. It's all falling into place.'

'You're going to tempt fate with words like that.'

'Fate is on our side, Princess. We're meant to be.'

He leans in, his lips making for mine.

Suddenly, there's a series of yells. By the time we've both turned, it's too late. Lucca has come charging into the room, looking beyond raging.

'You absolute fucking bastard!' he bellows at Reid. 'BASTARD!'

'What did I do?' Reid calls back. 'WHOAH!' he yells, seeing a gun in Lucca's hand.

The Fae start to panic, looking at the weapon aimed at Reid.

El appears in the doorway, looking at the situation with wide eyes.

'Go stand behind El,' I tell Rhea quietly, nudging her towards the door.

If Lucca is coming apart at the seams, I don't want Rhea in his line of fire. Not if she's part of the reason his heart is breaking. Rhea goes and stands with El by the door.

Reid's light knocks the gun from Lucca's hand, burning his skin and making him roar in even more anger.

'What the fuck is wrong with you?!' Reid bellows.

'Why are you covered in so much blood?' I ask, a lump forming in my throat as I see Lucca's shirt soaked red.

He sobs angrily, his teeth clenched and every ounce of hatred being sent straight to Reid.

'How could you?' Lucca hisses at Reid.

'What the hell have I done?!' Reid snaps back.

'After all the shit you've pulled. All the cruelties and vindictiveness I have seen from you over the years, I never thought for one second that you would ever be this evil to one of your own. There's no end to your black heart, is there? You should be careful, Raven. When he's done with you, he'll be just as disgusting to you too.'

'I don't-'

Lucca interrupts me.

'The blood is Tessa's,' he says. 'From two gashes cut into her wrists, Reid.'

The entire room falls silent. It's as if the air has been sucked out of the room.

'What?' I gasp. 'Tessa slit her wrists?'

'She's still alive,' he tells me. 'I got to her in time.'

'Why... why would she-'

'Why the fuck do you think? Ask your sadistic Mate over there why.'

Everyone looks at Reid.

'What did you do?' I ask him, knowing that I fear his answer.

'Nothing she didn't deserve,' he says heartlessly. 'Her petty jealousy was tiresome. But her actions were unforgivable. Her messing with you sent you straight to Ivan. It brought back those Dark Fae that killed dozens of the Fae you saved. It's why our location was compromised, and we had to leave the farmhouse.'

'What did you do to Tessa?' I repeat.

'He made her watch,' Lucca says. 'Forced her to stand and watch him fuck you in the great hall after promising to be the mother of his children. She told you. She said watching you together broke her heart, so you forced her to watch as you fucked Raven. Reid said he would exile her if she looked away, made a sound or left.'

I feel sick. Utterly disgusted. Because there are no lies in his words, and when I look at Reid, he refuses to meet my gaze.

'She was in the room?' I look at Cyrus. 'You knew she was there?'

'She needed to learn a lesson,' Cyrus says, also avoiding meeting my gaze. 'And realise that there was no point in pursuing Reid. She put you at risk. That's not gonna happen again. Not now.'

I avoid Reid as he tries to take my hand.

'Don't. Don't you dare fucking touch me.' I recoil, desperate to get as much distance between us as possible. 'You make me sick. Like, actually sick. I want to throw up.'

'Tessa will be fine. Blood loss-'

'You used me. You both used me to hurt her. To humiliate her.' I look at them both. 'To humiliate me!'

'We didn't humiliate you. It was-'

'What the fuck is wrong with you?' I whisper in angry disbelief.

Again, Reid steps towards me. I can hardly see him as tears fill my eyes, burning with their betrayal.

'I didn't give you my consent. I didn't agree to have someone watch me like that. To see you and me so...' My stomach turns as I remember our session in the hall. They kept making me watch Cyrus and Reid seemed to keep looking at the door. 'I thought you were watching to make sure no one walked in. But you were watching her, weren't you?' I clutch my stomach as it turns. 'You weren't even with me when you were inside me. You were screwing me with hatred for her.' He takes another step, insisting that what I'm saying isn't true. Not even close. 'Don't.' Another step. 'I SAID DON'T!' I scream, my voice echoing around us again and again. I look at them both.

'Tessa needed a cold hard dose of reality,' Cyrus tries. 'Words don't work with her. She had to see. And her jealousy put everyone at risk. She would never have stopped interfering.'

'And what about me, huh? Did I have to be involved in your sick little game? What you did was cruel to her. But what you did to me was a betrayal of everything I have tried so hard to put in place so I can be with you two.'

'She had to be punished.' Reid says. 'So I punished her.'

'She tried to kill herself, Reid! Because of you!'

Reid looks at me with those dark eyes unblinking. Uncaring.

'That's what happens when someone tries to get between us, Raven,' he says. 'When someone tries to hurt you. They get punished.'

'Is that right?' Lucca laughs. His eyes are wide and his voice is unhinged. 'You punish them? Is that what you do?' He throws an unsteady arm towards the door. 'Then why the fuck is Ahriella still walking about, huh? Why does she have safety, food, and freedom, and yet it is your ex that lies in bed with slit wrists? Of all the people in this palace, Ahriella deserves your fucking punishments for what has happened to Raven.'

'Lucca. Don't-'

Lucca yells over me.

'Because if the girl who sold the woman I loved to Jonah, to be repeatedly beaten and raped, was living under *my* roof, I don't think she would be living all that long. If the girl who handed the woman I loved to the Authority and left her to be gang raped in the woods as she screamed for help, if the girl who turned her friends against the woman I loved and made her the punching bag of the entire school for years, she would be the one bleeding to death. Not my ex, who is only lashing out because we all know what awaits her when she returns. And whose fault is that, huh? Whose fault is it really that Tessa is terrified of returning home without you as her husband?!'

He gasps in angry breath after angry breath.

'How dare you leave Ahriella in peace and punish Tessa. Jonah's obsession with Raven is Ahriella's fault. He raped Raven right in front of you, and yet she is allowed to just... she's...'

Lucca's words fall silent as a low, demonic growl starts. It reverbs off the walls and the floor, travelling around us like a menacing gale.

We face the door where Rhea stands.

The growl is coming from her.

'Rhea?' El tries, tentatively reaching out for her hand. 'Are you-'

Rhea's head shoots up and she meets my gaze.

'You let her live?' she growls at me, her voice so low the room seems to vibrate. 'You let her come back with us?'

Rhea turns and leaves, running out of the room.

We all run after her, listening to the growls become roars and the gentle tapping of her feet turn into the slamming of monstrous footsteps.

I run. I run so fast after her my legs burn. Claw marks appear on the walls. The stone floors are dented and broken from where her weight has blasted into them as she passed.

Then screaming begins. Terrified screams that travel up from the great hall, accompanied by demonic yells of pure rage.

I call Rhea's name and dodge the hands that try to stop me from chasing her.

I burst into the great hall and stop.

The room is in carnage. Absolute carnage. Rhea isn't Rhea. She's the Dark monster from all our nightmares. Her long, taloned arm sweeps anyone in the way far across the room. Many are thrown across tables, and others barely get out of her way in time. At the far end of the room is her target.

Ahriella, who is being led back to her cell by the guard.

Ahri turns and screams as she sees this gigantic form heading towards her. The guard is tossed away as if nothing, leaving her exposed.

Rhea grabs Ahri by the ankles, lifts her high, and then starts hammering her into the stone. Again and again, smashing her body into the floor, each time leaving patches of blood in her wake. Ahri's wails are cut short with each hollow thud.

'RHEA!' I scream, running to try and stop her. Reid wraps his arm around my waist and holds me back.

Rhea drops Ahri, bloody and broken, to the floor. But she's still alive. A mangled mess, but still breathing and still conscious. As the others in the hall try desperately to escape this terrifying creature, Rhea stands over Ahri, snarling and snapping her teeth.

Her fingers wrap around Ahri's leg, and she squeezes. I hear the bones snap from here, even over the commotion of the others and Ahri's agonising cries.

I plead with Reid to let me go. I thrash and threaten. Only when my wings emerge and a shield blasts into him does his grip ease. Free, I run towards my sister.

Rhea opens her massive jaws, shouts a shrill cry of rage, and bites down on Ahri's head.

I watch as she pulls it off and tosses it away.

It rolls and lands at my feet.

Ahri's eyes fixate on me before all light leaves them.

I look down at her severed head. The last moments of fear are etched on her face.

And with a deep breath, I push down any grief I might feel for her. Any pain at her loss. And I step over it.

I slowly walk towards my real sister.

'Rhea…' I try, my words soft as she stares at the headless corpse before her. 'Rhea, look at me.'

Her breaths are short and sharp. A constant growl emanates from her chest.

I keep inching closer, even as Reid and Cyrus hiss at me to get away.

I hold up my hand, silencing them.

'Rhea, look at me. Please.'

Slowly, her head turns in my direction. It takes all I have not to show any flicker of fear.

'Killed her,' Rhea snarls, her hand slamming down on Ahri's broken torso. 'Punished.'

'Turn back, Rhea,' I tell her, still taking small steps towards her.

When a stool scrapes against the floor, Rhea turns and shouts a massive roar at the child cowering behind it. Every bit of sound and movement makes her jerk and bare her teeth.

'Ahri's gone,' I tell her. You've punished her. You did-'

'Jonah,' she snaps, slamming her fist into the floor. 'Must be punished.'

Her head jerks with a whine.

'Voices.' She jerks again. 'In my head. Voices.'

Panic grips my heart.

'Don't listen to the voices. That's Ivan. Ignore him and listen to my voice, Rhea. Please!'

From behind, El takes my hand and places herself at my side. She looks up at her dark lover.

'Look at us, my love,' El says. 'You look at your sister and me and think of how much we love and care about you. Don't listen to the voices. You stay with us. We need you!'

Another step and we're close enough to reach out to her. As soon as I make contact, she swipes her arm and throws me away before releasing another scream. One so loud and filled with such hatred the flames in the room are extinguished.

Darkness begins to fall, and screams fill the void as everyone starts to run and panic.

The more they do, the more feral Rhea becomes. Tables are smashed and glass shatters. All I can see is darkness.

I'm pulled away suddenly by the Bond on my arm and crash into Reid's chest. Pinning me close, he creates his light in his hand and holds it high. Rhea is lashing out, throwing herself into the tables and chairs as her balled-up fists crash into the side of her head over and over. As she thrashes about, her massive form threatens to crush or maim anyone who can't get out of her way in time.

'Let go of me!' I yell at Reid as he grips me tighter. 'Get off!' I strike his chest over and over, but he's not letting go. Not at all.

My sister is fading. I can't lose her. Not again.

I focus hard and send a shield from my body, forcing Reid away.

Before anyone can stop me, I run to her. Beneath her, I stand tall.

'Rhea, look at me. LOOK!'

Reid keeps his light in his hand, ready to throw it. To kill my sister. I stand in his path. He'll have to kill me too.

Rhea covers her face with her gnarly hands, whimpering as she curls up in a ball. I hear her gentle sobs deep beneath the animalistic cries.

The room falls still as the others grab each other and skirt the room's edges. They all watch her, terror in every pair of eyes.

'Raven,' Cyrus hisses, watching my sister warily. 'Get your fucking arse back here right fucking now.'

I stop at her side and cautiously rest my hand on her leathery back, ignoring the furious demands to get back to the guys.

'Rhea. You are stronger than Ivan. Please. Please don't listen to him. Please don't leave me. We are so close to getting away from all of this. Once the Arch is finished and the portal is remade, we can go to our home realm and all these people will be safe. You and I will be safe! Together. Together or not at all.'

Her hand rests on mine. Our fingers gently entwine.

'Together...' she says.

'Together,' I repeat. 'Yes.'

'Together...' she says again, her fingers tightening around mine. 'Together. Together.'

'Yes. Rhea. Together.' I grimace as her fingers squeeze harder. I squeeze back. 'I'm right here. We're all right here.'

One of the children at the edge of the room collapses. He's held by one of the Fae women we pulled from Serge's brothel as the boy shakes and shudders. A man we freed from the factory goes down. His body convulsing and shuddering. A woman falls next, landing on the floor in a heap. All three gurgle and writhe.

Their backs arch and spit flies from their mouths. Their skin starts to change colour.

A low and dark laugh ripples out from Rhea before suddenly, her head shoots up with a twisted grin.

'Hello, Daughter of mine.'

Her hand crushes mine, snapping my fingers and making me scream. Reid throws a ball of light at her shoulder. It gets her off me and I manage to scrabble away as she stands tall, her gigantic frame stretching halfway to the ceiling.

Those who have fallen are still on the floor, their screams turning to roars.

I look at Rhea. But the golden and black eyes looking back at me aren't hers. They're Ivan's.

And he's got hold of her. He's using her power and turning the three in the room Dark.

'No. No stop!' I yell, watching the young boy turn first. 'Stop it.'

Rhea grins and peers down at me. Ahri's blood stains her teeth.

'It seems not all of your pets have been protected by your blood. They're mine now.' She looks past her shoulder at the three creatures. 'Kill them all.'

The three Dark Fae disappear into the shadows and start slashing. The screams and panic turn my blood cold.

Someone screams for light. Others scream for help.

'So,' she snarls in my face. 'You have a portal here. And where is here, precisely?' She looks around. Without the flames above, it's too dark to see.

Reid throws more light and charges towards us. Rhea falls back as he hits her in the shoulder and Cyrus engulfs me in black smoke before pulling me away.

But Rhea gives chase.

'STOP!' El screams, planting herself between us, her hand held high. 'Rhea. I know you're in there. I know it!'

'The lover,' Rhea growls, looking down at her.

'That's right. Her lover. I love you, Rhea. Completely. Do not let him win!'

Rhea's mouth opens wide. Her lips pull back and she lunges for El.

From the shadows, Lucca jumps between the pair.

'NO!' he screams, holding his arms out wide and his wings even wider as he uses his entire form to protect El.

Rhea's teeth find his neck. Lucca is shaken about, as if in the mighty jaws of a fierce dog. He tries to fight his way free of Rhea's grip but screams in pain as his flesh tears and blood splatters the floor. Rhea tosses him away into the shadows, showering the floor, Cyrus, El and me in a thick layer of his blood.

El's scream as she watches him disappear into the darkness sounds like her soul is being torn from her body. With a firm swipe from Rhea, she's tossed out of the way and follows Lucca into the chaos. I wipe Lucca's blood from my mouth and eyes and stare into the surrounding darkness, hearing death and destruction all around me. I'm drowning in it.

Lucca...

I reach out my hand and send out my shield. It hammers into Rhea's body as it spreads further across the hall. It travels through the surviving Fae, leaving them untouched. But when it meets a Dark Fae's form, it hurtles them away.

The shield glimmers around us, and the surge of power from my body reignites the flames in the ceiling, illuminating the great hall once more.

And what I see...

My heart breaks as I take in the bodies on the floor. The three Dark Fae have attacked us hard. I count maybe ten survivors of those who were trapped in here.

The rest...

In the corner, El holds Lucca in her arms. She screams in misery, rocking his body back and forth.

His face is torn to shreds. His neck oozes blood. His chest is cut to ribbons. Reid runs to their side and falls to his knees. Reid's trembling hand rests on Lucca's cheek. There's no way he'll survive. If he's not dead already, it will be minutes.

El throws back her head and lets out a blood-curdling, grief-stricken cry.

Lucca.

'Look at you,' Rhea says.

I pull my focus away from El holding Lucca and aim it at my sister, who just tore him to pieces.

'Your wings.' Her head tilts to the side as Rhea's stolen form looks over my shoulder. 'I have missed those beautiful wings.'

I can't seem to think. My body is frozen, and all I seem able to do is keep my shield up to protect as many as I can. But I know my wings have emerged at my back.

Cyrus steps ahead. His dark wings are spread wide, too, and smoke emanates from his whole body.

'You can't have Raven,' Cyrus tells him.

'We'll see,' she snarls back. 'I've gotten everything else I want.'

From behind them, Ezra and his men launch an attack. Swords and daggers slash and stab at the creatures.

'Wait,' I try, but my voice is quiet and can't be heard, shock still gripping my very core. Ezra plunges his sword through the gut of the smallest Dark Fae. The child. 'NO!' I cry, rushing forwards. 'STOP!'

Cyrus uses his Bond-tether to drag me back.

'I can save them! I can–'

'You can't! You can't save them.' He grabs my face with both his hands. 'You can't save them.'

The three creatures are killed.

They all turn their weapons to Rhea.

Every Fae left standing does the same. Those with powers. Those without. They face her, ready to kill.

'No,' I try to shout, watching as they descend on my sister.

Cyrus holds me back as they all yell and charge her.

But Rhea spins and runs. She doesn't fight but sprints away.

I force my way past Cyrus and chase after her. The shield falls as I pass through it, and I dodge as hands try to grab and stop me. Rhea leaves behind cracks in the stone as she moves as fast as possible. I follow them and soon realise she's heading to the exit.

I scream her name as loud as I can. I plead with her to hear me. To come back. To force Ivan out of her mind.

She keeps on running.

I reach the vestibule and see her at the bottom of the staircase, heading straight for the Black Mirror.

The two guards at the exit try to block her path. They're swatted out of her path like flies. And as I run down the stairs, she leaps through the mirror.

'RHEA!' I scream, running full pelt after her.

My arms suddenly get yanked back as both the boys pull on the Bond. I collide with the marble staircase and get dragged up them, each step slamming into my side as I pass.

But my determination... my desperation... they know no bounds.

I pull back with all my might. I pull and I pull, screaming in agony as I feel them pulling back.

With a roar, I fall back and tumble down the stairs, as they release me simultaneously.

I turn and I run to the mirror. I leap through without a moment's hesitation, emerging in the caves. I pull myself out of the lake before beating my wings and making for the exit. I follow the sound of Rhea's shrill and monstrous roars echoing through the tunnels until I see a small hole in the top of the cavern above. I make for it and soar upwards, breaking out of the stale air below and into the clear night sky above.

I scream once more as the Bond returns, and I'm pulled down with such force I plummet to the ground like a rock falling from space. Wind howls in my ears. Hair whips my face. I reach out and try to fight back, but I can't. I slam into the ground, winded and devastated, left looking up at the sky, watching through the canopy of trees above. Reid and Cyrus land on either side of me and look down as I stare blankly past them.

I expect Rhea to keep flying away.

But she doesn't.

She stops mid-air and looks down at us with a twisted smile before releasing a mighty roar into the air.

A roar which is returned tenfold by the hundreds if not thousands of Dark Fae surrounding us. The boys look all around as we see the golden eyes glimmer in the darkness.

From the bushes Authority Agents emerge, all twisted with demented powers, making them mutated and monstrous. Somewhere between human and Dark Fae.

'How...' Reid breathes. 'How are they here?'

'Something to ask back inside the palace,' Cyrus says, swiftly scooping me up in his arms.

They start to charge.

'GO!'

The boys take flight and make for the caves, a stream of scrambling monsters giving chase.

THIRTY

Once back through the Black Mirror, we're met by armed men with weapons ready. Cyrus lowers me to my feet and faces them all. Everyone is bloody. Everyone is distraught and angry.

'Where is she?' Ezra asks. 'Rhea. Where–'

'Outside,' Reid replies. 'With an army of Dark Fae and Ivan fucking Walker.'

'How?' Ezra asks with a deep frown. 'I don't–'

'They knew we were here,' Cyrus spits, pinning me closer to his body. 'Someone brought them here. We're completely surrounded.'

'He can't get through, right?' I look back to the Mirror, but Cyrus's grip on me is so tight I can't turn. 'The enchantments mean he can't get through.'

'Do you think this will keep him out forever?' Cyrus snaps, nodding to the shimmering mirror. 'He'll get through. Ivan knows magic. He knows science. We'll fall. We will all fall if we haven't already.'

Brennan appears. His clothes drip with blood and the palace shakes from what sounds like an explosion outside. He doesn't even look away from Reid as he walks quickly over.

'What do we do?' he asks.

'Precisely what we planned. We fix the portal and get the fuck out of here.'

'Is Lucca okay?' I ask Brennan, terrified that I know the answer already.

'No.' He shakes his head. 'He's not got long. I'm amazed he's still with us at all.'

'I want to see him. I have to-'

'He's with El,' Brennan tells me. 'Let them be alone.'

'I'm so sorry,' I whimper. 'She didn't mean it. It wasn't Rhea.'

'We fix the portal,' Cyrus says. 'Now. Everyone who is able needs to get to the Arch room. We don't stop until it's completed. He doesn't get any more of us. He doesn't get Raven. We go home as planned.'

'If he follows us through?' Brennan asks.

'We destroy the damn Arch on the other side. Seal it off for good.'

'What about the Fae still here?' I demand, jumping as the ground trembles again. 'We can't just abandon them.'

'Watch me.' Reid says, turning to face Cyrus. 'Get her somewhere safe. The Portal is our priority now. We go home. Do you agree?'

'I agree,' Cyrus agrees.

'You heard us.' Reid yells his words at those gathered around. 'Everyone to the Arch room. We don't stop until it's complete. You men,' he says to Ezra's guards. 'You protect the Mirror. If anything manages to come through, kill it.'

Everyone rushes off, making for the Arch room as ordered.

Reid takes my face in his hand.

'Look at me, Raven Rivers.' I pull my gaze to his blood-streaked face. 'I want you to know. I need you to know.' He leans close, his voice a soft whisper. 'No matter what happens. I want you to know that I love you. And there is no other soul in this universe or the next that I will ever cherish more.'

His lips rest on my cheek and he presses a firm kiss on my skin. 'Remember that I love you. No matter what.'

Before he gives me a chance to say a thing, he runs up the stairs and joins the others, leaving Cyrus and I standing in the painful quiet of the room.

In silence, I'm marched to the bedroom.

'Why am I in here?' I ask, looking at the empty room. 'You said we need to fix-'

'You need to stay in here where it's safe.'

'What? No! El needs support, and Lucca... Lucca needs...' A sob swells in my throat. 'I have to do something.'

'You are. You're staying here where it's safe. Where I know you will be for when the time comes.' He swallows and repeats the words in a whisper. 'For when the time comes.'

'Why would Lucca tell Rhea about that stuff? Why would he do that? He knew I was keeping it a secret. That her knowing would-'

'I don't think we'll ever be able to ask him, Princess.'

He stands at the door, gripping the handle as he looks at me. Pain and loss swim in the dark pools of his eyes. Like everyone else, he's splattered with blood and looks harrowed.

'I love you,' he says in barely a whisper. When he blinks, a tear slides down his cheek. 'These past few weeks with you have been the best of my entire life. Your smile is, and will always be, the most beautiful thing I have ever seen. I hope I'll get to see it again.'

'Why does you and Reid telling me that you love me, sound like you're both saying goodbye?'

'Not goodbye. Never goodbye. Because you are ours, and we are yours. Forever. I wish I had scooped you up that day I first saw you in the alley. I wish I had taken you away where no one would have ever found us and kept you hidden. Kept you lost to the world. Kept you mine and mine alone. I need you to hear me say these words, and I need you to know that I meant them. I love you, Raven. My Raven.'

'Cyrus. I lo-'

He closes the door before I can say it back. He closes it and locks it.

I sit on the edge of the bed, knotting my fingers together as I stare at the wall.

We fix the portal and pray we do so before Ivan arrives with his army to claim this place.

I have no doubt he'll break through eventually. None whatsoever.

The fire spits and hisses as it burns. Beyond the locked door, I sometimes hear people rushing about. There are three guards outside. I hear them talking. Each time I try the door, they refuse to open it and insist I wait for Reid or Cyrus to fetch me.

They have no hope of getting the portal back up and running without my powers. If I run off or die, we're all fucked.

I'm so numb by it all.

Lucca. I have no idea if he's alive or dead.

Rhea. She's lost again.

Am I supposed to feel angry at her? That she went Dark? That she killed Ahri? That so many of the Fae we risked everything to save, have been killed or maimed by her?

Our last safe place on earth will fall because she is under the control of Ivan Walker once more. Ivan Walker, whose creatures are already here waiting outside.

How? How does he know we're here?

And what lies beyond the portal is as much a mystery to me as anything else.

I try to keep myself busy. I wash off the blood from my skin. I change my clothes. I pace the room, reliving the last few hours repeatedly. And ask myself the same damned questions over and over again.

The door opens, making me jump and my heart hammer in my chest.

I turn to see Reid standing there.

He steps inside and closes the door. I see the guards look inside briefly before Reid closes and locks the door.

'What happened?' I ask him, terrified to hear what he has to say. 'Is the portal fixed? Is Lucca okay?'

Reid walks towards me, stopping when he's in front of me. His hand rests on my cheek and he smiles.

'Is it time?' I ask, watching that smile. He stares at my lips as his thumb traces back and forth across my cheek. His entire presence isn't right. Even the way he breathes is off. 'Reid? What happened?' I rest my hand on his chest, feeling his heart hammering away beneath my palm. 'Are you okay?'

His fist slams into the side of my face. I didn't even see it coming, and it landed with considerable force. I hit the floor, and he's on me before I can do a single fucking thing. His fingers knot in my hair. He lifts my head, and *SLAM!*

My skull meets the stone with a thud.

My body goes limp. My ears ring as blood rushes through them. The room spins wildly around me, and I can't hold my weight as he hoists me to my feet. I stumble as he drags me across the room, my feet tripping and dragging behind me. Hair is torn from my roots as he pulls me without care, and with a swift motion, his arm sweeps the table clear of the books and plates, and I land face down.

I'm so dizzy. So uncooperative. I don't understand why he's laughing. If this is because he's angry, why does he laugh?

My attempts to speak are a slurred mess. It takes all I have to stay conscious.

I barely register that my trousers are being removed. Only when I see him toss them to the floor do I know he's stripped me. His hand grips the back of my neck, and he forces himself inside me with a victorious yell.

I want to be sick. I want to fucking die as Reid, the man I love and who declared, with truth, that he loves me too, rapes me.

Tears stream down my face as I try with all I have to stay awake. His hands pin me down, and each thrust is so hard the table jars forwards.

I reach back and grab his hand.

And all I can think is... why are you doing this to me?

Why?

'Reid...' I cry. 'Stop! Please... STOP!'

He suddenly starts to choke and withdraws. I roll off the table and land on the floor, my entire body shaking and my heart broken into a million pieces. I look back.

Reid is pulling at a belt around his neck, trying to get free of it. He thrashes against the person at his back, who is relentlessly pulling and pulling.

Against Tessa.

Her face is contorted with anger as she pulls and pulls. The veins in his neck bulge, as do his eyes which become more and more bloodshot. Reid creates deep scratches on his neck as he tries to get free. But he can't. He falls to his knees, foaming at the mouth before his arms go limp and his eyes roll into the back of his head. Only when he falls still does Tessa let him go.

He falls on his side, unconscious and still.

Tessa looks at me. There are cuts on each of her wrists that have been sealed with heat, and blood stains her skin and the pale pink gown she wears.

'You okay?' she asks coldly. Avoiding eye contact with me.

I just sit there. Half naked and stunned. Broken and lost.

She makes her way to where my trousers lie in a heap and silently hands them to me. I shake so much I can't get them on.

'Let me help you,' she offers, her eyes still avoiding me.

Carefully, she guides each leg in and holds me up as I get them over my hips. Kneeling, we face each other. She's so pale and looks ready to pass out.

We then turn to Reid on the floor.

'How could he do this to me,' I whimper. 'Why?'

'I thought the same thing earlier,' she says. 'But about Lucca. Not Reid.'

'Lucca?' I repeat.

'I went to see him after I saw you with Cyrus and Reid in the great hall.'

'I didn't know you were-'

'I went to Lucca's room,' she cuts in. 'I was so angry I wanted to leave. I wanted him to come with me. I knew he and El were having trouble and thought maybe we could leave together. Because we had both been spurned by our lovers, maybe we could be happier together.' She speaks so blankly and without much emotion at all. Like she's drained of all energy and will to carry on. 'Lucca hit me over the back of the head, cut my wrists, and left me on the floor.'

She looks at her wrists. The skin around the cut is red raw and blistered.

'Lucca did this to you?' I shake my head, unable to comprehend it. 'He... he said... he said...' I think back. He said Tessa had cuts on her wrists. Not that she did it to herself.

'I cauterised the wound after he left and then I passed out. When I came to, the attack had happened. I came to find you.' She looks back at me. 'I think I was going to try and kill you,' she admits, her voice deadpan. 'I thought you had turned even Lucca against me. But when I came in here and saw Reid holding you down... I knew something wasn't right. Reid would never... he would never...' She swallows and looks at the floor. 'I grabbed him and took him down. Reid would never have done that.'

'He did. Reid-'

'I'm not as strong as Reid. Even at full strength, I wouldn't stand a chance. I'm down on blood. I'm struggling to stand. There's no way I could have taken Reid down. No way.' She looks back at him again. 'He would never do this to you. And Lucca would never do that to me.'

'They're... they're being controlled?'

'Maybe.' Tessa crawls towards Reid, watching him closely. 'Wait... hold on.'

She unbuttons his shirt.

'His markings,' I breathe, seeing nothing there at all. Not a single mark.

'I knew of a man who could do this in the First Kingdom,' she says. 'To take another's face and wear it as their own. To mimic their voice too.' She sighs tiredly and shrugs. 'He was a High Lord in your mother's kingdom. And Ahriella's Grandfather.'

'Ahriella...' I whisper.

'I heard her mention a power was stolen from her. I heard that Jonah took it. Powers can be inherited, so...' Again, she shrugs and nods towards Reid on the floor. 'If you put it all together.'

I see it now. The body before us isn't Reid's. It's nowhere close to him. Not in size or shape. And not in cruelty.

But I know a man whose body matches this one.

'Jonah...' I breathe.

I crawl towards him too.

'We've been missing the man from the factory since we arrived,' Tessa says. 'My guess... *he's* the man.' She nods to him. 'Planted there, perhaps. I don't know.'

'Let's know for sure.' I grab his head and call my power. I have to fight the urge to crush his skull.

I live it all as he did. It's revolting to see as he sees. To live even a second in his life. The images flash before me and tell his sordid story.

Of him hunting and catching Ahri, putting her in that chair and stealing her gift. I watch him slowly cut off her hand with a dull saw and keep it so he can use it on me.

I see him in the Authority bar below the bedroom we portaled into the night we went to the factory. He pulls himself away from the grotesque scene of three Fae surrounded by drunk bastards and watches Cyrus's black smoke seep over the road. He follows it to the factory, watching as Cyrus materialises and peers inside a high window before leaving.

He goes inside and kills a Fae man to take his place with his stolen face.

He watches me fight the spider creatures. He never looks away. I see it all from his eyes as I fight for not only my life but for his, too, protecting him from one of the creature's spawn.

He comes through the portal and returns to the palace.

He's terrified as he passes through the Black Lake and so relieved when he emerges.

Rhea is his target. It becomes clear that they are hiding the truth from her about my past, and that if she ever found out, her emotions would get the better of her. So he knows what to do. Rhea needs to know.

He mimics Lucca's face whilst he's passed out. But Tessa discovers him in Lucca's room as he changes clothes. Tessa suspected him. She knew something wasn't right. So Tessa has to go.

And then to the Arch room.

He spills the secret. He watches as all hell breaks loose. He watches the real Lucca arrive and leap between El and Rhea.

He watches Ivan take Rhea and knows his mission is complete.

And then he waits. When he sees me being put in the room alone, he can't resist. The compulsion is too strong. To destroy my feelings for Reid and hurt me in the process is just too much to pass up.

So he wears Reid's face.

And he comes for me, just as he always did.

I let go, gasping and shaking before I tell Tessa everything. She barely reacts as she listens. She sits on her knees, utterly defeated, broken and completely lost.

'I know this is all terrible for you, Tessa. I know you have lost so much, but we have to work together.'

'I've lost everything,' she snipes back. Slowly she gets to her feet and looks down at me. There's no kindness in her eyes. 'Don't you dare patronise me. I don't want your pity. I did not stop that bastard through any care for you. I stopped him because it was the right thing to do. That's all.'

'We'll fix the portal and return to the Fae Realm. Everything will be okay. I know it.'

She sneers at me and lets out a hateful scoff. 'No. It won't. You have no idea. None at all.'

'What do you mean?'

'How have you never seen it, in all this time? It's been right in front of your stupid little face.' She laughs now, a jeering, mocking laugh as she looks at me on the floor. 'When I return home, I am worthless because of you. I am married. My husband still lives. I am abandoned. Spoiled. No man will accept me. No man will marry me. No respectable one, anyway. When I return, I have no option but to serve as a maid or whore to earn my keep. All because you have stolen my Lord and my home.'

'That's not going to happen, Tessa. I won't let it. I promise you!'

'You look, but you do not see,' she says, hissing her words. 'If you think for one second you will have any say in what lies beyond the portal, you are a fool.'

'Why? What do you mean, I look but don't see?'

She stands over me. Hatred etching over every inch of her face as she lifts her skirt and shows her knee where a series of knots wrap around it in black ink.

'My promise, to never betray my Lord's orders. The orders of my husband. I swore never to tell the secrets of his missions, so I can't tell you.'

'Missions?'

'Elanor. Lucca. Brennan. Reid and Cyrus. They were no ordinary team. They were the best. The best killers. The best spies. The best saboteurs the Thirteenth Kingdom had ever known.' She steps closer to me, and I know the dark pleasure on her face is about to break me. 'Why is it, Raven, that of all the Fae that came over in the event, all were from the First Kingdom? All, except a team of trained killers. A highly skilled team of murderers, all from the Thirteenth Kingdom. The kingdom whose Lord and master stood opposed to your mother?'

All the air leaves my lungs as her words sink in.

'Fix the portal. And we shall see what awaits us both on the other side. Either way,' She sighs. 'You and I are fucked.'

'They would never let Reid's father hurt us, Tessa.'

'Reid's father wasn't in the First Kingdom. We were. Think about that. Or better yet, seeing as I can't tell you. Perhaps you should ask someone who was there.'

'Who?'

'Your mother, of course. Fates above. You are slow.' With an eye roll, she turns and leaves.

As the door closes, I sit in silence. But nothing inside me is calm or quiet. A million things flash before my eyes, my memories of the many times something jarred inside me and made me feel uneasy.

'My mother...' I whisper. My wings emerge and swoop around me. My fingers dance across their surface as they glisten. My eyes turn golden as I call upon my power. 'Mother,' I breathe, closing my eyes. 'Mum. Show me the truth.' I take a shuddering breath. 'Who are they to you?'

The chandelier above my head trembles. The floor shakes. The flames in the fireplace double in size and heat. Everything is lost to a flash of white, and the room fades away. The bed where I slept in my lover's arms. The table where the man of my nightmares raped me.

I drop back my head and let it consume me, letting out a long, frightened exhale.

THIRTY-ONE

I return to the bedroom, my hand gripping my chest as I openly howl a cry of utter despair, expelling the sheer pain of it all. The horrendous truth that has been hidden in plain fucking sight all this time.

I slam my hands over my mouth to try and stop it. To stop the scream from tearing me apart or reducing the palace to rubble.

I fall forwards and cry as I have never cried before. There's no anger in my heart at this moment. I am sure anger will come, but now all I have is utter heartbreak. As I let out sob after sob, I hear a gentle whoosh. I lift my gaze a little and watch as black smoke forms before me. His feet first, then his legs. His waist. His chest and then his face.

Cyrus looks down at me on the floor.

'What happened? I felt-'

I create a shield between us as he takes a step closer. I watch him.

I hate him.

I love him.

He looks at the form of Reid on the floor. As he does, Reid runs into the room, breathless from his sprint.

'Is she okay? What happened? You were so upset. My heart felt like it was broken into-' Reid sees himself on the floor, trousers around his ankles and a belt around his neck.

The confusion between them both is clear.

'What the fuck...' Reid whispers.

'It's Jonah,' I manage. Every word forced past the desperate need to sob. 'He's wearing your face.'

'What... What did he-'

'He raped me. He beat me, and he raped me.' I feel the blood seeping down from the blows he delivered. I see them watch it fall as they take in every injury. 'Just as you wanted to do to me.'

My words leave me in a croak. A broken and dry strain carries a soft sob I can't hold in.

'What the hell are you talking about?' Reid hisses. He storms towards Jonah. I extend my portal and cover him, blocking his path.

'Lower the shield. You lower it and let me tear him-'

'Why? He has done nothing to me you had not planned to do yourself.' I try to stand tall, but nothing inside me has pride. Nothing has strength. I manage to get to my feet and sway. That's all. I face them, hating that the tears keep spilling down the same cheeks they have kissed so many times.

'What are you talking about?' Reid asks, trying to sound lost, but I hear it. I feel it, in fact. The dread. I have felt the same dread on and off since we arrived here. Since the prospect of returning to the Fae Realm became not only a possibility but our only way to survive.

'I hate how you can sense my emotions,' I tell them, resting my palm flat over my breaking heart. 'I loath it. How you can spy on me. Feel what I feel when I want to hide my misery from you. I can feel yours too. The dread you have felt. The anxiety you have endured. It's been so strong I have tapped into it repeatedly without knowing. I thought it was Tessa. But it was you.' I look at them both. 'Even as you both declared your love to me tonight. It wasn't because you feared death. No. You knew, one way or another, you would lose me. Because when we returned home, I would learn the truth. And I would never forgive you.'

'Whatever has been said to you–'

'Not said. Shown. Now I know why you didn't want me to look into my mother's memory. It wasn't because of how it affected me. It was because of the things you feared I would see.'

They look on in silence.

'My mother called you to the kingdom for protection. Ivan's disgusting experiments were discovered. He had fled, leaving my pregnant mother all on her own–'

'Raven. What you think you saw–'

'She called you, and you came. But you didn't help her, did you? You didn't protect her.' My lip trembles as hatred, disgust and anger threaten to swallow me whole. 'You looked at her bump. At the life inside it, and you sneered in disgust.' I see their faces now as I did in the memory. How they stood before her. How they drew their swords and rested them over her stomach.

'Whatever you saw in the memories,' Reid starts. 'It's not–'

'I saw the truth. I saw you. Both of you. You told the kingdom that she could not be trusted. That she was Ivan's wife. That she was the one who brought him to your world. You told them that she was in on it!' I slam my foot into the marble, shattering it underfoot. 'You were the shadows beyond the bars that held my mother prisoner. Tell me. Would you have at least tried to have loved me?' I ask. 'After you convinced the kingdom to imprison my mother and wait for me to be born before you execute her for treason?'

'Raven. Whatever–'

'Would you?'

'No,' Cyrus admits before Reid can attempt any more bullshit. Cyrus's dark eyes are locked hard and fast on me as he stands in the doorway. 'I had no intention of trying to love you.'

I refuse to let the sting of his words show. I look to Reid.

'Did you?'

Slowly, he shakes his head and looks at my feet.

'She invited you. She called you for help.'

'She summoned us like a pair of dogs, Raven. We were not men who were summoned. We were not men to be owned.'

'Owned by me, you mean.'

'By anyone,' Reid says quietly. 'We were young. Full of anger and raised to fight in wars. Not sit at a child's side to take orders. We saw an opportunity and we took it.'

I walk towards them, still sealed up tight and safe in my shield.

'I know what you thought. I felt her fear. I felt her terror as she heard you discuss your plan. Your sick, twisted fucking plan!' I yell my words, and even as the room shakes, they don't move a muscle. 'I heard you. Once I was born, you planned to kill my mother as a traitor. I would become the Queen, and as my Bonded Mates, you would have regency until I came of age. Until my ageing slowed, so what... eighteen? You would have eighteen years to rule as you see fit.'

'Raven,' Cyrus tries. 'Please-'

'As your father saw fit, I should say. It was his rules you wanted to put into place. It was his kingdom you planned to elevate.'

'My kingdom,' Reid says. 'My home, which was poor and for-gotten.'

'Because your rules and laws were barbaric. My mother would never give wealth or support to a kingdom that treated its people so savagely.'

'We didn't see it like that at the time. My father's way was all we knew. It was-'

'Your words. While you stood outside my pregnant mother's cell as she clung to her bump in the cold and the dark? Do you remember them?'

'It wasn't-'

'Do you remember them?!'

The room trembles again, and yet, they don't flicker.

'She heard you. *"We'll breed the girl as soon as she starts to bleed and secure a strong and extensive bloodline in our name. Should get three or four kids out of her before she matures and can inherit the throne."'*

'Raven, please,' Reid tries, watching me with his arms hanging loosely by his side. 'Please let me-'

' *"And then we kill the bitch. And keep her throne for our sons to inherit. Secure it in our name for the rest of time."* That's what you said. That's what you planned.'

They wince at my words and close their eyes.

'That's what you wanted to do to me? Breed me? Kill me? Keep me in that cell my entire life?'

Their silence is both devastating and infuriating.

'You wanted the throne so much, you were really-'

'It never happened, Raven,' Reid tells me, finally getting the courage to look at me. 'We were young and stupid. All we saw was a chance at power. A chance to rule the entire Kingdom. All Thirteen. To lift up our home and-'

'Inflict your father's laws on the innocent. To hold me hostage and breed me. To steal our children and then kill me! Oh my goddess...' I lean over and start retching, my hands gripping my knees as I throw up on the floor. I rest my hand on my side. 'The promise. The promise you wanted about having your children.

You still want to do it, don't you? Is that what awaits me over there? A life of giving you children as I live in a cell?'

'No. No, of course not!' Reid rushes up to the shield and presses his hand against it. 'That was then. So much has changed. Everything!'

'I can't trust you,' I cry. 'I can't-'

'It never happened, Raven.' Cyrus stands beside Reid and his palm rests on the shield too. 'We both know, without a doubt, that we would never have hurt you like that. As soon as we saw you, all we wanted to do was protect you. To keep you.'

'Reid Triggered me, and you both threatened me for weeks. *"Do as I say or else".* You would have hurt me as you planned.'

'Nothing happened, so *"what if's"* are a waste of fucking time. All that matters is what *is.* And what *is,* is that we love you. More than anything in this entire fucking world.' Cyrus slams his fist into the shield. 'Now, you tell me if that's a lie.'

'Ivan came back for her.'

They both swear angrily at my refusal to bend.

'He took my mother from your cell with ease. He had tunnels under the palace.'

'We didn't know-'

'He took her to the human world and locked her up. He made the chair and he shoved her into it with Rhea and me inside her. He turned it on. He turned it on and stole Rhea's power of the portal to feed to his machine. The machine that stole the Fae. To bring them here and lock them up in the cities.'

'Ivan wasn't...' Reid sighs heavily. 'He wasn't supposed to-' His words get stuck in his throat. 'When your mother disappeared and the Bond we felt with you died, we never realised just how much you mattered to us until that moment.'

'Yeah. Your fast track to the crown had gone.'

'No.' Cyrus shakes his head. 'Our hearts had broken.'

'It was a month after the Bond died that the event happened,' I carry on. 'Why were you still there? Why were you the only members of the Thirteenth Kingdom that came over in the event?'

Reid and Cyrus share a look.

'Tell me. Tell me the truth right now or-'

'Tessa,' Reid says, closing his eyes. 'We were there because of Tessa.'

'T-Tessa?' I repeat.

'The Queen was gone. As was her heir and her husband. We had no real claim to the throne any longer. The First Kingdom wanted us gone. My father wasn't ready to give it up so easily.' Reid's forehead rests on the shield as he watches me.

'Tell me,' I urge.

'You had a brother,' he tells me. 'Older. From your mother's first husband, who died in a drowning accident before she met Ivan. She had a son with him.'

I bite down on my lip to hold in anything I feel.

'He inherited,' Reid continues. 'My father made a deal with him that I would marry his daughter in a bid to unite our two kingdoms in peace. But it was a lie. We did not want peace.'

'I had a brother?'

'Yes.'

'You married his daughter?'

'Yes.'

'Tessa. She's my niece?'

He nods slowly.

'She was pliable and easily manipulated. Tessa was so desperate for attention that she obeyed any command. So I married her. I married her and returned to the Thirteenth Kingdom as agreed. A First Kingdom princess married to the son of the Lord of the Thirteenth Kingdom. To the world, it looked like a treaty.' He shakes his head and admits. 'It wasn't.'

'The night of the Event, we returned to the palace to...' Cyrus's face scrunches up as he fights the urge to lie or shut up. 'To kill Tessa's father. With him dead, she would inherit.'

'You planned to kill my brother?' My head spins. Is there no end to this?

'We did kill him,' Cyrus admits.

I clutch my middle as it feels the stab of yet another fucking betrayal.

'We killed him. And then...'

'You ended up here.'

Cyrus nods.

'So you got what you wanted.' I step back, lost in disbelief. 'Did Tessa know you killed her dad? My brother?'

'As I said,' Reid mutters. 'She's very pliable. All I had to do was ask, and she led me straight to him. The promise of a crown was too tempting. Do you see now why I went to such lengths to get her to leave you be? I didn't want her to-'

'You killed my brother. You planned to kill my mother. And you planned to keep me your prisoner. That's all before I was even born. The list goes on even after that.'

'I know. I know what-'

'My mother called you because she trusted that you would love and protect me as a Bonded Mate should.'

'We do,' Cyrus insists. 'We fucking do now!'

I look at them lost. 'Now is too late. If you had protected her as she wanted you to. If you had stood by her side, let her have me and help watch over me as I grew, I would have loved you. I would have loved you fiercely and completely. You would have had me any way you wanted because you did, boys. Both of you had me in every way a man can have a woman. Mind. Heart. Body and fucking soul. I would have given you children. I would have helped you raise your kingdom to greatness without anyone suffering at a tyrant's hands. No one would have been stolen. The Fae wouldn't have fallen. We could have had everything if you had just accepted our destiny.' I step back again. 'If you had just accepted me. But power is all you see. That's all that matters.'

'No. No, it's not.'

I scream as Jonah's hand reaches out and his fingers wrap around my ankle. He pulls me down and throws himself on top of me. His face is still Reid's, but I see Jonah in his eyes.

As the boys yell and shout for me to lower the shield, I look up at Jonah.

And I am done.

I think I'm just... broken.

I slam my fist into his face, and the pathetic man falls off me. My wings spread as I throw myself on top of him and look at my lover's copy beneath me. I do as Jonah did and slam his skull into the stone. Again. And again. And again, leaving behind a palette of red.

He has no iron to weaken me. I don't hold back for fear he is the man I love.

And I have nothing left to lose. All I cared about lies in ruin, along with my broken heart.

Beneath the table lies the shards of one of the glasses Jonah threw to the floor before he bent me over.

I take it.

'This face is not yours,' I tell him. 'I'm taking it back.'

I start to cut. He thrashes and claws at me as I drag the glass around the edge of his face. And as I cut, I see Reid, Cyrus, Jonah, Ivan, and all who have twisted me and bent me, right up until this moment. The moment I break in two.

I cut and I carve and slice and I dice. His screams echo all around the room. The squelching, as I slowly pry his flesh from muscle and bone, is beyond satisfying.

My fingers slip in the thick blood gushing through my fingers.

He stops moving, unconscious but alive. With a final grunt, I tug. His face now rests in my hand. I grip it tight and laugh before spitting in his eyes.

Bloody and panting, I stand and face the two men beyond the shield.

'Is the Arch fixed?' I ask.

Reid looks at the glass in one hand and the sagging flesh of his face in my other.

'Is it?' I repeat.

'Almost,' he tells me. 'Any minute.'

The palace shakes and shudders so much we all stagger. The roof releases clouds of dust and the stones grind together as everything vibrates around us.

I feel it, then. The warmth of power. The call of the portal.

'The Arch is complete,' I whisper, watching the specks of dust fall down the golden shimmer. My eyes rest on Reid and Cyrus again. 'If I create the portal with the Arch and we destroy the other one in your realm, Rhea will be left behind. All the Fae here will be left.'

'We have no other choice. If we don't, Ivan can follow us through.'

'She's my sister. Those people are my people.'

'We have tried to save as many as possible for you, Raven. But we can't save them all. One day, you will learn to make portals between Realms. We can return-'

'In decades. Centuries. That's how long you said it would take to master such power. I won't leave her under his control. Not again.'

Reid takes a long breath. 'You will, Little Bird.'

'I'll make the portal. But I will stay.'

Reid slowly shakes his head as Cyrus lowers his.

'You can't force me.'

'We can. And we will. As soon as you step into the portal, you will travel through. You will be in the Fae Realm, and we will follow. And then we will destroy it. There's no other way.'

'There is.' I drop the flesh on the floor. 'I kill Ivan and get my sister back.'

I reach out my hand and blast the pair with my shield, forcing them back. They hurtle through the open door and crash into the hall. I run. I run with all my might, sprinting out of the door and leaping over them as they reach out for me. I collide with the wall and push myself off it, urging myself on harder and faster.

They give chase, running after me with ferocious determination, crashing into corners and leaping over any obstacle that gets in their way.

They pull on my Bond and I scream as my arms get yanked back. Still yelling, I slide back to them, returning to their feet.

Reid is on me in a second, pinning me down as I thrash and shout beneath him.

'Ivan has a fucking army out there. You won't last a minute. And then he will hunt us down and kill us all. Every single one of us. Every man, woman and child will die in this place. Is that what you want?'

'I want him dead!' I spit in his face. 'I won't do it. Not for you. Not after all you have done.'

'You will do it, Little Bird.' He looks up at Cyrus who has pulled out a needle from his pocket. 'Now.'

The syringe plunges deep into my neck and I feel weak and dizzy as the liquid courses through my bloodstream.

Cyrus sweeps the hair from my face as he kneels beside me. Both of them look at me beneath them.

'Sense our truth, Raven,' Cyrus says. 'We love you. Both of us. More than anything. We don't know what would have happened if your mother had remained in the Fae Realm. We're blessed never to find out. Because we know, without a doubt, that we would never hurt a hair on your head now.'

'I'm hurting, Cyrus.' I sob weakly under them. 'You're destroying me.'

'We're saving you,' Reid corrects. 'This battle is lost. We have no chance here. Back home, we do. We'll fix this. You'll forgive us, and we will rule as one.'

'Your father rules,' I reply weakly, fighting against the effects of the sedative.

'We'll fix it,' Cyrus insists. 'All we have to do is go home. We'll fix this. You'll see.'

He lifts me in his arms.

'I told you once before. We are not heroes. If it means saving you, we will let this realm burn. That includes your sister.'

'I'll never forgive you for this.'

'You will. One day. And we're patient men, Princess. When we want to be, we can be extremely patient.'

He carries me towards the Arch room.

THIRTY-TWO

*C*yrus holds me tight as I quietly cry in his arms. I hate that I have the urge to sink into him for comfort. That it's his actions that have caused this pain. His embrace, Reid's too, would have eased this devastation.

But this devastation is of their making.

How could they do this to me? To anyone? How could they plan to inflict such a fate on my mother and me?

How?

We walk through the endless halls and corridors and arrive at last at the Arch room. Outside, the Fae all linger. So few are left. They're hurt and traumatised, with the blood of the fallen still drying on their skin.

They all fall silent as I pass, limp in Cyrus's arms.

He carries me inside and walks quietly down the raised pathway to the Arch.

It's complete. Its surface shines with perfection. Not a hint of a crack or chip. It's healed. The structure towers twenty feet high and five feet thick. It's immense and glistens with endless colours.

'Cyrus,' I try once more. 'Please.'

We pass Brennan, who stands with his hands cupped together in front of him, his head low. We pass Tessa, who watches the space before her with glazed and unfocused eyes. We pass El, who kneels on the ground with Lucca's mangled body groaning in her lap. Tears stream down her face in silence as she avoids meeting my gaze.

We approach the Arch where Ezra stands, his hands in his pockets and a sympathetic expression as he looks at me in Cyrus's arms.

'I am sorry it came to this, my Queen,' he says.

'Bite me,' I slur back.

'How do we get this thing started?' Reid asks, keen to get this over with.

Another explosion, and we all watch the ceiling as small chunks and clouds of dust drift down.

'Place her under the Arch,' Ezra instructs, stepping aside to let Cyrus pass.

Cyrus walks beneath the structure and gently places me down, resting my back against its sleek surface.

My head lolls as the sedative continues stealing my strength. He lifts it and sweeps the hair from my face.

'You wait, my love. When this is over, we will show you a world you could only imagine in your dreams. We will fly over the ice mountains on the Emerald island. We'll swim in the crystal oceans of the midnight sea. We'll touch the stars and make you see the heavens every night.'

He smiles a hopeful smile. A loving smile.

I have none to offer in return. Just more tears.

Cyrus leans in and kisses my lips. I don't return it.

'I love you,' he tells me. And I sense no lie. 'I will devote the rest of my life to making you happy. You have my word.'

Again. No lie.

Another kiss lingers on my lips. I watch him, unblinking. His eyes remain open, too, and the betrayal he sees in my eyes breaks him.

He stands and steps back, wiping the tears clear.

Reid kneels before me next.

'You have my heart, woman.'

'Keep it.'

'It's yours. I will take your retributions when the time comes. But I will never back away. I will never abandon or betray you again. This is the last time I break your heart. This is the last time you will cry because of us.'

'I won't make the same promise to you, Reid. I will make you cry. I will break your black heart.'

'As I said. It's your heart. Do with it as you see fit. Because it loves you completely. And one day, I know you will forgive–'

'You will regret this. I will make sure of it.'

He goes to kiss me. I move my lips away. So he plants his final kiss on my cheek.

'I'll see you when we get home,' he whispers. 'And then we will be free of all this.'

'Free?' I manage. 'How can freedom start with pain and betrayal?'

'It always does, my love. Pain. Blood. Death. Betrayal. There's no such thing as freedom without it.'

Reid returns to his feet and steps clear of the Arch, taking his place beside Cyrus.

I look at each of them in turn. All of them who proclaimed friendship and loyalty. My final gaze resting on El.

'You will abandon Rhea?' I ask her. 'You'll leave her–'

'Lucca needs a healer. If he doesn't get home now, he'll die.' She lowers her head and clings to Lucca's wheezing form. 'I owe him that much, Raven. I'm sorry.'

The Arch room doors are closed, sealing us in.

'Ready?' Ezra asks.

The boys share a look and ready themselves for an answer.
But someone beats them to it.

'Ready, Ezra.'

Everyone turns to Brennan.

He pulls out a gun and fires it twice, shooting both Reid and Cyrus in the back. They fall with a yell, their skin burning and a silver trail travelling up their necks through their bulging veins.

'I am very ready, indeed.' Brennan smirks. 'Finally.'

THIRTY-THREE

*B*rennan smiles as both Reid and Cyrus groan and struggle to move. They're on their knees and fighting with all their might to stay up. Cyrus tries to make his smoke, and Reid attempts to make his light.

Nothing happens.

Brennan looks at his gun and grins.

'Iron darts,' he admires. 'Not lethal. Sends powdered iron through the bloodstream. Bet it hurts, huh boys?'

Brennan walks towards me, the gun still in hand. He points it at El as she tries to stand and fires it into her shoulder.

Her yell echoes around the hall as she falls back down and screams against the pain. The same silver trails travels up her neck as the iron in her body spreads.

Brennan shoots Tessa, too. She goes down silently, already so broken and defeated she barely has the strength or will to scream.

Brennan stops when he reaches me. He crouches down, and smiles.

I know that smile. No one else holds such malice and cruelty in a smile.

'Ivan...'

'A little bit formal. But I suppose asking you to call me Dad would be a bit of a stretch.'

As I watch him, his face changes. Brennan's features disappear, and I shudder as I face my father instead.

'So many wonderful gifts your kind has. It's a disappointment that they are wasted on vermin like you. Good thing I'm here to change all that.'

Ezra's men turn their weapons to Reid, Cyrus, El, Lucca and Tessa. Their swords are different. Not a shiny steel, but a deep grey. They're iron. The handles are jet black and made of a material that protects them from the blades' effects.

'Make a move, fellas,' Ezra says with an amused smile as he watches Reid and Cyrus still try to stand. 'I will have my men hack the women into pieces before your eyes.'

'I should be insulted you thought me so stupid that I would ever allow you to get this far.' Ivan laughs and shakes his head, that nasty cackle echoes around the room. He tucks my hair behind my ear. Whatever drugs the guys injected me with make my movements sluggish as I pull away from him. I can hardly move at all. 'You think you got to this palace and fixed the Arch without my help? My sweet daughter. I thought I raised you smarter.'

'Where's Brennan?' I ask.

'Where you left him,' Ivan shrugs. 'In pieces. Back at the Farmhouse. I'm afraid he didn't survive the attack. He's probably filled with maggots by now. Poor Brennan.' He turns to face Reid. 'Some best friend you are. I've been here this whole time, and you didn't realise I wasn't the man you loved like a brother?'

'You killed Brennan?' Reid manages, still struggling with the effects of the iron coursing through his veins.

'If it makes you feel any better, he called your name as he died.'

I watch Reid sink as he realises that his friend is gone. And then the anger rise as it sinks in that Ivan has been here this whole damn time.

'It's been kind of nice if I'm honest,' Ivan sighs. 'Getting to know you all. Learn your weaknesses. See the kind of woman you have become. Watch you live in the hope that you'll escape and be free. It was amusing.'

'Fuck you.' I raise my hand, ready to make a shield.

Ivan puts the gun to my stomach and fires.

I scream as the dart penetrates me and seeps its poison. Fire spreads through me, burning and searing as it is pumped around my body. I yank the dart out and drop it to the floor. But the damage is done. My powers are lost, and pain consumes me. I force myself to be quiet. I won't give Ivan the satisfaction of hearing my agony.

Ivan leers over me. 'If I didn't need you to complete the Arch, you would have been in chains weeks ago, Daughter. I knew where you were the entire time and I let you remain free. If you can call living in squalor free. But only your hands could find the right stones that belonged in the Arch. The portal wielder is the only one who can sense the powerful stones in its structure. Without your help, it would have taken us decades to fix.' He looks at the structure above us. 'It looks bigger than it did when I strapped your mother into the chair beneath it all those years ago.'

'My mother?' I repeat, still struggling against the iron's agony.

'Oh yes. This palace was my home away from home. There was an ancient Arch back in the First Kingdom. It took me here. This is where I performed many of my early experiments. The chair I used with your mother is outdated technology.' He runs his hands against the Arch's smooth surface. 'This is far improved. I thank you for your help in creating it for me.'

'I would never willingly help you,' I spit.

'I know. That's why I let you think you were winning. It's amazing how much of a motivation hope is. Even if slight. You did this in a matter of days. If I had forced your hand and held you captive, I doubt you would have ever helped me. No. I needed you to have time to fall in love with those morons so you would have something to fight for. Something to lose. I needed you to fall in love so you would want to save them.' He scoffs and rolls his eyes. 'You work so much harder when it's to protect the ones you love, so I hear. At least, that's what Jonah always said.'

'Jonah raped me.'

'He has his issues. But I can't deny him what he wants. He's like a son to me. So loyal. So dedicated.'

'I'm your daughter!'

'No. You're my creation. Nothing more. Loving you would be like loving this Arch. I can be proud. I can be impressed. I could never love you or it.'

'Where's my sister?' I demand.

'Oh, she's well out of the way. Of all of you, she was the one I needed to ensure was gone before I started the portal up. No way she would have let me do this if she was here. I'm not sure I could control her if she truly tried to fight against me. A powerful creature, that one. She's safely locked in iron. But Jonah did a fantastic job pushing all the right buttons to get her to turn Dark for me. If that sadistic little bastard is good at anything, it's pushing the right buttons. Where is Jonah?' He looks at Ezra, who shrugs.

'I can look for him if you like, Sir?' Ezra offers.

'Send one of your men. I do like having Jonah around. He's just the right level of psychopath. That, and he's got powers I don't want to go to waste.'

Ezra gives the order, and one of his men leaves to find Jonah.

'You betrayed us,' Reid snarls, staring at Ezra. 'You lying piece of shit!'

'Me the liar?' Ezra laughs.

He holds out his hand and creates Reid's light. He admires it for a moment before releasing it. The light slams into Reid's shoulder, making him roar in pain and sending him down with burnt flesh.

'You thought I didn't know?' Ezra scoffs. 'That I had a power inside me that you refused to acknowledge? That you lied to our father about and told him I had no gift? That you refused to Trigger it back home and elevate me to the position of High Warrior?'

Ezra creates a stream of black smoke. It collides with Cyrus's chest and knocks him down, gasping, to the floor.

Ezra laughs and admires his hand.

That's not possible. To have two gifts like that? How?

'Cool, huh? All it took was for me to come here in search of Ivan. A couple of days is all it took before I Triggered. And Ivan's men kindly provided me with all the Gilt I needed. That any of my men could need.' He throws me a wink. 'But your blood did the trick with its more permanent solution. Thank you, *My Queen.*'

I watch him with such anger, loathing every word. Every betrayal.

'Lucca would have heard your thoughts.' Reid says painfully, returning to his knees. 'He would have-'

'No. He wouldn't. And your whore of a princess wouldn't have sensed my lies either. And believe me, there have been a lot. No. None of your power would have worked against me.'

'He's a Mimic,' Cyrus realises. 'He can take on other's powers when they're close. Uses them against them. I knew whatever you could do, it was going to be powerful. Fucker.'

'Yes. I am a mimic,' Ezra says proudly, puffing out his chest and lifting his chin high. 'I must have given off quite the aura when you sensed my power. Mimics are very rare. If I had been Triggered as the law dictated, I would have even outranked Elias.'

'Is that why you have done all this?' Reid glares from Ezra to Ivan. 'You side with Ivan because I didn't Trigger you?'

'I sided with him long before that, big brother.' Ezra roars with laughter, his maniacal chuckles forced out with menace. 'Father and I both. Where do you think Ivan got all his equipment for his experiments? Who do you think helped Ivan steal the First Kingdom? Emptying it so we could claim it for our own? After all, we couldn't rely on you actually going through with the whole murder and kidnap plan. Father knew deep down that you would end up letting him down. That you would lose us the crown. So he asked me to help with plan B. And I succeeded. Ivan and I emptied the entire First Kingdom and sent everyone to this hell hole.' He gives a bow to an ungrateful crowd. 'You being sent over was a very happy coincidence. We have the throne now, Elias. Father and I.'

'And you will keep it, Ezra,' Ivan says. 'As long as you hold up your end of our arrangement.'

'Arrangement?' I repeat.

'I helped them take your realm. They help me take this one. This is no average portal. It is your magic. My science. Ezra and

I placed my technology inside the Arch as we rebuilt it. The Fae Realm is of no consequence to me. This world is. This world is mine. And with a steady supply of Fae delivered to me each year, I can take their powers to sell to humanity and turn them into my own twisted mutations who will obey me at every turn. I can rule this realm. I can be king of the world.'

'This portal will send over more Fae?' I ask.

'The Seventh Kingdom,' Ezra says proudly. 'They are Ivan's next shipment.'

'I won't start it. You need my power. I won't-'

Ivan lets out a fake sigh and shakes his head. 'All it needs to function is your blood.' He pulls out a knife. I watch it as he grips it tightly. 'I'm sorry about this, Raven dear. But I'm afraid that before I start the machine, I'm going to need them back.'

'W-what back?' I force myself to reply, frozen with dread.

'What you stole from me.' He gives a nod to my back. 'I'm going to need my wife's wings back.'

With that, he plunges the blade into my side, burying it deep and then twisting it. I scream, and the pain makes my wings emerge. He wastes no time. Ezra's men surround me, and I'm thrown face down on the floor.

'NO!' I scream, trying to get them away. 'DON'T!'

They pin me down and tear off my shirt. Through them, I see Reid and Cyrus try to come to my aid, but more of Ezra's men surround them and keep them away with swords to their throats. They still try with all their might. I lock eyes with them as I'm held down.

'No. No-no-no-no!' I cry. Flashbacks of my mother's death hit me hard as it becomes clear that I am destined for much the same fate. 'Don't!'

That's all I manage before Ivan kneels beside me and starts cutting.

The room fills with my screams as he hacks at my beautiful wings. Blood sprays over us as I thrash against the men holding me down. My throat burns as I cry and plead.

But my father never listened to my pleas for mercy.

The pain becomes too much and I go limp.

My body rocks back and forth as Ivan saws through flesh and bone.

Reid and Cyrus roar my name and keep trying to get free.

They won't. They can't.

And it's too late anyway.

Ivan stands. The cutting ends, and he steps back, my wings in hand.

He wipes the thick layer of blood spray from his face and looks down at me.

I can't move. I lie on my front and feel the pool of blood grow around me.

'Raven...' Reid whispers, horrified at what he's just seen.

He and Cyrus are as pale as death, and neither can look away.

The room trembles. A pulse emanates from my body, making me jolt and convulse onto my back.

Everyone steps away from me and clear of the Arch.

A golden shimmer spreads over each end of the Arch, slowly spreading and sealing me inside.

The surge leaves my body and I slump, gasping in a desperate and painful breath.

Ivan gestures to the men guarding Reid and Cyrus.

'Release them. Let them say goodbye. Let them know what happens when they stand against me.'

Reid and Cyrus scramble to the arch as soon as they are free.

Cyrus collides with the barrier and looks up at it, searching for a weak spot or gap to get through. There is none, so he starts throwing his fist against it.

Blood spills freely from my back and the stab wound on my side, soaking me and surrounding me in red. It seeps out beyond the portal and meets their knees.

Reid and Cyrus throw their body against the shield, slamming into it repeatedly.

Nothing. Not a scratch. Not a mark. Not a tremble.

I reach out and rest my hand against the barrier between us. It's not mine to control. Not mine to create or destroy.

I'm trapped. Sealed in.

'Cyrus. Reid,' I groan.

Together, we watch as my fingertips begin to glow brighter and brighter

'What's happening?' I whisper.

Cyrus punches his fist into the shield. 'LET HER OUT!'

'It's begun,' Ivan says in an excited whisper, holding my bloody wings to his chest.

'What are you doing to her?' Reid looks at me with desperation. 'What are you doing?'

My body still glows. Brighter and brighter. I lift my hand. Particles of glimmering light from my fingertips drift into the air.

I watch as more and more of my hand disintegrates. I Watch myself flake away slowly, bit by bit, becoming the same as the many portals I have made over the last few months.

I let out a scream. It tears through my throat and bursts from my lungs. I feel that same pain I did back in the chair. When I was strapped down, torn apart from the inside, over and over. Every cell and molecule is alight in unrelenting agony.

I watch my fingers dissolve into dust and float upwards to the top of the Arch.

'Stop!' I cry, looking at them both with utter desperation. 'Please! Make it stop!'

'You don't have to kill her to make a portal, Ivan!' Cyrus yells. 'She can make it work. Stop!'

'Not this portal. She doesn't power it, you fools.' Ivan looks at me with a twisted sense of pride. 'She creates it. Her essence. Her body. Her soul. Her magic. All of it. She *is* the portal. Just as Rhea's power created the portal before her.'

'Her blood!' Cyrus tries. 'You need it if your powers are to remain and-'

'Her magic is all I need. And she is about to become pure magic. I will syphon off all I require whenever I need. Just as Ezra did when I created the first portal using Rhea's power. He took enough to recharge the portal in your realm, just in case something were to happen to me and I did not return. Which I didn't, thanks to my daughter blowing up my factory and putting me in a coma. And everyone else will have the synthetic blood, which not only makes them strong, but controllable too. Science meets magic.'

I try to hold it in. The pain. The despair. It wants to swallow me whole.

A wind picks up around me. The stones in the Arch begin to glow. The gold dust begins to swirl with the gust, taking more and more of me as it does.

'No. No. No-no-no-no...' Reid watches me as his hand settles at his neck. He looks down. The Bond. Our Bond. It's fading.

'NO!' he roars, resuming his attack on the shield, throwing all he can at it. 'NO! You can't take her! You can't!'

But there's no way through.

They both throw themselves at the barrier between us, giving all they have to try and break through.

I press my hand on the shield between us. What remains of it. My markings are fading with theirs. Our Bond is ending.

Tears stream down their faces.

More of me fades. The pain is beyond anything possible to describe.

Sobbing and desperate, Reid falls to his knees and looks on helplessly.

'I don't want to die,' I quietly cry. 'I don't want to die, Reid. I don't want to. Cyrus... please... I don't want... I don't...'

Gold specks rise from my chest. I'm fading. A moment, and I will be nothing but dust.

Reid and Cyrus look on and openly sob, watching with horror as I disappear before their very eyes.

'Hold on, Raven. We... we can save you!' Reid weeps.

'Save my sister,' I tell him. 'Save them all.'

That's all I manage before the pain becomes too much. My words turn to screams.

My legs fade. My middle. My arms.

The doors explode from their hinges as Rhea charges in. Her monstrous form stands tall as she scans the room. Her eyes land on me.

'NO!' she screams. 'RAVEN!' She charges forwards, barrelling through the men that try to stand between us.

She's back!

Rhea... she's back! She doesn't go for the glimmering shield. No. She crashes into the Arch itself. The whole thing trembles. Another crash and cracks begin to appear.

It starts to break.

The gold slows and starts to sink back into my body. The pain eases as I piece back together.

A third attack, the Arch will fall!

She runs forwards with all her might.

But screams as Ivan shoots her three times with the iron dart gun. She falls, but not entirely. She turns as he goes to reload and raises her enormous claws, ready to strike Ivan.

The Arch shimmers and mends itself whilst she's distracted.

My body fades again, more and more as I seep into the portal.

The pain... so much pain...

I take my final breath and fall limp. Fall into nothing. Become... nothing.

I am dust, swirling in a void of torment. My soul, body, everything I am... scattered to the wind.

Reid and Cyrus are the last things I see before everything goes a blinding white. The sound of crumbling rocks and shouting rings in my ears. Of screams and death and destruction.

They yell my name. They yell it with all their might.

Pain claims me. Pain and darkness as black as Ivan's soul.

A final whisper follows me.

We love you.

Sorry.

Followed by a lifetime of screaming and pleading to die.

And never being heard.

THIRTY-FOUR

*A*nother blinding flash of light. Another explosion. The vacuum of nothing but agony is suddenly filled with colour and sensations as I'm thrown back together again. My body lands with a thud on the ground. My ears ring and my vision is a blur.

I lie there, groaning and in too much pain to contemplate moving.

I have no idea how long it is until I gain enough strength to force myself up. My arms keep buckling under my weight, and I repeatedly fall flat on my face with each attempt to stand.

With a determined grunt, I slam my palm into the ground and push myself up, ignoring how my arms tremble and how my head spins so much that it makes me want to hurl.

Up. I'm up.

I raise my head and blink my vision clear.

The Arch is gone. The whole room. The palace.

A night sky now twinkles overhead. Stars, so bright and clear, they could be diamonds on a midnight canvas. A gentle breeze dances over my body.

I stand, my legs unsteady. I'm naked. My entire body, not a stitch of clothing. And not a single mark on my skin. No hint of the Bond markings. No scars. No bullet wounds or stab wound.

Nothing.

My hair falls to my knees in a tangled and filthy mess, at least ten inches longer than it was.

I'm in a deep crater. I look up at the steep slopes surrounding me. With my first step, my legs wobble, and I fall into the dirt.

My head hammers with a sudden influx of voices, all yelling and whispering or hissing. The piercing bombardment makes me scream. Clinging to my head, I pray for it to stop. I cry and shout, demanding it just fucking STOPS!

The silence of the night returns as quickly as the voices arrived, and I slowly blink open my eyes.

The unmistakable snap of a twig has my head shooting up, and I watch the ridge of the crater surrounding me with bated breath.

Another rustle. Another snap.

I think of Ivan. Ezra. His soldiers.

And all I want to do is tear them to pieces.

A figure leaps down from above and lands before me. His wings spread wide as he withdraws a sword from a sheath at his hip.

I raise my hand and create a shield around me.

But he drives the blade into the earth below and steps back.

He lowers his hood and smiles a familiar smile.

'L-Lucca?' I step closer to the shield, staring at the impossible man before me. 'You're alive? H-how?'

'Welcome back, Pup,' Lucca grins. 'My Goddess. Am I glad to see you.'

His face is a mess of deep scars, and his left eye is covered with a black leather patch. His lips are a mangled mess and his neck is littered with deep teeth marks carved into his flesh.

'How? How are you healed?' I ask, utterly confused.

'It took a while. Lots of disgusting medicine and ointments that burned like hell but-'

'It just... it all just happened... time? Lots of...' I groan again and pinch the bridge of my nose as those whispers start again. The deafening, chaotic whispers of words I can't hear or understand.

'You okay?' Lucca steps forwards, but the shield still separates us. 'Pup?'

It goes again. Just as quick. I stand and face Lucca. He surveys me with absolute awe.

'I can't believe we finally got it to work,' he whispers. 'I can't believe we finally got you back.'

'W-we?'

He looks up.

'Some friends and I.' He holds out his hand. 'Let me show you.'

I hesitate.

'How can I trust you? You could be wearing Lucca's face.'

'What face?' he laughs, gesturing to the deep scars. 'You seen this thing? Not much of a face left, Pup.' He watches, and I don't ease on the suspicion. 'And wings,' he says, pointing at his wings at his back. 'They can't fake the wings. Please. Trust me. I swear. No lies here, Pup. It's me. And you can trust me.'

I lower the shield and he slowly steps forwards, offering me his hand.

'Where am I?' I ask.

'I will show you.'

He takes off his jacket and wraps it around me. It smells of firewood and smoke. Of dirt and sweat. It's more of a cloak. He wraps his arms around my waist and takes flight.

The air on my face. The way it forces itself down my throat and fills me up. It's bliss. We land on blackened grass and scorched earth. It smells like ash and fire. It still smoulders and emanates heat when I rest my bare feet on it.

I hear another rustle as the brittle grass crunches underfoot.

I turn and come face to face with a small army. All dressed in black with swords at their hips and some with wings at their back. At least a hundred of them. Maybe more.

'W-who are they?' I turn back to Lucca. 'Where am I? How are you alive? Where's my sister? Where's-'

'There's a lot you need to know. I get that. I'll tell you everything. But we need to move. Now. They would have seen that explosion.'

'Explosion?'

'You came out with a rather large bang, Pup.' He looks at the crater. And then at the perfect circle of charred earth surrounding it. 'They'll be coming for you. And you cannot be here when they do.'

'Who? Ivan?'

'No.'

'Ezra? If it is, let him come. I'll kill him.'

'Come with me. I'll explain.' He glances briefly into the surrounding woods, shielded in darkness. He tries to keep that Lucca smile in place. But he's scared.

'Where is everyone? Where are El and Rhea? Where are the guys? Where are we, Lucca? I don't-'

'You are in the Fae Realm, Pup,' he says. 'On the outskirts of the Second Kingdom where we found the carcass of an old Portal Arch. Lost to time and-'

'T-the Fae Realm?' I repeat, cautiously glancing back over my shoulder at the copious amounts of armed men behind me. I look back to Lucca. 'How am I in the Fae Realm?'

'We found a hidden portal Arch in the empty lands that make the borders. One we remade. One we bastardised and contorted. One that pulled you out. But you arrived with one hell of a show, and they will be coming for you.'

'Who?'

He pauses and takes a deep breath which he holds as he hesitates.

As an animal roars in the distance, everyone turns to look at the treeline behind us. Many of the men face it completely, ready with their swords.

'Dark Fae are coming?' I ask.

'That's not Dark Fae,' Lucca replies. 'That sounded more like Gedora.'

'A what?'

'Like a wolf fucked a dragon and had a baby. Nasty fuckers. And as big as a car. Not something you want to mess with. They usually stay in the swamps and marshes, but times as they are, they're getting braver and breeding like fucking rabbits. Along with all the other nasties that seem to have decided to breed and migrate.'

The same roar repeats. This time with several others to accompany it.

'We have to go, Pup.'

'I'm not going with you until you tell me. We were just in the Arch room. Everyone was there, and now we're here? Did they get left behind? Does Ivan have them?'

'No,' he says with a sympathetic frown. 'They didn't get left behind. By some miracle, you sent us all home. You got us back here. Safely.' He chews his lower lip, hesitating. 'A lot has changed since you died.'

'Died...' I whisper.

'I'll show you.' He holds out his hand. 'You can trust me.'

I hesitate.

'I'm a unicorn. I hate chocolate. And I have three feet.'

The familiar effect of a lie sweeps over me at his words. He sees my body's reaction.

'You can trust me. You can sense my lies, right?'

I nod.

'I'm not going to hurt you. I have risked everything to bring you back. Please. Take my hand. I will show you.'

I grip his hand, and we take to the sky.

We stay there, and he shows me what was once the Second Kingdom of the Fae lands. I recall the pictures in the book Ezra showed me. The book showed images of endless flowers and trees. Buildings made from nature and moss over every surface. It was Spring eternal.

Now, it's blighted by large buildings of grey stone that billow out smoke and grit from their immense chimney stacks. In the dim light, I see enormous banners draped from the tallest of the buildings.

Banners of Golden eyes.

Authority banners.

He returns us to the ground.

'They lost you,' Lucca says. 'And they lost themselves. They're the enemy now, Raven.'

'Who are?' I look at him. 'Who is?'

Lucca swallows and looks painfully out at the scene before us. 'Reid,' he admits. 'And Cyrus. El and Rhea as well.'

'What?' I whisper, my voice trembling as the words leave me. 'Reid took El as his wife.'

'No... No he didn't...'

'Cyrus took Rhea as his. So much has happened since you have been-'

'How... how long have I been gone, Lucca?'

A siren begins to blast in the heart of the kingdom.

'We need to go.' Lucca's fear is evident in his voice. 'I'll explain everything that's happened, Pup. I swear it. But if you stay here, you will end up lost again. And both the Fae and Human Realm will be lost for good.'

He goes to move. I refuse to budge.

'How long have I been gone, Lucca?'

He takes in a deep and shuddering breath.

'Two years, Pup,' he says. 'It's been two years.'

'T-two years?' I repeat. 'This makes no sense. This is madness.'

'Do you remember anything after the Arch activated? Where you... I mean... were you okay?'

'I remember... Rhea. She came back. She...' Violent flashbacks assault me, and those voices reappear in my head, screaming and wailing so loud I groan and cover my eyes.

Lucca's hand rests on my shoulder.

'Pain,' I tell him.

'You're in pain?' he asks. 'Your head?'

'There was just pain.' I lift my gaze and meet his. 'Constant pain. It felt like it lasted forever. And voices. So many voices screaming and shouting. It felt like I was in the chair. Constant... I lost track of time. I didn't...' The voices fade, returning me to the night's silence.

'You were in pain the whole time?' he asks in a whisper. 'For two years?'

Lights appear on the horizon, and the siren increases in ferocity. A figure runs up to us.

'Tessa?' I ask, utterly lost as I see her. She's lost the dresses. Her hair is scraped back, and she wears weapons instead of jewellery.

'We have to go, Lucca. Now! If they get her back, we are all done for.'

Tessa looks at me, her eyes briefly scanning me before she turns her focus back to Lucca.

'If they catch us, they will kill us. We just interrupted their trade and stole their machine. We have to move!'

'Kill us?' I repeat. 'They want to kill us? W-what trade? I don't understand!'

'As I said. A lot has changed. Please, Raven.' Lucca takes my face in his hands and searches my eyes with pleading desperation. 'We have to go!'

I look back at the city.

This can't be true. This has to be a nightmare! Hundreds of winged warriors appear in the sky and start heading straight for us.

'We have to go!' Lucca yells, pulling on my arm. 'Now, Pup! Trust me! Please!'

All I can do is slowly nod. My eyes remain glued to the figures far in the distance, and I wonder if one of them is Reid or Cyrus.

I walk around Lucca and look up at the sky.

As I do, I fill with such wrath and rage that the ground trembles beneath my feet. The trees shake. The men stagger on the uneasy ground as it cracks and rocks below them.

I scream, releasing a blast of power that explodes from my body like a shockwave. A wall of gold and black expels from me and goes straight to the incoming Fae in the sky. It hammers into the trees, knocking them down in its wake, and finally crashes into the Fae far in the distance, hurtling them backwards.

The air and ground fall still as I take a deep breath. My fists are clenched, and my nails dig hard into my palms. A trail of destruction lies between the Second Kingdom and us.

Destruction to match my broken heart.

'They are all together. All married. As I suffered. As I screamed. They fell in love with another?' I can't comprehend it.

'Pup...' Lucca whispers.

I turn to face him with devastated and angry tears seeping from my eyes.

'What in the name of the Goddess...' he whispers, staring at something just behind me. 'How?'

I look.

I have wings.

Enormous, jet black and solid wings. Unlike the ones Ivan cut from my body which were thin and shimmering, these are formidable. Lethal.

All strength leaves my body and my legs go limp.

Lucca catches me and scoops me up in his arms.

'We'll fix this,' he says. 'Now you're back, we can save everyone. We can fix it all. Our Mates included.'

Lucca takes flight.

And we flee into the night.

End of book two.

I hope you enjoyed Fall of the Fae.

Please take a moment to leave a rating or a review on Amazon or Goodreads.
Every single one helps me in an incredible way.
Amazon: https://mybook.to/fallofthefae
GoodReads: https://www.goodreads.com

Let's connect!
Follow me on

Facebook: https://www.facebook.com/hellomjlawrie/

Instagram: m.j.lawrie_author

TikTok:https: https://www.tiktok.com/@mj.lawrie_author

Or join my mailing list: https://www.mjlawrie.com/

Also by
M.J.LAWRIE

The Last Witch Series

A dark, paranormal fantasy romance series.

The Verity Duology

A dystopian, romance, fantasy.

The Stolen Fae series

A dark, MFM, paranormal romance fantasy.

 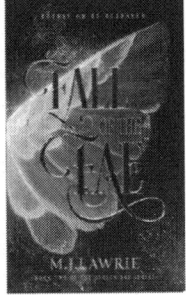 

Printed by Amazon Italia Logistica S.r.l.
Torrazza Piemonte (TO), Italy

52461167R00252